Also by Anna Schmidt

WHERE THE TRAIL ENDS
Last Chance Cowboys: The Drifter
Last Chance Cowboys: The Lawman
Last Chance Cowboys: The Outlaw
Last Chance Cowboys: The Rancher

Christmas in a Cowboy's Arms anthology

★COWBOYS & HARVEY GIRLS★

TRAILBLAZER

ANNA SCHMIDT

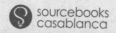
sourcebooks
casablanca

Published by Sourcebooks Casablanca, an imprint of Sourcebooks,
Inc.
P. O. Box 4410, Naperville, Illinois 60567-4410
(630) 961-3900
Fax: (630) 961-2168
sourcebooks.com

Printed and bound in Canada.
MBP 10 9 8 7 6 5 4 3 2 1

WANTED:

Young women, 18–30 years of age, of good moral character, attractive, and intelligent, as waitresses in

HARVEY EATING HOUSES ON THE SANTA FE RAILROAD.

Wages $17.50 a month with room and board. Liberal tips customary. Experience not necessary.

Write Fred Harvey, Union Depot, Kansas City, Missouri

Chapter 1

September 1898

GRACE ROGERS HAD MADE HER DECISION, AND SHE would not be talked out of it. Not by her mother's tears and not by her father's refusal to even speak of the matter. It was time to go, time to do her part to help her struggling family. Time to seek the adventure she'd dreamed of her whole life. So, after supper, while her siblings scattered to attend to evening chores, she lingered at the table.

"Papa, Mama, I have some news." She pulled the advertisement she'd clipped from the paper from her skirt pocket and handed it to her father. "Mr. Fred Harvey is seeking young women of good character to work in the restaurants and hotels he's established along the railroad line heading west."

Her mother wiped her hands on her apron as she peered over her husband's shoulder.

"I have applied and been invited for an interview in Kansas City. They sent me a ticket for the trip,"

Grace continued as she handed her father the reply she'd received. "And if things don't work out, they'll pay for me to come back home."

"But, Grace, you have a teaching position here as soon as Miss Barker retires next year," her mother said. "And what about Buford? Are you just going to walk out on him?"

Buford Kestner and Grace had been sweethearts since seventh grade, and everyone had always assumed they would marry. But over the last year or so, Buford had followed in the footsteps of his father and older brothers, drinking to excess.

"Buford and I have decided to stop seeing each other, Mother. You know that. He's taken up with Sissy Portman."

"Only because you're being so unreasonable." Lines of worry creased her forehead and pinched the corners of her mouth. "And who exactly do you expect to pay for all this? Ticket or not, you'll have expenses. What will you do for food?"

"The company is paying for everything."

"And then?"

"Well, assuming I pass the interview, I'll be enrolled in training for a month at the headquarters in Kansas City, then I'd be assigned to one of their locations out west. The pay is twice what I could earn here, and my room and board are included."

It was precisely because Grace knew that every single penny counted if they were to keep the farm from going on the auction block that she had decided to apply for the position. At nineteen, she was the eldest of six, and it was her responsibility—or so she felt—to do whatever she could to help her family. Surely her parents couldn't argue with that.

Her mother turned to the dry sink. She stood there a moment, head bent, then drew in a breath and began washing the supper dishes, swishing the water in the speckled tin dish pan with unnecessary vigor.

Grace looked pleadingly to her father, who hadn't uttered a word since reading the letter. "Papa?"

"I got chores," her father muttered as he left the room, leaving the letter and advertisement on the table.

Grace picked up a flour sack turned dish towel and took her place beside her mother, wiping each dish dry as her mother handed it to her. And all the while, Mary Rogers kept up a steady stream of objections and questions. Finally, as Grace set the last coffee cup on the shelf, she turned to her mother and said, "I have to try, Mama."

Even then, Grace understood nothing was yet settled, at least for her mother. "Sleep on it, Grace," she said. "By morning—"

Just then, her siblings all raced back inside, talking over each other and arguing about the next morning's chores.

"Shush," their mother commanded.

Grace kissed her cheek. "I'll get the twins ready for bed," she said. "Good night, Mama."

By the following morning, her mother had come up with even more reasons why Grace needed to come to her senses. "What will people say?" she demanded. "A waitress? On the frontier? And these so-called Harvey eating houses? How are they any different from a tavern or saloon? You'd be nothing more than a barmaid, living among a bunch of ruffians, outlaws even. It's all well and good, Grace, with you being out there while we're here dealing with the whispers and gossip."

Grace bit her lip to keep from laughing. Mary Rogers had never cared a whit for what others might say. But she sobered immediately when she saw that her mother was near tears.

Footsteps in the hall had both women looking toward the door. Grace's father stopped short of entering the room, his expression questioning whether anything had changed.

Her mother wiped away fresh tears and scurried from the room. "You talk to her, Jim. I have no more words."

Jim Rogers leaned his full weight against the doorjamb of the room Grace shared with her sisters, watching her move between the single drawer in the bureau that held her clothes and the open carpetbag on her bed.

"You're determined, are you?"

"Yes, sir." Her voice shook as she folded the last piece of her meager wardrobe and laid it carefully in the bag. "Papa, I can send money back and help carry us through these hard times."

"That's not your job, Gracie. Your job is that teaching post. Your job is to marry up and be a good wife and mother. Your job is—"

"And what if I want more?" She glanced up at him, trying to judge his mood. The night before, he had left her sitting at the kitchen table, dismissing her with his silence. And now, he looked weary, as if life itself were a burden too difficult to bear.

"More what?"

She searched for the words that would end in his blessing. "More life," she said softly. "You always said..."

He shoved his lean body away from the door. "Don't be telling me what I said in the past, Grace. You were a child, and children deserve their chance to dream. But now..."

"This isn't a dream, Papa. It's a real opportunity. I'm nineteen years old, so if not now, when? Not only will I be able to send money, but, Papa, think of the adventure. I'll get to travel to a whole new part of the country. I'll see things I would never be able to here."

He picked up the letter confirming the interview she'd left lying on her bed and read it again. "I heard something about this outfit," he mumbled, turning the single sheet over as if expecting there to be more on the back. He released a long breath, looking first at the floor, then out the window behind her, and finally settling his gaze on the carpetbag. "I'll take you to the station," he said as he folded the letter and handed it to her. He walked away, his receding steps heavy with defeat.

Grace squeezed her eyes shut. Her parents thought she was off on a fool's errand, but in time, they would realize she was doing this for them, for the family. She hurried to check the small room for anything she might have left behind, then carefully pinned her hat to her upswept hair. She wound the strings of her purse around her wrist and lifted the heavy bag, carrying it out the door. Outside, her mother stood with her arms wrapped in her apron as if to ward off a chill, although it was uncommonly hot for late September. It was apparent she knew her husband had agreed to what she clearly saw as madness.

"I'll write every day, Mama," Grace promised. "Besides, I don't have the job yet. Chances are I'll be home before the week is out."

"You'll get the job," her mother grumbled. "They'd be fools not to take you on." She smoothed the collar of Grace's jacket, then took hold of her wrist. "Don't be talking to strangers," she warned as she shoved a large silver safety pin and a small mesh bag half filled with coins into Grace's hand. "Pin this to your camisole," she whispered, as if robbers might be just around the corner.

"Mama, I—"

"Don't be so proud, girl," her mother snapped. "If you're determined to do this, at least be smart about it."

"Yes, ma'am. Thank you." She hugged her mother. That money was the savings it had taken months to accumulate, and it had been earmarked for shoes for her oldest brother, Reuben, who seemed to grow a couple of inches every month. She hugged each of her siblings in turn, whispering promises to write and eliciting their promises to be good and tend to their chores, and silently vowed to replace the money and then some at her first opportunity.

Her father pulled the buckboard to the front of the house. The team of plow horses snorted and pawed the ground, impatient to be on their way. Her mother placed a sack of food inside her carpetbag, and Reuben hoisted it into the back of the wagon as Grace accepted her father's callused hand to climb up next to him.

When she was settled, he clicked his tongue, and they moved forward. Grace twisted around so she could wave her handkerchief, and kept waving until the dust from the road hid her family from view.

She looked at the road ahead and felt a twinge of excitement. She was on her way. She was going to do something that would contribute to her family's well-being and, at the same time, give her a chance to explore new places and meet new people. She trembled with the possibilities.

They rode in silence for much of the way, but as they neared town, her father cleared his throat. "You can always come home, Gracie. Don't go gettin' it in your mind that if these folks don't have the sense to hire you straight away, that's somehow a failure on your part. That's on them. You come on home. Nobody's gonna think less of you for trying. And if you do take on this work, remember what your ma and me taught you. Anything worth doing is worth doing right. And when they pay you, don't go sending that money back straight away. You're likely to have needs, so take some time to settle in and get your bearings." He fell silent for a moment before adding, "I appreciate you wanting to do your part, Gracie, but your mother and I have weathered hard times before. We'll get through this as well."

This was probably the most her father had ever said to her at one time. He spoke softly but quickly, as if he had a lot he wanted to say all at once. They were even with the station now, and Grace saw a few other passengers waiting patiently on the platform. She nodded to neighbors who had come to town to buy supplies or maybe to stop by the bank. Her father had been one of those only weeks earlier, going to see about a loan that had never materialized. The set of people's shoulders and the slightly skittish looks on their haggard faces spoke louder than words. The summer had been unusually hot and dry. Crops had shriveled in the fields. Hopefully, spring would bring better weather and the new crops would thrive, but they had to get through the winter first. And to do that, her family sorely needed the fifty dollars the bank had denied them.

Her father pulled the wagon up to a hitching post, set the brake, and climbed down. Grace followed, smoothing the skirt of her best navy-blue serge Sunday suit. Would it do for meeting the woman who was to interview her once she reached Kansas City?

"Train's comin'," someone shouted.

Her father took her bag from the wagon and led the way to the station. Inside, she presented the voucher the company had sent for her ticket to Kansas City. Max Branson, the stationmaster and a man her family had known their whole lives, looked at Grace's father as if to ask if he was sure about all this. It occurred to Grace that the entire town would likely be buzzing long before she reached her destination, voicing their opinions about her decision. She was pretty sure most would side with her mother.

Outside, the train's engine hissed steam, adding to the noise of people boarding and shouting their good-byes. Her father handed her the bag and kept his eyes on the wooden planks of the platform. She gripped the cracked leather handles with both hands.

"'Board!" The conductor moved along the platform, herding people onto the two passenger cars.

Grace set her bag down and wrapped her arms around her father. He stiffened and then softened as he returned the embrace. "Remember what I said," he whispered, his voice breaking.

Unable to speak, Grace nodded, kissed his weathered cheek, grabbed her bag, and hurried to climb the iron steps leading to the last passenger car. Although she'd been sent vouchers for first-class travel as well as for food, the stationmaster had told her there was no first-class coach on this train and her food voucher was no good either. Her father had handed over payment for the one meal the train would stop for between here and Kansas City. Grace felt embarrassed. She had worked so hard to convince her parents that the Harvey Company would cover all expenses, and already that was proving not to be true.

The train started to move as she lurched down the aisle. She quickly found a seat next to a heavyset woman who scowled at her but gathered her belongings closer, leaving Grace a sliver of space on the hard wooden seat.

Grace tried rubbing a film of black dirt from the window so she could get a glimpse of her father, but by the time she managed it, the platform was empty. It was hard to believe that in just a matter of weeks, if she passed the interview—and the training—she'd be on her way to her new life somewhere west of Kansas City. The dreams she'd had as a girl of travel and adventure were actually coming true.

In time, the rhythm of the train and the monotony

of the view through the window lulled her into
sleep, so when it stopped with a jolt, she sat up and
looked around.

The heavyset woman picked up her belongings
and waddled down the aisle, practically at a run. The
conductor announced the stop as "Twenty minutes!"
Grace stood and waited politely as the other passengers
made a mad rush through the car. Earlier, the conductor had reminded them the train would stop once on
its way to Kansas City. The food they'd paid for when
they bought their tickets would be waiting for them,
but they needed to eat and get back on the train. "We
keep to the schedule," he'd told her as he moved on
to the next car.

A woman grabbed Grace's arm.

"Come on, honey," she said. "Don't want to be last
in line." Once they stepped off the train, the woman
continued her instructions. "You'll want to head
straight for the washroom so you can relieve yourself,
then get in line to grab your food and make it back to
the train before it pulls away again."

"But Mr. Harvey's establishments…"

The woman shrugged. "This ain't no Harvey place,
honey."

And it wasn't. The owners claimed they had fallen
behind and the food would not be ready for another
twenty minutes, meaning even though passengers had
paid in advance, they had to choose between forfeit-
ing their money or missing the train. The thing that
surprised Grace was that no one complained. They just
grumbled as they filed back onto the train. She wondered if this was so normal that travelers took it in stride.

She also wondered if maybe the Fred Harvey Company had oversold what she could expect from them.

As the train picked up steam, she shared the food her mother had stashed in her bag with the woman who had helped her, as well as others seated around her. By the time she arrived in Kansas City, her stomach was growling, and she was feeling hot and a little dizzy as she made her way through the crowds. A passing carriage splashed mud on her skirt, and she knew her hair was in serious need of repair. By the time she found the Harvey Company headquarters and presented herself to a young man seated at a large reception desk, she was convinced there was no chance she would be hired.

What a mess I've made of this, she thought.

"Grace Rogers!"

A young woman stood in an open doorway calling Grace's name, apparently not for the first time.

"Here," she said, raising her hand the way a student might in school.

"This way, please. Miss Culver is waiting."

Miss Culver was about Grace's mother's age, but any similarity ended there. Fashionably dressed in a rose-colored skirt topped by a high-necked, lace-collared blouse similar to day costumes Grace had admired in the Sears, Roebuck and Co. mail-order catalog, the woman's smile was both welcoming and concerned.

"Oh, my dear," she exclaimed. "I see you've had a time of it already." She led Grace to a straight chair and poured her a glass of water from a beautiful crystal pitcher. "Drink this and catch your breath," she instructed. She stood by for a moment to make sure Grace drank the water, then took her place behind a large desk. Miss Culver folded her hands and said, "Now then. Tell me, Grace Rogers, why do you want to be a Harvey Girl?"

An hour later, Grace's head was still spinning but for an entirely different reason. Miss Culver had asked so many questions—about her background, her experience, even her hopes for the future. But when she handed Grace an official-looking document and said, "Sign here, dear, and welcome to the Harvey Company," Grace felt like shouting for pure joy. She'd done it!

Her hand trembled as she signed the contract stating her intent to accept the terms of employment Miss Culver had explained. The contract was for six months, the first month without pay while she was being trained, although she would be housed and fed. After successfully completing her training, she would leave immediately for whatever eating establishment she was assigned.

"Miss Trevor will take you to be measured for your uniforms and show you to the dormitory where you'll stay for the next month," Miss Culver explained, ushering Grace to the door. "Come the end of next month, all going as planned, you'll be on your way to your new position. Congratulations."

Four weeks before she would begin earning the money she intended to send home.

It seemed so far away.

Nick Hopkins was anxious to get back to the ranch. The yearly October trip to Kansas City was a necessary evil that went with his job as foreman of a large cattle concern just outside Juniper, New Mexico. At least negotiating with the railroads over the price of beef to be served along the routes had gotten a lot easier now that Fred Harvey's outfit had convinced the railroad to let them take over the food service part of the business. Old man Harvey might be a stickler for doing things proper, but at least he was honest.

The train back to Juniper this time around was unusually crowded, even in first class. All Nick wanted was to find a seat he didn't need to share so he could stretch out a bit and get some much-needed shut-eye. The city was noisy and far too bright for his tastes. He longed for the dark quiet of New Mexico.

As the train jolted forward, he found his balance and looked down the aisle. He spotted one empty seat, but it was one of those situations where the seats faced each other. The other side was occupied by a young woman. What if she wanted to chatter on about being on her way to visit some relative or maybe meet her intended? She looked nervous, her arm firmly locked through the handles of her carpetbag. Her gaze darted around, and she twisted the frayed strings of her cloth purse in her fingers while she took in her surroundings.

Still, it was the only available seat, so he moved forward and nodded to her as he placed his bag in the overhead carrier. He sat with his back braced against the window and stretched out his legs. Then for good measure, he folded his arms over his chest and lowered his hat over his eyes. That should give her the message.

She cleared her throat.

He opened his eyes to slits and studied her below the brim of his hat. She had fixed her gaze on the passing scenery and set the carpetbag on the seat next to the window, but she was still fiddling with that purse. Every once in a while, she would shift in her seat, touching the carpetbag as if to assure herself it was still there.

He shut his eyes tight.

She continued to fidget.

He'd never get any sleep if the woman kept up her squirming and twitching. "You'd be more comfortable if you let me put that bag of yours up in the rack," he said.

She studied him with eyes that were large with surprise—or maybe shock that he had dared speak to her. Blue eyes, the color of a New Mexico sky at noon.

"No, thank you," she said primly. Her gaze skittered away to a man seated across the aisle, and then Nick understood the reason for her nervous fidgeting. The man was grinning, his bloodshot eyes roaming brazenly over her. He was clearly a man of means, but his expensive suit was unkempt. He was traveling with a woman Nick assumed was his wife and three squirming children. They were all well-dressed, but the man was clearly drunk, and the woman looked exhausted. With a worried frown, she continued to glance between her husband and the younger woman.

Nick sat up, leaned across the aisle, and spoke directly to the harried wife. "Those are good-looking kids, ma'am," he said.

His words had the effect he expected. Her husband drew himself up to his full stubby height and glared at Nick. "Mind your business," he muttered. He switched seats to sit next to his wife, putting himself out of the line of sight of the girl, and ordered his three children to sit on the seat opposite and be quiet.

Nick shrugged, leaned back, and once again lowered his hat over his eyes.

"Thank you," the young woman across from him whispered as she bent down and pretended to straighten the hem of her dress. She was wearing gloves that looked new, but the single feather in the small hat perched on her honey-colored hair could use replacing, and the rest of her traveling outfit had seen better days. Maybe the gloves had been a going away gift. In spite of himself, he was curious.

"Where you headed?" he asked.

She hesitated.

"Just passing time," he assured her as he sat up again and faced her, setting his feet on the floor and his hat on the seat beside him.

"New Mexico," she replied.

He smiled. She was a cautious one. "New Mexico's a big place."

"So I've heard."

"You visiting family?"

"No." She turned to the window.

Okay, she didn't need to hit him over the head. He got it. They'd switched roles—now she was the one who wanted no conversation. No skin off his nose. He leaned back and closed his eyes. Still, in spite of his determination to mind his own business, there was something about her that piqued his curiosity. After a moment, he said, "I manage a ranch just outside Juniper. That's a little north of Santa Fe."

She frowned and tightened her grip on her purse. "That's nice."

He leaned forward and spoke in a low voice meant for her ears only. "Just a word of advice. The more you fiddle with that purse of yours, the more you'll make unsavory sorts wonder just what you've got in there that you're so scared of losing."

Her mouth opened and closed a couple of times, and she glanced around the car as if looking for an escape. Just then, the conductor started down the aisle, calling for tickets, and Nick saw her breathe a sigh of relief.

She handed over her ticket and motioned for the conductor to lean in closer, whispering something to him.

"Sorry, miss. We're pretty full up. A few passengers are scheduled to leave us at the supper stop. Maybe after that," the man replied as he took Nick's ticket and punched it. He studied Nick for a moment and grinned. "Mr. Hopkins! Haven't seen you on board in a while."

Nick grinned. "It's Ollie, right?"

The conductor nodded. "Good to see you, sir." He turned back to the young woman and leaned in close, but Nick still heard his words. "You're in good hands, Miss. Mr. Nick Hopkins is a fine gentleman." He turned to punch the tickets of the family across the aisle.

❧

Nick Hopkins might be a fine man, and a handsome one, but he was nevertheless still a stranger. On the other hand, his comment about her purse was probably no more than him trying to offer some advice. He did seem sincerely concerned, the way he'd thwarted the unwanted attention of the man across the aisle. But still, a girl needed to take care. She looped the strings around her wrist again and allowed the purse to rest against her side.

She glanced at him and saw his lips quirk in what might have been a smile before he turned his attention to the window. His skin was tanned to a burnished gold except for a lighter stripe across his forehead. His head was probably usually protected—her father had the same line on his face for the same reason—though in the cowboy's case, it would have been by that black hat on the seat next to him. His thick, chocolate-colored hair kept falling over his forehead even though he repeatedly brushed it back with his fingers. He needed a shave, but there was something appealing about the stubble of whiskers. He was tall; that much was evidenced by the fact that even when occupying a seat meant for two, he seemed to need more space. He had broad shoulders that stretched the limits of the dark-gray sack coat he wore. The tan cotton shirt underneath it was in need of a good ironing. His trousers were a dark brown and his boots black, with fancy tooling.

"Do I pass inspection?" he asked, jarring her back to reality—and the realization that she had been studying every inch of him.

Her cheeks grew warm and red. "I…"

He waved away any excuse she might offer. "Look, Miss…" He waited.

"Rogers," she said, her voice cracking. "Grace Rogers." She saw no harm in giving him her name, and she didn't want to be rude.

"Pleased to make your acquaintance, Miss Rogers." He hesitated, then added, "Like Ollie said, I'm Nick Hopkins. I wonder if you would do me the honor of joining me for supper?"

The offer was more tempting than it should have been. She had looked forward to dining in a real Harvey eatery, but even though her first-class ticket included meals, having dinner with this stranger— even paying her own way—simply would not do. "I have food with me. Apples and cheese and some bread." She nodded reluctantly toward the carpetbag and the sack of food inside it that Miss Culver had given her at the station.

"But did you ever eat in a Harvey House, Miss Rogers?" he asked.

"Yes. In Kansas City." She took pleasure in his surprise. He probably saw her as some country bumpkin. She straightened her back and shoulders and met his gaze directly for the first time. "You see, I work for the organization." She flashed the practiced smile she'd developed in training.

His return smile took her breath away. How could any man be this good-looking? She felt her cheeks begin to turn pink, but she shook off the attraction. She had no time for flirting. She was on her way to a *job*, a new life that would hopefully provide adventure for her and much-needed financial assistance for her family.

Still, she couldn't help but cast him a quick look from beneath her lashes.

"Well now," he drawled. "In that case, it seems to me it would be to your advantage to try as many of Mr. Harvey's establishments as possible. You could look at things from the customer's view and see how the one we'll be stopping at soon is different from the one where you'll be working."

"Oh, there are no differences, Mr. Hopkins," she replied, parroting the information she'd absorbed during her training. "At least not when it comes to service and quality of food. Our organization adheres to the same standards no matter where we are. It's the Harvey way." As the train pulled into the station, Grace pressed her hands over her skirt. "Enjoy your meal, Mr. Hopkins," she said brightly.

Nick Hopkins grinned and stood. He reached past her and took her carpetbag from her, lifting it into the overhead rack, then stepped back to allow her to go ahead of him. "If you change your mind, Miss Rogers…"

A dozen different thoughts flashed through Grace's mind. She reminded herself that going with this man might be construed as breaking the strict rules for conduct set forth in her training. She reminded herself of her mother's warning not to talk to strangers. She reminded herself that she had no time for exploring a possible friendship—or more—with a man.

She was a Harvey Girl now and, as such, represented the high standards of the company. "I won't," she said, "but thank you for your kind offer, sir." With that, she made her way to the exit.

The establishment was a far cry from the place her train to Kansas City had stopped. Greeters met passengers at the entrance and discreetly directed them to the appropriate washroom. By the time Grace returned to the dining room, Mr. Hopkins was already seated at a table near the door. He looked up, arching an eyebrow and nodding toward the empty place across from him in question.

She hesitated. The truth was, now that she was actually standing in the dining room filled with people, it struck her that she was alone and knew no one—other than Mr. Hopkins. Where would be the harm in sitting opposite possibly the most handsome man she'd ever seen, a man who also appeared to be quite intelligent and genuinely concerned for her welfare? After all, the conductor had vouched for him.

On the other hand, given how strict Mr. Harvey's standards were for his employees, how did she know someone wouldn't be watching and report her? Maybe Mr. Hopkins worked for Mr. Harvey and was supposed to be testing her.

She straightened to her full height—just over five feet—scanned the room quickly, and made her way to a vacant chair at a table occupied by two other women. Seating herself, Grace smiled up at the waitress in her pristine uniform: a black dress covered by a crisp white pinafore apron, black shoes polished to a sheen, and black hose, all topped off with a perky white bow in her upswept hair. "Milk, please," she said and watched as the waitress set her coffee cup next to its saucer, its position a simple cue to the girl who served the beverages.

As soon as the waitress walked away, the drink girl arrived, glanced quickly at the way the cups had been set, and poured coffee for Grace's tablemates, leaving a full pot on the table in case they wanted refills. Moments later, she delivered a tall glass of milk to Grace, presenting the beverage on a small silver tray. A girl could be fired for simply carrying a glass or plate to a customer. Serving on a tray was the Harvey way.

This is my future, Grace thought, *not some cowboy who is far too handsome for his own good.*

"Oh, sweetie," one of her tablemates whispered as soon as the drink girl left. "Are you sure? I wouldn't turn that down if I were you." The one speaking nodded toward the cowboy who had snapped open his cloth napkin and was smiling up at a waitress.

Grace kept her attention focused on the two women sharing her table. One was slim and tall, with blond hair that was so pale, it was almost white. Her friend was petite with curly light-brown hair that framed her delicate features.

"That man?" Grace glanced briefly at Mr. Hopkins. "I don't know him. He took the seat across from me on the train." She hoped the slight lift of her shoulders could be interpreted as "What could I do?"

"Still…"

The brunette, seated across from Grace, rolled her eyes. "Pay no attention to Lily. She's never seen a man she hasn't pictured as her Prince Charming. I'm Emma Elliott, by the way."

"Grace Rogers," Grace replied, taking in each of her tablemates with the introduction. "I just finished my training with the Harvey Company. I'm on my way to Juniper, New Mexico, to start work."

Lily grinned. "Welcome to the crew. We're Harvey Girls as well. Just got transferred down to New Mexico. Frankly, I can't wait. If that cowboy is any example of the local fare, I'm gonna be one happy lady."

Emma smiled. "Lily Travis, you are all talk."

They finished the first course—a wedge of iceberg lettuce covered in the Harvey Company's homemade dressing—and then gave their attention to the manager, who entered the dining room carrying a large tray balanced on the flat of one hand held high above his head. Beef sizzled on the tray, and the irresistible aroma spread throughout the room. He set the tray on an empty table and was immediately surrounded by the waitresses who waited for him to carve and portion out the servings that they delivered quickly to their tables. The food was piping hot and smelled delicious.

Conversation throughout the dining room petered out as everyone enjoyed the food. The waitresses passed through the dining room offering second helpings, and the manager assured everyone they had plenty of time to enjoy their meal. He would let them know when it was time to board the train. Grace couldn't help thinking about the difference between this meal stop and the one she'd experienced on her way to Kansas City a month earlier.

By the time they'd finished dessert—a quarter of warm apple pie, because the Harvey way was to divide a pie into four slices, not the usual six—Mr. Hopkins was no longer in the restaurant. On their way out the door, Emma came alongside and hooked her hand through Grace's arm. "The couple sitting across from us left the train here. There's room if you'd like to sit with us," she said. "We're at the far end of the first-class car, near the sleeping berths."

"Yes, thank you," she told Emma. "I'll just get my bag." Mr. Hopkins was standing on the other end of the platform. If she hurried, she could collect her bag and make the move before he was aware she'd decided to change seats.

"The conductor will take care of that for you. Come on." Emma led the way to the train, only stopping to speak to the conductor. He nodded and assured Grace he would take care of moving her luggage as soon as everyone was on board.

Just then, Lily came rushing from the station. "Saw someone I knew and had to say my goodbyes," she said, but what Grace noticed most was that the lively young woman had evidently taken a moment to apply rouge to her cheeks and lips.

"So it's the rushing about that is to account for the sudden glow to your cheeks…and lips?" Emma asked drily as she led the way down the aisle to their seats at the far end of the car.

They settled in, and the train moved slowly forward. Then Lily gasped. "Oh my," she whispered and immediately put a hand to her hair as she looked up with a coquettish smile.

"Ladies." Grace was seated with her back to the new arrival, but she knew that voice—a little husky, very deep. Mr. Hopkins stepped forward and looked down at her. He was carrying her bag. "I'll just store this above for you. Give everyone a little more room."

Grace's cheeks flamed with embarrassment. She kept her eyes on the toes of his black boots as she nodded. "Thank you," she managed.

"You could join us," Lily offered. "There's plenty of room for four."

Grace's head shot up.

Mr. Hopkins chuckled. "That's mighty kind of you, Miss...?"

"Travis," Lily said as she offered him her gloved hand as if expecting him to bow and kiss it. "Lily Travis. And where are my manners? This is Emma Elliott, and of course you've already met our friend, Grace Rogers."

Grace wondered how she could have missed Lily's Southern drawl. Then she realized the accent was for the benefit, no doubt, of Mr. Hopkins. After all, she'd said she was originally from Chicago.

"Nick Hopkins," he said as he nodded to Emma, who stood and shook his hand as firmly as any man might have.

"Thank you for taking such good care of Miss Rogers, Mr. Hopkins," she said. "We'll be fine for the remainder of our journey."

Grace might have expected the cowboy to be upset, but instead he nodded and tipped his hat to each of them. "Ladies," he said again. "I look forward to seeing the three of you again." And with that, he strode up the aisle, seemingly impervious to the need to steady himself against the movement of the train.

Grace realized she had turned around to watch him leave. Behind her, Lily sighed. "That is one good-lookin' man."

Emma took out some knitting and began to work. "That is one dangerous man, ladies. If you value your jobs, I would advise keeping your distance." She fixed her gaze on Grace. "Especially you."

"Why me especially?" Grace would have thought Emma would be far more concerned about Lily.

"Because that man has his eyes on you. Not me and, despite her efforts, not Lily."

Lily stuck out her tongue at Emma and then grinned. "Never mind men. The three of us are going to have a grand time in Juniper, I just know it."

But as the train clicked off the miles, Grace realized dismissing Nick Hopkins was not as easy as Lily seemed to think. She found herself recalling little details about the man, like his smile and the way he kept brushing his hair off his forehead. Far more intimate details than seemed proper for a Harvey Girl.

Chapter 2

THE TRAIN PULLED INTO THE JUNIPER STATION JUST after sunrise. The three women had moved to their sleeping berths a little after nine, but Grace had been too excited and nervous to sleep. At first light, she scooted close to the window and peered out, trying to see through a mist of steam as the train slowed for the final approach to the station.

"Grace, are you awake?" Emma whispered from the berth across from hers. "We're getting close. You should dress and get to the washroom before the hordes descend."

Grace had never bothered to undress, sitting up through the night studying her training manual and writing her mother about the train, the restaurant stop, and her new friends. She had decided not to say anything about Mr. Hopkins. She stepped into the aisle. Lily yawned and stretched as Emma gathered her toiletries and walked unsteadily down the length of the car to the washroom.

Once they had all taken their turn in the washroom and gone back to sit in the passenger car, Lily lowered the top half of the window, stuck her head out, and looked around. The train slowed to a stop, and she ducked back inside and shrugged. "Seems like a nice enough place," she reported. "Lots of people milling around. I saw the hotel just across the street and some shops down the other way." She gave Grace a sly grin. "I also saw your Mr. Hopkins, stepping off the train the second it stopped and heading into the station like he owned the place."

"He is hardly *my* Mr. Hopkins," Grace protested, flustered. She turned her attention to retrieving her bag—one she had to lift with two hands and that Nick Hopkins had handled as if it were empty. She set it on the seat, put on her hat, and jabbed the long hatpin firmly through it and the twist of her hair.

"Ready?" Emma asked.

Grace took a deep breath, let it out, and nodded. *I'm actually here*, she thought, unable to control a giggle of delight.

After making arrangements for their luggage to be delivered, the three women walked across the platform and through the bustling station to the main street beyond. The October early-morning sun was already as warm as summer in Missouri. They paused, looking up and down the street as they took in their surroundings. The town was nowhere near as large as Kansas City had been, but there was still a fair amount of traffic. Wagons, buggies, and men on horseback wove their way up and down the dirt street. Emma pointed out two saloons, already open for business even at this early hour. A large mercantile dominated one side of the plaza, its assortment of wares spilling onto the boardwalk outside its double doors. Nearer the station was a blacksmith shop. Nick Hopkins stood there, holding the reins of a beautiful black horse while he laughed at something the blacksmith was saying.

He did have the nicest smile.

Emma tugged at her sleeve and pointed across the street to where Grace saw a sign announcing *Welcome to the Palace Hotel—A Harvey House Establishment*. The building was impressive, constructed in the adobe style common to the area, its reddish-brown clay walls inset here and there with aqua ceramic tiles that reflected the morning sun. The grounds surrounding the hotel set it off to perfection, large planters overflowing with desert foliage set at intervals along the covered walkway that ran the length of the front of the hotel.

"Oh my," Grace whispered and hurried forward without a thought for whether or not Emma and Lily were following, anxious to see the inside of this place. It had already exceeded even her wildest hopes for what she might find in New Mexico. Once she added these details to the letter she'd started on the train, her parents would have to agree that she had made the right choice in coming here.

The morning breakfast rush was just ending when they reached the hotel. Men in business attire and others dressed in the rougher clothing of ranch hands or railroad employees tipped their hats politely and stepped aside as the three women entered the spacious lobby. Emma took charge as usual, approaching the desk. The man behind it, dressed in a black coat and striped morning trousers, topped by a white shirt with a stiff collar and bow tie, looked up.

"May I be of service, miss?"

"We are the new girls," Emma said, gesturing to Lily, who had wandered away to look around, and Grace, who stood frozen to the spot next to Emma, trying hard not to gawk. "I'm Emma Elliott."

"And I am Aidan Campbell," the man replied, "manager of this hotel and eating establishment."

Grace realized Mr. Campbell was technically the boss of every employee working in the hotel. She smoothed her hair and stood a little straighter, hoping to make a good impression.

"You're Scottish," Emma said with a smile. "I recognize the hint of—"

"Miss Kaufmann, our head waitress and dining room manager, has been expecting you." Mr. Campbell snapped his fingers to gain the attention of a young man dressed in a uniform of red and black. The bell-boy hurried forward. "Please escort these young ladies to Miss Kaufmann's office and then return to take care of their luggage." He turned back to Emma. "I assume your belongings will be delivered from the train?"

Emma fished around in her bag and produced a coin. "Yes, please see that the porter receives this, with our thanks."

"Unnecessary," he said, staring at the coin Emma held out to him.

"I insist."

Grace realized she liked Emma more and more. Here was someone with the confidence and poise not to be intimidated by others. She might do well to model herself on Emma's example. Mr. Campbell took the coin with a slight frown. He was clearly not a person who was accustomed to being contradicted. Grace filed that snippet of information away as well.

"A bit full of himself, that one," Lily muttered as they followed the bellboy down a back hallway and through a door that led to the kitchen.

The gangly youth led the way through the kitchen, where cooks and dishwashers dodged around each other preparing the last of the lunches, and on to the open door of a small room. He paused and cleared his throat.

The woman seated at the desk looked up, then stood. "So, they're here at last," she sighed.

"Yes, miss." The boy stepped aside and hesitated.

"That will be all, Tommy," the woman said.

The bellboy nodded to the trio and then hurried back to the lobby.

Meanwhile, Miss Kaufmann stood just outside her office and studied the three young women. "Names?"

"Emma Elliott." Emma had to shout to be heard above the din of pots and pans behind them. The smell of food cooking was a reminder that they had skipped breakfast in order to have more time in the washroom.

"Lily Travis."

"Grace R–R–Rogers."

Miss Kaufmann walked in front of them as if inspecting her troops. She circled them as a group before stopping to study Lily more closely. "Is that lip rouge, Lily Travis?"

Grace followed Emma's lead of keeping her eyes on her shoes while Miss Kaufmann produced a clean white handkerchief and handed it to Lily. "Clean it off, and let's have no more such foolishness."

To Grace's surprise, Lily did as she was told, murmuring, "Yes, ma'am," as she scrubbed her mouth clean.

"We're a bit short on dorm space here at the Palace. I'm afraid the three of you will share a room on the top floor, end of the hall." She indicated a back stairway. "When in uniform, you will use this rear door as your entrance and exit path to and from the hotel. I do not ever wish to see any of you in the lobby or other public areas unless you are as properly attired as any of our guests. Is that clear?"

"Yes, ma'am," they replied in unison.

"In addition to my duties overseeing the counter and dining room, I am also your housemother. My room is at the top of the stairs, and I am a light sleeper. Curfew during the week is ten o'clock. On Saturdays, it is midnight. The bath is across the hall from your room and shared by all the young ladies employed here. There are uniforms and shoes waiting for you in your room. Please go wash up and change. Don't dawdle. I need you in place for the lunch hour."

Grace's hands were trembling, and Miss Kaufmann took note. "As the new girl, you'll take a post behind our lunch counter to start. I assume you've been properly trained in the serving of beverages?"

"Yes, ma'am," Grace whispered.

"Speak up, child, and smile." She gave Grace a rather gruesome showing of her own teeth, and Grace heard Lily cover a snort by pretending to cough. "Well, off with the three of you. We have four trains a day coming and going on our weekday schedule with people needing to be fed in a timely manner, along with all the locals and railroad workers. No time to dillydally." Miss Kaufmann flapped her hands at them as if she were shooing away flies.

Dismissed, they hurried up three flights of tiled steps and were a little out of breath by the time they reached the top floor. They followed a long dim hallway past a series of closed doors to the one at the end of the hall that stood open. Crowding into the small room, they saw three narrow beds that took up most of the space. On each bed lay a uniform—high-neck black dress, white apron and petticoat, black stockings, and the trademark white bow they would wear in their hair.

"What if our uniforms don't fit?" Grace said as she studied the polished shoes next to one bed. During training, she had worn her own shoes, and truthfully, she dreaded breaking in new ones.

Lily shrugged. "I assume they took your measurements and shoe size during your training. Emma and I are transfers, so those are for you. We have our shoes already." She lifted a foot to show the toe of her shoe, then took her uniform and headed across the hall to the bathroom.

"Don't dawdle," Emma called after her in a perfect imitation of Miss Kaufmann's instruction before turning back to Grace. "We should start changing. Knowing Lily, we'll barely have time to relieve ourselves and wash our faces before we have to race downstairs again." She closed the bedroom door and began removing her traveling clothes.

Grace followed Emma's lead. Not only was Emma confident, she was older and more experienced, having worked for the Harvey Company for five years. She understood what it would take to make a success of the position. *Like a big sister*, Grace thought and then allowed herself a little smile of pleasure as she pulled on the black stockings. Back home, she'd always been the oldest. It might be nice to have someone she could rely on.

Emma dressed quickly, clearly well practiced at putting on the uniform. While Grace was fastening the buttons on her dress, Emma stepped across the hall and knocked loudly on the bathroom door. "Time's up, Lily," she called and then came back to help Grace fix the white bow in her hair. "Perfect," she announced as Lily exited the bathroom, carrying her traveling clothes, which she dumped on her bed instead of hanging on the hooks provided as Grace and Emma had done.

"Ready, girls?"

Emma rolled her eyes and indicated Grace should use the bathroom next. As she closed the door, Grace heard Emma say, "Lily, I'm guessing this job is important to Grace—and her family. Please don't lead her astray."

"I would never," Lily protested as she closed the door to the bedroom.

Grace wondered why Emma felt the need to caution Lily. True, Lily was outspoken and free-spirited, but she'd certainly shown Grace nothing but sincere friendship. She opened the door to the shared bathroom and gave no more thought to Emma's warning. The view before her made her giggle with pure delight.

During her training, Grace had experienced the convenience of an indoor toilet and hot water on tap, neither of which they'd had back on the farm. But in *this* bathroom, there was a bathtub that looked large enough for two and stood on feet that looked like a lion's paws, a toilet with a pull chain to empty it, and a sink with faucets marked as hot and cold, plus a basin deep enough for washing one's hair. She was well used to sharing a room with her sisters no bigger than the one across the hall, but a real bathroom? That was living in luxury as far as she was concerned. Just wait until she wrote Mama about this!

Once downstairs, Emma and Lily were directed to the main dining room while Miss Kaufmann walked with Grace to the lunch counter just off the lobby. The large U-shaped counter was made of gleaming black marble set on a highly polished mahogany base. Swivel chairs set on metal posts secured to the floor lined one side. Each place was set with a cup and saucer, a pristine white linen napkin, and a gleaming set of cutlery, waiting for the next customer to arrive. The serving side of the counter had storage underneath, outfitted with wire baskets to hold fresh napkins and silverware and space for stacks of cups, saucers, and juice glasses. The plates and bowls would come from the kitchen, depending on what the customer ordered.

Two of Fred Harvey's trademark huge silver-plated coffee urns sat on the second black marble counter behind the first, along with an array of tempting pastries and pies displayed on glass pedestals, each covered with a spotless glass dome. Grace knew she and a polishing cloth would have more than a passing acquaintance in short order with all that glass and silver. Two of the chairs at the counter were occupied, and given the number of people milling around in the lobby, it seemed likely the rest would be filled soon enough.

Grace swallowed her nerves and tried to concentrate on the instructions Miss Kaufmann was giving.

"For now, you will be on beverage service," she said, waving a hand at the coffee urns. "Cups, saucers, spoons, napkins, sugars, and creamers." She moved quickly along the open shelving indicating the location of each item. "Miss Forrester here will take and deliver food orders and set the cups." She stopped speaking and stared a moment at Grace's trembling hands. "You do know what I mean when I say 'set the cups,' Miss Rogers?"

Grace forced her hands to be still by flexing them at her sides beneath the cover of the fullness of her apron. "Yes, ma'am." She cleared her throat. "I mean, yes, Miss Kaufmann."

"Very well." She still did not seem convinced. Grace had visions of the head waitress going straight back to her office and dictating a telegram to headquarters in Kansas City that the new girl simply would not do. "Miss Forrester, let me know if there are issues."

"Yes, Miss Kaufmann," the other girl assured her, seeming to swell with importance. But when Miss Kaufmann had gone, she turned to Grace. "Just to be clear, my name is Polly, and I am in charge of things here at the lunch counter."

Grace stuck out her hand. "Pleased to meet you. My name is—"

Polly ignored her outstretched hand. "I do not have time to learn all the names. There's work to be done. Assuming you recall your training, I'll set the empty places with cups to indicate a customer's choice of beverage. Tell me what each person has ordered."

She'd just gone through four weeks of demanding training and answered the same doubt from Miss Kaufmann. Was she to be tested yet again? Grace stiffened slightly, wondering just how far Polly's authority extended.

They moved to the first setting. Polly set the cup upright on the saucer. "Coffee," Grace said and moved on to the next place where Polly turned the cup over. "Hot tea." Polly set the next cup upside down but tilted against the saucer. "Iced tea." The final cup was also upside down but completely removed from the saucer. "And milk," she said.

"Impressive. Of course, there is not yet the pressure of the rush. You'll need to keep your wits about you." Polly pointed at the giant urns. "As for these"—she took the cup set for coffee and turned to the urns—"we do not leave pots of coffee or tea at the counter as we do in the dining room. You fill the cup three quarters full in case the customer uses cream and sugar," she explained. "Of course, in time—if you last—you'll get to know the regulars and their preferences." She set the cup and saucer on a small silver tray, then opened the door to a refrigerated section below the urns and removed a glass pitcher of cream. "Never prepare the creamer in advance and leave it sitting out," she instructed. "No matter how busy we are."

Grace nodded. It had been the same in training; otherwise, she might have suspected that Polly was either testing or deliberately misleading her. "Thank you, Polly. I really appreciate this. I think I can manage now."

"Good. Now reset these places with clean dishes, and remember, you are to serve beverages only. I will handle everything else," Polly said. She glanced at the entrance to the café and suddenly broke into a radiant smile. "I'll take this one," she said, thrusting the tray into Grace's hands. "Dispose of this." She hastily moved to the end of the counter.

"Hello, Polly…and Miss Rogers."

That voice. Grace spun around and looked directly into Nick Hopkins's deep-brown eyes. *The color of black coffee*, she thought before she realized Polly was scowling at her.

"Hello," she murmured. The small tray shook, and the cream sloshed dangerously close to the rim of the pitcher.

"Oh, for heaven's sake," Polly muttered as she relieved her of the tray and disposed of the dishes in a dance of efficiency before turning back to their customer. The smile returned as she posted herself directly between Grace and Nick, setting a fresh cup and saucer in place as she did—cup turned upright. "So good to see you back, Mr. Hopkins," she said. "Will you be having your usual order?"

"Just coffee today. How 'bout you let Miss Rogers serve me? I expect she could use the practice and a friendly face on her first day here." He grinned at her.

"I wasn't aware the two of you were acquainted," Polly said as her smile stiffened into something that appeared quite painful.

"Met on the train from Kansas City. Isn't that right, Miss Rogers?"

Admittedly, she had hoped she hadn't seen the last

of Nick Hopkins, but this was her first day. Could he not see he was making matters worse? "I'm still in training," she managed. "Miss Forrester is—"

"Not at all," Polly said. "The customer has made a reasonable request that should be your privilege and pleasure to fulfill." She stepped aside and disappeared around the corner, leaving Grace on her own. Grace had the suspicion that Polly had not gone far and would be silently observing every move and every word.

She set his cup and saucer on a tray and went to the urns.

"By the way, I take it black, but just to give you the practice, how about you bring me some cream and sugar as well? If you like, of course."

"Yes, sir," she replied and turned to face the shelves. There were the creamers, but where were the sugar bowls? She scanned the shelves.

"Two compartments to your left," she heard Nick mutter softly.

She retrieved one of the small silver bowls filled with lumps of sugar as well as a pair of miniature tongs, and set the cup below the spigot of the urn. This was going better than she'd hoped. Nick was obviously a regular at the counter and was giving her tips to make her job easier. She relaxed and touched a finger to the lever as she'd observed Polly do. But Polly evidently knew exactly how much pressure to apply. Grace did not, and the coffee came rushing out like a creek breaking free of its ice bonds in spring. It spattered onto the counter and worse, onto her pristine white apron.

Polly was at her side instantly. "Go and change," she hissed. "I'll do this."

Mortified, Grace hurried around the corner and into the kitchen on her way to the back stairs, nearly colliding with a young man carrying a tray loaded with clean dishes.

"Whoa, Nellie," he said as he steadied his tray, but he continued to block her way. He glanced at her apron, and his laughing eyes turned sympathetic. "No need to go all the way upstairs. The girls keep clean aprons right over there." He jerked his head toward a row of hooks near the exit to the back stairway. "Go on. I'll just set these down and be right back to help you."

By the time he returned, Grace had removed the soiled apron and dropped it in a laundry bin that was already nearly full of tablecloths, dish towels, and other linens. At least laundering her uniform was one less thing Grace needed to worry about. She slipped a fresh apron over her head, trying not to muss her hair or ribbon. The man returned as promised and stepped behind her to tie the sash. He was not much taller—or older—than she was, but there was little doubt he was far more experienced. She could feel him whipping the sashes into a proper bow as if he'd done it dozens of times before.

"Name's Jake Collier," he said. "I'm the kitchen manager. And you are?"

"Grace Rogers. Thank you, Jake." She was close to tears, certain that Polly would report the incident to Miss Kaufmann. "I can't lose this job," she blurted.

Jake stepped around to face her. "Who says you will? Polly? She probably set you up. Those urns can have a mind of their own—takes a special touch.

Everybody makes mistakes, but you'll catch on soon enough. Now give me that smile I know is hiding somewhere behind those big blue eyes."

She couldn't help it. She smiled, sniffing back tears before they could overcome her.

"There you go," Jake said. "Now get back out there and show Polly you're here to take her job if she don't watch out."

The idea was so preposterous that Grace hooted a laugh and realized she felt better. Of course, there were going to be people like Polly who might try to intimidate her, but there would also be people like Emma and Lily and now Jake who would be there to help her make sure the Pollys of the world did not succeed.

When she stepped back to the counter, Polly was serving three men at the far end. Nick Hopkins glanced up, clearly surprised to see her back so soon.

"Would you like more coffee, Mr. Hopkins?" She was fully aware that Polly was watching her.

"Thank you, miss," he replied.

She discarded the dregs that remained in his cup before very carefully touching the lever on the large silver urn. This time, it obeyed her, and she allowed coffee to dribble into the cup until it was precisely three-quarters full. She presented the fresh coffee to him with a triumphant smile. "Will there be anything else, sir?"

He grinned at her. "That'll do fine, miss—just fine."

Grace continued to smile as she turned to address a customer who had just arrived and taken the remaining seat at the counter. "May I offer you some coffee, sir?"

"Orange juice," the man muttered.

Grace froze. Mr. Harvey's rules said that anyone

ordering orange juice got it freshly squeezed and the glass set on a bed of crushed ice, and that posed a whole new set of issues. She looked at Polly—who had heard the man order and was now smirking at her. Instead of stepping forward to help, Polly deliberately turned her back to speak with the businessman seated at the opposite end of the counter.

"Yes, sir," Grace said, her voice faltering. She edged a little away so that she was closer to the corner that led to the kitchen, praying that Jake might be there to rescue her yet again.

"Tray, juice glass—shelf to the right," Nick muttered under the guise of blowing on his coffee to cool it. "Oranges are in the bowl above the fruit press there."

She followed his whispered instructions, her hand shaking a little as she removed the bowl and caught sight of the press to her left. The confidence she'd felt when she conquered the coffee urn faded. She located a knife and cutting board and sliced oranges, willing herself to concentrate so she would make no more mistakes. She set the glass in place to catch the juice as she pressed it from the fruit. In less than two minutes, she had filled the glass. Pleased with herself, she placed the glass on a tray and prepared to serve the man when she heard Nick clear his throat on the word, "Ice."

As if by magic, Jake came around the corner just then and set a shallow bowl of shaved ice on the counter next to her before retrieving the used orange peels and juice extractor to take back to the kitchen for cleaning. Grace set the glass in the center of the shaved ice and presented it to her customer. "Miss Forrester will be here to take your order shortly, sir."

The man studied her, then grinned. "How about you take my order, missy, and maybe later, you'd also enjoy taking orders of a more private—"

Nick Hopkins was on his feet in an instant, standing just behind the man. "Maybe you need to find some manners, cowboy. She may be new, but there's no cause to disrespect her."

The man glanced over his shoulder, clearly recognized Nick, nodded once, and turned back to his juice. "Didn't mean nothin' by it, miss. Just my way."

"Miss Forrester will be with you soon to take your order, sir." Grace began wiping the counter as Jake appeared to reset the citrus press with clean parts ready for the next order. He grinned at her and gave her a salute to let her know she had done well.

"Thank you, Jake," she murmured, then turned to Nick Hopkins's vacated seat to collect his cup and saucer and the coins he'd set beside them to pay his bill. He'd overpaid by ten cents.

"Mr. Hopkins—"

"See you again, miss," he said as he tipped two fingers to the brim of his hat and walked away. Three times that morning, he'd stepped in to help her, and it occurred to her that having Nick Hopkins around might not be so bad.

The minute the train pulled into the station, Nick had intended to pick up his horse from the livery and head straight for the ranch, but he'd gone to the lunch counter on a whim. He could get coffee at the station or one of the saloons. He certainly didn't need to walk across the street to the hotel. But aware that she was over there, he couldn't deny he was curious. More than curious—he was attracted.

Fess up, Hopkins, he thought. *This is a lot more than idle curiosity.*

These Harvey Girls were not the usual sort of females seen in these parts. Men had settled the West, built the towns, established law and order. Even now, they outnumbered the women by a margin of probably ten to one. One or two men he knew had resorted to sending back east for what had come to be called a mail-order or catalog bride, desperate for a woman's help in managing the house and easing the brutal loneliness that was life on the frontier. Others found solace in the arms of the girls in the saloons— soiled doves, they were called—but a man would rarely consider marrying a girl like that. So when Harvey's girls started showing up, men in the area took note, even going so far as to agree to wash up, put on a clean shirt—and a jacket if they wanted to eat in the dining room—and leave their pistol at the door for the privilege of spending an hour enjoying good food and the smile of a pretty young waitress.

Nick had been as drawn to Fred Harvey's waitresses as any other red-blooded male would have been. A couple of times, he had invited Polly Forrester out to a band concert on the plaza or sat with her on the veranda of the hotel on a Sunday afternoon. Polly was nice enough, but Nick wasn't looking for anything permanent. He'd tried to be clear about that with Polly. He'd not once held her hand or tried to kiss her. He'd explained to her that he had plans—plans that eventually included marriage and family, but that was down the road a ways. She'd assured him she understood and talked about her own ambitions for a career with the Harvey Company.

After leaving the counter, Nick mounted his horse and rode out of town. He mused about the three women he'd met on the train. Emma Elliott would make a success of her new assignment. Everything about her posture and restrained smile said she understood the rules and had no intention of breaking them. Lily Travis, on the other hand, was trouble tied up in a shirtwaist that tested the limits of its button front, with cheeks and lips far too perfectly rosy to be genuine. And then there was Grace Rogers, the new girl. The one yet to be tested. What was her story? She was young, and yet she'd taken this job hundreds of miles from home without knowing a single person. That alone was a sign she had a spirit of adventure, and Nick admired that.

But it wasn't just her spunk that had her coming to mind more often than any female he'd ever known. The way she'd stood her ground in refusing to have dinner with him had made him smile—and made him tell Ollie he would move her carpetbag when the conductor came to collect it. And what about heading over to the hotel for coffee, telling himself he just wanted to see if she'd gotten settled in?

Admit it, Hopkins, he muttered. *Where Miss Grace Rogers is concerned, you're finding it hard to keep your mind on your work—and the future you've mapped out for yourself.*

In the distance, he saw some of the men he

managed working the herd. He waved his hat in greeting. Later, they would all gather in the bunkhouse for their nightly card game, and he'd hear all about what had happened while he'd been in Kansas City. That should do the trick when it came to getting his mind off the perky waitress and back onto the job—and the life—he loved.

He spurred his horse to a canter and headed over the rise that would lead to the Lombardo Ranch, which he'd managed since he was seventeen years old. It was a good job working for good people. After his folks died, the Lombards had taken him under their care. They'd given him the responsibility for managing their large land holdings and herd, and they had encouraged him to think beyond just working for them the rest of his days. He felt a loyalty to them that was hard to explain, but at the same time, he looked forward to the day when he might have a place of his own. He had his eye on a little patch of land in a valley not far from the Lombard place, and he'd finally managed to put aside enough of his pay to make a down payment. All he needed was for the bank to approve a loan, and since John Lombard had offered to cosign that loan, Nick was pretty sure the bank would allow him to buy the land. So first land and stock of his own, then a proper house, and maybe after that…

He was back to thinking about Grace.

That first night, as Grace sat in bed writing her family, gunshots rang out from down the street. All three of the women rushed to the window and witnessed two men staggering unsteadily in the street, waving pistols in the air and yelling obscenities at each other.

Lily raised the window and leaned out for a better view.

"Lily, get back in here," Emma instructed. "You're in your nightgown! Not to mention you could be shot by a stray bullet." She herded them into the hall, away from any windows, where Miss Kaufmann, Polly, and the other girls were already gathered, seemingly untroubled by the ruckus outside.

"Welcome to the Wild West," Polly said sarcastically.

"Does this happen regularly?" Grace asked.

Another girl snorted. "Just every night. They'll calm down directly, and then we can get some sleep."

Lily chuckled. "There was a time back in Chicago before I became a Harvey Girl when I worked for the Marshall Field department store," she told them. "I worked in the tearoom, and our customers were mostly society ladies dressed to the nines with apparently more money than they knew how to spend. One day, this man came in. He was wearing a suit that looked like he'd slept in it, and when he sat down at one of my tables, he placed a large revolver on the table. You should have heard the titters and outright screams from those women."

"What did you do?" Grace asked as she realized they had all forgotten about the ruckus in the street.

Lily shrugged. "I told him we preferred firearms be left at the door, used a napkin to pick up the thing, and handed it to the maître d'."

"And what did the customer do?"

"It was a tearoom, so he ordered tea and cakes," Lily replied with a grin.

All the girls laughed, and soon others were sharing tales of their experiences. Grace listened intently to all the stories, but truly, they only made her miss the farm and her family. She'd been so excited about the adventure of being on her own that she'd failed to realize how lonely that might be.

When they could no longer hear anything from the street, Grace turned to Emma. "I'm going to bed." She had spent most of the previous night sitting up on the train, and then she'd been on her feet serving customers at the lunch counter much of the day as the trains came and went. And when there weren't any customers around, she'd spent hours cleaning and polishing the silver coffee urns, marble counters, and glass display cases. She was exhausted and more than a little homesick, and morning would come all too soon.

Back in their small room, she picked up the letter she'd been writing to her mother when the whole thing started and set it aside. The hours since she'd arrived in Juniper had been so full of new experiences. She needed some time to find the words to relay them to her parents, words that would send the message that she was all right and had made the right decision.

But had she?

Chapter 3

NICK HOPKINS WAS ALREADY SEATED AT THE LUNCH counter when Grace hurried to her post two days later. The three girls had overslept, and Lily had spent so much time in the bathroom that Grace had only had the time to run a damp washcloth over her face and brush her teeth before following Emma and Lily down the back stairs.

"Good morning, Miss Rogers," Nick said with that smile that made Grace's pulse jump in her throat. "Take a moment," he said softly, studying a menu that, as a regular customer, he must surely already know by heart. His cup was once again turned upright, so Grace turned away to prepare his coffee.

"Think I'll start with some orange juice, please," he added.

She smiled. He was testing her to see if she'd gotten any more confident. Expertly, she sliced oranges, placing the halves one by one on the citrus press until she had a glass filled with juice. She scooped ice from a bucket Jake had left next to the press, filled the shallow dish, set the juice glass in its center, and presented it to the cowboy. "Will there be anything else, sir?" He grinned at her, his eyes sparkling with respect. She had impressed him and found she wanted to keep on surprising him with how competent she was. "The chef has prepared his famous orange pancakes this morning or—"

Polly came all the way from the far end of the counter. "Get the customer his coffee, Grace," she instructed through gritted teeth, then turned to Nick. "Your usual, Mr. Hopkins? Eggs over easy with bacon and toast?"

"No thanks. Just the juice and coffee." He kept his eyes on Grace.

Polly glared at her but went back to her customers. Lily had told her she'd heard that Nick had taken Polly out once or twice.

"She's not one who would appreciate competition," Lily had said.

"I'm hardly competition," Grace had protested, but Emma had sided with Lily.

"You don't mean to be, but Nick Hopkins has taken a shine to you, and Polly will not like that."

So Grace forced herself to take a deep, steadying breath before she prepared Nick's coffee. Polly was watching her every move, but Grace was determined not to allow that to force her into hurrying and making a mistake.

He had finished the juice by the time she brought his coffee. "Will that be all, sir?"

"Yes, thanks."

She moved on to serve a man and woman who had just taken seats at the counter. The couple was barely aware of her, they were so wrapped up in each other.

"Newlyweds," she heard Nick mutter. She glanced his way and saw that he was grinning at her. Polly also saw him grin. It was pretty clear she did not like it.

Later, long after Nick Hopkins had paid his bill and left and Grace had served coffee or juice or both not only to the newlyweds but to the steady stream of customers who followed, she stole a quiet moment for a quick break. She was standing in the small yard outside the kitchen door, her eyes closed as she breathed in the remarkably clear air, when Jake stuck his head out the door.

"Miss Kaufmann wants to see you." He held the door open for her, and it did not escape her notice that he looked worried.

Grace straightened the bow in her hair and checked her apron for any small stains, then wove her way between the preparation counters and dishwashing sinks until she reached Miss Kaufmann's office. She knocked lightly on the open door.

"Ah, Grace. Come in, please."

Since she had not been invited to sit, Grace stood with her hands clasped in front of her while Miss Kaufmann walked to the open door and closed it. She returned to her desk chair, sat, and let out a long sigh as she studied a paper before her.

"Grace, you are new to this. I understand that, and because of that, I am inclined to give some leeway."

Scanning her brain for any misdeed or failure to perform her job, Grace recalled the hours she'd spent the day before polishing silver and glass. It seemed every time she thought they were perfect, she'd discovered another smudge. "I can do better. I mean, I tried to polish the coffee urns to the best of my ability, but admittedly, I—"

Miss Kaufmann stared at her. "This has nothing to do with performance of your duties, Grace. This is about the matter of a young man."

What young man? The only male Grace had befriended in the short time since she'd arrived in the hotel was Jake in the kitchen. "Jake has been kind to me, but I assure you—"

"A customer," Miss Kaufmann interrupted. "Nick Hopkins to be specific. You do know who he is?"

"Yes, ma'am, but—"

Miss Kaufmann held up her forefinger, silencing Grace. "You know the rules, Grace—rules about fraternizing with the customers while on duty. Should you care to see this young man outside of your hours, that is acceptable. However, while you are wearing that uniform, I expect you to conduct yourself properly. I understand the line between friendly professional service and flirtation is thin, but there is a line, and assuming you wish to continue your work here, I would suggest you keep your distance from Mr. Hopkins."

"I have not encouraged any—"

"Perhaps not, but I have received word that he seems somewhat smitten with you. It is hardly unusual. The men in this town seem to make it a habit to test the new girls, especially those as pretty as you are."

It was a compliment wrapped in a reprimand, and Grace was unsure which she should address. "I can hardly—"

"Avoid the man?" Miss Kaufmann smiled. "Ah, but

you can. Beginning tomorrow, Polly will be the one to serve Mr. Hopkins. In time, he will get the message that he has overstepped, and the issue will resolve itself. In the meantime, keep your distance. Do I make myself clear?"

"Yes, ma'am."

"Very well. You may go, and let's have no more discussions of this nature in future, shall we?"

"No, ma'am. Thank you, ma'am." She wondered if she should curtsy but instead turned and left the office.

Jake was waiting just outside. "You'll need to watch yourself around Polly," he said in a low tone meant for her ears only. "She's got her eye on Nick."

"You heard?"

His cheeks reddened with embarrassment. "Yeah." He motioned to the recently washed plates and bowls he was inventorying just outside Miss Kaufmann's office. "Can't help it if the walls are thin as paper, and Miss K has a voice that could call pigs to supper."

Grace felt a bubble of laughter well up and stifled it by covering her mouth with her hand. She squared her shoulders and went back to her post serving customers at the lunch counter, returning Polly's smirk with a bright smile. Once again, she reminded herself that she'd been in Juniper less than three days, and in spite of getting off on the wrong foot with Miss Kaufmann—and Polly—she had found friends in Lily, Emma, and now Jake.

Later that night, she sat up in bed, going over the handbook she'd been given in training. She had almost memorized the entire training manual word for word. Despite Lily's teasing and Emma's assurances that she was doing just fine, she was determined to succeed in her position. The thrill of being on her own was one thing, but she would not lose sight of her true purpose to do her part for her family. She had a goal in mind—leaving the lunch counter as soon as possible for a position in the dining room. Away from Polly—and from Nick.

In the meantime, Nick Hopkins continued to show up at least once a week, and every one of those mornings, Polly sashayed her way down the counter with her bright smile to wait on him. Grace told herself she should be relieved. With Polly serving the cowboy, there was little danger Grace would be called back to Miss Kaufmann's office. But the truth was, she missed their brief encounters. He was someone who perhaps she could trust, the way he'd murmured helpful clues to her that first day and the way he'd come to her defense with the customer who'd tried to flirt with her. He could be a friend, like Jake was. But even though Polly's jealousy was misplaced, there was little Grace could do. Hopefully in time, she could win the other Harvey Girl over.

It didn't take long for Nick to realize what had happened. Grace barely looked his way when he sat down at the counter these days. He'd come to town for his appointment with the bank, and he was in the mood for celebrating. Bank president Jasper Perkins had approved the loan. Of course, the letter of recommendation Nick had handed him from Mr. Lombard had helped. Mr. Perkins was married to Mrs. Lombard's sister, which probably also worked in his favor. No matter how it had happened, he had the loan, and that meant he had the land.

Walking out of the bank, he'd wanted to share his good news, and he'd thought of Grace. He hardly knew her, but something told him she would understand what this meant to him. After all, they were both following a dream, and he knew she would appreciate his excitement. So he headed for the hotel. But to his disappointment, it was Polly who stepped forward to serve him.

"You look happy," she said as she prepared his coffee.

"Had some good news," he replied, looking past her to where Grace was preparing a cup of tea for a customer at the far end of the counter.

"Care to celebrate with a slice of apple pie?" Polly shifted slightly so that she was blocking his view of Grace.

He smiled at her. "Not today, thanks. I need to get back to the ranch." He downed his coffee and laid a coin on the counter.

Polly frowned, and he knew she was disappointed. He didn't know what he could do or say. When it came to the way a female mind worked, Nick had to admit he was often at a loss.

On his way out, he tried to get Grace's attention, just to nod or offer her a tip of his hat if nothing else. But she kept her focus on her customer, casting a quick glance toward Polly, and he understood. It was evident Polly was the jealous sort, and Nick knew she hadn't liked the attention he'd given Grace. Probably best to keep his distance—from both of them. He didn't want Polly getting any ideas that things went deeper than friendship between them, and he didn't want to get Grace in trouble.

On his way home, he made a detour to ride out to the land he'd had his eye on for some time now, so it was coming on dark when he rode into the yard at the ranch. As he passed the main house, John Lombard and his wife, Rita, motioned for him to stop.

"Well?" Rita demanded.

Nick grinned. "I got the loan, thanks to you folks, I'm sure."

"Nonsense," his boss said. "Your hard work and reputation as a man of good moral standing and integrity—that's what got you the loan."

Nick was glad for the shadows of the night. He didn't take compliments easily, and he could feel a blush coloring his neck and cheeks. "I'd like to tell the men," he said, nodding toward the bunkhouse.

"Of course. Congratulations, Nick," Rita said.

Nick unsaddled Sage and turned the horse loose in the corral as he strode to the bunkhouse, which he realized seemed unusually quiet as he opened the door.

The other hands were all seated around a worn plank table, and they looked up as he entered. Nick understood that in many ways, his getting the loan would be a kind of victory for them as well. Most cowboys aspired to have their own place someday, but few ever got the chance to fulfill that dream.

"Well?" Smokey Sanger demanded.

"Got it," Nick replied with a wide grin.

The men all cheered and stood to pat him on the

back and make room for him at the table. As soon as he sat down, two of the hands set a large cake in the center of the table and handed him a knife.

"Don't be chintzy with the pieces," Slim instructed. "We've been waiting all day to cut into this cake."

As he divided the cake, he told them about his meeting with the banker. "My knees were actually shaking," he admitted, and he saw by their expressions that they understood how difficult it must have been for a ranch hand—even a foreman—to walk into a bank and ask for a loan.

"Well, at least you'll still be close by," Slim said.

"Oh, you'll not be rid of me so easily," he said. "Got to make those payments every month until that loan is paid off, so I'm not going anywhere."

"Shucks," Smokey muttered, and everyone laughed.

Later after the night riders had left to watch over the herd and the rest of the hands had bedded down, Nick took Sage to the barn to brush him down. It had been a good day. Most of his days were, but this one had been special. He had set out a plan, and today, he'd made a huge first step toward realizing that future, and he still found himself wanting to share his good news not just with his friends at the ranch but with Grace. He thought about the way her eyes would widen and she would smile up at him, delighting in his success.

Why Grace? Why not Polly?

Because he was pretty sure Grace would understand what this meant to him and be happy for him. "Best keep your distance," Jake had advised.

Trouble was, when it came to Grace, Nick didn't want to keep his distance.

Blessedly, work filled Grace's days. Even after the lunch counter closed late in the afternoon, there was still so much to be done. In addition to the endless regimen of polishing, she was responsible for restocking the shelves with cutlery and dishes and wiping down the counters and high stools, not to mention every other surface in the place lest Mr. Campbell walk by and run his finger over a windowsill or chairback and find it dusty. With all that, she spent a part of every evening cleaning her shoes or mending a tear in her hose. And she was determined to keep her promise to write to her family every day.

Late one afternoon, three weeks into her time at the Palace Hotel, Grace was finishing her chores when Jake brought over a load of freshly washed cups and saucers and set the tray on the counter. He remained there watching her sort flatware and check each piece for spots. "Hey, Grace, I've been thinking about this picnic Mr. Campbell's taking us on this Sunday."

The lunch counter was closed on Sundays, and the dining room was open only for the noonday meal. "Since this is my first such outing, Jake, what should I expect?"

"Well, as soon as the dining room closes for the day, we'll all get changed and meet in the yard. Mr. Campbell's hired horses for the ride up into the hills and on into a little canyon by a waterfall. We'll build a campfire and have our supper there."

"It sounds exciting."

"You should be sure to tell Lily—and the other girls, of course—to bring warm coats. It gets cold this time of year once the sun goes down."

"I have to say, I'm not sure horseback riding is something that will appeal to Lily. She's more of a city girl," Grace said.

"Yeah, I thought about that. Don't let her back out, okay?"

"You could ask her to go yourself."

Everyone on the staff was well aware of Jake's crush on Lily—a crush he was prevented from acting on because of the Harvey code that forbade staff from becoming romantically involved.

The color deepened in Jake's ruddy cheeks. "Now, Grace, you know the rules. But this being a group thing…well, I thought maybe we could at least get a little better acquainted. Will you encourage her to be there, please?"

"I'll try, okay? No promises."

Jake grinned and did a silly little jig as he returned to the kitchen. Grace laughed and started putting away the cups and saucers.

"What's so funny?"

She spun around. Nick Hopkins stood at the counter.

"We're closed, Mr. Hopkins," she managed, though he had to be aware of the fact already.

"Yep. Just saw you working away here—on your own for once—and thought I'd see how things are going."

"Everything is fine. However, if Miss Kaufmann or Mr. Campbell see me speaking to you—"

Nick started backing toward the door. "Just wanted you to know Jake told me about Miss Kaufmann calling you in and…well, I'm sorry if I did anything to make trouble for you, Grace. Just wanted to be sure you knew you had somebody watching out for you. I mean, not that you need looking after. You're perfectly capable of—"

"Did you really come to check on me? I mean now?"

He nodded, opened the door a crack, and looked both ways. "But I'm going."

"Thank you," Grace murmured as he slipped through the opening and headed away. She set down the stack of saucers she had been holding and walked to the window that overlooked the street. She pushed aside the lace curtain and watched as he mounted his horse. He spotted her then, grinned, and tipped his hat as his horse trotted away.

"Well, well, well." A voice behind her had her jumping away from the window and spinning around, prepared to defend herself. It was only Lily leaning against the door that led to the dining room, and Grace relaxed.

"It was…Mr. Hopkins."

"I heard. He stopped by to see how you were doing. How sweet." She sighed and pushed herself away from the door. "Honey, Nick seems like a genuinely nice guy all wrapped up in a package of gorgeous, and he's obviously got a thing for you, but…"

"I think he sees me as a little sister—somebody who needs a protector," Grace said as she returned to her work. "It's nothing more than that."

"Oh, Grace, trust me. That man does not see you as his sister."

Grace sought some opportunity to change the subject. "Speaking of men seeking to get to know us better, Jake and I were talking about Sunday's outing. Sounds like we'll be riding to a little canyon nearby where we'll—"

"Horses? No one mentioned horses." Lily looked horrified. She lifted her skirt to her ankles. "Trust me, Grace, these legs were not made for sitting on a horse. They are intended for carriage rides with wealthy gents intent on giving me the moon and stars, should I ask."

"And just how many such 'gents' have you met out here in New Mexico?" Grace teased. "Come on, Lily. Everyone's going. It will be fun."

Lily sighed. "I'll need to go shopping." She brightened slightly. "I saw a pair of boots in the window at the mercantile. They cost a fortune I'm sure but—"

"I'm sure there's no dress code."

"I always dress for the occasion," Lily announced and returned to the dining room with a dramatic sweep of her hand.

Grace finished her list of chores and climbed the stairs to the third floor. She changed out of her uniform and into a calico dress before lying down on her bed and staring at the ceiling. She closed her eyes but could still see Nick Hopkins grinning at her as he tipped his hat and rode away.

"No!" She let out a groan of frustration before grabbing the last letter she'd received from home and hurrying downstairs to the small room off the lobby where guests and properly attired staff could write letters or read one of the books in the hotel's collection. She would write her mother and enclose the fifteen dollars she'd set aside from her first paycheck. What did she need money for? Her food, room, and uniforms were provided, and while her personal wardrobe could probably use some improvement, it was serviceable and would certainly do for now. Soon, when the weather turned really cold, she would set aside money for a warm coat and, of course, put aside enough for Christmas presents for Emma, Lily, and Jake, in addition to those she would send her family.

Mentally adding up the expenses she could foresee, she thought perhaps she should heed her father's advice and not be quite so generous in what she sent home at first. Ten dollars each month for the five months she'd earn a paycheck during her contract would be fifty dollars—money her family could count on regardless of how the crops did or whether taxes rose. And after her contract was up, perhaps Miss K would want her to stay on. Perhaps she would earn a raise—Emma and Lily both made a dollar a month more than she did.

She pulled out a sheet of the hotel's stationery and dipped the pen in the inkwell.

Dear Mama,
    I met the most wonderful man.

She crumpled the paper and tossed it in the waste bin.

There was no sight more calming and inspiring than a New Mexico sunset, as far as Nick was concerned.

He liked nothing better than to sit astride his horse at the top of a mesa and watch the whole show. Streaks of purple and orange filled the western sky as the fiery orb of the sun sank behind the jagged peaks of the Sangre de Cristo mountain range. He stayed until the glow faded and the stars popped out, then clicked his tongue and turned Sage toward home, humming to himself as he rode.

Had Grace Rogers ever found the time to enjoy a sunrise or sunset or anything about this wild and wonderful country? She seemed always to be there behind that counter, the perky white bow that was the signature of a Harvey Girl perched on her hair—hair he had once mentally compared to a New Mexico sunset, with its streaks of gold, and eyes he had once compared to a New Mexico sky at noon. Eyes so full of wonder and innocence that he'd felt driven to make unnecessary trips into town to make sure she was all right.

Who was he kidding? His attraction to Grace Rogers had very little to do with playing the protector. It was a lot more carnal than that. His first thought that morning when the other cowboy had flirted with her had been, *Back off, buddy. She's mine.*

At night watching over the herd or lying in his bunk, he saw her perfectly proportioned body, imagined details of her curves beneath that black uniform, thought about rolling down those black stockings to reveal the creaminess of her thighs…

"You're getting way ahead of things, Hopkins," he muttered to himself as he rode back to the ranch. Neither Grace nor any of the women who worked for Harvey were meant to be trifled with. They were women of a high moral standard. Women who tended to end up married to men with money, like bankers or ranch *owners*, not hands. Of course, he was a foreman, and he made a good salary…

Married?

He shook his head and chuckled. "Who said anything about married?" He had a plan for his life, and marriage would be a part of it eventually, but there were still a lot of steps along that trail. First, he had to pay off the loan so that once he owned the land, he could get himself settled and make sure he could truly provide for a family. Set up a proper house. Have some savings to fall back on. By the time he accomplished all that, he suspected Grace Rogers would be long gone—off to some better position in the Harvey organization or married with a family of her own.

He rode up to the corral and dismounted, slinging the saddle over the split rail fence. "Boys," he said by way of greeting to the two cowhands leaning against the fence, smoking their cigarettes and talking. The men had finished bringing the herd down from the high pastures for the winter. Some of them had since moved on to other jobs farther north, and the ranch was down to the few hands who had made it their permanent home.

"The boss man was looking for you," one of them said. "Want me to brush Sage down?"

Nick nodded. "Thanks." He handed the reins to the cowhand and headed up to the main house.

John and Rita Lombard were sitting near a small fire pit in the courtyard enjoying the night air. "Hello, Nick," Rita said. "Did you eat?"

Nick smiled. The woman was always trying to feed him. "Yes, ma'am." He turned to John. "You wanted to see me?"

"I know it's not your job, Nick," John began, and Nick tightened his grip on his hat. Every time his boss started out this way, Nick was pretty sure he was going to be asked to do something he'd rather not.

"What do you need, boss?"

"Aidan Campbell has this idea about arranging for a little thank-you outing for his employees this coming Sunday. His plan is for them to head into the canyon near the waterfall for a campfire and picnic supper."

"Okay." To Nick's way of thinking, taking a bunch of people who had rarely, if ever, been on horseback out into the wilderness any time was a bad idea, but clearly, the plan was already under way.

"So he needs a guide."

"I'm sure I can spare one or two men. You want them to do the cooking?" Nick did a mental roll call of his men. Slim and Smokey would probably be best.

"Well, that and I'd like you to lead the tour. You know this territory better than anybody, and with them setting out late in the day and not returning till after dark—"

A bunch of tenderfoots on horseback after dark is asking for trouble, he thought even as he said, "I'll set it up. Anything else, sir?"

"Not unless Mrs. Lombard can persuade you to come in for a cup of coffee and a slice of her spice cake."

"Sounds tempting, but planning out this picnic

thing will take some doing. How many will be going, do you think?"

His boss shrugged. "Work with Aidan Campbell on that. Have a good evening, Nick."

"Good night." Nick put on his hat and walked back to the bunkhouse. There was always the possibility Grace would not be on the excursion. On the other hand, there was every possibility she would be. He'd need to be sure not to pay her special attention, since her bosses would also be along for the ride.

"What're you grinnin' at?" Smokey glanced up from the nightly poker game when Nick entered the smoke-filled room.

"Boys, who would like to go on a little picnic excursion with the staff from the Palace Hotel?"

It took a moment for the men to process the fact that "staff" included the Harvey Girls, and then every hand shot high in the air.

Nick laughed and pulled a three-legged stool up to the table. "Deal me in. Last three to stay in the game win."

"That include you?" Smokey asked.

"Nope. I'm in already."

"I figured," Smokey said, chomping down hard on his cigar. "So that means three spaces up for grabs. Somebody deal the cards, and let's get this decided."

On Sunday, the kitchen staff and waitresses met in the covered walkway that ran the length of one side of the hotel.

"I see you're all well-prepared for our outing,"

Mr. Campbell announced once they were all gathered. Most were carrying an extra coat and a blanket or shawl.

A commotion at the kitchen door drew everyone's attention as Lily appeared and joined the group. As was her habit in her off-duty hours, she was dressed in an outfit that came closer to costume than regular attire. Grace knew she had spent the last of her paycheck on the boots she'd admired at the mercantile. She wore a beige split skirt in a fabric far too fine for riding in canyons and across desert land, a pristine white blouse trimmed with deep-red piping, and a wide-brimmed hat that hung down her back by its thin leather laces. Her hair was pulled back at the nape of her neck, the white-blond curls cascading over one shoulder. She was a perfect picture, but Grace realized her friend had little idea what a ride over dusty trails and through shrubs with nettles and burrs that could cling and scratch might do to her outfit.

Grace glanced at Emma, who raised her shoulders slightly as if to say "too late now." Emma and Grace were more appropriately dressed in split skirts suitable for riding, sensible shoes they'd worn enough to shape comfortably to their feet, calico blouses that had seen many washings, and hats that, like their shoes, were well-worn and more serviceable than stylish. Like the others, they had brought coats and blankets. As they left the room, Emma had grabbed Lily's coat as well.

"This way," Mr. Campbell instructed as he led them around the side of the hotel to the rear yard where three cowboys were posted next to a line of horses and two burros loaded with supplies. Grace felt a bubble of excitement knowing she would finally have news to fill the pages of her letter home. Lately, her days had all been so much the same that it was hard to come up with anything to write about. She'd tried describing her customers, especially the regulars, but her mother had written that while they enjoyed hearing about Grace's roommates, they'd just as soon hear no more about these strangers. She'd said nothing about the money Grace had sent.

Tonight, she would have something to tell them, she thought as she joined the others in mounting up. She looked up to see Nick Hopkins watching her from his position at the front of the line. She still hadn't told her mother anything about Nick. She had gotten as far as writing that she'd met someone—a true gentleman who stopped by the hotel often to make sure she was doing all right. But she'd thrown that letter away as she had her first attempt. After all, it had only been six weeks since her arrival in Juniper, and Grace understood that in her mother's eyes, that was far too little time for Grace to be going on about some handsome ranch hand who made her heart beat faster every time she thought of him.

As he led the party away from town, Nick tried his best to remain professional. He made a point of moving Sage through the group, talking to different Harvey employees. Most he knew, and a few he didn't. But somehow, Grace always seemed to be within range. He was aware of her even when she was behind him. He could pick out her voice from the general chatter and found that he often lost the thread of the conversations he might be having, trying to hear her words. Whatever she might be sharing about herself with someone who wasn't him.

She was an experienced rider—that much he'd gleaned from watching her mount without help. He liked the way she leaned forward when they stopped at a creek to let the horses drink. She stroked the horse's neck, combing her fingers through its mane. Unconsciously, he removed his hat and combed his fingers through his thick hair as he watched her from several yards farther downstream.

"You look real pretty, Hopkins," Smokey teased.

Nick slammed his hat back in place and turned his horse away from the creek. "Let's head out, folks," he shouted. "Got a fair way to go."

He urged Sage to the head of the line, passing Grace without looking her way, but it didn't matter. He was aware of her even when she was somewhere else. Determined to focus on his job, he mentally ran through the logistics of the trip before climbing the steep trail that would lead them to the entrance to the canyon. He caught up to the cowboy handling the burros. "Slim, you go on ahead and set up the campfire. I'll bring the supplies."

Slim nodded and took off, glad to be rid of herding the sometimes stubborn burros along the narrow trail.

"I got this, boss," Smokey said, coming alongside. "One of the ladies back there is having a little trouble with her horse."

Nick glanced back and saw Lily Travis struggling to

get her horse moving forward. He also saw Grace next to her, offering advice.

"Stop pulling on the reins, Lily," she was telling her friend when Nick got to them. "If you do that, the horse thinks you want to go backward, not forward."

Lily looked frankly terrified, and Nick realized she'd probably never been astride a horse in her life. He brought Sage up alongside her. "How about you just hold onto the saddle horn there and give me the reins, Miss Travis?"

"And then what?" Lily asked, her voice trembling.

"Then I'll lead you along the path until we reach the campsite. On the way home, maybe you and Gr— Miss Rogers can switch mounts. Paint there is a good deal more docile and knows the way back to town."

"Oh, Lily, let's just switch now," Grace said.

Nick noticed she didn't look directly at him but kept her focus on her friend. Ever since he'd stopped by to assure her he wouldn't do anything that might cause her trouble, they'd been shy with each other, exchanging sidelong glances and half smiles whenever he came to the counter.

"No," Lily decided, handing Nick the reins before gripping the saddle horn with both hands. "I'm hoping it's not that much farther?"

"Maybe twenty minutes," Nick said.

Lily groaned.

"Twenty-five if we don't get going," he added.

Grace expertly positioned her horse next to Lily's on her other side. "I'm right here, Lily."

Lily nodded to Nick. "Lead on," she said with a dramatic sigh.

All chatter had stopped around them, everyone waiting to see how the scene would play out. As soon as Nick clicked his tongue and Sage started walking slowly up the trail, the others relaxed. Nick led Lily's horse to the head of the group, and behind him, he heard laughter and talk pick up once again. He was aware that Grace had followed, and he had to admire the way she kept up a running conversation with Lily in an attempt to ease her friend's fears.

"I wasn't more than seven or eight when my father set me on a horse, and I remember thinking how I would never get the hang of being astride something so large. But once you understand that the animal is looking to you for direction—that you are in charge—"

Nick glanced over his shoulder. Judging by the stiff set of Lily's body, Grace was only making matters worse. "Miss Travis, do you know any camp songs?"

"Camp songs?" Lily repeated.

"Yeah. Songs folks might sing around a campfire?"

Lily snorted a laugh. "I'm from Chicago. I've sat around a campfire about as often as I've been astride a horse, Mr. Hopkins." After a pause, she added, "If you know any such tunes, however, I'm always willing to learn."

Nick smiled. Lily couldn't help herself. She was a natural-born flirt, and she was definitely flirting with him. Well, where was the harm? Especially if it took his mind off Grace.

"Oh, give me a home," he sang, raising his voice so those following him could hear, "where the buffalo roam..."

He wasn't much of a singer. In fact, his men often

teased him about his off-key renditions when they were out with the herd. But to his surprise, from his position riding in a buggy with Miss Kaufmann, Aidan Campbell took up the tune. The hotel manager had a strong baritone and urged those around him to join in, coaching them in the words until everyone was singing the chorus.

"Home, home on the range." Their voices ricocheted off the rocky cliffs, and when he looked back, Grace caught his eye and nodded toward Lily. The woman was swaying in the saddle in time to the music, completely relaxed. Grace smiled at him, her eyes sparkling with gratitude.

He tipped two fingers to the brim of his hat and eased Sage to a walk as they started their descent into the canyon. Her direct smile had completely unnerved him. It was a private moment between just the two of them, one she clearly did not regret. He had thought her attractive before, but now he saw just how beautiful she was. And he also realized how much trouble he was in if he allowed himself to dwell on that fact. For with that came the logical next thoughts—that smile, her lips meeting his, his fingers trapped in her sunlit hair, his—

"Hey, boss!" Slim was riding up the trail toward him and was practically in front of him before he realized it. "Want me to start the cooking right away or wait till—"

Nick cleared his mind of thoughts of Grace. He was in charge of this expedition, after all. "Start now, and build up the fire. Once the sun goes down, we'll need the warmth." He turned in his saddle and addressed the others. "Okay, folks, almost there. Keep an eye out on your left for your first glimpse of the falls. In the late-afternoon sun, it's quite a sight."

He knew the exact moment the first of the group saw the falls—a cascade of pulsating water iridescent in the sunlight, spilling over a high granite cliff into the narrow and deep canyon below. Their gasps and whispered comments were unmistakable. Nick smiled, more than a little pleased with himself for having planned the route and timing with just this moment in mind. He looked back at Grace.

She stared at the scene with a look of such serenity and joy that it took his breath away. She met his gaze. "It's wonderful," she said, her voice just above a whisper as if they had entered a church. "I could never have imagined anything so beautiful."

I could, Nick thought as, for the moment, everyone else seemed to fade away. Their eyes met and held.

"Hey," Jake Collier shouted from his position at the back of the line. "How about giving the rest of us a chance to see what all the fuss is about?"

This has to stop, Nick warned himself. She had a contract to fulfill, and he had worked too hard saving for the day he could buy his own spread to have that undone by a pretty smile and a pair of sky-blue eyes that set his heart thundering like the roar of the water as it tumbled over the edge.

Chapter
4

By the time they'd dismounted and turned the horses loose in a roped-off area, Grace could smell the food the cowboys were preparing. The cook from the ranch had driven the chuck wagon to the site earlier, and now dinner was almost ready. Grace joined Emma, who was spreading a white linen tablecloth over a large, flat rock. "Nothing but the best for us Harvey folks," she joked.

Grace helped unpack the plates and flatware. No wonder the burros had moved so slowly. The weight of all this must have made climbing the steep trail daunting. At least with the food devoured, they'd have an easier time of it on the way back.

"How do you plan to handle things today?" Emma asked in a low voice meant for Grace's ears only. "Mr. Hopkins has—"

"Mr. Hopkins has a job to do," Grace said. "He has the responsibility for everyone on this expedition and certainly will not have time to concern himself with me. Besides, is there any reason he and I can't be friends? We're not breaking any rules."

"He's coming over," Emma said and, before Grace could stop her, moved away to help one of the other girls slice bread.

Grace concentrated on unpacking the last of the plates and rolling flatware in napkins. She was aware of his proximity the way she might have felt the hint of a breeze had there been one.

"Grace?"

She turned to him with a bright smile—her Harvey Girl smile. "Quite a fancy picnic," she commented.

He grinned and shook his head. "Aidan Campbell has some strange ideas when it comes to these things. And yet it is kind of nice."

She concentrated on her task. He said nothing more, just watched her as she worked. The air between them felt heavy with words unspoken and thoughts unshared.

"Was there something you needed, Mr.—"

"Nick," he corrected. "You're off duty, Grace."

"I'm also being observed by others," she replied softly, glancing at Polly and Miss Kaufmann, who stood under a tree not three feet away. "Still, I do wish—"

"What do you wish, Grace?"

She wished she could tell him what his friendship meant to her. "I wish I…we…" She shook off the attempt and smiled. "I wish you would help me unpack all these serving platters and trays."

"My pleasure."

They worked in companionable silence. When his hand accidentally brushed hers, she did not startle or pull away. "Now what?" she said, hands on hips as she surveyed the stack of large metal trays leaning against a boulder.

"Smells like the food's ready," he said. "Hey, Slim, if you and Smokey are ready, Miss Rogers can bring you trays for the potatoes and corn."

Slim gave a sign, and Nick picked up the trays, handing them to Grace. This time when their fingers brushed, his lingered, and Grace ducked her head to hide the blush she felt rising to her cheeks as she hurried to deliver the trays to Slim.

Behind her, she heard Nick clap his hands for attention before announcing, "Folks, we're about ready to eat. Once we have, those who aren't too full are welcome to join me to walk to a special point perfect for catching the last of the sunset on the falls."

Grace heard a general chatter of excitement and pleasure as she handed Slim the trays. He accepted them with a shy smile and began loading them with baked potatoes and ears of corn. "Thank you, miss."

She waved to Emma and Lily, who were already in line for food, and joined them.

"Hey, no cuttin' the line," Jake teased.

Grace blushed again and looked around to see if anyone truly minded. Of course, no one did, so she relaxed and prepared to enjoy the meal with her friends. This was their first true break since they'd arrived in Juniper and her first chance to have a good look at this wild country. It was so different from the farm fields of Missouri. She planned to eat quickly so she could take a walk on her own and really take it all in. She'd brought her journal along to make notes and some rough sketches, some to send home in her letters for her brothers and sisters to enjoy.

The group sat on the flat rocks that formed a rough circle around the campfire. Slim and Smokey wove their way among the group offering second and third helpings. It was refreshing to be served rather than be the server. But anxious for an opportunity to explore the area and perhaps make some sketches to send her siblings, Grace ate hurriedly and refused seconds.

"I'm going for a short walk," she told Emma and Lily as she took their plates and stacked them on hers.

"Not by yourself," Jake protested as he leaped to his feet.

She looked around, hoping perhaps Nick might agree to accompany her, but he had disappeared. "I'll stay right in the area, I promise. I just want some time to—"

"Our Gracie is one who needs her time alone," Lily explained. "Emma and I have learned not to take it personally. She'll be fine." She patted Jake's hand, and he was so startled and pleased that he sat down again.

"No farther than hollerin' distance," he warned.

Grace laughed. "You think you could hear me above this din?" She glanced around the circle where several lively conversations were in progress.

"No more than where we can see you then," Jake bargained.

"I'll be fine." Grace carried the dirty dishes to the chuck wagon and handed them to the cook. "Lovely meal," she said. "Thank you for all the trouble you took."

"No trouble at all, miss."

She pointed to a narrow path behind him. "Where does that go?"

"The falls. That's the trail the boss will take you folks on to see the sunset."

If she got an early start, she'd have the advantage of seeing it in silence, treasuring the moment before sharing it with the others. She'd have time to make a couple of sketches she could color in later. The cook had left his post to offer the guests more coffee, so Grace started up the well-worn trail, taking care to find secure footing with each step. And because she was so focused on her footing, she was almost upon Nick before she realized he was there.

She looked up as a shadow darkened her path. There had been no storm or rain predicted, and yet they'd been told how suddenly bad weather could come over the mountains and strike without warning. Nick stood at the top of a rise, hands on his slim hips.

"Grace?"

"Oh, hello. I—"

"You shouldn't be roamin' around out here on your own." He had pushed his hat back, and she saw a slight frown crease his forehead.

This was a new side to Nick Hopkins. She was used to the man who smiled and flirted so easily—the man who seemed unruffled by anything life might send his way. But this man looked worried. Lily might have tried charming him out of his mood, but Grace felt only annoyed. After all, there was such a thing as being overly protective.

"I just came to see the falls," she said.

"I told everyone I would bring the group up together."

"I know, but I had hoped to enjoy some time alone before you and the others—" Taking a step forward without testing her footing and setting off a small avalanche of loose dirt and rock, she pitched forward to keep herself from skidding backward and off the trail entirely.

Nick was there in an instant, his hand gripping her upper arm to keep her from the mortification of falling face-first into the dust and dirt. Using both hands, he hauled her up and forward until her clenched fists rested on his chest. Their faces were no more than an inch apart, their breaths coming in syncopated huffs. She met his gaze, and in that moment, she knew something was about to change between them— something she hadn't realized she'd been hoping for.

"Are you hurt?" His voice was husky.

She shook her head but made no other move. His eyes lingered on hers. Did she move half a step closer, or did he? Did she speak aloud the single word that would answer the question in that gaze?

Yes.

Before she could further analyze the moment, he closed the distance, settling his lips on hers as his grip on her arm softened. Her fists unfolded until her hands were flat against the pounding of his heart.

His kiss was no assault but rather tasted of tenderness and frustration and the knowledge they both understood that this should not be happening. He pulled back.

"You okay?" His voice shook, and he had trouble

looking directly at her. Clearly, kissing her had not been planned. It just happened—out of the blue, like an unexpected storm.

Unable to speak, she nodded. "You're right. I should go back," she finally managed. She turned to go.

"Wait," he said softly. He stepped to one side of the trail. "Just over that rise. Best view around."

She hesitated, but with a sweep of his hand, he invited her to see for herself. So she stepped around him and climbed the last few steps of the trail, emerging onto a flat area where the mesas and cliffs dropped deep into a canyon. In the distance, the falls plummeted from their apex to the river far below, the tumbling water sparkling like a thousand precious jewels in the light of the setting sun.

"Oh, Nick, it's so…" she whispered as she turned back to thank him.

But he was gone.

Idiot.

Nick berated himself, kicking up dust as he stomped back down the trail to gather the rest of the group for the hike up to see the sunset.

You just had to kiss her, didn't you?

He touched his tongue to his lips. The taste of her was there—something sweet he couldn't define, something that had brought him up short and stopped him from going further with the kiss.

"Everybody's ready to see the falls, boss," Slim said as Nick stormed past. "You okay?"

"Yeah. Let's go so we can get them back to town before it gets much darker and colder." He paused for a moment, composing himself and pasting on the easy smile that was expected. "This way, folks. First the sunset, and then coffee and pie before we head back to town."

The others rushed forward, forming a single line as Slim led them up the trail. Emma Elliot stepped away from the group and said, "Did you happen to see Grace, Mr. Hopkins? She said she wanted to take a short walk, but I'm starting to worry."

Nick's smile tightened. "She went ahead on her own. She's up there at the falls waiting for you."

"I see," Emma replied as she studied him more closely. "She's all right?"

Nick feigned nonchalance. "Last I saw of her, she was." He turned away to herd the others along, and thankfully, Emma rejoined the line.

The distance from the picnic site to the top of the ridge was short, and he could already hear gasps of wonder as those at the head of the line caught their first glimpses of the waterfall at sunset. As soon as Aidan Campbell started up the trail at the end of the line, Nick glanced around. Smokey and Cooky were already setting up the pie and coffee service. The men were as anxious as he was to finish their duties and get home.

Nick deliberately avoided looking for Grace when he reached the top of the trail. The way he was feeling, anyone with eyes would know at once what had happened. He didn't want to cause her trouble, so he focused on the other girls, smiling at their attempts to fully express the beauty of the scene before them and giving a blushing Slim the credit for having discovered this view in the first place. "At least he was the one who showed me," he said when Slim stuttered a protest.

As the red-orange sun slipped below the horizon, everyone started back down the trail, anxious to wrap themselves in the coats and blankets they had brought along. Somehow despite his determination to keep his distance, Nick found himself walking behind Emma, Lily, and Grace. Lily chattered on, questioning how they were ever going to find their way back to town once dark set in, and suggesting maybe they should just skip pie and coffee and get on their way. She sure was a nervous little filly.

Emma rested her hand on Lily's waist. "We'll be just fine, Lily. Mr. Hopkins and his men will see to that. Isn't that right, sir?" She called this last over her shoulder in his direction.

"Yes, miss."

"But it's already getting colder and darker and—"

"We have these things out here called stars," Nick said, deliberately giving his words a teasing flair in order to lighten the mood before Lily's nerves affected others. "I'd say between those and the full moon, there's enough to show us the way."

"It is lovely," she admitted. "No wonder Mr. Campbell chose you to lead this little expedition, Nick. You are quite gifted at setting the proper mood and alleviating the fears of silly females like me."

Nick ducked his head, embarrassed at such a compliment delivered within hearing of his men. He would have to endure their teasing later. He glanced at Grace. He sure hoped she shared Lily's high opinion of him.

The pie and coffee were a perfect end to a successful expedition, and Nick was finally starting to calm down when Grace sought him out.

"That cannot happen again, Nick," she said softly, her voice shaking a bit. "Anyone could have come by and—"

"I assume you are speaking of the kiss—the one we shared?"

"I did not... I simply..."

"You're really going to tell yourself you didn't kiss me back?"

By the light from the campfire, he realized her lip was trembling. "I most certainly..."

"...did," he finished for her. Then he relieved her of her coffee cup and took it back to the chuck wagon. "Time to mount up, folks," he shouted.

I did not kiss that man, Grace fumed on the ride back to town.

Oh, but you did, she thought, recalling her murmured assent. She was grateful for the darkness, the necessity to go single file down the trail, and most of all Lily's constant jabbering that kept everyone else—including Nick—focused on reassuring her.

"Not long now," she heard him say as he led Lily's mount at the head of the line. There was such patience and kindness in his tone. *He's such a decent man*, she thought. On the other hand, could she afford to become distracted from her true purpose in coming to Juniper? And what of the future? Once her contract ended, she had always thought she would return to the farm. Surely it would be foolhardy to allow herself to become entangled in a romance with Nick when there was no future in it. *Oh, but when he kissed you…*

Not that she'd never been kissed. Buford had started kissing her when they were twelve, but by the time they had stopped seeing each other, she had to admit the one thing she would not miss for a minute was his wet, slobbery mouth on hers.

Nick's kiss had been different. She struggled to put her finger on why it had been so special but failed. It had all happened in a moment—a moment so brief, it was hard to believe she hadn't imagined it. But the reality was that he had kissed her—and she had savored that kiss.

They rode into town, light spilling over the entire party from the streetlamps and saloons. She watched as Nick dismounted ahead of her and helped Lily from her horse. She studied the breadth of his shoulders, the ease with which he lifted Lily, and most of all the professionalism he continued to show the entire group while carrying out his duties as the leader of their expedition. Nick Hopkins was a mature man, confident enough in himself and his abilities that he could easily focus on the needs of others.

Still, she couldn't help being disappointed when Nick showed no sign of even nodding good night as she filed past him with the others. Indeed, he seemed to deliberately turn away to speak with one of his cowhands as she approached. Then just as she passed, his hand brushed hers, and she heard him say, "Good night, Grace."

"Good night, Nick," she murmured and allowed their hands to remain in contact for a brief second more.

When Nick did not come to the hotel, not the next day nor indeed all the next week, Grace told herself this was a good thing, that putting time between their kiss and seeing each other again would ease the awkwardness. Surely they both realized what a mistake it had been. But the more days that passed without him coming to the counter, the more Grace looked for him.

"Are you unwell, Grace?"

She had not seen Miss K approach. The morning train had just departed, and Grace had been lost in thought as she tended to her usual duties of wiping down countertops and polishing silver.

"I am fine, Miss Kaufmann." Admittedly, she was slower than usual in performing the chores. She doubled her efforts to put a shine on the coffee urn.

"I thought perhaps after our delightful outing earlier this week…"

Grace realized that Miss K's concern was genuine. In the weeks she'd worked at the Palace, Grace had come to admire the head waitress. Miss Kaufmann had a good deal of responsibility and yet, in spite of her strictness, she took an interest in her "girls."

"It was lovely," Grace agreed.

Miss K cleared her throat, signaling she had business to discuss. "Grace, one of the girls in the dining room is leaving us. That leaves an opening for a beverage girl. Would you be interested?"

She would be on the same schedule as Lily and

Emma—and away from Polly. Nick rarely if ever ate in the dining room, so perhaps, as much as she looked forward to seeing him, that was another plus. She could concentrate on why she had taken this job in the first place. Working in the dining room meant a higher wage and larger tips. "Yes, ma'am, I would."

"For now, I'm afraid I need you to pull double duty—mornings and lunch at the counter and evenings in the dining room. That would just be until a new girl arrives to take your place at the counter."

"That would be just fine." She could hardly wait to share her good news with Emma and Lily—and Nick.

"Very well. We'll start the new schedule tomorrow, so why don't you take the rest of the day off?"

"Thank you so much." Grace grinned.

Miss K returned her smile and actually walked with her into the kitchen. "You should go change and get out and enjoy yourself. You're going to be quite busy in the coming days."

On her way to the back stairs, Grace passed Jake. "I'm to be the dining room drink girl starting tomorrow," she told him, unable to keep the news to herself a minute longer. "And I've been given the rest of the day off."

Jake smiled. "Well, go on with you then. Get changed and get out of here. Go shopping, or just sit in the plaza and write your folks the good news. Not every day somebody around here gets promoted."

Grace ran up all three flights of stairs. She changed from her uniform to her favorite dress, braided her hair into one thick plait that hung down her back, pinned on her hat, and grabbed pencil and paper so she could write her parents.

Outside, the weather was the usual New Mexico combination of sunshine and dry, clear air. Grace stood at one corner of the town plaza considering the park benches scattered along the paths. She chose one with a view of the hotel, with the idea of making a sketch of the scene for her siblings. She worked intently, glancing between her paper and the hotel, trying to get the proportions right. She was aware of people passing, the clip-clop of horses and rumble of wagons, even the whoosh of the two o'clock train pulling into the station behind her. But she ignored it all as she carefully drew and labeled the different parts of the hotel and grounds.

Finally satisfied, she sat back, flexed her fingers, and considered her work. The bell in the church chimed three times, and she realized she'd been sitting and sketching for over two hours. "Surely you aren't going to waste this gift of a day sitting here," she muttered to herself as she gathered her things, packed them away in her satchel, and stood. Grace allowed her gaze to roam over her surroundings and settled it on the mercantile, a place she had not permitted herself to explore in all the weeks she'd been in Juniper lest she be tempted to spend her money on something frivolous. But this was a special day, and perhaps a small treat to mark the occasion was exactly what she needed. She shouldered her satchel and walked with purpose across the plaza and onto the warped boardwalk that led to the shops.

The double doors were closed, no doubt to keep out the constant dust, and a small brass sign attached to the outer wall read *Mr. Frank Tucker, Proprietor*. A bell jangled as she stepped into the cool dimness of the store. Goods of every sort filled the aisles, making it difficult to see the proprietor or other customers.

"Be right with you," a male voice called out from the back of the store.

Grace followed the sound of conversation, passing bins of colorful candies and thinking she could buy an assortment to share with Emma and Lily to celebrate her promotion.

Of course, as she made her way down the aisle, it was hard not to pause and examine the shelves with an eye to gifts she might send her family for Christmas. Here was a rolling pin made of marble instead of wood. It would last forever, no matter how many pies her mother made. And there, a display of pipes and tobacco for her father. Farther along, she came to a selection of bandanas for her brothers and wooden pull toys and rag dolls for the twins. She glanced at the prices and calculated the total along with what it might cost to send everything by post.

Too dear, she thought as she reached the end of the aisle. To one side was a potbelly stove surrounded by a semicircle of worn wooden chairs. To the other was a long wooden counter with a large cash register at one end and a roll of brown wrapping paper and a large spool of twine at the other. Mr. Tucker was gathering supplies from the bins of flour, sugar, and other foodstuffs displayed along the wall behind the counter. He was a short, stocky man of maybe fifty with a snowy white beard that she had to admit reminded her of Santa Claus.

And waiting for the order to be filled…was Nick Hopkins. Both men turned. The store owner smiled.

Nick didn't. He simply looked up and then back down at the list he carried.

"Grace," he said softly.

How she loved the sound of her name coming from him!

"Good day, miss," the owner said. "Just finishing this order, and I'll be right with you. Got a new shipment of ladies' hats in just yesterday if you'd care to have a look." He motioned to the far wall.

Grace had no interest in a new hat, but the far wall put distance between her and the shop window. She and Nick hadn't really had a chance to speak since the company outing—since the kiss. And yet she so wanted to revive the easy friendship they'd shared before that night. Maybe they could steal a moment or two to talk, away from prying eyes. He glanced at her, and she smiled, then walked over to examine the hats. She fingered the round brim of one hat, the bright red feather of another as she waited.

"This one, I think." Nick was behind her, reaching up and over her to take down a cocoa-brown straw hat trimmed with a turquoise moiré ribbon held in place by an engraved silver button. "It matches your dress and brings out the color of your eyes."

Grace turned to respond and barely stifled a gasp. He was standing too close, looking at her too intently, his gaze holding hers, his eyes questioning exactly where they stood with one another.

She wished she could give him an answer, but to do that, she'd first have to know herself.

Instead, she ducked beneath his arm, still outstretched to retrieve the hat from the wall display.

"I came for penny candy, not a hat," she said with a laugh she hoped would lighten the moment. Perhaps they weren't ready to be alone away from curious eyes after all.

It worked. He grinned and stepped aside, offering her a little bow as he led the way back to the counter. "Frank, Miss Rogers is in the market for a selection of your candy."

"Licorice sticks, peppermints, lemon drops, butterscotch…or perhaps these nice chocolate creams?" the store owner offered. He pointed to a display of luscious-looking chocolate bonbons arranged on a plate under a clear glass cover.

They did look tempting, but when she calculated the price, she decided the penny candies were the wiser choice. "Perhaps an assortment of the hard candies and licorice," she said. "Three of each, please."

"No chocolates then?" Nick asked.

"They are far too dear," she explained. "Perhaps another time," she added, not wanting to hurt the proprietor's feelings.

The shopkeeper smiled at her. "Is this some kind of celebration, Miss Rogers?" he asked as he dropped the various candies into a paper sack.

"I just got a promotion," she blurted, unable to control the smile she knew was spread across her face. The way Nick's eyes brightened, she knew he was truly pleased for her.

"You're a Harvey Girl, are you?" Mr. Tucker asked.

"One of the best," Nick said. "What's the promotion?"

"I'm to serve the beverages in the dining room

beginning tomorrow, though I'll be continuing my duties at the lunch counter as well for the time being. That's why Miss Kaufmann gave me this afternoon off."

"Well now, that's just swell," Mr. Tucker said as he handed her the bag of candy. "So how about you allow me to give you this on the house? My way of congratulating you?"

"I couldn't."

"It's my pleasure, Miss Rogers. I hope to see you back in the store soon—maybe taking another look at that hat?"

Grace blushed. Mr. Tucker was a good salesman, that much was clear. "Thank you. Maybe not the hat, but I will need to do some Christmas shopping later." She folded the top of the bag closed and stored it in her satchel. "Thank you, sir."

Mr. Tucker turned to Nick. "Well, Hopkins, you gonna just stand around all day or walk this young lady back home while I load up your wagon?"

"Oh, I'll be fine," Grace rushed to assure them both, all the while edging toward the exit. As much as she would enjoy a stroll across the plaza with Nick, she felt perhaps this was not the time. What if Mr. Campbell or Miss Kaufmann saw them and decided she was perhaps not serious enough for the new position after all? There certainly were a number of other girls Miss K could have given the opportunity. "I have some time and thought I would explore the church and... Nice to meet you, Mr. Tucker. Good day, Nick," she called as she turned and fled the store.

Chapter 5

NICK CAME TO TOWN ONCE A WEEK TO BUY SUPPLIES for the ranch. Mrs. Lombard gave him her list, and he added it to what he needed to replenish for the hands and himself. He'd told himself he was in town on ranch business and that business only. To that end, he had eaten a hardy breakfast with the other ranch hands and chewed on some beef jerky during the ride in so as not to be tempted to stop by the hotel.

Ever since the picnic, Grace had been a constant presence in his thoughts—and his dreams. Everywhere he went and everything he did, she was there. More than once, the other cowboys had teased him about daydreaming, speculating on who the lady might be. None of them had guessed Grace. Most had thought it might be Lily, once Slim told them all how Nick had given her special attention during the ride to and from the falls.

Knowing the trouble he'd caused for Grace with her employers with the special attention he'd paid to her those first days after she came to the Palace, he'd really tried to keep his distance. And repeatedly when he found himself thinking of her, he reminded himself that his plan for the future didn't leave time for a serious romance just yet. But lately, he'd begun to rethink his plan. Why wait for each thing to fall into place? He had a good job, and there were separate quarters for the foreman, although he'd always preferred to live in the bunkhouse with the other men. But there was certainly no reason he couldn't marry and start a ranch at the same time. In fact, having someone to work alongside him would probably be better than going it alone, and from the little he knew of her, it seemed to him Grace would be the perfect helpmate. In the past, he'd known men who had courted a Harvey Girl on her time off. The key was to respect the rules set up for her at work, but when she was off duty, what was the harm in getting to know her?

He barely listened to Frank's chatter as the two men loaded the supplies into the back of the buckboard. That was until he heard Frank say, "Pretty little thing, isn't she?" The older man was studying Nick closely, his eyes squinting in the late-afternoon sun.

"Who?" Nick asked.

Frank just laughed and clapped him on the shoulder. "You know damned well who." He nodded toward the church. "Saw her step inside there. Good place for two young folks like you to talk, maybe get to know each other a little better?"

"You're a hopeless romantic, old man," Nick muttered as he climbed onto the seat of the buckboard and unwrapped the reins.

Frank shrugged. "Romantic? Realist? Who says you can't be a realistic romantic?" He headed back toward the store. "You're not getting any younger, Nick, and take it from me, a girl like that one won't come along twice."

The best way out of town meant driving the wagon around the plaza—past the church. Nick was tempted to heed Frank's suggestion and stop, but instead, he made the full circle until he was back at Tucker's store.

Once inside, he slapped down payment and ordered half a dozen chocolate creams boxed and tied with a ribbon.

Frank filled the order, then passed Nick a scrap of paper and pencil.

"What's this for?" Nick asked.

"I figure maybe you'd like the candy delivered? Or were you just planning to bust into the church and declare your love for the lady? If you ask me, that'll get you nothing but scaring her off for good."

Frank had a point.

Nick held the pencil poised over the paper.

"Just say 'Congratulations' and sign your name," Frank advised. "Make it about the promotion. Give the girl a way out if she wants it. I'll drop the candy and note by the hotel on my way home."

Nick took the advice. He knew Frank had his best interests at heart. "Thanks." Once he'd signed his name, he looked around as if trying to decide his next move.

"You should head back to the ranch," Frank said. "Be dark before you get there."

Nick nodded and left. As he walked back to the wagon, he saw Grace leaving the church. He raised his hand in greeting, and although she hesitated, she returned the gesture and continued standing on the church steps watching him. Nick climbed onto the seat and loosened the brake. "Let it play out, Hopkins," he advised himself, although what he wanted more than anything was to change course, walk to meet her, and ask her straight out if she might be feeling what he felt for her. He knew he'd have his answer in a heartbeat, just by looking in those eyes. They were like a mirror to her thoughts.

Friendship, he reminded himself firmly. *Take it slow—for now.*

Once inside the quiet, dark church, Grace chose a pew toward the back, sat down, and closed her eyes as she tried to calm herself. This attraction to Nick Hopkins was risky. And yet…

Repeatedly since arriving in Juniper, she had reminded herself of her stated purpose in leaving home. But as a girl, she had often dreamed of travel and adventure and the freedom to make her own choices. And if she was brutally honest with herself, yes, she had imagined a day when she would meet a man like Nick—kind and understanding and, of course, handsome. Now she had, and he seemed as attracted to her as she was to him. But the timing was wrong.

Nick's life was here in New Mexico. Where was her future once she completed her contract? She'd always assumed she would return home, her itch for adventure scratched and her determination to help her family fulfilled. All those weeks earlier when she'd boarded that train, it had never occurred to her that adventure might include meeting the man of her dreams. She had confided her growing feelings for Nick to Emma, and the older Harvey Girl had offered encouragement.

"Grace, you have every right to see Nick or any other man not employed by the Harvey Company when you are off duty. The only thing Miss Kaufmann and Mr. Campbell will be watching closely is your conduct—and his, around you. If things go too far…" She shrugged. "But then who knows? There are plenty of stories of Harvey Girls breaking their contracts to marry."

"Marry! Oh no, Emma," Grace had protested. "It is far too early. I mean, we barely know each other. He has plans, as do I. Marriage? Not at all."

Emma had only smiled. Just then, Lily had returned from her nightly toilet, smelling of her signature lily-of-the-valley soap as she swirled into the room like a breath of spring air. "And what have the two of you been plotting in my absence?" she teased. "Such serious faces, it must be something dire."

Grace had told Lily about her feelings for Nick, and as usual, Lily had brushed all doubts aside. Now, Grace smiled as she realized how comforting it was knowing Emma and Lily were in her life and on her side. Maybe things could work out after all. Why shouldn't she enjoy Nick's company when she was off duty? Certainly, other Harvey Girls had beaus they saw when not on duty, men who worked for the railroad or men from town.

Of course, Polly would be upset, but perhaps in time…

Grace opened her eyes and focused on the beautiful interior of the church—the light coming in through the large stained-glass window behind the altar, the high-gloss polish of the wooden pews, the—

Polish!

She stood and practically ran to the exit. Had she finished polishing the coffee urns before Miss Kaufmann had given her the offer? She thought so, but what if—

Grace blinked in the bright sunlight outside the church. Across the plaza, Nick was just climbing onto the seat of his buckboard. He raised a hand to her. She hesitated, then returned his greeting and stood there watching as he drove out of town.

The urns!

She ran across the plaza, and when she entered the ornate lobby, Mr. Campbell glanced up and smiled. "Congratulations, Grace," he called to her.

"Thank you, sir. I just want to check something at the lunch counter."

She opened the doors that led to the lunch counter and squinted in the dimness. Twin silver urns caught what light there was. Grace moved behind the counter and examined them more thoroughly, inspecting them for any sign of a smudge or fingerprint. Finding none, she heaved a sigh of relief.

"You're quite welcome." Polly Forrester stood in the doorway leading to the kitchen. "I understand you've been promoted," she added. "You seem to have wheedled your way into becoming everyone's pet around here."

"I... Thank you, Polly, for polishing the urns. When Miss Kaufmann came to speak with me—"

With a wave of her hand, Polly dismissed anything Grace might say. "A word of warning, Grace. Nick is not the marrying kind. He has plans. He wants a place of his own, and he's made it clear that comes before anything—or anyone—else." With that, she left.

Grace wondered if perhaps Polly was upset because she had been working at the lunch counter far longer than Grace had. On the other hand, Polly truly thrived in her position as a sort of assistant manager of the lunch counter. It seemed to Grace that the other waitress might actually see serving drinks as a demotion.

Putting Polly out of her mind, Grace busied herself checking to be sure everything was in perfect order for the next day. She was just replenishing the supply of juice glasses when Jake stuck his head around the door from the kitchen. "Package for you, Grace." He held out a small cardboard box tied with a red ribbon and then lingered, his curiosity getting the better of his manners.

Grace untied the ribbon and opened the box. "I can't imagine who—"

She opened the folded paper on top of the wax paper liner and immediately felt the heat rise to her cheeks as she read Nick's brief message.

"Secret admirer?" Jake asked.

"Just a friend congratulating me on my promotion," she replied as she spread the wax paper to reveal six perfect chocolates. She offered the box to Jake. "Have one," she invited.

He peered at the sweets and shook his head. "Too fine for the likes of me," he said. "You enjoy them, Grace. You've earned a treat, hard as you've been working."

Grace laughed. "Nobody works harder than you around here, so I insist."

Jake studied the candies. "Do you think they're all the same?"

"Only way to find out is if we each try one." She took a chocolate and bit into it. "Peppermint," she announced.

Jake did the same, only he popped the entire piece into his mouth. "Yep, peppermint as well."

"What's going on?" Lily asked as she swept down the stairs, still tying her apron in preparation for starting the dinner shift.

"Grace has a secret admirer," Jake reported.

"Not so secret if you ask me." Lily peered into the box. "Ooh, chocolates!"

"Have one," Grace invited, and she didn't have to ask twice. Like Jake, Lily picked one and ate it whole, licking her fingers as she savored the sweet taste. "Heaven," she moaned. "I am telling you, Grace, if you let that man go, you are the world's greatest fool."

"He simply... We saw each other at the mercantile, and he heard me tell Mr. Tucker about my new position."

"Uh-huh. And of course, every time a Harvey Girl gets promoted, he runs out and buys her chocolates," Lily teased.

"He's a very nice man," Grace said defensively.

"He's a man all right, and, honey, that man has his eye on you." Lily pinched Grace's cheek and then hurried to the dining room to tend her tables.

Grace watched Jake follow Lily with his eyes. How wonderful it would be if Lily felt for Jake as he so obviously did for her. But Lily had made it clear she saw the kitchen manager only as a friend—nothing more. Grace touched Jake's hand, calling his attention away from Lily. "Well, I have the rest of the evening free before I start double duty tomorrow," she said, "so I think I'll take advantage and get some rest."

"Thanks for sharing your chocolates," Jake said as Grace started up the stairs. "Say, Grace, there's a concert on the plaza in the evening day after tomorrow, and it being Sunday and all... I mean, with the dining room not open, maybe you, Emma, and Lily might like to go?"

"I'll ask them. Sounds like fun. Thanks, Jake."

As she climbed the stairs to the third floor, she couldn't help but wonder if Nick and some of the other cowboys might come into town for the music. "Stop this," she whispered, but as soon as she was inside her room, she took out Nick's note and read it again. She rolled the red ribbon around her fingers before storing both it and the note in the box where she kept her journal and a locket with the one photo she had of her parents.

By the time Grace finished her double shift the following day, she was completely exhausted. She was pretty sure a smile was permanently embedded in her face after hours of filling drink orders for the steady stream of customers who had packed first the counter and later the dining room. Usually, there was a lull just after the lunch rush, but the two o'clock train had brought a tour group—all of them excited and all of them hungry. By the time that group left and she'd served beverages to the dinner guests, she was beginning to think maybe agreeing to the double shifts had been a bad idea. All she wanted was a hot bath and sleep.

But when she returned to the room she shared with Emma and Lily following her bath, her roommates were deep in conversation, and whatever the topic, it looked serious. Emma was uncharacteristically near tears.

"What's happened?" Grace asked. She headed across the room and sat next to Emma, who was clutching a telegram.

Lily glanced at Emma, who nodded. "It's all right. I trust Grace. You can tell her."

"Emma has had some bad news," Lily said. "A man she knew when we worked together in Omaha has decided to join up with Roosevelt's Rough Riders to fight in Cuba."

"I thought he loved me," Emma sobbed. "Why would he do such a thing? Deliberately place his life in danger when—"

"Perhaps he won't be chosen to go," Lily offered as consolation.

"He's already been chosen, and why not?" Emma declared. "He's tall and strong and an expert horseman, which is precisely what Roosevelt wants in his men."

"He says he loves you," Lily reminded her, reaching for the telegram clutched in Emma's hand. "Right here," she added as she smoothed out the paper.

"If he loved me, he wouldn't be doing this. Arrogant boy, that's what he is." Emma stood and began pacing the small confines of the room. "Well, two can play this game. He's punishing me because I refused to marry him on his terms. Well, what about my terms?"

Grace was unsure what she could say to comfort her friend. She had never seen Emma so upset. Of the three of them, Emma was always the one who seemed in perfect control. How could any man fail to see how strong and capable she was? But perhaps that was the problem. Some men didn't like women who spoke up, who had opinions of their own. Grace's mother had warned her of that often enough. "Emma, do you truly love this man?"

Emma stared at her, lips moving but no sound coming out. As tears leaked down her cheeks, she shrugged. "I thought I did," she blubbered. "And I thought he—"

"Then write to him at once. Beg him to reconsider. Ask him to come here so the two of you can—"

Emma snatched up the telegram and handed it to Grace. "He's already gone, Grace. He sent this right before boarding the ship taking them to Cuba." She collapsed onto the bed and covered her face with her hands.

Lily gathered Emma in her arms. "Then we must pray for his safe return," she said.

Emma pushed Lily away, rolling away from them and curling herself into a protective huddle. "I don't want to talk anymore," she announced. "Thank you both. I'll be fine by morning. Good night."

Grace exchanged a look with Lily, who covered their distraught friend with a blanket before lowering the wick on the single lamp that lit the room and climbing into her own bed. Grace followed her lead, but she knew neither of them could ignore the soft sobs coming from the bed by the window.

She lay awake for some time, listening to Emma sniff back her tears. Emma's heartbreak got Grace to thinking. Not that she and Nick were serious or anything, but what if they were?

Emma had clearly trusted her young man, believed he wanted her as much as she wanted him. But he had wanted something that didn't include Emma, and he had chosen that over her. Nick had plans—a place of his own, according to Polly. Grace wondered where love might fit into that picture. Was Nick capable of choosing a piece of land or a chance to start his own ranch over the possibility of true love? Was that something all men did—put what they wanted in life ahead of what would be best for the women they loved?

He really should just stay at the ranch. Nick had half expected some word from Grace. She could have sent some thanks for the chocolates. He needed a sign.

"Come on, boss," one of the hands urged. "Let's go into town and blow off some steam. That concert's on tonight."

"You fellas go on. I've got work to do."

"You're sure?"

Nick grinned. "No," he admitted. "Maybe I'll see you if I get caught up on these ledgers."

He heard the men ride off and turned his attention back to updating the columns of figures, but his mind wandered. He kept hearing music that wasn't there and seeing Grace, all dressed up and enjoying herself. He shook off the image and turned back to the long line of numbers on the page. They blurred, and he rubbed his eyes. Maybe the boys were right. Things were slow this time of year, and the ledger could wait until morning. Opportunities to get away for a few hours were rare enough in his business, so why not take advantage?

He stood and stretched and realized he smelled of work and sweat. He stripped down to his waist and washed himself. As he dressed, he spied Slim's bottle of hair tonic on the shelf above the cowboy's bunk. He splashed a couple of drops in one palm, rubbed his hands together, and then ran them through his thick hair. It smelled like limes. Pulling on a clean shirt, he bent to study his reflection in the small mirror that hung on a nail near the bunkhouse door. Probably could use a shave, but that would take some time, and he had a half hour's ride into town. He finished buttoning his shirt, stuffed the tails into his trousers, hooked his suspenders over his shoulders, and grabbed his hat and jacket from the nail above his bed before heading out.

Outside, the black sky was dotted with stars, and the air was cool and dry. When he discovered his horse already saddled and waiting for him, Nick laughed out loud. The boys had clearly bet on him coming into town. He'd have to buy them a beer—and then he'd have to see if Grace was among those listening to the music in the plaza. The boys were right. It was a night to forget about work.

He heard the band as he reached the edge of town. Just past the hotel, a crowd had gathered around the bandstand. Was Grace there? And what if she was?

What would he do? What would he say? He'd sent her the candy, but she hadn't replied, and now he was worried that he'd made a mistake. Maybe she had someone back home. The truth was, he knew very little about Miss Grace Rogers.

"Well, there's a remedy for that, Sage," he muttered as he dismounted and tied his horse to the hitching post outside one of the saloons. Before he did anything else, he might as well buy his men that beer.

Grace had just walked over to the crowded plaza with Emma, Lily, and Jake when she caught sight of Nick—and then saw him enter the saloon. Disappointment welled in her chest. Of course, he was a grown man, and men were known to indulge, but somehow, she'd never thought of Nick as a man who might frequent a saloon.

Silly.

But she couldn't help thinking about Buford. The smell of whiskey had been on his breath all the time those last months they'd stepped out together. He'd taken to carrying a small bottle with him. "Tonic," he'd told her with a grin as he took a swig. When she'd protested, he'd offered the bottle to her, suggesting it might help "loosen her up some." When she refused and she told him how much his drinking bothered her, he'd walked away, and the next time she saw him, he'd been snuggling up to Sissy. Grace had thought herself well rid of him.

But Nick was another matter. She'd thought better of him.

"Are you chilled, Grace?" Jake studied her with concern, and she realized she'd crossed her arms tightly over her chest, pulling her coat tighter.

"No. Just so many people and close quarters." She smiled and released her grip on herself.

The musicians had just started a new tune, one that had a few people dancing and everyone else tapping their toes or clapping hands in time to the lively beat. Some even sang along, and Grace felt her disappointment in Nick Hopkins melt away. After all, she hadn't joined the Harvey Girls to find a beau, had she? She looked at Jake, Emma, and Lily, their arms linked as they swayed and sang, "Ta-ra-ra boom-de-ay."

Emma held out her free arm to Grace, and she eagerly joined their circle, raising her voice with theirs on the chorus. Her friend had said nothing more about the man who'd left for Cuba, but Grace was well aware that Emma's normally sunny smile didn't quite reach her sad eyes these days. It was good to see her out enjoying the music.

The song ended, and the band leader announced a short break, pointing out a table where ladies from the local church were selling hot chocolate. "I'll get us some," Jake volunteered.

"I'll go with you and help carry," Lily said.

Grace turned around to say something to Emma and found herself facing Nick instead.

"'Evenin', Grace." He removed his hat and gave her a slight bow. "Miss Emma," he added.

"I'll go tell Jake we need one more cup of cocoa," Emma said and hurried off before Grace could protest.

"Are you enjoying the music?" he asked, leaning closer to be heard over the chatter of the crowd surrounding them. He did not smell of spirits. He actually smelled of limes.

"Yes. Thank you for the chocolates," she said shyly. "That was very thoughtful." She glanced nervously to where she could see her friends gathering at the hot chocolate stand. They certainly seemed in no hurry to return. Lily even raised her cup to Grace before turning away.

"Pretty noisy here," he said. "Could I persuade you to come sit with me on that bench over there? We can still hear the music once they start up again, and I'd like to ask you something."

She was intrigued in spite of her earlier concerns, but she still hesitated. "I don't know. My friends—"

"I'll be sure they see where we're going." He made eye contact with Emma and pointed to the bench on the far edge of the plaza, then turned his attention back to Grace. "Okay?"

"If Miss Kaufmann or Mr. Campbell—"

"Grace, you are not working now, and that gives you every right to sit with me—if you choose to do so."

He was right, of course. "Very well," Grace said and started threading her way through the crowd until she reached the bench. She had barely seated herself when he sat down next to her, and suddenly, the bench seemed far too small for the two of them. She arranged the skirt of her dress so there was a clear space between them and folded her hands in her lap. "Lovely evening." She sounded prim even to herself and so forgave him when he lost the obvious battle and broke out with a warm, charming smile.

"It is that. Not too many left that will be suitable for band concerts here on the plaza." He cleared his throat. "I was wondering how you might feel about the two of us stepping out together, getting to know each other."

She uttered the first word that popped into her head. "Why?"

Her question apparently startled him. For the first time since she'd met him on the train, he seemed unsure of himself. Her heart went out to him, because she understood that kind of uncertainty. Seeing each other socially was uncharted territory, not unlike the day she'd left the farm and boarded that train for Kansas City.

"Why?" he repeated. "Well, the thing is, Grace, I like you. I thought maybe you liked me in return—at least as a friend. Seems to me like the next step might be to get to know each other a little better."

His sudden discomfort made her smile. "I thought we had already started down that road when you kissed me without so much as a how do you do."

His head jerked up, but when he realized she was teasing him, he relaxed. "Well now, Miss Rogers, seems to me we already cleared this up. I kissed you and you kissed me back. And now I'm asking to know more about you. It may be the cart before the horse, but it is what it is. Are you interested?"

"Yes." The word was out before she had allowed herself to fully consider the ramifications of agreeing.

"That's swell, Grace. And I want you to know, if you ever…that is, if some other guy…" He hesitated. "I mean, is there another guy? Maybe back home?"

There was something truly endearing about his sudden stumbling for words. She placed her hand on his. "There's no one, Nick, so how about we just see how it goes? How about I start? What made you become a ranch hand?"

He let out a long breath and relaxed against the back of the bench, his arm stretched out behind her. "I love the life—the land. I grew up on a ranch, and I guess it's all I know."

"It seems like it might be demanding work."

He shrugged. "I guess, but it's never the same. No two days are alike, and that's pretty special." He looked at her. "My turn. Tell me about that family back in Missouri."

"There are eight of us," she said. "My parents, of course, and then there's me, Reuben, Angie, Walt, and the twins—Darcy and Douglas." She ticked the names off on her fingers.

"And what's it like living in Missouri?"

She laughed. It felt so good to let down her guard, just talk like any two people might. "Missouri is a lot different than living here. For one thing, what folks here think of as 'cold' is like a spring day for us. And there's snow—I do miss snow."

"Sometimes it snows in the mountains," he told her. "Maybe we could take a ride one day."

"I'd love that."

"Well, okay then. It's a date." He scratched his chin nervously. "I didn't mean…that is—"

"It's a date," she said. "A new adventure I can look forward to."

They fell silent.

Finally, he said, "Do you like it here, Grace?"

"Oh yes. Very much."

"You don't miss the farm?"

"I miss my family terribly, but what I don't miss is the struggle…and the solitude."

"Jake told me you took this job so you could maybe help make things back home easier."

Grace nodded. "It's not much, but it feels good to be able to send what I can. My father was refused a loan we sorely needed, so if I can send fifty dollars over the time I'm here, that will make a difference. And just being here, I've taken some of the burden off my folks. One less mouth to feed and all."

"What will you do once your contract with the Harvey Company ends?"

She released a long breath. "I've been thinking about that a lot. I enjoy the work, and I've made wonderful friends. The truth is it would be hard to go back to life on the farm." She shrugged. "It can get pretty lonely."

"It can be lonely here as well—unless you happen to meet somebody special." He took her hand between both of his.

Nick Hopkins was flirting with her. It was unsettling yet exhilarating. Grace cleared her throat and sat a little straighter. "What about you?" she asked brightly. "I mean, do you have plans beyond this?"

Big mistake, she thought when he looked at her for a long moment before answering.

"I've got plans," he replied slowly, his eyes meeting hers. "Nothing unusual—land of my own. A house." He paused as if deciding whether or not to say more, then added, "Someday a wife and family."

Polly had said he wasn't the marrying kind. Apparently Polly was wrong.

In spite of the fact that they were seated on a park bench with people all around, the moment seemed suddenly far too intimate. Grace glanced around and saw people leaving. "I should go." She stood and offered him her hand for a handshake at the same time that he stood and offered her his arm.

He stood. "Grace, I may be nothing more than a simple cowboy, but I know enough to make sure you get back to the hotel safely."

"I doubt I'm in any real danger, Nick."

And just then, as if to prove his point, a trio of drunks staggered out of the saloon that stood between them and the hotel.

"I don't believe in taking unnecessary chances." He tucked her hand in the crook of his arm.

She glanced up at him. "And yet you've decided to risk spending time with me," she teased, wanting so much to end the evening with that smile turned her way.

"I said 'unnecessary,' Grace. Where you're concerned, I believe any risk is well worth taking." His eyes roamed over her face before dropping to her mouth.

Was he thinking of kissing her again? Was she thinking the same thing? "We should go," she said, but she seemed incapable of moving. The cold night air thrummed with the possibility that he might touch her cheek or kiss her again—both of which she longed for.

"Shall we?" he asked softly, and she took the first step. He matched his long stride to her shorter steps and saw her as far as the kitchen entrance. "Good night, Grace," he said as he placed her fingertips against his lips. "I have to be out on the range for the next week or so, but if you're available, I was thinking maybe we could do something a week from today."

Caught up in the warmth of his lips touching her fingers, she barely heard the invitation.

"Grace?"

"I'll see if Lily and Emma can go."

He released a long breath and looked beyond her toward the sky. "Grace, don't get me wrong. I like Lily and Emma just fine, but it's you I want to get to know."

"And you need to understand that I have a reputation to protect, one that, if sullied in any way, would cost me my position here. That, Nick Hopkins, is a risk I am unwilling to take." She slid her hand free of his and knew she sounded like a schoolmarm lecturing a recalcitrant student, but surely he could appreciate that.

The man chuckled.

"Good night," she said primly and turned to go.

He caught her arm. "Wait. I'm sorry. It's just sometimes you have this way of talking that confuses me. I mean, I like it. I like the way I think I've got you figured out and then you go and surprise me again."

She forced herself to look away. The man was impossibly handsome—and impossibly charming. If she wasn't careful…

"Next week after church, Lily, Emma, Jake, and I will be pleased to see you, Nick. Good night." Before he could protest her determination to include the others, she hurried inside and shut the kitchen door. Two of the kitchen workers glanced up from their chores. They nodded and went on with their work, but when she saw Jake, he cocked an eyebrow at Grace as if expecting a report.

"Good night, Jake," she said and ran up the back stairs. But once she reached her room, she had to face the fact that Emma and Lily would not be so easily dismissed.

"Well?" Lily demanded the minute Grace closed the door.

"I had a nice evening," Grace said as she removed her hat and gloves, "and that is all I have to say on the matter."

"Well, la-de-da to you too," Lily grumbled as she flopped onto her bed.

"Give her time, Lily," Emma advised. "This is all new."

"The least she could say is if she plans to see him again."

"I'm right here," Grace said, since the two of them seemed to be discussing her as if she were still out with Nick. "All right, I'll say this. We talked and—"

Lily sat up, her face eager for details. "And kissed?"

Did a brush of his lips on her fingers count? "No. What I was about to say is he has suggested we all go out next week after church. The two of you, me—and Jake," she added with a sly glance at Lily.

Lily frowned. "Why do I think this was all your idea? Not the two of you going out but you insisting on including us in the plan?"

Grace shrugged. "If you'd rather not go, I guess I could ask a couple of the other girls."

"Did I say anything about not going? We're in

favor of anything that gets us away from work for a few hours, right, Emma?"

"Next Sunday?"

"Yes," Grace said, taking note of how Emma's cheeks had turned a most becoming pink. "But if you have plans—"

"Actually, I promised to attend an organ recital at the church."

To Grace's relief, Lily's attention had shifted from her to Emma. "Promised who?"

"Aidan—Mr. Campbell. He's been most kind, Lily," she added defensively.

"You and Aidan Campbell?" Lily was clearly dumbfounded.

"Not like that," Emma snapped. "He heard me say I was going and said the organist is a friend, so perhaps it made sense for us to attend together."

"That's good, Emma," Grace assured her. "I'm sure you'll enjoy that much more."

"So Jake and me, and you and your cowboy," Lily mused as she studied her reflection in the mirror. "And me with nothing to wear." She sighed dramatically.

"I thought you found Jake's attentions unwanted," Emma said.

"As you well know, Jake and I are a lost cause as long as we both work for Fred Harvey. Grace and Nick on the other hand?"

Both Lily and Emma grinned at her.

"Oh, for heaven's sake. I'm going to take a bath," Grace said, grabbing her nightgown and toiletries and heading for the door. "And when I return, let's have no more talk of romance, understood?"

Emma nodded as Lily gave her a sharp salute. But the minute the door closed behind her, she heard her roommates giggling and whispering, and she knew it was all about her—and Nick.

Chapter 6

THE SATURDAY BEFORE GRACE'S DATE WITH NICK, Miss Kaufmann called Lily, Grace, and Emma to her office. "Mr. and Mrs. Lombard, owners of the Lombardo Ranch, are planning a large party to celebrate their anniversary. They've asked for some of our staff to serve at the party. I thought perhaps the three of you might be interested?"

"Me as well?" Grace blurted. "I mean, surely there are others who—"

Miss Kaufmann smiled. "You as well, Grace. The new girl arrives later today, and since the party is a week from today, Mr. Campbell has decided the lunch counter will be closed and we will only serve the noon meal in the dining room. Actually, serving at the party is child's play compared to the usual afternoon rush here. The food service there will be buffet style. Mainly, you will be passing among the guests serving champagne and clearing dishes." She shrugged. "How hard could that be?"

How hard indeed.

"I would be happy to be of service," Emma said.

"Sounds like fun," Lily added.

Miss Kaufmann turned to Grace. "You'll be paid a regular wage, and knowing the Lombards, I suspect that will come with a generous tip."

"Thank you for the opportunity," Grace murmured.

"Excellent." She turned to go and then looked back at them with a twinkle in her eye. "Did I mention that the party will be a masquerade ball? Everyone—including you girls—will be in costume."

"But—" Grace protested. How was she to bear the cost of a costume, much less have time to make something, even if she could afford fabric?

"Not to worry, Grace. As I mentioned, the Lombards are generous people. An appropriate costume will be delivered for each of you in plenty of time for alterations." Outside, a train whistle blared. Miss Kaufmann clapped her hands together. "Back to work, girls. The eleven o'clock train has just arrived."

As she returned to her post, Grace realized she was smiling and feeling lighter than she had before Miss Kaufmann spoke with them. *A party!* She had seen Mr. and Mrs. Lombard before when they came to dine at the hotel. Mrs. Lombard had a sunny disposition and was very friendly to everyone. Mr. Lombard was quieter but certainly seemed nice enough. It would be such fun serving their guests.

Of course, the Lombardo Ranch was where Nick worked. There was no reason to believe they would even cross paths. He was a cowboy, so he'd be out watching over the herd, wouldn't he? On the other hand, as their foreman, his employers might have special duties for him—duties that included him being at the party. A girl could only hope.

She scrubbed hard at the marble counter until it glistened, and all the while, she hummed to herself and wondered what her costume would be.

"We're to be dressed as ladies-in-waiting," Lily moaned later that night as the three of them sat in the kitchen eating a late supper. "Mrs. Lombard will be the queen, and her female guests, princesses. I mean, we may as well wear our Harvey uniforms."

"Well, Miss K could hardly approve our wearing some off-the-shoulder gown," Emma teased.

"I don't see why not," Lily huffed. "Certainly, the three of us would make better-looking princesses than Mrs. Lombard's friends, who are old."

Emma laughed. "And that, dear Lily, is precisely why we are to be properly covered. How would it be if Mr. Lombard's friends spent any time ogling the three of us?"

"You mean the way Mr. Fields and Mr. Perkins do now?" Lily replied.

"Miss K said we might even be paid extra for the evening," Grace mused.

"Well, of course we will," Emma assured her. "Not a great deal, but every bit helps, does it not?"

Grace had confided in Emma and Lily her plan to send as much money as possible back to her family. "Yes. I'm hoping the money I've sent already has started to make a difference."

"Your mother doesn't say?"

Grace shook her head. "And I don't know how to bring it up when I write her. I just tuck what I can in with the letter and send it with the hope that it will help."

Lily stared at her. "Please do not tell me you are placing actual cash in your letters?"

"Well, yes. I mean, how else—" Grace saw Emma and Lily exchange looks of alarm.

"You need to wire the money, Grace," Emma said. "You go to the telegraph office, pay them the money, and they send a wire to your hometown operator, who then pays out the money to your family."

"How much have you sent already, honey?" Lily sat next to her and wrapped her arm around Grace's shoulder.

Grace mentally added up the amounts she'd sent since starting her work at the hotel. Money she'd accumulated in tips over the several weeks she'd been working at the lunch counter, plus the ten dollars from her first paycheck and repaying the money her mother had slipped her the day she left. "I don't know. Almost twenty dollars, I guess."

Emma sighed. "Nothing to be done now," she murmured.

"But if the money has been stolen, surely a crime has been committed," Lily said. "We should tell Mr. Campbell, perhaps even report this to the sheriff."

A shudder of despair shook Grace to her core. "I suppose." But she had worked so hard for that money, and now it was gone. What had been the point of leaving home in the first place? She was humiliated and embarrassed. "I don't want anyone else to know of this," she said firmly. She looked from Emma to Lily. "I mean it. The money is gone, and it's my fault. Going forward, I will know better, but even if I did report the loss, it was cash—I have no proof."

"But—" Lily was clearly ready to protest her decision.

Grace gave Emma a look of pleading. "Please? Can't we just keep this between us?"

Emma patted Grace's hand. "Don't upset yourself further, Grace. You made a mistake. We all do from time to time—even Lily."

Lily gave them both a look of mock surprise. "Me?" she protested, and then she hugged Grace. "You're right, Gracie. Nothing to be done at this point. Live and learn has always been my motto. So what do you say we dwell on something less somber— like the party?"

"We are not guests of honor, Lily," Emma reminded her. Grace was grateful for the shift in focus away from her. "Jake told me because the ball is a masquerade, everyone will wear masks."

"Ooh," Lily trilled, already distracted. "Mysterious and exciting." She lifted her hand to cover the bottom half of her face and wiggled her eyebrows.

Emma and Grace broke into peals of laughter, and Grace's felt her spirits lift. These women were her friends. They did not judge. They listened and con-soled, and then they made her smile. "Why on earth would Mrs. Lombard want her guests in masks?" she asked as she carried her supper dishes to the sink.

"I heard she grew up in New York City where such parties were common," Lily reported, lower-ing her voice to a stage whisper. "Word has it Mr. Lombard will do whatever it takes to keep her happy out here in the Wild West, and I suppose recreating a party of her youth is one of those ways."

"Wouldn't it be wonderful to have someone love

you that much?" Emma said. "I mean, most of the men I know—including those in my own family—are more interested in what a woman will do for them. I'd give up a lot to find a man like Mr. Lombard."

"Don't let Mrs. Lombard know that," Lily teased, "or she might change her mind about having us serve at the party."

Grace had stopped listening to the details of their conversation. The minute Emma had started talking about the kind of man Mr. Lombard was, Grace's mind had shifted to Nick. He was awfully good-looking, so maybe he just took it for granted that women would fall all over themselves to do his bidding.

No, she decided. Nick was too much like her father—a good, decent man who cared about others, a man who, with any luck at all, was starting to care for her beyond the bounds of simple friendship.

"Now, Nick, about the ranch hands," Rita Lombard said as she bustled around the large kitchen serving up coffee and pie.

She was getting to it now, the reason why she'd insisted he have supper with her and the boss as soon as he had come in from a week on the range. Nick was pretty sure he wasn't going to like what she was about to say. "I'll make sure they're on their best behavior, ma'am."

"Oh, they'll have to go a step more than that. I need at least half of them—and you—at the party. We're expecting a number of single young ladies, as it turns out. Daughters of the other ranchers plus their friends, and they're all excited to get dressed up and dance and such."

John Lombard groaned.

"What was I to say?" Rita protested. "You men have all sorts of chances for adventures. Have a heart. These young ladies deserve an evening like this, and I say the more the merrier, and as long as we can provide well-mannered young men to attend to them—"

"Attend to them?" John roared. "Well-*mannered*? Rita, these are cowboys! It's rare for them to take a bath more than once a month. You can't—"

Rita held up one finger. "They are gentlemen and will conduct themselves as such for the evening. Nick will make sure everyone knows what's expected, won't you, Nick?"

What could he say? "Yes, ma'am."

The boss stood and clapped him on the back. "Sorry for dragging you and the boys into this thing. Let them know I'll make it up to them, okay?"

"And I've ordered costumes for all of you," Rita added with a coquettish smile.

Nick could not hide his alarm, and both of the Lombards laughed. "Come on, Rita, stop teasing the man, or we'll wake up tomorrow with nobody to run the place." John walked Nick to the door. "I hope you and the men take some time to enjoy this fandango, Nick. It's been a long, hard year, and you've done good work. We appreciate that."

"Thank you, sir, and as for the party, we won't let you down."

The two men shook hands, and Nick walked to the

bunkhouse, mentally running through the list of the unsuspecting hired hands waiting there. Who would he choose to watch over the herd and who to go to the party? Slim, Cooky, and Smokey had been on the trip to the falls, so he could count on them. Besides, Rita had said half a dozen. There were only three other men in residence, now that the seasonal hires had moved on for the winter. Could any of them dance a proper waltz?

Could he?

This whole business was getting out of hand, and he'd be glad when it was all over and he could just get back to work. The west was changing—and not for the better, as far as Nick was concerned. *Fancy dress balls?* What next?

He had no choice but to deal with it though. Aidan Campbell might have some thoughts about how best to get his men ready. He'd get to town early when he went to call on Grace and speak to Campbell about the party while she finished her shift.

On Sunday, he asked to borrow the buckboard, filled the back with hay, and had Hattie, the Lombards' cook, pack a picnic for six. Hopefully, Grace had encouraged Emma to invite someone as her escort for the outing. And with both her roommates matched up, he'd have more time alone with Grace—or at least that was the plan.

But when Nick reached the hotel, it seemed Campbell had other ideas. "Miss Elliott and I were to attend a concert, but that has been canceled," the hotel manager said. "Therefore, it occurred to me that with all of us scheduled to work the Lombard party, this might be a perfect opportunity to discuss the plans while we all enjoy this lovely afternoon."

Once again, what could he say? "Sure."

"Excellent. I'll meet you at the kitchen exit." Campbell hurried off, presumably to get his hat.

The last thing Nick had expected was a chaperone. Of course, Grace had insisted on including Emma and Lily, but he suspected they were on his side in this—or at least on the side of romance. Campbell was another matter. The way this day was going, Nick half expected Miss Kaufmann to join them. But then he walked around to the back of the hotel and saw Grace waiting for him, and his disgruntled mood vanished.

She wore a green calico dress, faded from the sun and multiple washings. Her hair was pinned up and under the straw hat she'd worn on the train. She sat alone on the bench outside the kitchen exit, her hands folded in her lap and her face turned up to the sun. Her eyes were closed, and she was so lovely that Nick stopped to stare at her, not wanting to disturb the portrait of serene beauty before him.

Just then, Lily and Emma came bustling out the kitchen door, Lily's voice carrying across the yard. "Really, Emma, I don't know what your problem is. Would you rather stay cooped up in that tiny room? You really need to learn how to have some fun. Sometimes you're as stuffy as Mr.—"

The rest of her sentence froze on her lips as Campbell stepped outside. He was half turned away from the group, giving final instructions to his assistant manager, who hovered just inside the kitchen door, pencil and paper in hand as he scribbled notes and nodded.

"Well, looks like we're all here except Jake," Nick said as he approached the group. Grace was standing now, apparently out of respect for the manager's presence.

"Right here," Jake called. He spotted the wagon Nick had parked behind the hotel. "A hay ride? Great idea." Without waiting for the others, he strode over and spread the blankets Nick had brought from the ranch over the piles of straw. He offered his hand first to Emma, then Lily, and finally Grace. "Ladies, your carriage awaits," he said, then looked at Aidan, apparently realizing for the first time that the hotel manager was part of the outing. "Sir." He extended his hand to Campbell as well. "Nice you could join us," he managed.

Nick swallowed a chuckle. If nothing else, this was going to be an interesting afternoon. He walked over to the wagon and prepared to close the flap at the back. "You know, folks, you might all be more comfortable if somebody rode up front with me." He focused his attention on Grace and, when no one else volunteered, extended his hand to her. "Miss Rogers, would you do me the honor?"

Other than Lily hiding a delighted smile behind a gloved hand and elbowing Jake, no one spoke. Grace hesitated, then allowed Nick to lift her from the wagon. He was tempted to prolong the time spent with his hands nearly encircling her small waist but was keenly aware of Campbell watching.

"The view's better from up front," he said, speaking loud enough so that it seemed he was speaking to the whole group.

"I like the view back here just fine," Jake said, his eyes on Lily.

"Stop that," she hissed, glancing at their employer. "You'll get us both sacked."

Nick had just helped Grace up to the front seat when Aidan cleared his throat, gaining everyone's attention.

"I have something to say that may make our venture today a good deal more enjoyable," he announced.

Grace turned to look back at him, and everyone else gave him their full attention.

"Today, I am simply Aidan. Tomorrow, we will resume the formalities, but whether or not you believe it, a man in my position needs time like this to enjoy the company of charming friends. So, may we all just relax and relish the time we have to be free of responsibility? Jake, that goes for you as well—just friends out for the day, all right?"

Nick glanced at Emma, Lily, and Jake. Their mouths were open, but clearly, they were speechless. "Sounds like a great idea, Aidan." He climbed aboard and took up the reins. "Lily, you're in charge of entertainment—singing should it be called for, games, that sort of thing. Jake, you scope out a good place for our picnic, and Emma, you take charge of the food. Aidan, on our way home later, I'd be obliged if you took the reins."

"You've forgotten Grace," Lily protested.

"Oh yeah—Grace." Nick pretended to be stymied, then snapped his fingers and grinned. "Grace is our navigator."

She laughed. "I don't know the first thing about where this road leads or what might lie beyond the edge of town."

"Ah, but when we come to a fork in the road, Grace will choose this way or that," Aidan offered. "We have a plan, so let's be off."

If anyone had told Nick it would be Campbell himself who set them all at ease, he would have laughed long and loud. But looking back at the man who had shed his usual morning coat and stiff collar for canvas trousers, a homespun shirt, and suede vest, he realized Aidan Campbell was not at all the prim and prissy man he and the other hands had thought. Beneath the rolled-back sleeves of his shirt, Nick noted muscular forearms, which spoke of physical labor and a man able to defend himself should the need arise.

Once they had left town, Nick turned the team toward the road that led west to Santa Fe. The route was lined with scrub sagebrush and different varieties of cactus. Nick heard Jake working hard to impress Lily with his knowledge of Santa Fe, while Aidan attempted to engage Emma in conversation without much success.

"See that plant?" Nick nudged Grace as he pointed to a low-growing cactus near the edge of the trail.

Grace shuddered. "It looks so prickly. I mean, I would hate to accidentally fall on something like that."

"How would you feel about eating it?"

She stared at him. "Eat it?"

"It's called a prickly pear cactus, and most women in these parts know how to make a right fine jelly from the fruit. It's too sweet for my taste, but most folks like it."

"What are those ones that look like they have fingers?" Grace asked.

"Cholla—also known as 'jumping' cactus."

"Why jumping?"

"Well now, the cholla is about the meanest, sneaki-est cactus in the desert," Nick explained. "They can grow to eight feet tall, but no matter how small or big they are, they have these needles that seem to jump off them if you so much as touch them with the toe of your boot."

"Ouch," Grace said.

"Ouch indeed. Those needles seek moisture—like your skin—and when they find it, the point can curve, locking the needle in place and making it the very devil to remove." He let that sink in, then added, "On the other hand, the blossoms give us some of the most impressive color you'll find in a desert, especially in spring."

She sighed, and for the first time since he'd helped her up to sit beside him, he realized she had relaxed. "It's like a different world, so different from Missouri," she said. "It's lovely in its own way, isn't it?"

"In spring when everything is in bloom, it's pretty special," he agreed. "Even at this time of year, if we get a solid, soaking rain, you'd be amazed at the color."

"Have you lived out here your whole life?"

"Most of it. I guess I was somewhere around six or seven when my folks came west."

"From where?"

He smiled. "My parents were city folks. They came from Philadelphia, and to hear my pa tell the story, they didn't know the first thing about ranching. But they learned, and taught me and my brothers as well."

"No sisters?"

"Nope. Ma always said she was outnumbered by Pa and the four of us boys, but I think she liked it just fine."

"You haven't told me much about your family," Grace said.

"My mother died when I was twelve. Pa had some bad years after that and eventually sold the ranch and went to work for the Lombards. He was killed in a stampede when I was seventeen. The Lombards gave me his job, and I stayed."

"Your brothers?"

"Married and scattered around the country." He glanced over his shoulder toward the back of the wagon. "Everybody doing all right back there?"

There was a general murmur of agreement before the four passengers returned to the debate they were having about whether or not a mountain lion was the same as a bobcat.

"All I know," Lily said, "is I would just as soon not see either one."

Nick chuckled and turned his attention back to the road ahead. "Jake, we're getting close to chow time, so any time you see a spot…"

"There's a nice grove of cottonwoods by a stream not too far from here," Jake replied. "Maybe quarter of an hour if you can get those nags to move a little faster."

Everyone laughed as Nick snapped the reins and let out a shout that had the team of horses picking up the pace and Grace grasping his arm to steady herself. He looked at her hand clutching his upper arm and then at her. "Shucks, miss, if I'd known holding on would be your reaction, I would have snapped those reins a mile or so earlier."

Her cheeks turned a most becoming rosy shade. She pulled her hand free, clutching the edge of the wooden seat instead as the wagon swayed from side to side. But the motion of the wagon could not stop her shoulder brushing Nick's, no matter how hard she tried to keep her distance. Truth be told, since she was smiling, Nick figured she kind of liked it.

Following Jake's directions, Nick pulled the wagon off the trail and drove over uncharted desert to the creek and its grove of large shade trees, including one that had fallen so that it rested in the creek. As soon as he pulled to a stop, the others climbed down from the rear. Emma and Lily set about choosing a spot to lay out the food, assuring Aidan they knew how to do a picnic "the Harvey way." Meanwhile Jake unharnessed the horses so they could drink from the creek and graze. Nick climbed down and held out his arms to Grace. Hesitation played across her face, but then she scooted across the seat and leaned down to place her hands on his shoulders as he took hold of her waist and swung her to the ground.

He wondered what it might be like to dance with her. *Must have that goldarned party on my mind*, he thought as he released her. She hurried away to help the other women while he decided to give Jake a hand with the horses rather than follow.

"I guess you musta heard about this fandango the Lombards are throwin'," Jake said as if he'd read Nick's mind. "You know Lily, Emma, and Grace are working the party, right?" He continued without waiting for an answer. "Wish I could be there. Might be a good chance to steal some time alone with Lily. You thinkin' about maybe trying to find some time with Grace?"

The man had a way of babbling so much that sometimes Nick didn't catch every word, but he heard that last bit. "Why would I do that?"

Jake stared at him. "'Cause you're sweet on her. Everybody knows that. At least for you and her, it's all on the up and up. If I want to see Lily—"

"We're just getting better acquainted," Nick corrected.

Jake shrugged. "Acquainted…courtin'… An apple's still an apple no matter if it's red, green, or yellow," he observed and led the horses to the creek.

Nick fiddled with the harness, keeping his eye on Grace all the while. She was laughing at something Lily had said, her head thrown back, exposing the line of her throat. In spite of his determination to take things slow with Grace, he couldn't seem to block out the image of trailing a row of kisses from her chin to the place where her dress was closed by too many little buttons.

Get a grip, Hopkins. His attraction to Grace could not be purely physical. She wasn't the type to take that lightly. She was interesting and smart, and he enjoyed spending time with her, but that was as far as things could go—as far as he could allow them to go, at least until he had something solid he could offer in the way of a future. But he couldn't deny that the more time he spent with Grace or even just thinking about her, the more flexible his plans became. After all, by the time her contract ended, he'd be that much closer to owning the land he'd picked out closer to Santa Fe. Taking a ride past that land was one of the reasons he'd chosen the route he had today.

Nick was used to girls and women who followed a man's lead, making sure any dreams they had melded with his. Grace was different. He might have figured out a plan for the future, but then just maybe in her plan, he was the one who didn't fit.

"Nick, are you coming to eat or not?" Emma stood by the creek, hands on hips. "Wasn't this whole picnic your idea?"

He grinned at her and waved. "Comin'," he called back and pretended to make one final check of the wagon before striding across the grass to join the others.

Hattie had outdone herself this time. There was enough food to feed twice their number—tortillas, a variety of relishes, bean salad, pickles, fried chicken, and potatoes wrapped in burlap to protect them. Aidan spread the blankets from the wagon on the bank of the creek while Lily found a private spot to remove her shoes and stockings out of sight of the others. She was now dangling her bare feet in the cool water as she enjoyed her meal. Jake took a seat next to her and clearly was not thrilled when Aidan sat down on Lily's other side. Emma fussed with the food, urging everyone to come back for seconds and thirds, while Grace perched on a boulder near the others to enjoy her meal.

"May I join you?" Nick could not seem to keep his distance. He could easily have stayed close to Emma, watching over the food to keep any insects or other critters away and making conversation as the two of them ate. But no, he went straight to Grace.

"This rock is hardly large enough for me," she said, smiling up at him.

"No matter." He plopped down on the ground next to her.

"Emma, come join us," she called, motioning for her friend and making room for her on the rock she'd just declared too small for two. She was as skittish as a newborn colt, and yet she kept watching him.

As she chatted away with Emma about the food, he stood and cleared his throat. Both women looked at him. "Seconds, Nick?" Emma asked.

"Thought I'd take a walk." He focused his gaze on Grace. "Care to join me?" The way he said the words, he knew they came out as more challenge than invitation.

Before Grace could answer, Emma relieved them both of their tin plates. "You two go along. I'll just wash up these dishes." She headed for the creek.

"Comin'?" Nick asked, deliberately softening his tone. "I've got something I'd like you to see."

They walked along the bank of the creek without speaking. She lifted her skirts when they caught on a burr or shrub. Once, she stumbled and he reached out to steady her, then immediately released her.

"You seem pensive, Nick," she said when the silence between them became uncomfortable.

"Just thinkin'," he replied. They had come to a place where the creek narrowed and a row of rocks made a path for crossing. He went ahead of her, holding out his hand to make sure she made it safely to the opposite shore. "See that land there?" He pointed to a place in the distance where the mountains rose behind a stretch of open flatland nestled at the base.

She nodded.

"That's the parcel I aim to own. Got a loan, and I'm making regular payments."

Her smile was radiant. "Oh, Nick, it's perfect. I can imagine a house just there in that cove of the foothills, and look how the creek winds all through it. It's beautiful."

He couldn't seem to take his eyes off her. "Yeah," he murmured. "Beautiful." He took a step nearer and, although her expression sobered, she did not move away. He fingered a strand of her hair that blew in the cool breeze. "Look, Grace, the thing is...well, I've been thinkin' maybe—"

"Are you going to kiss me again?" she asked.

"I was thinking pretty seriously about it. Would that be all right?"

She nodded. "I think I would like that." She reached up to touch his cheek.

He closed the distance that remained between them, wrapping her in his arms as he lowered his lips to hers. She cupped the back of his neck and closed her eyes, and suddenly, he was having trouble breathing. "Grace," he whispered as their lips met. So much for keeping things simple.

The first time he kissed her, it had been a shock to them both. This time, they knew what was happening. She'd given permission, and he fully intended to savor the moment. He stroked her closed lips with his tongue. To his surprise, she opened to him. He understood the action was purely instinctive, so he hesitated, giving her a chance to change her mind. But to his delight, her tongue flicked his.

She couldn't know what she was doing to him, and he pulled back, planting kisses on her cheeks and eyelids in a desperate attempt to maintain some control. Campbell wasn't that far away, after all, and although they had walked some distance from the others before crossing the winding creek and Nick was fairly certain they could not be seen, he would not compromise Grace's position.

"Hey," he said, his voice and breathing unsteady. "We should head back before Aidan sends out a search party."

"Yes." She stepped away and put a hand to her hair to check for any damage. "Thank you for sharing your dream with me, Nick." She motioned toward the land. "I hope you get everything you want."

He had no words, so instead of talking, he took her hand and did not let go until they were close to where they had left the others. To Nick's surprise, Emma, Aidan, and Jake had all joined Lily to wade in the shallow creek water. They were laughing and splashing water at one another, and judging by his soaked clothing, it was apparent Jake had fallen at least once.

"Well, finally," Lily shouted when she spotted them. "You put me in charge of entertainment and then disappear?"

"What's the entertainment?" Grace asked.

"Tag—you're it," Lily replied as she splashed Grace with water.

"Not fair," Grace squealed. "I still have my shoes on."

"Take them off," Emma instructed, pointing to a place where the trees grew so close together, they provided a screen. "And you as well," she added, turning on Nick and splashing him before pointing to a place where Aidan's and Jake's boots stood near a large, flat boulder.

Nick hobbled on one foot and then the other as he cast off his boots and socks and stepped in the cool water. Lily and Emma squealed and hid behind Jake and Aidan, and the game was on.

Once they straggled out of the creek, damp and chilled, there was enough food left for them to share a light supper before starting back. As they gathered at the wagon, waiting while Jake and Nick hitched up the team, Lily sighed and then spun in a circle.

"What a wonderful day," she shouted, her face raised to the sky.

The others laughed and prepared to take their places for the ride home. "You drive the team," Nick said, handing Aidan the reins. "Grace and I will ride in back."

"And leave me up here alone?"

"We'll sing to keep you awake," Lily volunteered, pulling the blanket Jake had handed her closer around her shoulders.

"More likely you'll all be sound asleep before we've gone half a mile." Aidan turned to look at them. "Miss Elliott, would you be so kind as to ride up here with me and keep me from drifting off and leading us astray?"

Emma hesitated, then nodded.

Once everyone was settled, Aidan clicked his tongue, and the team lumbered forward. Lily rested her head on Jake's shoulder, and the expression on Jake's face needed no explanation. The man looked like he'd died and gone straight to heaven. Nick envied him, as Grace seemed intent on making sure no part of their bodies touched—not even their shoulders. She carefully arranged the blanket so that a furrow a man could plant corn in separated them.

She was a strange one all right. One minute, she was kissing him as if they had been lovers for weeks, and the next, she was sitting upright, stiff and tense as the wagon rocked from side to side. He leaned closer, daring her to scoot away.

"Relax, Grace," he whispered. "I'm not going to kiss you in front of the others, although I doubt they would even notice."

"Oh, they'll notice," she whispered back. "At least Lily and Emma would, and I'd not hear the end of it for days."

Nick let out a breath and struck up a conversation about the weather in a normal tone that invited the others to take part. Emma and Aidan took the bait, and finally, Grace relaxed enough to allow their shoulders to meet and sway in rhythm to the movement of the wagon. He reached between them and took hold of her hand, interweaving his fingers with hers.

And when she did not pull away, he smiled.

Chapter
7

THE DINING ROOM WAS EXTRA BUSY THE FOLLOWING week, but Grace didn't mind. The busier they were, the more likely she could be promoted from serving beverages to full waitress, and that would surely mean another small raise in her wages.

At night, Lily could talk of nothing but the Lombard party. Emma and Grace listened patiently as she chattered on about who might be there, naming some of the wealthy ranchers and businessmen who often had their dinners at the hotel.

"You are being unkind to Jake," Emma noted one night as she repaired a snag in her stockings.

"Jake and I are just buddies—friends," Lily proclaimed. "We've talked, and he knows I could never feel that way about him. He's a nice guy but…"

Emma bit off a thread and examined her handiwork. "That man is head over heels in love with you, Lily, and you know it. Is it so impossible to imagine a day when the two of you might find a way to be together?"

When Lily didn't come back with her usual snappy comment, Grace looked up from the letter she was writing and was surprised to see Lily's chin tremble as she bit her lower lip. Grace set her pencil and paper aside and stretched out a comforting hand. "Lily, what is it?"

"I can't be with Jake," she blubbered. "The truth is I can't be with anyone."

Grace and Emma glanced at each other and then focused on Lily. "Why?" Emma asked, laying her handwork aside.

Lily tugged at a loose curl of hair. She was not looking at them. "I'm married," she whispered, and the floodgates opened as she threw herself down on her bed, covering her face with her pillow.

Grace looked at Emma, who sat frozen and open-mouthed, her eyes pinned on Lily. "Married?" she finally managed in a whisper.

Lily let out a fresh wail that Grace took to be affirmative. She tried to find her way through the thoughts rocketing like fireworks through her brain. "But you can't be. I mean, we aren't permitted."

Lily sat up, throwing the pillow aside. "I lied, Grace. No one knows."

"But then where is your husband?" Emma placed her fist against her lips as a fresh thought came to her. "Oh, Lily, tell me there are no children."

"There are no children," Lily confirmed. "He didn't stay long enough for that."

"How did you meet?" Grace's question might have been inane, but there were so many missing pieces to what Lily had just shared. Perhaps starting at the beginning might make sense of it all.

Lily sniffed back a sob. "It was before you and I met, Emma. Before I knew there was such a thing as a Harvey Girl, I was down on my luck. I'd been let go from the job at Marshall Field's, and I was barely getting by. I was cleaning rooms at a hotel, thinking of taking a job in a saloon as one of the dancehall girls, when suddenly, there he was. He was a guest, a businessman, always immaculately groomed and well-dressed. One day, the bellboy handed me a note. It was from him, inviting me to meet him for dinner."

"You didn't?" Emma was clearly shocked.

"Obviously, I did," Lily admitted. "I mean, if you had seen the man, all charm and perfect manners, you would have gone as well. Yes, even you, Emma Elliott."

"I don't understand. You had dinner, but how did you end up married?" Grace felt an actual chill.

Lily sighed. "We met every night, and it wasn't like what you might be thinking. He took me to a concert and bought me presents, sent me flowers. Oh, there was kissing, and after a couple of nights, things got pretty heavy between us, if you get my meaning. But when he wanted to…you know, I refused."

"Good." Emma seemed to breathe for the first time since Lily's stunning announcement.

"I told him the only way that would ever happen would be if we were properly married." Her tone was defiant, and then her expression changed to one of disbelief. "The next night, we met as usual, and he took me straight to a justice of the peace, put a ring on my finger, said the words, and called my bluff."

"So you spent the night with him?" Emma was aghast.

"We were married," Lily replied, stressing each word. "We *are* married—at least as far as I know.

Nothing really happened. I mean, we were naked and all, but he'd had so much to drink that he fell asleep before—"

"Where is he now?" Grace asked.

Lily shrugged. "Don't know and don't care. The morning after our so-called wedding night, I awoke to a note on the pillow next to me, claiming he had business back east and would be in touch. That was three years ago, and I've not seen hide nor hair of him since." She started to cry again, softly this time, the tears dropping unnoticed onto the pillow she clutched.

"But, Lily, if you never consummated the union, you can get an annulment," Emma protested. "He's not worth your tears, Lily, and he certainly does not deserve to ruin your life."

"So your answer is that I should seek an annulment," Lily fumed as she stomped around the room. "Brand myself forever with that? I did nothing wrong. When does he face the music? When does he have to endure finger pointing and whispers and gossip?"

She was right, Grace thought. It was Lily who would pay the price of her mistake in trusting this man.

With a long shuddering breath, Lily pulled herself together. Calmly, she turned to face them. "So now you understand why I can never be with Jake…or anyone else. All I have are my fantasies, girls, so please, could we just not talk about something for which there is no solution and allow me to enjoy what might have been?"

What could they say? They were her friends, so they would do what Lily asked. "But the man is not worth it," Emma muttered.

Later, after the three of them had said their good

nights and settled under the covers of their own beds, Grace lay awake staring at the blackness surrounding her. She thought about Nick and the way he had kissed her. Was he like Lily's husband? Did he think he could simply take what he wanted when he wanted it? No, she decided, it wasn't the same thing at all. Nick was nothing like the horrible man who had wronged her friend. He was a gentleman. And yet when Nick had walked her to the door of the hotel following their outing, he had said something about wanting to see her again but without all the chaperones.

She took that to mean he wanted to be alone with her, and when they were alone, past experience showed he would want to kiss her. She could not deny she wanted that as well. But what if he wanted more, like Lily's husband had wanted from her? She imagined Nick opening the collar of her dress, touching her exposed throat, kissing her there—and other places. She squirmed in the bed, trying to relieve the strange and oddly thrilling ache that spread from between her thighs up through her body.

"Grace!"

Emma getting out of her own bed and shaking Grace's shoulder brought her fully awake. "What?"

"Lie still or get up," Emma whispered. "It's like sleeping in a room with a whirling dervish!"

"Sorry," Grace muttered and turned onto her side, forcing herself to remain perfectly still until she was sure Emma was asleep. Then she slipped out of bed, found paper and pencil, and curled up on the floor near the window. Working with the light from the street, she started a letter to her mother.

Dear Mama,

   I want to tell you about a wonderful man I've met. He has the kindest eyes and the most winning smile, and when he touches my hand, it feels like we were meant to be together.

She paused, chewing on the end of the pencil. She realized what she really wanted to tell her folks was that with each passing day, she was less and less sure that she wanted to return to the farm. It felt as if her life was in Juniper now. She loved her family dearly, but what would she do in Missouri? By now, someone else had taken the teaching position, and when she thought about marrying and settling down, it was Nick she saw herself with. That might not work out, of course. But if she went back to the farm, it never could. She folded the letter into quarters, crept back to her bed, and placed the letter in the box that held the picture of her parents and the ribbon from the box of chocolates Nick had sent her.

Grace had never been to such a grand party as the one the Lombards hosted. The large house and courtyard were alive with the wavering flames of dozens of candles. A quartet of musicians played classical selections in the front parlor, while in the courtyard, a trio provided livelier music for those wishing to dance. The food rivaled anything Grace had ever seen, even at the hotel. The guests were all dressed in costume, the upper halves of their faces covered with masks. Grace moved among the clusters of guests with a silver tray filled with crystal glasses of sparkling cider. In spite of her determination not to, she caught herself searching the crowd for Nick. She had already recognized one of the men who'd taken them on the trip to the falls weeks earlier, but she did not see Nick.

She focused on the younger women, many of them single. After all, Nick and his men had been given the assignment of dancing with the unaccompanied young ladies.

And then she saw him—or rather the back of him, his broad shoulders accented by a white shirt covered with a black leather vest, the unmistakable way his hair curled just slightly over the shirt collar. Her tray tipped dangerously, but she recovered as she recalled the feeling of her fingers entwined in that thick hair when he'd kissed her. He turned with his partner, gazing down at the woman in his arms, and Grace saw that he wore a black half mask that made his smile even more appealing.

"Just doing his job," Lily whispered with a nod toward the dance floor. She passed Grace and moved on to serve a gathering of businessmen engrossed in conversation on the veranda.

And I should get on with mine, Grace thought. She smiled brightly and offered cider to two women about her age who were watching the dancing. They each accepted a glass, and as Grace moved on, she heard one whisper, "Who is he?"

"I have no idea," her friend replied, "but I wouldn't kick that one out of my bed, believe me." The two giggled as they edged closer to the dance floor, no doubt for a better look.

Grace was tempted to tell them that Nick Hopkins was simply doing his job, and if there was anyone at this party he would think of taking to bed, it would surely be her, not them.

"Well, aren't you a pretty little thing." The man blocking her way was her father's age and obviously drunk. "How about a dance, little lady?"

Blessedly, that was the moment the tune ended. Grace smiled politely. "I'm so sorry, sir, but I'm part of the staff." She held up the tray to prove her point.

To her surprise, the man relieved her of the tray and placed his broad hand flat against her back, guiding her to the dance floor. "I said I want to dance, missy," he muttered and motioned to the musicians to strike up a tune. He pulled her tight against his barrel chest, and his cheek resting against her temple was wet with perspiration. She tried to put distance between them as he moved her awkwardly into a waltz, but any attempt in that direction seemed only to fuel his determination to hold her as close as possible. "Do you know who I am?"

She tried to smile. "You're wearing a mask, sir, but—"

"I am Jasper Perkins, and I have more money than you'll ever see, girlie, so count your blessings I chose you tonight."

"It's my pleasure to dance with you, sir…"

His laugh was too loud and made him slobber slightly. "This ain't about dancing. This is about you meeting me later. Top of the stairs, end of the hall. I'll be waitin'."

Grace was sure she was going to be sick. And then

Mr. Lombard was there, his hand on Mr. Perkins's shoulder. "Jasper, there you are. We need you for the card game." He was smiling, but Grace noticed his eyes were cold as ice. "My foreman will finish the dance for you. Come along." He led the man away.

Grace turned to bolt from the dance floor and found herself facing Nick instead. He held out his arms to her. "Shall we?" he asked.

"I have to—"

"Don't run, Grace. Never run. Hold your head up. Smile. That's my girl."

He spun her to the music as others who had witnessed the scene settled back into the rhythm of the dance. And in his arms, she felt safe, but she resisted the inclination to rest her cheek against his chest. The tune ended, and the dancers dispersed. Jake, who had wrangled a position on the serving staff, picked up the silver tray Perkins had disposed of so unceremoniously.

"You okay, Grace?" he asked.

She nodded, swallowing the bile that burned in her throat and forcing a smile. Mrs. Lombard threaded her way through the guests. Grace was sure she was about to be dismissed for the evening.

"My dear," Mrs. Lombard said, taking Grace's hand between both of hers. "Please accept my apologies. Jasper is—well, aside from being my brother-in-law, he is an ass, pardon my language." She turned to Nick. "Please see that this young lady gets some air, Nick, and a chance to recover her nerves."

"Yes, ma'am." Nick took hold of Grace's elbow. "Come on. Let's start by getting you some of that fruit punch."

"I'm fine," she protested.

He grinned. "Sorry. Boss lady gave me orders, Grace."

The punch helped. Nick even joined her, and it occurred to Grace that they must look like two more guests enjoying the party. They each wore a mask, and although she was dressed in the garb of a lady-in-waiting, it was no less a costume than that of those women who were clothed as princesses or fairies. The two young women who had been watching Nick dance stared at her standing so close to him, their mouths open in surprise. She resisted the temptation to raise her punch cup in a toast to them.

"Now we walk," Nick said, once again taking hold of her arm and tucking it through the crook of his elbow.

"Walk where?"

"Away from here," he replied.

Willingly, she followed him away from the throng of guests, away from the candlelight, away from the music and chatter. He led her past the corral and on toward the bunkhouse and a *banco* just outside the door. "Sit," he instructed.

"You're being very bossy for a man wearing a silly mask," she noted, but she sat and removed her own mask.

He grinned. "I thought it might make me more mysterious—more appealing."

"Well, you certainly caught the attention of at least two of the single young ladies at the party."

He frowned and removed his mask, discarding it and running his fingers through his hair. "I hoped to appeal to you."

"Why?"

He signed heavily but kept his gaze on the corral. "Look, you and me—well, we've each got plans for the future, and it seems to me they may not be plans that travel the same trail, and yet…"

"And yet?" She touched his hand.

"I like you, Grace Rogers. I like you a lot."

She considered whether in this case honesty was indeed the best policy and decided it was. "I feel the same and have no earthly idea what to do about it."

"I can think of one thing," he said, leaning closer.

"Please don't. Your men are likely to—"

"My men are either out tending the herd or up there at the house enjoying the party in spite of all their grousing." He took her hands in his. "We're quite alone here, Grace. We could kiss, and nobody would know." He hesitated and then, to her surprise, pulled back. "Sorry. You're probably thinking I'm no different from old man Perkins."

She touched his chin, turning his face to hers. "You are nothing like that horrid man, Nick. You've been thoughtful and gentle, and you respect a lady even if she is only hired help."

The music drifted faintly across the yard that stretched between them and the party. Nick stood. "Dance with me?"

"Why, sir, I would be delighted." She stood and stepped into the circle of his outstretched arms—and this time she gave in to the urge to rest her cheek against his chest.

❦

Nick had been looking for an opportunity to speak privately with Grace when the boss had come up next to him and pointed to the dance floor. "Jasper's up to his usual tricks. I may need your help. He's drunk, and that means things can get nasty. I won't have him spoiling this night for Rita."

And that was when Nick had spotted Grace. The boss's brother-in-law had her clenched against his chest, and the expression on her face spoke of panic that bordered on fear. His boss led the way, but during the discussion that followed, Nick tightened his fists, only just holding on to his temper. Once John led the man away, it was all Nick could do to keep himself from wrapping his arms protectively around Grace and leading her from the dance floor. But that would not do. Not for her and not for Mrs. Lombard if guests began gossiping. So he did the only thing that seemed logical—he stepped in to finish the dance.

And now they were dancing once again, only this time as they swayed to the music, it was as if they moved as one. She pressed her cheek to his chest while he rested his chin against her soft hair. As the music came to an end, he spun her away and then back into his arms. Their faces were so close that a kiss seemed inevitable. She touched his cheek. He raised his hands to frame her face.

"You are a beautiful woman, Grace Rogers," he said as he kissed her temple and then her closed eyelids.

She laughed nervously. "A woman who should get back to work." She stepped away from him. "Thank you, Nick. I'm fine, truly. I'll just—"

He caught hold of her hand. "Remember that piece of land I showed you last week?"

She nodded.

"I've been making payments every week, and well, one day…"

He saw that she was genuinely pleased for him, sharing his joy. He also saw that she didn't understand why he was telling her this now. "I know we haven't known each other that long, but out here, things tend to be different than maybe they are where you come from."

"Different how?"

"I don't know. I'm not much good at words. I guess what I mean is folks out here tend to take action quicker than they might in places where things are more established, more certain." She was no longer trying to move away from him, and he took that as a good sign. "See, Grace, like I told you, I have this dream of owning my own spread. And along with that come other things—important things."

"Such as?"

"A wife. Kids. A family." He barely managed to get the words out. "Look, Grace, I know up to now, maybe we've been headed down different paths, but lately, I've been thinking. I mean, do you think you might consider us walking together? Maybe not right away but some day. I mean, once I've cleared the land and built a cabin and gotten a start on a herd and you've put together the money your pa needs… What I'm trying to say is, could you see yourself thinking about sharing that with me someday, Grace?"

They were linked only by his hand holding hers, but the spark that connected them as they stood facing each other was undeniable. She bowed her head. "Nick, I not only have responsibilities to my family, but also an obligation to the Harvey Company."

"But someday?"

She looked at their joined hands. He held his breath. "Yes. Someday," she agreed. She looked up at him and smiled. "And now I must go. Lily and Emma will be frantic."

"All right, but first, let's seal the bargain." He stepped closer. "Someday?"

She offered him her handshake.

He chuckled as he pulled her close. "Afraid a simple handshake won't do, Grace."

She took a half step and touched his face. "We could seal our bargain with a kiss," she suggested.

He kissed her, tentatively at first, not wanting to do anything that might remind her of the encounter with Perkins. But when she wound her fingers through the thickness of his hair at the nape of his neck, he deepened the kiss.

The soft roundness of her breasts pressed against the hard muscles of his chest. He heard the sound she made signaling pleasure when he traced her lips with his tongue. His desire hardened into something far too dangerous to unleash at a time and place like this. But someday…one day.

He broke the kiss but not his hold on her.

"I have to go," she whispered.

"I know. Tomorrow?"

"Yes."

He understood neither of them knew what they

were agreeing to in that exchange. "And the day after that?" he called as she headed back toward the party.

"Yes," she replied.

"And the day—"

"Yes, yes, and yes," she shouted, and he heard her laughter blending with the music.

As she worked the rest of the party, Grace could not seem to stop smiling. Nothing bothered her—not having to mop up a spilled drink or having to console a lost child until her mother could be found in the throng of guests. She wondered if this could be love. She had never been in love before. Certainly, what she'd shared with Buford could not be called love, but what she felt for Nick was unlike anything she'd ever experienced. It made her deliriously happy, and at the same time, it drove her to distraction. How could things ever work out between them?

She had four months to go on her contract, and even sending her parents every penny she could save, it might still not be enough. If she married Nick, there would be no money to send home, because there would be no job. And with Nick, there would be a whole new set of struggles—challenges that might be more than what they felt for each other now could survive. Then what?

"Ready?"

She hadn't heard Emma come alongside her. "Yes. Let's go."

Aidan had sent a wagon to drive them all back to

the hotel. "I should have warned you girls about Jasper Perkins," Jake said once they were on their way. "He didn't…do anything, did he, Grace?"

So they had all seen her on the dance floor. "No. And Mr. and Mrs. Lombard were very kind and apologetic."

"Still, you should watch yourself around him," Jake warned. "He's not likely to forget once he sets his sights on you."

"He was quite drunk. I doubt he'll remember," Grace replied, anxious to close the conversation.

"He'll remember," Jake muttered. "Just watch yourself, okay?"

His warning was unsettling but not such that it could do anything to overshadow the memory of Nick's proposal of someday and the dance they had shared—and most especially the kiss. Grace settled back against the rough side of the wagon and smiled. Yes, what she felt for Nick Hopkins had to be love.

Later, when she told Emma and Lily what had happened with Nick, she did not exactly get the reaction she'd hoped for. Instead of being delighted for her, both of them seemed to be taken aback.

"But you need to be careful," Emma exclaimed. "I mean, things have already developed so quickly between the two of you, and kisses can—"

"What we're trying to tell you, my innocent friend," Lily interrupted, "is that soon—very soon—kisses won't be enough for him—or you, given the fact that you're obviously head over knickers for the guy. Kissing leads to touching leads to undressing leads to—"

"All right," Grace cried. "I'm not as innocent as

you may believe. I did grow up on a farm, after all. Why can't you just be happy for me? I thought you both liked Nick."

"Oh, honey, we are—we do," Lily assured her. "It's just that—"

A knock at the door stopped her from finishing her thought.

"Come in," Lily called.

To their surprise, Miss Kaufmann opened the door. "How was the party?" she asked.

"It was lovely," Emma assured her. "Thank you for giving us the opportunity to be there."

Miss Kaufmann smiled. She pulled an envelope from the pocket of her apron and handed it to Grace. "This came for you today. Time for bed, girls," she added as she left, closing the door behind her.

The letter was from her mother. Grace tore the envelope open and scanned the first page. "They did get the money I sent after all," she shouted before reading on. "And it was enough to buy new work boots for my brothers and feed for the livestock," she added, her voice rising with excitement. Lily and Emma joined her on her bed and leaned in over her shoulder.

Early on, Grace had realized that neither Lily nor Emma seemed to get mail, so she had begun sharing her mother's letters with them. Now they knew her siblings by name and age and were always anxious for news of their latest adventures. Grace's mother always asked after her friends, and it pleased her that her real family and the people she'd come to think of as family had a connection.

She had never written anything about Nick or even mentioned him by name. Lily had teased her about that. Tonight, she was glad her mother knew nothing of Nick. It would be hard to explain who he was and what he meant to her, when she wasn't sure she understood herself. Once she'd settled into her job at the hotel, she'd begun to see a plan for her future that went beyond just helping her family financially. But lately, she found herself planning a life right here in New Mexico—a life that included her friends and maybe even a future with Nick.

Miles away, Nick lay awake, his arms folded behind his head. He imagined he could still feel Grace's touch, smell the clean, pure scent of her, taste her kiss lingering on his lips.

John Lombard had suggested Nick start working on clearing and fencing his land in the spare time he would have over the winter. The ranch would not get busy again until calving time in the spring. Oh, there would be things to do—rounding up strays wandering off in the snow, mending fences, the usual chores. But there would be time enough to maybe get a start on a cabin. He pictured something with a loft and room for a kitchen garden, somewhere to hang clothes to dry in the sun. But mostly, he pictured Grace in the kitchen or sitting with him by the fire or out in the courtyard—or lying in their bed.

He swallowed a groan. His physical desire for her had become something that occupied his thoughts night and day. He wondered if it was the same for a woman. Did she want him? Did she think about lying with him as much as he did her?

In the bunk next to him, Slim snored loudly, something Nick and the other men had grown used to sleeping through. But not tonight. Tonight, every little movement or sound seemed magnified. Finally, Nick gave up, stood, pulled on his trousers, shook out his boots in case of a scorpion or other critter, tugged them on, and walked outside.

It was so quiet, as if the party had never happened. The sky was filled with stars. A horse whinnied. A night bird sang. Nick turned up the collar of his jacket, then closed his eyes, allowing the sounds of this land he loved so much to wash over him.

After a while, he walked up to the barn, lit a lantern, and pulled out a notebook he used to keep count of the Lombard herd. He turned to a clean page and began to sketch out the cabin he would build—the cabin perhaps one day, he would be able to share with Grace.

Chapter 8

GRACE SAW NICK EVERY NIGHT OVER THE NEXT TWO weeks. He sometimes came to her straight from the range, his clothes dusty and his skin musky with sweat. Sometimes, they would have only a few precious minutes before it was time for her to go, but he insisted one minute spent with her was worth hours of lost sleep. Whether they had the luxury of hours or only the moments they could steal before the church clock chimed ten, the evening always ended with the two of them finding a place in the shadows where they were unlikely to be seen or interrupted.

Lily, it turned out, had been right. Their kisses grew more passionate, and it seemed only natural for things to progress beyond holding and being held to touching and being touched. It wasn't long before they realized their place in the shadows no longer provided the cover they wanted for the passion that grew like a wildfire between them. One night, Nick had been waiting for her the minute she finished her shift, giving them over an hour to be together.

"I found a place where we can be alone," Nick

said. "But, Grace, you need to be sure this is what you want."

"I am," she assured him.

He took hold of her hand and led her through the rear yard of the hotel, through an area littered with discarded roofing tiles and other building materials, to a dilapidated shed. The door hung loose on its hinges, and the single window had been covered over with paper. "It's not much," he said once they stepped inside, "but we'll be out of the wind, and no one will bother us here." He knelt and stacked kindling and wood in the corner fireplace.

As the light from the fire unveiled the single room, Grace ignored the squalor and neglect and focused on a stack of burlap sacks. While Nick tended the fire, she took a few sacks, shook them out, and placed them on the dirt floor. She knelt next to him and ran her hand over his back. The shed might be shabby and barren, but the fire warmed her, and Nick was by her side. That was all she needed.

The place was so small that they sat with their backs against one wall across from the fireplace, their legs outstretched and their arms around each other. Words seemed unnecessary as he leaned in to kiss her. Watching her for any objection, he unbuttoned her coat. When he cupped her breasts through the fabric of her dress, she gasped but did not pull away. Instead, she wondered how she might touch him in such a way that he might experience that same shock of longing he inspired in her.

Every night, she hurried to change after her shift and slipped away, knowing Nick would be waiting.

One night while he was kissing her, she tunneled her hands under his shirt and ran her palms over the smooth coolness of his bare skin. He stepped away, his breath ragged. "Do you know what you're doing, Grace?"

She hesitated, searching for words that could possibly explain the urges coursing through her body. "It feels right," she replied.

He unbuttoned his shirt. Now exposed from the waist up, he placed her hands on his naked chest, the light of the fire playing over his muscles. She traced the outline of those muscles and watched as his pulse jumped in his throat.

"Grace," he whispered.

He began undoing the buttons of her dress, pausing between each to give her the chance to stop him. But the truth was, she wanted to know what it might be like to feel him touch her as she was touching him, with no barriers of clothing. When he had opened the bodice to her waist, he tilted her face so that even in the dark, she was looking at him. The night was cold, but there was a heat between them that made them oblivious to the weather.

"If we start down this road, Grace, we can't go back," he warned. "It's your decision. It has to be. I want you in every way a man wants a woman, but I will not take any part of you without you agreeing."

"I want that. I want us."

And still, he stopped short of fully making love to her. When she urged him to go further, he shook his head and rolled away from her. "Not here, Grace. Not yet."

"But someday?" she whispered, deliberately repeating the promise they'd exchanged at the Lombard party.

"Someday," he agreed.

One night as they sat holding each other and watching the dying embers of the fire, she nestled her face in the curve of his neck and said, "Nick, once I complete my contract, I've decided I'm not going back to Missouri. No matter what happens between us, this place and the people I've come to know feel more like home than the farm. That was my childhood home, but this...you..."

The way his eyes widened with surprise and his smile spread like a rising sun, she knew he was pleased. "That changes everything, Grace," he said as he ran his fingers through the tangle of her hair. "I mean, I didn't want to push you, and I've been telling myself you might just decide your place was back there with your family. But if you stay, then we—" He pulled her close for a searing kiss.

"Touch me, Nick," she whispered, needing more than ever the feel of his hands on her bare skin, claiming her. He eased her dress down to reveal her bare shoulders and expose her camisole. She knew he could see everything in the light of the fire, and his expression left no doubt of how he desired her. She kissed his throat, then his chin, savoring the scratch of his whiskers against her cheek, the play of rough on soft.

And then he was kissing her bare shoulder, easing the strap of her camisole off, exposing the tops of her breasts, moving lower, and kissing her there. Her nipples hardened and pressed against the soft fabric of her undergarment—again, rough on soft. She knew all she had to do was offer the slightest resistance and he would agree it was too much. But the truth was, she had never in her life wanted anything more, never wanted any man in this way, never even thought of being with a man this way. Not until now.

Not until Nick.

But it was Nick who pulled away. He sat up from where he had gently laid her back on the floor, his bare back glistening with sweat in the glow of the fire. He released a long breath.

"Grace, I have to go away for a while on ranch business. It might be a month or more. But when I return—"

A chill ran through her whole body. Suddenly, she found herself thinking of Lily's so-called husband. She sat up and pulled her clothing closed. She wanted to ask him why now and why he hadn't mentioned at least the possibility he might be called away. Surely he had known. Doubt replaced passion, and she had serious misgivings about telling him she planned to stay on in Juniper. "When do you go?" She forced herself to speak calmly.

"End of the week." He twisted around so that he was looking at her. "But, Grace, when I return—"

She shook off the questions and protests. "Tell me where you're going and why."

"California. Mr. Lombard thinks he can get a better price for his beef there, but he doesn't want anyone to know he's looking into new markets. The other boys will think I've gone to work on my land. I'll be back in plenty of time for calving and branding season."

"I see." It was a lie. She didn't understand any of this.

He took hold of her hand. "I love you, Grace. I honestly think I fell in love with you on that train ride. I know for sure I couldn't seem to stop thinking about you or coming around to the hotel to check up on you. I know I've spoken often about having all these plans for my life, but then I met you and… All I want is for us to marry and raise a family and spend the rest of our lives together." He hesitated, searching her face for answers she didn't have. "And I'm not forgetting that you have responsibilities to your family or that your job at the hotel is important. Just tell me you feel as I do, Grace, and together, we can find a way to have everything we both want."

His expression was so earnest, his need for her to believe in him—in them—there in every line. She framed his cheeks with her hands.

"Oh, Nick, do you have to ask? My feelings are written on my face, in every kiss we ever shared. Yes, I love you, and yes, together, we can make it all work out." She practically threw herself into his arms, the movement so sudden and unexpected that it caught him off balance and ended with the two of them lying on the blanket, laughing with the joy that comes with youth and the belief that dreams could come true.

But then the laughter died. He turned on his side, settling his weight on his elbow as he stroked her hair away from her face. "So lovely," he murmured as their lips met, their mouths opened, and their tongues waltzed to the music of the crackling fire. He had taught her well, for she knew exactly what made him gather her closer and deepen the kiss. He lowered his mouth to her breast, suckling her until the fabric of her camisole was soaked before moving on to kiss her throat, the lobe of her ear.

He moved over her, and the bulge of his undeniable desire pressed against her. She cast aside her doubts. "Love me," she whispered, her lips against his ear.

Bracing himself above her on his forearms, he studied her face. "Marry me," he countered.

"Yes. By the time you return, I'll have only weeks left on my contract and then—"

"Marry me before I go, Grace. You're not a woman a man just takes, and I won't be the one who does. We can be married before I leave. There's a judge I know over in Santa Fe."

"But—"

He lay down and pulled her to his side, laying out the plan. "Friday. We'll leave right after you finish work for the day. We'll be married and back before anyone knows."

"It's two hours to Santa Fe and another two back," she argued. "Add in time for even a simple ceremony, and it would be impossible for me to be back before curfew."

"We'll stay overnight. Emma and Lily will cover for you. They've had to before." He tweaked her nose, reminding her of the night they had gotten so wrapped up in each other that the church bell had tolled quarter of an hour past curfew before they realized she was late. "Don't you want to marry me, Grace?"

It was the first sign of uncertainty he'd shown. She stroked his hair. "I have a contract, Nick."

"Answer the real question, Grace."

"Yes, I want to marry you more than I have ever wanted anything in my life."

"But?"

She blushed with the intimacy of the question she was about to raise. "But what if we marry and then we…consummate that union, and while you are gone, it becomes obvious that I…"

His grin was infuriating. "Grace, there are ways. I mean, we can, as you say, consummate the union without—"

She slapped his chest. "Don't you dare laugh at me, Nick Hopkins."

He held her close. "Shhh," he whispered. "We can have it all, Grace. Just say yes and trust me."

She rested her cheek against his bare chest, her mind racing as she tried to consider every possible thing that might go wrong. What if someone saw them in Santa Fe? What if the judge refused to marry them? What if she got caught sneaking back to her room? What if, in spite of his assurances, she ended up pregnant? "I don't understand the rush," she said. "I mean, if the point is to be legally wed before we…you know…then why not marry once you return?"

"Because the truth is, I'm not sure I can wait that long to make you mine. The way I see things, this time tomorrow night, we could be husband and wife in every way."

"Are you planning to add hours to the day? By the time we go, find the judge, marry, and return—"

He kissed her into silence. "Just say yes, Grace," he said. "Say yes, and I promise you the wedding you deserve—the life you deserve."

"You're a madman, Nick Hopkins."

He grinned. "Ah, but you can't resist me any more than I can you, so let's make this happen."

He was right, of course. She felt the thrill of the adventure that was what life with Nick promised to be. "Yes. Yes!"

He let out a whoop of delight and rained kisses over her face, continuing to explode with yells of joy between each kiss.

Laughing, she pressed her fingers to his mouth. "I have to go," she said, standing as she did up the buttons on her dress and then twisted her hair into a loose knot.

He stayed where he was, watching her. "Friday," he said, standing to hold her coat for her and then sealing their plan with a kiss. He would stay behind and make sure the fire was out while she ran the short distance from the cabin to the hotel's kitchen entrance and up the back stairs just in time to bid good night to Miss Kaufmann and try to figure out what on earth she was going to tell Emma and Lily.

Mrs. Nicholas Hopkins. Grace Hopkins.

It was all happening so very fast, and yet having come to the decision to stay in Juniper, marrying Nick was just one more piece of the puzzle of the life she'd always dreamed of falling into place.

Nick was nervous. Friday had to have been the longest day he'd ever drawn breath, and now as he waited for Grace, he mentally went over every detail of the plan.

He'd sent a wire to Judge Elton Brill, a man only a year or two older than Nick, who was married to a friend from Nick's childhood. Brill's reply had arrived just that morning. It contained the address in Santa Fe where the judge would meet Nick and Grace at the appointed time. A horse and buggy were ready to go. No one would think twice about seeing the couple off for a drive in the country.

The only problem was that Grace was late.

Nick paced outside the hotel, willing the kitchen door to open and her to come running out, full of breathless apologies. But what if she had changed her mind? What if she didn't come? What if—

Suddenly, he heard the familiar creak of the door, heard her telling someone she'd see them later, and then there she was. She was wearing the dress she'd worn on the train—her best dress, she'd told him. And that ridiculous little hat that made him smile. He hoped she never got rid of that hat.

He watched her for a moment as she stood there, pulling on her gloves and then looking around, not seeing him at first, and then when she did, smiling and giving him a little wave. They met in the middle of the yard, and it took everything in him not to wrap her in his embrace right then and there.

"Ready?" he asked, and when she nodded, he offered her his arm and walked sedately with her over to the livery. He helped her up onto the seat before climbing in next to her, took the reins and snapped them.

"We're off," she said as if she could not quite believe it.

He took hold of her hand. "No regrets?"

"No. I did some figuring last night. Assuming we can keep our marriage secret long enough for me to complete my contract, I'll still be able to keep my promise to send all fifty dollars. We'll make this work, Nick."

"That's my girl," he said and grinned at her. If they'd been away from people shopping and going about their business, he would have put his arm around her and kissed her.

Once they were out of town, she rested her head on his shoulder and watched the sun set behind the mountains in the distance. It would be dark by the time they reached Santa Fe, and shortly after that, they would be married. She sucked in a breath as if she were about to plunge into deep water and realized it was an apt analogy.

"You cold?" Nick asked, tucking the edge of the lap robe tighter around her legs.

"No. Just excited."

"And a little scared?"

It was one of the things she realized she loved about this man. He seemed so in tune with her thoughts, and he cared what she might be thinking. "Are you?"

He chuckled. "Yeah. It's a big step."

Maybe he was the one having regrets. "Nick? If you don't… I mean, we can turn back. If you—"

To her surprise, he pulled the buggy to a stop, turned to face her, and cleared his throat. This was it then. He had changed his mind and been too much of a gentleman to say so, but now that she had given him permission to...

"Are you listening to me, Grace?"

She'd been lost in her thoughts, aware of the murmur of his words but not really hearing what she feared he might be saying.

"I love you. I want to be with you. Not just for a night on the floor of an abandoned cabin but forever. I want to wake up to your face and go to sleep to the feel of your breath on my bare skin. I want to sit across from you at meals and watch as you tell our children stories at bedtime. Darn it, woman, I even look forward to arguing with you, mostly because I figure making up will be worth the trouble."

"Still, there is so much we don't know," she cautioned, afraid to take him at his word.

"Grace, I'm of age, and so are you. My guess is that for some time now, you've had the notion in mind to find a man to spend your life with. I know the thought's been there for me. Finding a woman, that is. I've looked at this thing from every side, and what I know for sure is that I'd be a fool to walk away from a chance to be with you. Our timing might not be perfect, but then timing rarely is. This is our moment, and I'm asking you to be real sure you want to grab on to it."

I do. Oh yes, I do. The words rang so loud in her brain that she was sure she had spoken them aloud. Tears of pure joy rolled down her cheeks.

"Grace? Are you crying? Oh, honey, I never meant—"

She wrapped her arms around him and pulled him

close. "Don't try and back out now, Nick Hopkins. A promise is a promise, and you promised me a proper wedding. Now let's get going before the judge decides you've changed your mind."

He kissed her, and in that kiss was all that would remain unspoken between them. They would marry tonight and face together whatever tomorrow and all the tomorrows to come might bring.

By the time they reached Santa Fe, the shops had closed for the day. The building that held the judge's chambers looked deserted except for a single light in a window on the first floor near the entrance. Nick helped Grace down from the buggy, and they walked together to the rough-hewn double doors that marked the entrance to the building. Nick raised a knocker and let it fall twice. Voices and footsteps echoed from inside, and then the double doors swung back.

Judge Elton Brill greeted them with, "You're late, Hopkins."

A woman hurried past him, kissed Nick's cheek, and grasped Grace's hands. "I'm Clarissa," she said. "Pay my husband no mind. He seems convinced that his title gives him special dispensation when it comes to rudeness. Come with me, Grace. I expect you'd like to freshen up a bit before we begin."

"Clarissa," her husband protested.

"Elton, this is a wedding, not a sentencing. Show some patience and common kindness. Don't you have papers that Nick should sign?" She actually shooed him away before leading Grace through a narrow doorway and into a small room lit by kerosene wall sconces. In the center of the room was a table, and on that was a hand mirror, a hair brush, combs, and ribbons for arranging hair. "Sit," Clarissa instructed. "Let me do something special with that beautiful hair."

"How do you know Nick?" Grace allowed herself to relax as Clarissa brushed out her hair and then expertly braided and arranged it, talking around a row of hairpins she held between her lips.

"Nick and I grew up together. His pa and mine owned small ranches next to each other. We were back and forth between each other's houses all the time. And then when I married Elton, he and Nick got on like a house afire. Pay no attention to my husband's gruffness. He's just worried that maybe the two of you are rushing things a bit."

"We love each other and—"

"—don't want to give into the temptation of putting the cart before the horse?"

Grace was glad of the shadows in the room and hoped they hid her embarrassment.

"I had to remind Elton that we had done exactly the same thing—run off in the middle of the night to be married, that is—and we were a lot younger and stupider than you and Nick are. I expect the two of you have thought this through."

Grace wasn't sure that was a question, so she didn't supply an answer. "It's kind of you and the judge to do this for us," she said.

"Are you kidding? I was thrilled. Not every day I get to put on a wedding. Elton and I have got all boys—not a daughter in sight—so I'm doomed to play the mother-in-law role. But when I heard about you and Nick…" She took a step back and admired her handiwork before passing Grace the mirror. "I figured a veil was out of the question, you in street clothes and all, but the ribbons make a nice substitute, don't you think?"

They did indeed. Grace stared at her reflection. Clarissa had woven the white satin ribbons in with her hair, wrapping the resulting braids around to form a sort of crown. "It's so pretty," she exclaimed. "Thank you. I look—"

"Like a bride, so let's not lose the moment." She handed Grace a small nosegay of flowers and then opened the door to the hallway. "Ready?"

Grace wasn't so sure, but apparently, Clarissa didn't notice.

"Wait here until you hear the music, then walk straight down the hall. The door to Elton's chambers will be open. No chance of taking a wrong turn." She kissed Grace's cheek and hurried away so she could be waiting with her husband—and Nick.

Seconds later, Grace heard the strum of a guitar, and she followed the sound. At the door to the judge's chambers, she hesitated, taking it all in. The judge stood in front of his desk, wearing the formal robes of his office. Clarissa stood to one side of him with Nick at the other. The room was lit by about a dozen candles. Furniture had been pushed aside to form a short aisle from the door to the desk, and Grace followed it. She was aware of passing a youth who provided the music and two women who might be the boy's sister and mother. They smiled shyly at her and then slipped from the room, closing the door behind them.

She locked her gaze on Nick and somehow moved

forward. He stared at her in some kind of disbelief, as if seeing her for the very first time. When she reached him, he took her hands in his and whispered, "You are so beautiful."

The judge cleared his throat, and they turned to face him. He opened a small book covered in black cowhide and lifted away a red satin ribbon that marked the page before he began to read the words.

"Dearly beloved…"

In spite of her determination to savor every second of her wedding, Grace barely heard a word the judge said. She spoke the vows as instructed, answered the query "Do you take…" and heard Nick do the same. When the judge called for the ring, Grace almost turned to him to explain that there had been no time, but then Nick reached inside his vest and produced a thin silver band. He had truly thought of everything.

Her heart swelled with emotion as he slid the band onto her finger and repeated the words Elton prompted. "With this ring, I thee wed."

And seconds later, she heard the judge start to utter the final words, "By the power vested in me, I now—"

She was in Nick's arms before the judge finished. They were kissing, and there was music again, livelier than before. Music that made her want to dance and laugh and share this incredible joy she felt with the world. Clarissa clapped in time to the music, and Nick lifted Grace and spun her around. He was laughing as well, and the expression on his face mirrored what she was feeling inside. They were married. From this day forward, they were one.

After he set her down, Nick shook hands with the

judge but still held Grace close with his arm around her waist. Elton had shed his robe and was looking far less intimidating in shirtsleeves and a vest. He was even smiling.

Clarissa kissed first Grace and then Nick on the cheeks. "There's more," she said with a twinkle. "After all, what's a wedding without a reception to follow? Come with me."

"But we really should start—"

Clarissa linked arms with her husband and led the way to the door. "Resistance is futile," the judge warned.

The room where Clarissa had fixed Grace's hair had been transformed. More candles had been lit and the table set with a small cake and four crystal glasses. Next to it was a stand that held an ice bucket and a bottle of champagne. Clarissa took the bottle from the ice and handed it, dripping, to her husband. "You open, and I'll pour," she instructed.

"Beware of what you've just stepped into, my friend," the judge teased Nick as he pulled the cork from the bottle with a satisfying pop. "Clarissa was never this bossy when we were courting. All sweetness and smiles, she was."

Nick laughed. "Clarissa was always this bossy, and you know it. It was her spirit that got you hooked in the first place."

When they each had champagne in hand, they raised their glasses. "To Grace and Nick," the judge said. "May their life together be filled with adventure and challenge and above all, the abiding love they will need to see them through times of sorrow and times of joy."

"To Grace and Nick," Clarissa chorused.

It was not the wedding she had imagined, but it was one Grace would certainly never forget. She regretted the absence of her parents and siblings, but perhaps one day, she and Nick could travel back to Missouri and have a small celebration there.

The guitarist's mother and sister cut the cake and served each of them a thin slice. As they ate, Grace turned to Clarissa and her husband. "Judge Brill, I'd—"

"It's Elton, Grace. Nick is our dear friend, and now we look forward to getting to know you as well."

"See, I told you," Clarissa added, poking her husband in the ribs. "Once he gets out of that robe, he's really just regular folks."

Nick set his plate on the table. "Well, Grace and I need to get started back." On their way to Santa Fe, he had pointed out a spot where they could spend the night under the stars and the rolled canvas and other supplies he'd loaded onto the buggy for just that purpose.

"Nope." This time, it was Elton who protested their intention to leave. He took out his gold pocket watch and checked the time. "The way I see it, you have a good eight hours before dawn, time enough for you to get Grace back to her job and you on your way to California. Clarissa and I have a wedding present for you." He actually winked at his wife. "Follow me."

On his way out the door, Elton plucked his suit coat and a derby hat from a hall tree inside his chambers, then led the way across the plaza and into the elaborate lobby of the renowned La Casita Hotel—another Harvey property. "Wait here," he said as he and Clarissa approached the desk.

"What's going on?" Grace whispered.

Nick must have had some idea, given the way he was grinning. "I think we're about to spend our wedding night in one of your employer's finest establishments instead of camping by the creek," he replied as he watched the desk clerk hand his friends a key.

"But what if someone sees me—us?"

"No one knows us here, Grace, and we'll be gone before first light."

Clarissa and Elton were coming their way, both smiling broadly. Clarissa handed Nick the room key. "The desk clerk will make sure your horse and buggy are properly stabled for the night and ready to go tomorrow morning." She patted his hand closed around the large brass key. "Be happy, my friend," she murmured, and Grace saw tears glisten on her lashes.

Elton bent and kissed Grace's cheek and then shook hands with Nick. "Let's go, Clarissa," he said as he steered his wife to the door.

"Good night," Clarissa called, looking back over her shoulder.

Nick and Grace waved. "And thank you both," Grace added.

When they were gone, Nick led the way to the stairs, and they climbed together to the second floor. "This way," he murmured after checking the number on the key and signs on the wall.

Once inside the room, they were suddenly shy with each other. Nick took her coat and his and hung them in a small closet, then went around opening doors and drawers, discovering a washroom with sink and toilet and a desk with a fold-down writing surface and three shallow drawers. Grace walked to the window and parted the heavy drapes to reveal a view of a church, its stained-glass windows dark. They both avoided looking at the bed that dominated the room.

"There's a gift for you," Nick said. He pointed to a white box tied with red ribbon on the bed.

Since he was still all the way across the room from her, Grace had to ask, "How do you know it's for me? It could be for you, or both of us."

Nick chuckled. "Only way to find out is to open it."

They approached the bed from opposite sides of the room. He slid the box toward her. "There's a card."

She opened it, read the message, and smiled. "It's for me—from Clarissa. She says she figured I didn't have a chance to pack."

"Open it."

Once the ribbon was untied and the lid set aside, Grace dug through what seemed to be masses of tissue paper until finally, her fingers closed on fabric—a fine, creamy-white lawn. She held up a nightgown trimmed in lace with ribbon closings. She immediately began putting it back in the box.

Nick reached across and placed his hand on hers. "Go put it on," he said softly. He nodded toward the bathroom. "Go on."

She took her time, mostly because her hands were shaking so badly, she had to struggle to unfasten the buttons on her dress. When she was down to her undergarments, she hesitated, staring at the beautiful nightgown she'd draped over the edge of the sink. It was so thin, Nick would see everything.

Well, isn't that the idea?

She could hear him moving around outside the door. She heard his boots hit the floor as he shed them, followed by the creak of the bed. She wondered if he was as nervous as she was.

"Grace, are you all right?"

"Yes."

"Awfully quiet in there," he added.

"I'll be out in a minute."

That seemed to satisfy him. Turning away from the small mirror over the sink, she quickly shed the rest of her clothing. Naked now, she folded each undergarment and stacked it with her dress before putting on the nightgown. The long sleeves covered her arms, a lace ruffle brushing the backs of her hands. The neckline barely covered her shoulders until she tugged on the ribbons to gather the fabric closed. She tied each of the ribbons that ran from her neck to her waist, imagining Nick opening them again—unwrapping her as if she were the gift.

She drew in a shuddering breath and turned away from the mirror before releasing the pins, ribbons, and combs Clarissa had used in her hair, dropping the pins in a small glass dish that sat on a shelf over the toilet. Lock by lock, her hair tumbled down her back. She lifted the weight of it and pulled it all over one shoulder. And when she finally raised her eyes to the mirror, she barely recognized the woman staring back at her.

"Mrs. Nicholas Hopkins," she whispered, smiling at her reflection.

Chapter 9

NICK KEPT HIS EYE ON THE CLOSED DOOR. WHAT could be taking so long? He'd shed his clothes and turned back the luxurious satin spread on the bed in no time at all. Now he sat with his back against the cypress headboard, the covers—softer than anything he'd ever slept under in his life—pulled to his waist.

He was about to go to the bathroom door again when he heard a soft click, saw the knob turn, and watched as the door slowly opened. When she stepped into the room, he swallowed a gasp. She stood for a minute, smiling uncertainly, the light from the street outside the window silhouetting every detail of her body beneath the gown.

She fingered one of the ribbons. "Isn't it lovely?" she said.

"You're lovely," he managed. He patted the bed. "Come here."

"Turn out the light," she said, nodding at the lamp on the bedside table and not yet realizing he'd already seen everything.

"Grace, we're married."

"Then you come here," she said, stepping farther back into the shadows.

"Grace, I'm naked. Clarissa didn't send anything for me."

"Oh." The way she looked around, he was half afraid she might go running back to the bathroom.

"Hey," he said, pulling the sheet free and wrapping it around his waist. Barefoot, he crossed the room, pulled her into his arms, and kissed her. "This is me—and you." He ran his hands from her shoulders to her breasts. "Right now, we're not doing anything we haven't done before. Just fewer barriers." He kissed her throat. "Touch me, Grace," he whispered.

She placed her palms flat on his bare back.

He untied the first of the ribbons, then two more, and spread the neckline of the gown so that her shoulders were exposed. He kissed her there and, nudging the gown lower as he went, trailed kisses across the rise of her breasts. She wrapped her arms around him, urging him closer. He grasped her bare waist, and as he lifted her, the gown fell away, and he let the sheet drop as well.

Cupping her hips as she wrapped her legs around him, he carried her to the bed. Gently, he laid her down, her hair fanned over the pillows. His breath caught, and his desire swelled to a near breaking point as he straddled her, resting his weight on his hands, flat to either side of her face. But was she ready? Did she understand?

"Grace, the first time can be—"

She placed her finger against his lips to shush him and then trailed that finger down his chin, his throat, his chest, and on until she touched him intimately, spreading her fingers over the length of him. "Teach me," she whispered.

He didn't need to be asked twice. "Well, for starters, if we want to really enjoy this, you need to stop touching me in that particular way."

She jerked her hand away. "Sorry."

"That's kind of the advanced lesson. First, we need to be sure we're both ready."

"I'm ready, Nick. I—"

She gasped as he touched her in a way that was both shocking and thrilling.

"Not quite yet," he murmured. "Soon," he promised. "Very soon."

Grace had no idea what was happening to her. All she knew was that she was certain that at any minute, she might explode like a skyrocket. But when her body jerked in an involuntary spasm and Nick immediately stopped the exquisite torture, she grasped his hand before he could pull free of her. "Don't stop," she whispered.

He shifted so that he was not only massaging her down there but also covering one nipple with his open mouth, allowing his tongue to play over the hardened and sensitive tip. She scraped his bare back with her nails, urging him closer—as if he could be any nearer than he was.

And then everything stopped. He raised himself onto his forearms and looked at her. "Ready?"

She was half crazed with the need for him to burst this dam of sensation he had created. "Yes." Her voice was a hoarse rasp.

Nick placed his hands under her hips and then lay over her. At first, it seemed impossible that their bodies could be made to connect in this most intimate way. He was tender and cautious. She was frustrated and impatient. She shifted beneath him, searching for the exact angle that would allow him full entry, full possession.

And then in one swift moment, they were joined—they were one. For an instant, they froze, and then slowly, he started to move, and she matched him in the rhythm of this dance she understood was the waltz of love.

∝∝∝

It was still pitch-black outside the hotel window when Nick woke her. He was entirely dressed except for his boots.

"Grace?" He touched her cheek, and she leaned into the caress and smiled.

"What time is it?" She pushed herself to a sitting position and stretched before realizing she was naked. Nick's hand hovered near her exposed breast.

"Nearly four." He allowed his finger to graze her nipple. "We have to go." His tone reflected the regret they both felt. The fairy tale of the last several hours had come to its end.

"I wish—"

He smothered her words with a searing kiss. "So do I," he whispered. "But we have to leave soon, or you'll be slipping past Miss K's room right when she comes out to start her day."

On her way to the bathroom, she stepped on the nightgown, now lying on the floor. She picked it up and, for a moment, glanced around. She had no luggage, and she could hardly return to the hotel toting the large gift box, but she would not leave it behind. In the bathroom, she washed herself, feeling the exquisite soreness that was evidence of her status as a newly married woman. She could not seem to stop smiling.

Before she finished dressing, she slipped the night-gown over her head and then put on the rest of her clothing over it. She wound her hair into a knot and anchored it with the combs and pins she'd removed the night before. She took the ribbons and wrapped them around her fingers before stuffing them inside her purse.

"Almost ready," she said as she opened the door. Nick had put on his boots. She sat on the small settee and reached for her shoes.

"Allow me, my lady." He knelt and raised the hem of her dress above her ankle. He kept his hand there for a second, stroking her calf, before reaching for the shoes. Using a buttonhook he had retrieved from the dresser, he concentrated on wordlessly attending to each shoe.

Grace watched, her eyes accustomed enough to the predawn darkness to see him bite his lower lip in con-centration. She found this so endearing and wondered how many little details she had yet to discover about her husband.

Husband.

"I don't want you to go," she murmured.

He stood, having finished the task, and held out his arms to her. "Then quit your job and come with me. We'll tell Aidan we're married, and that will set everything in motion. A honeymoon in California and then—"

The realities and practicalities of their situation hit her like a pail of cold water. "No, we need this time for me to complete my obligation to the hotel and my family while you get that much closer to paying off the bank loan without having to worry about providing for me."

He folded his arms around her and pressed her close to his chest. "I know," he said. "I know." There was so much they hadn't thought through—where they would live, how they would manage—and yet she had no regrets.

They stood like that for a long moment, and then he kissed her forehead and stepped back. "Ready?"

She nodded. He held her coat for her before picking up his hat and opening the door.

"Wait," she said and hurried back to the bedside table to get her wedding bouquet.

Nick grinned. "What are you gonna do with the flowers?"

"I'll come up with something, but I'm not leaving them behind."

Outside, the horse and buggy waited by the entrance.

"How did they know?" Grace asked as Nick helped her climb in.

He shrugged. "Elton and Clarissa leave nothing to chance." He tipped the doorman and climbed aboard, and they were off. "Well, Mrs. Hopkins," he said and then grinned.

"Well what?"

"Nothing. Just wanted to say the name." He urged the horse to greater speed, and suddenly, Grace knew exactly what to do with the ribbons and flowers.

She pulled the ribbons from her purse, then stripped the petals and leaves from all but one of the blossoms in the bouquet. That one, she wrapped in her handkerchief and tied with one of the ribbons before placing it carefully back in her purse. Then, as they rode away from the deserted streets of Santa Fe, she released the rest of the ribbons and petals in the air. "Hello, world! Meet Mr. and Mrs. Nicholas Hopkins," she shouted as she flung them high.

Nick laughed, wrapped his arm around her shoulder, and pulled her close. They drove that way until they reached the outskirts of Juniper. The sun was just beginning to win the battle to lighten the black skies to charcoal and then gray and then a rosy pink. Nick turned the buggy down a narrow, unmarked trail.

"This will take us to the back of the hotel," he explained. "I'll get as close as I can, but you'll need to make a run for it. There's a side door used by the housemaids. You can go in that way, through the laundry, and up the back stairs there. The entry to your quarters will be at the far end of the third-floor hall."

Grace stared at him.

He grinned. "Want to know how I know all that, do you?"

She nodded.

"Slim was courting a Harvey Girl a few years back and scoped out the whole hotel for every possible way to get her in and out."

"Is he…is she…?"

"She ran off with a peddler. Slim never got over it to this day." He pulled the buggy to a stop. "I'm not much of a letter writer, Grace, but…"

She framed his face with her hands. "Just send word you've gotten there safely and come back to me as soon as you can," she pleaded. She kissed him, memories of their night of lovemaking filling her thoughts as he wrapped his arms around her and deepened the kiss.

Too soon, he rested his head against her forehead. "I love you, Grace. And I know I have put you in a terrible position here, but I hope you have no regrets. As for me, if the time we've had together were all we were ever to have, I'd still take comfort in knowing we did it legal and proper. A woman like you deserves nothing less. And I swear I'll make it up to you. We're goin' to have a terrific life together—that's a promise I aim to keep."

"Just come back to me, and we'll figure out the rest together." For the first time, she understood the finality of what was happening. He would be gone for a month. She could not tell anyone—not even Lily and Emma—they were married. "I should go," she whispered as she leaned in and kissed the lobe of his ear.

Before he could come to help her, she stepped down from the buggy. "Go," she urged as tears threatened.

"I've got time. You go first. I want to watch and be

sure you get in before I leave." He motioned toward the back of the hotel. "Laundry door is there just past—"

"I see it." She blew him a kiss before grabbing her skirt in one hand and running quickly through the thickets of sage and juniper. It was still dark enough to conceal her movements should anyone be looking out. She was breathless when she reached the laundry door and turned the handle. The door opened, and she heaved a sigh of relief. Before slipping inside, she turned and waved and heard the jingle of harness in the distance as Nick left to return the buggy and board the train for California.

When she reached her room, Emma and Lily were already dressed for work and sitting on their beds. The minute she stepped inside, they stood.

"Where were you?" Emma demanded, her face twisted into a mix of irritation and concern.

"We fell asleep." It was not a lie—eventually, they had slept. "Did Miss—"

"You're fine," Lily said. "But if you don't hurry, you're going to be late, so get changed."

Grace grabbed her uniform and hurried across the hall to the washroom. By the time she returned, dressed and ready, Emma and Lily had left for their shift in the dining room. Grace found the locket that held the picture of her parents and pulled the chain free. She threaded it through her wedding ring and fastened the necklace around her neck, hiding any evidence under her dress. As she ran down the back

stairs, Grace heard the clock on the second-floor land-
ing chime the hour. She waved to Jake as she hurried
through the kitchen.

The new girl hired for the lunch counter had
not worked out, so Grace was still taking double
shifts. Polly scowled at her as Grace hurried to her
post, and as if the day weren't already off to a bad
start, seated on a stool was none other than Jasper
Perkins. Grace hesitated. The banker usually chose
to eat in the dining room. In fact, she could not
recall a time he'd come to the counter since she'd
started working there.

"Well, well, well," he said, eying her closely. "It's
you."

"Pardon, sir?"

He laughed—too loud and long enough to attract
attention. He glanced around, then lowered his voice
as he pretended to study the menu. "Now, girlie, let's
not play games. You might have been wearing a mask,
but I never forget a pair of eyes. Especially not eyes
like yours."

She picked up his cup, already set to signal black
coffee, and filled it. "May I take your order, sir?"

He scowled at her. Grace saw Miss Kaufmann pause
to glance her way as she passed through the lobby on
her way to her office. Perkins motioned Grace closer,
although she doubted Miss K could actually overhear
the exchange.

*If a customer makes any reasonable request, it is the duty
of a Harvey Girl to honor that request.* The words she'd
read time after time as she studied the manual came
back to her. Was this going to be a reasonable request?

She pressed her palms against the edge of the counter as he leaned in so that only she would hear what he said.

"What I want, missy, is time alone with you. I suggest you find a way to make that happen, or I promise you I can make your life a living hell."

Grace was so shocked, she straightened suddenly. Hot coffee sloshed over the back of her hand and spotted her apron. "I...excuse me, sir. I must change. I'll send another waitress to take your order."

She waved to Polly, pointing out the stains on her apron, and then fled to the kitchen. By the time she was safely away from the man, she was shaking so badly she could barely manage to untie the sash.

"Grace?" Miss K had paused in the kitchen.

"Mr. Perkins was placing his order when I accidentally... Polly has a customer, and Mr. Perkins is quite—"

"I'll go. Take your time."

"Please take care—"

Miss K gave her an odd, kind smile and left to serve the banker.

Grace ran through the kitchen and straight out the back door to the yard where she doubled over and forced herself to gulp fresh air.

At the party, Nick and Mr. Lombard had come to her rescue, but who was to rescue her now? The man had made a very definite threat. She had no idea what he meant by it, only that she was certain he was fully capable of delivering. He was one of the most powerful men in the community. A word from him could quite possibly be enough to get her fired.

Lily rushed outside. "Grace, you need to get back to your station." She was carrying a fresh apron and immediately began untying the bow of the soiled one and replacing it. "Miss K told me to come get you."

Grace allowed her friend to tie the bow on her clean apron before turning to face her.

"You look like hell," Lily said, never one to mince words. "When's the last time you had any real sleep? Certainly not last night. Well, you'd best tell Nick that you—"

"Nick's gone to California."

"For good?"

"For a month." Grace touched her hands to her hair, straightening the white bow. "I'm fine. Let's go before I get you in trouble as well."

"You gonna tell me what happened?" Lily asked as they walked back inside.

"Later." Grace pasted on her brightest smile and returned to the counter where Jasper Perkins was glaring at Miss Kaufmann and pointing to a plate of perfectly served eggs and bacon.

"I tell you, it's undercooked," he ranted.

Aidan hurried over. "Is there a problem, Mr. Perkins?"

"There is. Take this back, and have that girl bring me a properly prepared breakfast." He thrust the plate of food at Aidan and pointed at Grace. "And from now on, when I choose to dine in this establishment—whether here or in the dining room—I wish that girl to be my waitress. Is that clear?"

"Perfectly, Mr. Perkins," Aidan assured him. "We are so sorry for any inconvenience. Of course, your meal today will be compliments of the house."

"I should think so," Perkins grumbled as he sat back down and tapped his coffee cup with his spoon. "Could use a refill."

"Of course." Aidan motioned to Grace, and when she hesitated, he frowned.

As she picked up the coffee cup, dumped out what was there, and refilled it with fresh, she wondered if this was step one in Mr. Perkins's promise to make her life miserable.

Beneath the bodice of her uniform, she felt the press of her wedding ring against her chest. She forced her mind back to the happiness she'd felt just hours earlier and smiled. If she thought about Nick and not this horrible man, just maybe she could make it through the day.

Jasper Perkins showed up for breakfast and lunch every day that week and the next, and every day, he sat at Grace's station. He made conversation with her that to anyone else would seem simply like polite interest, but Grace was not fooled. Every comment was a veiled threat.

"Just heard Nick Hopkins had to go out to California," he said one day. "You must be missing him. Haven't the two of you been steppin' out?"

"We're friends," Grace replied with a tight smile.

Perkins snorted. "Friends? Is that what you young folks call it these days?"

She set his cup and memorized his order before returning to the kitchen. Harvey Girls did not write anything down. "Will there be anything else, Mr. Perkins?" she asked when she delivered the food.

"Now, missy, you know very well there's to be

something else." He spoke in a low voice covered by a smirk. "Question is when and where?"

Never and nowhere, she wanted to say, but she smiled and refilled his coffee before turning to go.

"Do not turn away from me, missy," he growled. "I asked you a question."

Suddenly, she saw a way out of this nightmare. She smiled apologetically. "When and where would be convenient for you and *Mrs*. Perkins, sir?"

Perkins looked at her for a long moment, but instead of being enraged as she might have expected, his eyes widened with something she hoped was respect. "Why, how about Friday evening?" He wiped his mouth with his napkin and pushed back his chair. "Shall we say seven o'clock?"

Caught off guard, Grace nodded. "All right."

"Excellent. I'll let Mrs. Perkins know to expect you. Come by the bank once you've finished your shift, and we can walk to the house from there."

But later that evening as she, Lily, and Emma prepared for bed and Grace told them about the dinner invitation, Emma frowned. "I don't like it."

"I don't either," Grace agreed, "but the truth is if his wife is present, perhaps—"

Lily rolled her eyes. "When does Nick get back?"

"He said it could be as long as a month, and he's only been away for a little over two weeks."

"Well, that's no good. We'll just have to come up with something else." Lily directed her comment to Emma.

Emma thought for a moment and then snapped her fingers. "I've got it. Mrs. Perkins has been after

Miss Kaufmann to recommend one of us to help her plan a tea she wants to give for the ladies' auxiliary at the church. Seems Mrs. Perkins is not exactly a social butterfly—more of a wallflower, if gossip can be believed, and nothing at all like her sister, Mrs. Lombard. The other women tend to forget she's even in the room and often leave her off their guest lists for lunch or tea or such. Apparently, she thinks she can impress them by hosting some grand event of her own."

"I don't see how—" Grace began.

"It's perfect," Lily interrupted. "Let's ask Miss K right now." She was out the door and down the hall before Grace or Emma could say anything more. Two minutes later, she was back, bringing Miss Kaufmann with her.

"Grace, Lily tells me Mr. Perkins has extended an invitation to you?"

"Yes, ma'am."

"This is most unusual."

"He's been quite insistent," Emma said quietly.

"I see. And you have resisted these overtures?"

"Yes, ma'am. Until today. I thought if I mentioned his wife, he might stop."

Miss K nodded and sat down on the end of Lily's bed. "Well, it's hardly the first time," she said more to herself than to them. "I believe Lily's suggestion that all three of you go is the wisest course. I'll speak with Mrs. Perkins tomorrow and arrange everything."

Grace felt as if a huge weight had been taken from her. "Thank you so much," she gushed.

"And beginning tomorrow, you will change stations with Lily."

The weight came slamming back. "Please don't do that," she pleaded. "I mean, it will raise his suspicions, and he has…he could get angry."

Miss Kaufmann pinned her with a sharp glance. "Has he threatened you?"

"I'll be fine," Grace assured her, deliberately avoiding the question, "once he realizes we Harvey Girls travel in packs." She tried a smile.

"You won't mind if I alert Mr. Campbell to the potential problem?" Miss Kaufmann asked as she stood and walked to the door.

"Not at all," Grace assured her. "Good night, Miss Kaufmann—and thank you."

"We are a family, Grace—the Harvey family. We protect each other. Do not try to do anything on your own." She included Lily and Emma in that last warning.

"Yes, ma'am," the three of them chorused as she left the room.

That night, Grace got the best night's sleep she'd had since Nick left, and when Jasper Perkins took his seat for lunch the following day, she greeted him with her best Harvey Girl smile and a full cup of fresh black coffee.

Chapter 10

Nick was worried.

On their wedding night, he'd gotten so caught up in the thrill of making love to Grace, he'd completely forgotten his intention to pull away in time. What if she was with child? She'd have to admit to the secret marriage and would lose her job. The money she'd budgeted for her family would stop. The two of them would have to make do with his wages, and he could barely afford the bank payments on the property, much less provide for a wife *and* child.

If there is a baby.

In his zeal to return to Grace as soon as possible, he worked extra hours to finish the business Mr. Lombard had sent him to do in California, and after just two weeks, he had everything the boss needed. He wired his employer and got permission to come on home on the next train. He arrived on Friday night, and the first stop he made was at the hotel.

"They've gone to the Perkins' place," Jake told him.

"They?"

"Grace, Emma, and Lily. Miss K made the arrangements. Something about Mrs. Perkins needing their help to plan some tea or something." He edged a little closer to Nick and lowered his voice. "If you ask me, the whole business is a setup to protect Grace."

Nick felt his throat tighten. "From what?"

"From who is more like it. Perkins has been giving Grace the business every day since you left."

"And she's there? In his house?"

"With Emma and Lily and his wife. Calm down, Nick. It's all handled."

"What time did they leave?"

"You just missed them. They walked over to the bank. Perkins thinks it'll just be him and Grace, but he's in for a surprise." Jake chuckled. "I'd sure like to be a fly on the wall for that."

Nick considered his options. It was a little after seven. If the girls were meeting with the banker's wife, then it was likely they'd walk back to the hotel around nine. He had time to get a shave and a shower and make himself presentable. Then he'd just happen to be walking by the Perkins house when they were ready to leave. Perkins would most likely volunteer to walk the girls back to the hotel, hoping to get his chance alone with Grace. It seemed to Nick that Jasper Perkins might be in for more than one unwelcome surprise this night.

He told Jake his plan, and his friend grinned. "I got a better idea," Jake said. "What if we tell Perkins we saw some ruffians hanging out at the saloon the ladies would have to pass on their way back? What if you, me, and maybe Aidan Campbell showed up, knocked on the door, and said we'd come to see the ladies safely home?"

Nick grinned. "I like the way you think, Jake."

Jake shrugged. "Not just good with running a proper kitchen, cowboy."

Nick left to get cleaned up and changed while Jake went to find Aidan and tell him the plan. At eight thirty, the three men met outside the hotel and started across the plaza and on up the street to the large house the banker had built on the edge of town. The house was ablaze with light, and as they approached the front door, Nick could see Emma, Lily, and the banker's wife seated in the front parlor. They seemed to be waiting for something—or someone. Neither Grace nor Jasper Perkins were in the room.

Nick held up a hand, signaling Aidan and Jake to wait in the shadows while he moved stealthily around the side of the house, peering through each window as he went. When he reached the kitchen window, he understood what had happened. Perkins was pressing against Grace, her back to the sink. She was whipping her head from side to side, trying in vain to dodge the banker's attempt to kiss her. Nick was about to call out when Grace's arm shot out, sending a small stack of china dishes crashing to the floor.

"What on earth?" he heard a woman's voice cry.

Perkins stumbled backward, wiping his mouth on his sleeve and glaring at Grace, who was now kneeling to gather the pieces of the broken crockery. Emma, Lily, and the banker's wife rushed into the kitchen.

"I am so sorry, Mrs. Perkins," he heard Grace say. "It's all my fault. I was trying to—"

"And you will pay for every piece, young woman," Perkins shouted. "That china was my mother's."

"Oh, for heaven's sake, Jasper," Nick heard Mrs. Perkins exclaim as she and Emma and Lily helped Grace.

He'd seen enough. He was going to get his wife out of that house—now. He ran back around to the front porch and banged on the door. Jake and Aidan took their places next to him, unsure of what had just happened. They could hear Perkins muttering to himself as he threw the door open and faced the trio with an expression somewhere between fury and confusion.

"Good evening, Mr. Perkins," Aidan said, stepping forward. "Sorry to interrupt your gathering, but there has been a bit of a ruckus at the Staghorn Saloon, and Miss Kaufmann was concerned that the girls would be accosted on their way back to the hotel."

"She asked the three of us to see they get back safe and sound," Jake added.

Nick could not speak. All he wanted to do was throttle the fat, red-faced banker—something his friends seemed to understand, the way they had positioned themselves between Perkins and him.

Nevertheless, Perkins focused his gaze on Nick. "I see you've returned."

"If the ladies are ready…" Aidan continued.

"The *ladies* are cleaning up a mess in the kitchen." Perkins stepped away from the door, an invitation for the three men to enter the house. "And I had every intention of seeing them safely home."

Aidan smiled. "Still, three is better than one when there could be trouble, don't you agree?"

Perkins let out a growl. "Dolly, the girls are leaving," he shouted. He began removing capes and cloaks from a hall tree and doling them out as Mrs. Perkins and the three Harvey Girls appeared.

Nick fixed his gaze on Grace, taking careful stock of her clothing and face to see if he could find any evidence that might tell him Perkins had succeeded in his assault. But when she realized he was back—two weeks sooner than expected—her smile of pure surprise and delight calmed him. He offered her his arm. "Miss Rogers, may I see you home?"

"Thank you," she murmured before turning back to Mrs. Perkins. "I hope we were able to help you, Mrs. Perkins. I think your ideas for the tea are quite wonderful."

The banker's wife blushed and then squeezed Grace's hand. "You are too kind," she said. "You're sure you're all right?"

"I'm fine. And I will replace the broken cup and plate."

"Don't be absurd. The truth is I always hated that pattern. Mr. Perkins has been promising me a new set of china for years now, haven't you, Jasper?"

Another growl.

"Well," Aidan said, once again taking charge, "we'd best be on our way. Wouldn't want Miss Kaufmann worrying about our best Harvey Girls now, would we?"

The six of them walked two by two as they headed back to the hotel. Emma and Aidan set the pace, maintaining a distinct separation between them as they hurried along as if they were late for an appointment. Lily and Jake kept up a lively conversation, punctuated by Lily's delighted laughter as she regaled the men with her version of the look on Jasper Perkins's face when the three women presented themselves at the bank. But all Nick could think about was the scene he'd witnessed through the kitchen window and the helplessness he'd felt to do anything to protect his wife.

"I'm so glad you're back," Grace said, hooking her arm through his. "I missed you terribly, and every day seemed more like a week."

"Did he…" He found he could not bring himself to finish the question.

"Nothing happened, Nick. I'm fine."

"Don't say nothing happened, Grace. I saw him put his hands on you." He stopped walking to allow the others to go ahead of them and give them some privacy. "Are you sure you're all right?"

"I'm fine, Nick. I promise."

"Good." He linked arms with her. They walked across the plaza in silence.

As they approached the hotel, Grace let out a long breath as if she'd been holding something back. "Nick, about Mr. Perkins, you aren't planning to…retaliate in any way, are you?"

"I'd like to, but no."

"Good."

"Not good, Grace. You think I want to let him get away with hounding you the way Jake says he has done? What if he's done the same to other women before you?" He clenched his fists. "Men like that with their big houses and money and—"

She tightened her hold on him. "He didn't hurt me, Nick. He can't hurt us, so please let it go."

But as it turned out, Grace had greatly underestimated

Jasper Perkins. Not two days later, Nick came to the bank to make a deposit for the Lombards and pay the third installment on his loan. As he passed the glass window of Perkins's office, the banker stood and came to the door.

"Hopkins, a word," he said before heading back to his desk, leaving the door open.

Nick weighed his options. There was a chance that Perkins had some business with Mr. Lombard he wanted Nick to deliver. More likely, he wanted to revisit the evening he'd tried to assault Grace. Nick stepped just inside the door.

"Close the door and have a seat." Perkins busied himself with some papers on his desk and did not look up.

Nick followed the man's instructions, shutting the office door and then sitting on the edge of one of the pair of wooden chairs that faced the banker.

Perkins took his time, deliberately making Nick wait. Finally, he leaned back in his chair, which squealed in protest under his weight as he stared straight at Nick.

"I'm afraid the bank needs to foreclose on your loan. As you know, times are hard, and the bank must look closely at every loan with an eye to how quickly—and likely—it will be paid off."

Nick's heart pounded as he saw his future with Grace slipping away. He cleared his throat and forced himself to steady his voice. "I've made payments on time."

Perkins ignored his protest. "It has come to our attention that you have recently traveled to California and, given the nature of your profession, we feel you are a risk to simply take off and leave us without payment for the land. After all, men of your kind, in your line of work…"

It was bull of the highest order, and Nick was sure Perkins knew it.

"Who is 'we'? I'd like to make my case in front of the whole group."

Perkins smiled. "Your case? Oh no, my boy, I'm afraid you misunderstand. The loan has already been foreclosed. You will get a portion returned from what you gave in payment over the last two months."

"A portion?"

"Interest. Fees. The bank has expenses to cover. You can of course pay the loan in full immediately…"

"You know darn well I can't do that."

"I believe my brother-in-law cosigned the note? Perhaps he—"

"I am not going to ask Mr. Lombard to bail me out on this. If my money's not good enough for you—"

"Now, now. Let's not lose our tempers, shall we? Perhaps we could come to some sort of gentleman's agreement and dispense with this entire unpleasant business."

"Such as?"

"We are men who each have something the other wants. You want land of your own. I have a purely paternal interest in a certain waitress you seem to have befriended. I understand her family has fallen on hard times, and I should like to become her benefactor."

Nick was on his feet before the man could say another word. He placed his hands flat on the banker's desk and leaned in so they were nose to nose. "You know what you can do with your loan, Perkins?" He closed his hands around papers on the desk, uncaring whether they had anything to do with his accounts or not, and wadded them into balls. He pushed away from the desk, still clutching the wadded papers, and dropped them in a wastebasket to one side of the desk before leaving.

Jasper Perkins did not come to the hotel all that week, and Grace relaxed back into the daily routine. Nick had come to town every evening since his return from California, and they spent those hours in the abandoned cabin. He looked exhausted these days, and she urged him to stay at the ranch and get some rest, but he insisted. The thing was, in spite of the privacy of the cabin, he resisted making love to her. They kissed and touched, and he even showed her ways they could satisfy each other that did not involve the full union of their bodies.

He also seemed distracted, and one night when she began telling him an idea she'd had for the house they would build on the land, he cut her short. "We need to concentrate on the here and now, Grace," he said. "A place of our own—well, that's down the road a piece."

"I know, but…"

She'd been snuggled close to him, her hand resting on his bare chest. Gently, he set her hand away and sat up. He ran his fingers through his hair and let out a long breath.

Her heart pounded. "Nick?"

"There's no land, Grace, and there's not likely to be for a long, long time."

She sat up next to him, their backs against the rough cabin wall. Despite the warmth from the fire, she pulled the blanket closer. "I don't understand."

He told her about the confrontation with Jasper Perkins. "He's won, Grace."

"But surely Mr. Lombard will—"

"I'm not going hat in hand to my boss to beg for rescue," Nick said through gritted teeth.

She understood male pride. Her father had certainly struggled with it before accepting her help. But she also understood that pride could quickly become foolish vanity. She was sure that the Lombards would be appalled at what their brother-in-law had done. At the party, they had treated Nick more as a member of the family than hired help. And the way they had supported his desire to own his own homestead only further demonstrated their admiration for him.

"So the land—your land—now belongs to the bank?"

Nick nodded.

"Does that mean eventually the land will be posted for sale again?"

Nick shrugged. "Probably. It sure doesn't do the bank any good just sitting there." He cocked an eyebrow at her. "Grace? What's going on in that beautiful head of yours?"

"I'm not sure. What if somebody else bought the land and they sold it back to you—you paid them, not the bank?"

He laughed, but there was no humor in it. "And you know somebody like that?"

"Well, no, but…"

He stood and buttoned his shirt. "It's late. We need to get you back." He reached for her coat.

In silence, they dressed, folded and stored the blanket, and extinguished the fire. And in silence, they walked back to the hotel. Just before they stepped into the circles of light made by the lamps that surrounded the building, Nick took her hand. He kissed her fingers.

"I don't want you worrying about this, Grace. I'll figure it out. You've got till February on your contract—plenty of time for us to work out a new plan. Right now, the important thing is that nothing spoils things for you."

"Meaning?"

"Meaning, Wife, it's coming on Christmas, and I don't want our first holiday together to be sullied by worries we can't do anything about." He wrapped his arms around her and rested his chin on the top of her head. "I've got some special surprises in the works," he said.

"Like what?"

He laughed, and this time, it was the full-throated laughter she loved. "Didn't your ma ever tell you it can't be a surprise if you know what it is?"

She gave him a coy smile. "It's just that with your work and mine, if I need to schedule time off or something…"

"I'll let you know in plenty of time," he assured her. Then he kissed her the way he'd kissed her on their wedding night, and for the first time in days, she dared hope everything would be all right.

On the Friday before Christmas, she picked up her pay and headed straight to the Western Union office to wire half of it to her parents. In her last letter, Grace's mother had urged her not to send money, assuring her that the family was fine. But there had been an undertone to the letter, something important missing. For the first time since Grace had left home, there was no note from her father scribbled at the bottom of the page.

She took the rest of her pay and went to the mercantile, where she selected small inexpensive gifts for her siblings, her parents, Lily, and Emma. But what to get for Nick?

In a case near the jars of penny candy, she spotted a pocketknife, inlaid with turquoise and something that looked like blond wood.

"That's a beauty," Mr. Tucker said, removing it from the case and handing it to her.

"What's the wood?" she asked as she ran her thumb over the casing.

"It's bone. Elk antler," he said. He took the knife from her and opened all the attachments—a blade, of course, but also two smaller blades and the tiniest pair of scissors Grace had ever seen.

It was perfect.

"I expect it's quite expensive," Grace said.

He considered the knife. "Is it for Nick?"

Grace nodded.

"I could make you a good price. You could pay it off a little at a time, and there'd be no interest." He held out the tag attached to the knife. "What would you say to half?"

"I couldn't afford to pay you half that number now, Mr. Tucker. Thank you, but—"

He chuckled. "I'm saying half the price, Grace. Pay it off however you choose."

"Yes," she murmured before she could change her mind. "Yes, thank you. I'll take it."

She handed the merchant all but a dollar of what remained of her pay to cover the cost of all the gifts and the first payment on the knife for Nick. Frank wrapped everything in brown paper and tied the bundle with heavy string before setting it on the counter.

"Pleasure doing business with you, Grace."

"Merry Christmas, Mr. Tucker!"

She fairly danced down the boardwalk, clutching the package to her chest as she imagined Nick's surprise when he opened his gift. She giggled with girlish delight.

"Well, hello, Grace. Have you been doing a bit of shopping for Christmas?"

The voice stopped her cold. She turned to find Jasper Perkins at her side, crowding her so that she had little choice but to allow his shoulder to brush hers as they passed others in the street. Her emotions seesawed between her hatred of the man for taking Nick's land from him and dread that he would remind her of what he no doubt saw as the unfinished business of that night in his kitchen.

"'Tis the season," she replied with a gaiety she no longer felt.

"That's quite a bundle. May I carry it for you?"

Grace clutched her package closer to her chest. "No, thank you."

He let out a sigh and placed his hand on her elbow. "Ah, I imagine you are upset about that unfortunate business with your friend, Nick Hopkins."

She tried to jerk her elbow free, but he tightened his grip.

"What if I were to tell you there was a very simple way you could make everything all right for Mr. Hopkins? An ill-timed mistake in the paperwork. No harm done. The land fully restored to his name?"

As he delivered these words, he smiled and tipped his hat to the ladies or nodded to the men they passed. He was without doubt the most despicable man Grace ever hoped to know. "I take by your silence and continued presence walking with me that I have piqued your interest," he continued.

She had to admit he had that part right. "I'm listening," she said.

"Grace, whatever you may think of me, I am not an unreasonable man. There is no future for the two of us—we both know that. All I want from you is one hour in my office after the bank has closed for the day. There is a back entrance where you can come and go undetected. I will be gentle, my dear, and once we have completed this assignation, I will not bother you again."

"I...how..." She was speechless with fury.

"You see," he went on as if she had neither tensed nor tried to speak, "it is your innocence that has the appeal for me. And once our hour together is done, that innocence will have been breached, and I will have no further need of you."

With a strength she had no idea she possessed, she wrenched her arm free of his hold, stumbled to the edge of the boardwalk, and vomited into the gutter.

"My dear!" Perkins made a show of concern as several people paused on their way to complete their errands. "She'll be fine," he assured them. "A little too much fruit cake."

He placed his hand on her back, and she shrugged him off, whirling to face him and wiping spittle from her lip with the back of her gloved hand. Her bundle of gifts lay in the dirt of the street. "Do not touch me," she growled. "Do not ever touch or speak to me again." She didn't care who heard, although given the way others continued on their way, she doubted they had caught the words she'd delivered in a feral whisper.

"Or what?" Jasper Perkins's face was very near hers. "Take care, girlie. I have been most reasonable and generous. So far. Give it some thought. I will wait for you tomorrow evening, my office. Use the rear entrance. I'll leave the door unlocked."

He retrieved her package and handed it to her.

"And if I don't come?"

He smiled the triumphant smile of the devil himself. "Then my promise stands. I will make your life a living hell, Grace. Taking Mr. Hopkins's land away is just a small sample of what I can do. Merry Christmas, my dear." He tipped his hat and crossed the street.

Chapter 11

GRACE DID NOT SLEEP AT ALL THAT NIGHT. PERHAPS IF she simply told Perkins that she was no longer a virgin, he would discard her as promised. She did not have to reveal that she and Nick were legally married, just that she was no longer chaste. She could reason with him, assure him she certainly did not expect him to honor his side of the bargain. Then she could help Nick find someone who would buy the land and sell it back to him. Everything would work out.

But the following day as she was finishing her shift, her nerves and the lack of sleep got the better of her. She dropped a soup tureen, smashing the crockery and splashing soup over the dining room floor and several surrounding white tablecloths. Fortunately, it was the end of the day, and the dining room was nearly empty of customers. Those that remained hastened to finish their meal and leave. Unfortunately, there had been other trying issues throughout the day, and when both Aidan Campbell and Miss K came running at the sound of the crash, Grace could see neither was in a forgiving mood.

Aidan moved to soothe the remaining customers while Miss K surveyed the damage and then turned her attention to Grace.

"I am so sorry. I—"

"You will clean up this mess, Grace. You will not leave until you have removed every spot from these tablecloths, scrubbed the floor, and reset the tables."

Behind Miss Kaufmann, Grace saw the clock ticking off the seconds and minutes. Cleaning everything would take hours, and Mr. Perkins would be furious. "Yes, of course. But—"

Miss Kaufmann cocked an eyebrow. "There are no buts to this situation, Grace. We simply cannot tolerate such carelessness. This is your doing, and I will not let you off easily. Get to work now."

So she missed the appointment with the banker, and when she finally left the dining room after scouring the floor, scrubbing the stains from the cloths and hanging them to dry, setting the tables with fresh linens and place settings, and then ironing and putting away the laundered tablecloths, she trudged wearily up the back stairs.

Emma and Lily were out for the evening. She entered the room, lit only by the light of streetlamps, and collapsed onto her bed. Something crunched beneath her head. She sat up and picked up a thick white envelope with her name scrawled across the front in an unfamiliar script.

She walked to the window and slid her thumbnail under the sealed flap. Inside was a single vellum card that read:

IT WOULD APPEAR YOU DO NOT HONOR YOUR
PROMISES, GRACE. BE ASSURED THAT I ALWAYS DO.
J. PERKINS

She shuddered. What could he do to her? The fact
that he had found a way to have this message left on
her pillow illustrated his power. The true question was
what *would* he do? Her imagination refused to stop
spitting out visions of just how much trouble she was
in. Perhaps he would hire a thug to accost and rape
her. Perhaps he would accuse her of something and
ruin her reputation, get her fired. Perhaps he would—

Stop this.

All she had to do was respond to his note, explain
what had happened, promise to meet him another
night.

And then what?

He would never listen to reason. She had been
foolish to think he might. Even if he believed that she
was unchaste, he would accuse her of leading him on,
of pretending to be something she was not—a Harvey
Girl of the highest moral character. She stood frozen
to the spot, gazing out the window at the bank where
he had waited for her.

She had tricked him once, and now he believed
she had done so again. He would want his revenge.
Earlier, he had taken that revenge out on Nick.
Somehow, he understood how important Nick was
to her. No, she realized, he would not harm her. He
would attack those she cared for—like Emma or Lily.

She could hear her roommates coming down the
hall, their voices soft. They were the best friends Grace

had ever had. She would not involve them in this as she had before. Jasper Perkins was her problem—and hers alone.

Nick was at loose ends. With winter setting in, Christmas less than a week away, and no land to clear and prepare for building the cabin he and Grace had dreamed of sharing, his days were long and boring. And as a result, his temper was short. That morning, he had argued with Slim over a miscalculation the hired hand had made regarding the count on the herd. A steer was missing, and he and Slim were out now riding the range, looking for a missing cow.

He saw the cowboy in the distance, covering a portion of the land that ran along a barbed wire fence that separated the Lombard land from its neighbor. "Tracks!" Slim shouted, and Nick spurred Sage to a gallop as he covered the distance between them.

The fence had been cut. "Rustlers," Slim said and glanced around as if expecting to see the culprits still in the area.

"Yeah," Nick replied. He dismounted and examined the wire. He'd been too hard on Slim. After all, over time, he'd made mistakes in the count himself. "Let's get this repaired before they get any more of our stock."

Together, they pulled the wire tight and twisted the ends to make the barrier secure again. They worked without talking—but also without the tension of their earlier argument. Slim would just let it go, but Nick knew he'd been unfair.

"Sorry about earlier," he muttered as they reattached the wire to the post.

Slim shrugged. "Been a few days since you last rode into town," he said. Then he grinned at Nick. "You missing that Harvey filly?"

Nick swallowed a chuckle, knowing the men had probably been talking about what might be behind his sour disposition. "Yeah, it's been a while. She's had work, and that snowstorm closed the pass between here and town."

"Pass should be open now." Slim looked up at the sun. "Been warm enough these last two days to melt a way through. Maybe you ought to think about going. Me and the others can handle things here. I mean, if you was to get stuck there by another storm or something."

Slim delivered this without looking directly at Nick.

"You suggesting I take a couple of days off?"

Slim tested other parts of the fence, looking for other points of weakness. He shrugged. "You seem wound pretty tight, Nick."

"I'll think about it," he said as the two men returned to their horses. "We're unlikely to get that cow back, Slim. Not your fault she went missing."

"I know." Slim turned his horse to head away from the ranch. "I'll just ride the whole fence line to be sure there aren't any other cuts."

"Good idea. You head north, and I'll do the south end."

"And then you'll get yourself cleaned up and smelling pretty and head to town?" Slim grinned. "Not sure me and the boys can stand one more night of you keeping us awake with your pacing."

Nick laughed. "All right. You made your point. I've got some shopping to do anyway. What do you fellas want for Christmas, Slim?"

"A foreman that don't growl at us like a grouchy ol' bear would be real nice." Slim spurred his horse and rode off.

By the time he'd checked the fencing and returned to the bunkhouse, Nick had decided to take Slim's advice. If the pass wasn't open, there were other ways to get to town—longer, but then he had always enjoyed his time alone riding the range with nobody to talk to but Sage.

He stopped at the ranch house and asked permission to take a couple of days off.

"Of course. Going over to spend the holiday at your land?" John Lombard asked. Nick had not told him about his encounter with Jasper Perkins or about the bank calling in the loan.

"Thought I might go into town."

John grinned. "Spend Christmas with your gal? She's a pretty one, Nick—and smart, from what I could tell. She's certainly a hard worker, and I know Rita thinks she's a right good match for you."

Nick felt the blush spread across his already wind-reddened cheeks. "She's pretty special," he said.

"Well, go on. Get outta here," John said. "And wish Grace a merry Christmas from us."

Nick washed up, combed his hair, and put on his hat. "Well, boys, I'll see you in a couple of days."

The cowboys looked up from their card game. They grinned, and Smokey let out a whistle. "You smell awful pretty for a cowpoke, Nick."

Nick laughed. "It was you taught me that's what the ladies like, Smokey." As he left the bunkhouse, he could hear the others turning their teasing on Smokey. He chuckled as he saddled Sage and realized Slim had offered exactly the remedy he'd needed to dispel his foul mood.

The pass was still closed, but as anxious as he was to get to Juniper and see Grace, Nick wasn't disappointed. Grace was working, so adding an hour onto his trip wouldn't make much difference in when he could see her—hold her, kiss her, make love to her. In the meantime, the longer way gave him time to think and to figure out what they were going to do once Grace's contract was completed. It would be two long months before they could be together openly and start living life as a married couple.

The first thing he did when he reached town was stop at the mercantile. He walked straight to the display of ladies' hats and plucked the one he'd shown Grace that day from the shelf. Then he looked around. The hat no longer seemed like enough. This was his wife he was buying a present for, not a girl he was trying to get to know. He spied some rolls of ribbon behind the counter. He thought about their wedding and the ribbons wound through her hair. Those had been white, but what if she had a whole rainbow of colors to use? "How do you sell those?" he asked.

"By the yard usually. Two cents a yard."

Nick counted the rolls and calculated the cost. "A yard of each. No, wait." He'd just seen a set of combs like the ones he'd noticed on the bathroom sink that night they spent at the La Casita Hotel. "Those?"

Frank understood he was asking the price. "They're kind of pricey, Nick—tortoise with mother-of-pearl inlaid and carved the way they are."

"How much?"

Frank named a price.

Nick checked the price on the hat.

"I can do better if you buy the hat and the combs together," Frank offered.

Nick was low on cash, having spent most of his pay over the last couple of months on the loan. Even though he'd received a voucher from the bank a week after his encounter with Perkins, the amount was less than half what he'd originally paid out. But this was Christmas, their first Christmas, and he wanted to give her something she would have forever. He pushed the hat aside. "Wrap up the combs," he said, reaching in his pocket for the money. "If the hat's still here for her birthday, maybe I'll come back for it."

He watched Frank place the combs in a case made especially for them and realized he had no idea when her birthday was.

How little we know about each other, he thought. And yet he had never met another woman—or anyone for that matter—with whom he could share anything or whom he could trust not to doubt him when he talked of his dreams for the future.

Frank was tying the package with lengths of red, pink, green, lavender, and white ribbons that he measured out and cut from the rolls behind the counter.

"Thanks," Nick said as he took the package and handed Frank the money. "You didn't have to."

Frank shrugged. He held up a finger and then

filled a paper sack with peppermint sticks, licorice, and chocolates before handing it to Nick. "Merry Christmas, Nick."

By the time Nick left the store, the sun was setting and most of the shops had already closed for the holiday. Grace would be finishing her shift. It was Christmas Eve, and neither the dining room nor the lunch counter would be open on Christmas Day. The way he saw it, they had all night tonight, all day tomorrow, and all tomorrow night to be together before she would have to be back at work. He made his way to their secret cabin, where he fashioned some juniper and sage branches into a makeshift Christmas tree. He untied all but one of the ribbons from the package and wound them through the boughs and then set the gift next to it. He would save the candy for the guys in the bunkhouse. He gathered dried sage and some cypress wood and stacked it, ready to light it once he brought her to the cabin. Last, he laid out his bedroll, covered it with a blanket, and headed for the hotel. They might face a lot of problems in the coming year, but he was determined to make this first Christmas one they would never forget.

Grace was exhausted. She had worked a full day after putting in extra hours the night before cleaning up the mess she'd made with the soup. She'd promised Emma and Lily that she would attend church services with the hotel staff. All the girls were going, as well as most of the men who worked in the kitchen. But all she really wanted to do was take a long, hot bath and climb into bed. This was her first Christmas as a married woman, and she was missing Nick. The combination of the weather and their work schedules had kept them apart. She had imagined giving him the pocketknife while they sat under the blanket on the floor of the cabin, having finished a supper she would have brought for them. She had imagined his eyes as he opened the present. She had imagined a lot more than that, and the truth was, the last thing she was feeling was anything even close to the spirit of Christmas.

"You can't not go," Lily protested when Grace tried to beg off attending the church service. "Everyone will be there. And I won't have you up here all by yourself moping."

"Come on, Grace," Emma urged. "It will take your mind off missing your family—and Nick."

"An hour," Lily exclaimed. "What possible difference can an hour make when you have all day tomorrow to sleep?"

"All right, but I'm having that bath."

The church was crowded, but Jake had saved seats for them in a pew near the back. There were candles and winter greenery on the sill of every window, their glow bringing the beautiful stained glass to life in spite of the darkness outside. The altar was trimmed with vivid red poinsettias and two large candelabras that held eight fat candles each. Grace felt herself relax as the choir entered their loft and the organist struck up "O Come, All Ye Faithful."

As one, the congregation rose, their voices blending with the harmony provided by the choir. As they sang, someone crowded into the pew next to Grace. She pressed closer to Lily to make room and then turned to share her hymnal with the latecomer.

Grace gasped, and Nick grinned back at her. Lily elbowed her on her other side, muttering, "It's a Christmas miracle."

He was actually there, sharing Christmas with her. Her heart swelled with joy. Following the hymn, everyone sat down again, and because of the close quarters, Grace felt her hip and shoulder pressed against Nick's. As they listened to the reading of the Christmas story from the book of Luke, Nick linked his fingers with hers.

After services as the throng of people left the church, Nick and Grace slipped away to the cabin. He had her cover her eyes as they approached and wait outside a minute, claiming he needed to light the fire. He returned, urging her not to peek as he led her through the narrow door. "Okay," he said. "Open your eyes."

The fire was already starting to warm the small space, and she saw the makeshift tree he'd created from branches and a rainbow of ribbons, then she noticed a gift-wrapped box.

"Merry Christmas, Mrs. Hopkins," he whispered, stepping behind her and wrapping his arms around her.

"Oh, Nick, let me run back to the hotel and get my gift for you."

"Tomorrow. We have this whole evening, and I don't want to miss spending a moment of it with you."

He led her to the blanket where he'd set up a meal of bread, cheese, apples, and cider. He took out his old pocketknife to peel the apples, the handle of the knife coming loose twice before he completed the task. She smiled, knowing the pocketknife she'd bought for him was going to be the perfect gift.

"Open your present," he said.

"But it's not Christmas yet."

"Close enough. Come on, open it." His excitement was boyish and irresistible.

She picked up the gift and fingered the ribbon before carefully untying the bow and opening the box. Inside was another box—a wooden one, polished to a high sheen. She opened that and drew in a breath. "Nick, they're so beautiful." She removed the pair of combs and examined their intricate design by the light of the fire.

He scooted over so that he sat behind her, his legs spread to either side of her, and he began removing the pins from her hair and letting it fall over her shoulders. He took the combs from her and began slowly combing through the long strands. When he was finished, he handed her the combs. "Fix them in your hair," he said. "Let me see how they look."

She did as he asked. "It's difficult to know exactly how to place them without a mirror. How's that look?"

"Almost perfect."

"Almost?"

"Well, you see, all that clothing up and around your neck and shoulders kind of ruins the effect." He knelt in front of her. "I think if we just open this…" He unfastened the jacket of her outfit and pushed it off her shoulders, studied her a moment, then shook his head. "Still too much," he muttered as he began opening the buttons that closed the bodice of her dress.

She shrugged out of it. "Better?"

"Getting there," he replied, his voice husky with desire. "Just maybe…" He untied the ribbons on her camisole, then sat back on his heels. "Needs something more."

She lowered the camisole so that her breasts were exposed. "How's this?"

"Perfect," he whispered as he reached for her.

She cocked her head and studied him with a frown.

He moved away. "What's wrong?"

"Well, seems to me you're overdressed, Mr. Hopkins. I mean with all this heat—from the fire and all."

He grinned. "Any ideas how you might remedy that?"

She pushed his coat away, and he pulled his arms free. Then she pushed the suspenders off those broad shoulders and tugged his shirt from his trousers, lifting it over his head and tossing it aside. She leaned forward and kissed his chest, allowing her tongue to glide over the ridges of his muscles the way he'd taught her on their wedding night. She delighted in the shiver that ran through him.

He laid her back on the blanket and knelt at her feet, removing her shoes, then her stockings, then her pantaloons. Naked under the skirt of her dress, she lifted her hips to give him access to remove that garment as well, but instead, he ran his palm over her bare legs, along the inside of her thighs, close to the fire already raging inside her, and then away again.

She tunneled her hand down the front of his trousers and found him every bit as ready as she was. "It's been too long," she whispered, lathing his inner ear with her tongue.

He propped his weight on his hands and kissed her.

Seconds later, they had both fully undressed, casting aside the various pieces of clothing as they tumbled together back onto the blanket. He rolled with her so that she sat atop him. She could feel the fullness of him pressed against her inner thighs. He pulled her to him for a kiss she wished would never end. Then slowly, he lowered her so that she could feel him sliding inside, easily, perfectly, as if they had been created to fit together as one.

She reached up and removed the precious combs, setting them aside as she shook out the mane of her hair. When she bent forward, her hair formed a curtain that sheltered and warmed them both. She started moving in a rhythm that seemed as natural and inborn as breathing. She thrilled to the realization that she was leading in this dance they'd created.

But at the moment when it seemed they might explode in unison, Nick rolled her to her back and pulled away.

"No!"

"Shhh," he whispered as he gathered her close. "I want it too," he said, "but the last thing either of us needs right now is a baby. We've been lucky so far, Grace, but I don't believe in tempting fate."

She knew he was right. They held each other for a long moment. He stroked her hair. She ran her fingers over his chest.

"But someday?" she whispered.

He chuckled. "Yeah, someday…and then someday after that and someday after that and—"

She rose onto her elbow and stared at him. "How many children do you want?"

He seemed to consider this, the light from the fire playing across his features. "Lots," he said finally. "Half dozen?"

She thought of her family—her five brothers and sisters and how together, the six of them had enjoyed so many good times together. "Sounds about right," she said and snuggled in next to him again.

"Could be," he mused as he wrapped a tendril of her hair around his finger, "this time next year, we might already have a start. I mean, you finish your contract in February." He counted the months on his fingers. "Yeah, next Christmas, we might have a little guy of our own."

"Or girl," she corrected.

"Sure—as long as she's as pretty and smart as her mother."

"And if she's plain and dumb as a rock?"

He shrugged. "I'll love her more, 'cause she'll need it."

"You're going to be a fine father, Nick Hopkins."

They dozed a little, waking when the fire burned low and they felt the chill of the night. Nick stoked the fire with the small supply of kindling left, and they finished their supper, warming their cider by setting the tin cups close to the flames. They dressed slowly, pausing between layers to kiss and caress. As Grace twisted her hair up and anchored it with the combs, they heard the church bells calling people back for midnight services.

Miss Kaufmann had given the girls an extended curfew for the evening, as long as they attended services and came straight back to the hotel after. As

Nick and Grace crossed the plaza on their way to the church, they became part of a line of people all moving in the same direction. Grace imagined them following this tradition for years to come—herself, Nick, and their children.

And then she saw Jasper Perkins walking to the church with his wife. Dolly Perkins waved to her.

Nick spotted the banker at the same moment. When it appeared the two couples were bound to meet as they entered the large double doors, Nick pulled Grace around to a side entrance. They were already seated when Perkins led his wife down the aisle to a seat near the front—in a pew reserved for the dignitaries of the town.

Nick fought to contain his fury at the very sight of Perkins parading down the aisle, greeting people as if he were running for office. On the other hand, he was determined not to permit the banker to spoil the perfect evening he and Grace were sharing. This was their first Christmas together, and he was not about to allow anything to tarnish that in any way. He'd felt Grace tense when she noticed Perkins, and now she sat next to him, her hands clenched in her lap. He reached over and pried one hand loose from the other, then covered her hand with his and moved closer so that she could feel the press of his shoulder against her.

It worked. She tightened her fingers around his and smiled. Just then, Lily and Emma came hurrying down the aisle to sit with them, followed by Jake and, surprisingly, Aidan Campbell.

"Merry Christmas, Nick," Lily mouthed.

Nick grinned. Grace was lucky to have friends like Lily and Emma. They would make sure nothing happened to her when he wasn't able to be there. Now that Perkins had punished him by foreclosing on the loan, maybe the older man would back off. Grace hadn't said anything about him continuing to stalk her. He relaxed and turned his attention to the front of the church.

The midnight service was one of soft music and the occasional solo by a member of the choir. There was no sermon, no nativity pageant. Just before midnight, the ushers came down the aisles and handed each person a small candle. Then as the organist played "Silent Night," young boys from the congregation dressed in white robes with red bows went from row to row lighting the candle held by the person on the aisle. That person lit the candle of his or her neighbor and so on until the entire church was aglow and the bells chimed midnight. As the music shifted into "It Came Upon the Midnight Clear," the ushers stood sentry row by row to allow each pew to empty as people left the church, still holding their candles.

Outside, there were calls of "Merry Christmas" as the congregants scattered and walked or rode back to their homes. It was Christmas morning, and above them, a black sky dotted with thousands of stars lit their way as one by one, the candles were extinguished.

At the hotel, the six friends exchanged holiday wishes and chaste kisses on the cheek.

"I'll see you in the morning," Grace whispered as she stood on tiptoe to kiss Nick's cheek.

"At the cabin," he replied.

"Yes, and don't eat anything. I'm bringing breakfast."

"And my gift?" He gave her a teasing smile.

"Only if you're good," she replied.

"Grace?" Miss Kaufmann stood in the doorway checking the girls in for the night.

Grace kissed him again and then ran to the door. "Merry Christmas, Miss K," she said as she followed the other girls inside and up the back stairs.

Nick stood watching until Miss Kaufmann closed the door. He barely felt the cold as he returned to the cabin where he bedded down for the night and smiled in the darkness as he imagined all the Christmases to come once he and Grace were truly together. He folded his arms behind his head and said to himself, "Hopkins, you are one lucky cowboy."

On Christmas morning, Nick was awakened by kisses fluttering lightly over his face. He opened his eyes and rubbed the sleep from them as Grace laid out a breakfast for them of cinnamon rolls, apples and oranges, and a large thermos of coffee.

"You'll need to cut the fruit," she said. "I brought some apples and dried apricots. We'll mix everything into the oatmeal." She nodded her head toward a pot warming by the fire, the combs he'd given her gleaming in her hair.

Nick dug in his pocket for his knife and came up empty. "I had it," he muttered.

"Try this." She handed him a package he recognized as coming from Tucker's store.

He grinned as he tore off the wrapping and opened the box. "Oh, Grace, it's a beauty," he said softly as he examined every blade and accessory.

He set to cutting the fruit, handing her the pieces to add to the hot cereal while he munched on a cinnamon roll.

"What shall we do today?" she asked, then laughed when he raised an eyebrow and grinned. "I mean besides that. What if we spend time with Emma, Jake, and Lily? They don't have any family around."

"Is it your plan to care for the entire world?" he asked.

"Just the corner of the world that holds my family and friends—and my husband."

As Grace had suggested, they spent the day with others from the hotel, and that evening, Aidan hosted a lavish Christmas dinner. Afterward, everyone seemed to find his or her corner for quiet conversation or to simply relax. Grace and Nick slipped away, back to their hideaway where they made love and talked about what joys the new year might bring for them.

It was the perfect Christmas, Nick thought as he rode back to the ranch after Grace had returned to the hotel. He recalled how surprised and delighted she'd been with the set of combs, and certainly the pocket-knife was finer than any he'd ever owned. But the best gift of all was the life he could see them sharing—the years stretching out before them with many such happy times to come.

Chapter 12

THE HOLIDAYS DISAPPEARED INTO THE UNUSUALLY cold and bitter winds of January, and the cabin was no longer a viable meeting place. Even with a fire and extra blankets, the winds whipped through cracks in the walls, and the ill-fitting single window and door made it impossible to do more than cuddle together. On top of that, the rustlers that had struck before Christmas returned. Since the ranch was operating with as few hands as possible, Nick took double shifts watching over the herd. If he got to town twice a week, he considered that a blessing.

Grace was still working double shifts. "Every penny counts," she argued when Nick protested that between her schedule and his, they would have even less time to spend together. As the days dragged on, assuming work and impassable roads didn't prevent Nick from making it to town at all, they had to make do with stolen moments when she was on break. They were both exhausted and frustrated and short-tempered. The only thing that gave Nick hope they would survive this rough patch was that her contract would end in just a few weeks. Then they could tell the world about their marriage and move into the foreman's quarters at the ranch. Without the need to save money for loan payments, he would have enough so that if Grace hadn't quite managed to send her family the full fifty dollars, he could make up the difference.

Between shifts at the ranch, Nick contemplated the possibility that he might just need to confide in the Lombards that he no longer had the land and that he and Grace had married. If the Lombards agreed—and he had every reason to believe they would—at least he could pass the long stretches between visits to town getting the foreman's quarters cleaned up, painted, and ready for Grace.

"Nick, boss man wants to see you up at the main house," Slim said as he led his horse into the barn where Nick was cleaning stalls.

Nick leaned the shovel and broom against the wall and turned up the collar to his sheepskin-lined coat. "Did he say anything more?"

"Nope. Just told me to have you stop by as soon as you were available."

At the house, Nick stamped the dirt and slush from his shoes and knocked on the door.

Rita Lombard opened it and smiled. "Ah, Nick. Come in. John is waiting for you in the library." She took his coat and hat and hung them on the hall tree that featured antlers as hooks. Nick had always liked that touch.

While Rita returned to the kitchen, Nick smoothed back his hair and entered the library. Odd that his boss was there instead of his office where the two men normally discussed business.

"Nick, come in." John Lombard greeted him by standing and indicating a chair near the fire. "Can't recall a winter this raw in some time."

"No sir." Something was off here. He was being treated more like one of the Lombards' guests than their foreman. He stood next to the chair.

"Sit," John instructed. Two leather winged-back chairs with thick wooden legs and arms faced the fire. Nick sat in one, and John took the other. "How are things going with you and that pretty waitress in town?"

"Okay."

John frowned. "Just okay? That's not going to please Rita. She's convinced the two of you are a match made in heaven. I should probably apologize for all the extra work you've had to take on. Rita says it stands in the way of true love and…"

"…and that simply will not do," Rita announced as she entered the room carrying a tray loaded with a pot of coffee, cups, saucers, and a plate stacked with pastries. Her husband was on his feet immediately to relieve her of the tray, which he sat on the raised hearth before pulling a straight-back chair into the circle for her.

She talked as she prepared coffee for Nick and her husband. "The thing is, Nick, as I am sure you know, John and I are quite fond of you. Not being blessed with children of our own, we've come to think of you as something of a son we never had."

Nick felt heat that had little to do with the fire rise to his cheeks. His hand shook a little as he accepted the coffee. "Thank you," he murmured, hoping to cover both the offer of coffee and the compliment.

"What Rita is trying to say, Nick, is—"

Rita interrupted. "Nick, if you have an inclination to ask Grace to marry you, you'll need a place to live, at least until you can build a cabin on that land of yours. The bunkhouse will simply not do, but as you know, there are quarters for you just off the kitchen." She sipped her coffee and pinned him with a direct gaze. "Gossip has it that Grace's contract with the Harvey outfit will end in just a few weeks. I would suggest that you propose before that happens, or else she's likely to sign up for another six months or longer, and then where will the two of you be?"

"I…" Nick swallowed and set down his cup. "The thing is, I no longer hold title to the land. The bank foreclosed the loan, so at the moment—"

"Perkins called in the loan?" John Lombard was not a man who shouted or ranted, but there was never a doubt when he heard news he did not like.

"Jasper?" Rita asked as if perhaps she had misunderstood.

Nick nodded. "Yes, ma'am. He said—"

"I don't give a hoot what he said." Rita Lombard had no problem letting the full extent of her feelings be known either. "John cosigned that loan. I'm going to contact my sister and tell her she needs to set her husband straight on a few things."

"Rita, calm yourself. Let's hear Nick out. Is there something more, Nick?"

One of the traits Nick had long admired about his boss was the man's ability to read people. He decided to confide in them. "Grace and I are already married," he said softly.

Rita gasped and then smiled and then frowned. "But she cannot—"

"No one knows. We thought we'd make it till her contract runs out, and in the meantime, I would get something built on the land so we could live there once she was done with Harvey." He lifted his shoulders and let them drop in a gesture of defeat. "Guess maybe we should have—"

"Well, this will not do," Rita muttered. "Not one bit."

John picked up a pastry and bit off half of it. He chewed slowly as he stared at the fire. "It must be providence, son," he said when he'd finally swallowed and licked powdered sugar from his fingers. "The thing is, Rita and I have been thinking quite a bit about the future, Nick—ours and yours. We aren't getting any younger. But we've built a good business here, and with no one to leave this place to... Well, we were hoping maybe you might reconsider building a place of your own. What if, instead, you stayed on here? You'd take on more responsibility, with a higher wage of course, and then one day..."

Rita reached over and covered Nick's hand with hers. "You're too old for us to adopt, Nick, but you've been like a son to us since your father came to work here when you were just a child. You've practically grown up here, and once you took on your father's job—you were still so very young." Tears welled in her eyes.

"Seventeen," Nick said softly, recalling those early

years, remembering how John Lombard had taken him under his wing after Nick's father was killed during a stampede. He shook off the memories. This was now. "I couldn't possibly—"

"Just say you'll give it some thought," John urged. "After all, given your circumstances, you need to make some plans, son."

Son.

Nick understood it was a generational term, and yet the way it so easily rolled off John's tongue, it felt like more.

"I'll think on it, sir," he agreed.

"And don't you worry about the secret you and Grace hold. We won't reveal it," Rita assured him as her husband stood, indicating the meeting was over.

Nick stood as well. "Could I ask one more favor, ma'am?"

"Of course."

"Please don't raise the issue of your brother-in-law calling in the loan with your sister. Just let it alone."

She started to reply, bit her lower lip as she squinted up at him, and then touched his cheek. "Jasper Perkins is a horrible little man," she said. "I told Dolly that when she married him, but she went ahead anyway. It is high time someone brought him down off that high horse."

"Please?"

She huffed a sigh of resignation. "Very well. Dolly has no power when it comes to her husband anyway, so what good would it do to upset her?"

The older couple walked Nick to the door and waited while he put on his coat and hat. He shook hands with John, and then for reasons he didn't fully understand, he gave Rita a hug. "Thank you both," he said.

Outside, he did not feel the bitterness of the wind but rather felt as if his lungs had been filled with fresh, clean air. Everything was going to be all right. He could hardly wait to tell Grace about the generous offer. That would have to wait, of course. He was on night duty now that Smokey was down with the grippe. But he would go to town at his first opportunity. Who needed sleep when your life was finally falling into place?

Grace could not remember a time when she had been so exhausted. Even the long hours she'd worked back on the farm with her siblings and father to sow or bring in the crops had never felt quite so draining. There were days when she did not recall making her way up the three flights of stairs and collapsing onto her bed.

Both Lily and Emma had been sick with colds that had them sneezing and coughing through the night. And since Miss Kaufmann worked hard to schedule the girls who were sick with duties behind the scenes rather than upset the customers, they were short-handed in the dining room. Grace had twice her usual number of customers to serve—with a smile.

Of course, the worst of it was that since Christmas, she had hardly had more than a few minutes alone with Nick, to the point that she had recently suggested it was foolish for him to ride all the way to town and back for such a short visit. He'd taken it the wrong way.

"Are you saying you'd rather not see me, Grace?"

"Not at all. But face facts, Nick. We are both frustrated by having so little time, not to mention privacy. I don't want to argue with you. Do as you like."

They were both overworked and on edge. The kisses and embraces they managed were rushed and had a sort of desperate quality to them that held none of the passion or sweetness they had shared before. Nick was constantly counting the weeks until she would be free of her obligation to the Harvey company, and she realized that irritated her. She would be giving up a great deal once her position came to an end—friendships, the pride she took in what she had accomplished, the promotions and money of her own, and the regular customers who requested her table and shared their news with her. And now that Jasper Perkins had robbed Nick of his land, where were they to live?

Jasper Perkins.

The mere thought of the man sent a shiver down her spine. He had made no further move since before Christmas, yet he continued to come to the dining room, continued to insist she serve him, continued to stare at her as if she were a piece of prime meat. She shuddered with disgust as she untied her apron and made her way through the kitchen. For the first time since Christmas, she had been given the supper shift off.

"Hey, Grace," Jake called.

She paused and waited for him to come closer. He was carrying a folded piece of paper. "A note for Lily?" she guessed and smiled. It was so sweet the way Jake sent daily messages now that Miss K had decided Lily was far too ill to leave her bed.

"This one's for you. A kid came by earlier and said Nick sent him. He wants you to meet up at 'the usual place' at six."

She took the paper. "That's not Nick's handwriting," she said.

"No. There was no note. I wrote down what the kid said in case I missed seeing you in person." He grinned. "Sounds like Nick might have something special planned." He handed her a small box tied with string. "The kid also brought this."

She untied the string and smiled. The box was filled with chocolates. Suddenly, she felt lighter. They just needed to get through this. There were challenges in every marriage, and this busy time was theirs. She offered Jake a chocolate. He popped it whole into his mouth and grinned. "Peppermint," he said as he headed back to work.

Upstairs, Grace told Lily and Emma the news, then took a long, hot bath, hoping it would revive her. She even considered borrowing a little of the rouge Lily kept hidden to give her pale face some color but decided no rouge would be able to withstand the kisses she and Nick would share. Somehow, he must have come up with an idea for making the cabin habitable so that they could have the whole evening together without freezing. As she soaked, the weariness that had stalked her for days eased. Back in the room, she dressed quickly.

"Take my coat," Lily croaked. "It's warmer."

"And cover your head," Emma instructed. "Can't have you coming down with whatever we've got."

She did as they suggested, hesitated at the door, and said, "I wish the two of you could—"

"No you don't," Lily said with a throaty laugh. "Besides, we plan to polish these off while you're gone." She held up the box of chocolates.

It was nearly dark when Grace hurried outside. She checked to be sure no one was around who might follow her or see her head down the path that led to the abandoned cabin. As she approached, a thin sliver of smoke rose from the chimney, and she imagined the fire Nick had built. He would have arrived early to make the small space as toasty as possible. She should have stopped in the kitchen and brought something for them to eat. Nick was always hungry after...

Her heart was hammering with both the exertion of breathing in the frigid air and excitement as she approached the door. She knocked, imagining Nick opening the door only wide enough for her to slip inside before wrapping her in his arms and kissing her with all the passion they'd shared on their wedding night.

The door remained closed, but not all the way. She smiled. So, he was playing a game, teasing her. She pushed the door open and stepped inside. The door closed behind her with a firm click. She turned, still smiling.

"Well, at last," Jasper Perkins said.

Grace gasped and instinctively pulled Lily's coat closer. She was incapable of speaking. The banker pointed a pistol at her and waved it between her and the fire.

"I have done my best to see to your comfort, my dear, although I must say your cowboy has poor taste when it comes to his choice of accommodations for a lover's tryst." He leaned against an empty barrel that had once held nails. She realized he was slurring his words, and in the close confines of the cabin, she smelled liquor. "Please stand there by the fire where I can see you plainly and remove your clothing—slowly."

"Mr. Perkins, you—"

He smirked. "The other option is for me to undress you myself." He cocked an eyebrow and then chuckled. "You do have the most expressive features, my dear. I can already see that of the two options, you are going to choose the former."

Somehow, she found her courage. "And what if I choose neither? What if I—"

She started for the door, but he blocked her way, pressing the gun against her stomach. "You have crossed me once too often, Grace. For the next hour, you will do exactly as I say. After that, we will each be on our way and never speak of this again."

She had no doubt he believed this was realistic. The man was drunk—and quite possibly insane. He moved the muzzle of the gun to her cheek, pressing the cold metal hard against her bare skin. "I am not going to violate you, Grace," he whispered. "You have already betrayed me on that front, have you not? What young couple comes to a hideaway as reclusive as this to share a few innocent kisses?"

The man was so vile that Grace thought she might be physically ill. "If you shoot me, how will you explain my death? Someone will hear."

"No one will hear. Isn't that why your cowboy chose this spot? So the two of you could cry out in your passion without fear of being discovered?"

Had he spied on them? The idea that Jasper Perkins might have been lurking outside the narrow window of the cabin watching them… "Nick and I are married," she blurted. What did it matter if she lost her position now? Perhaps Miss Kaufmann would even understand that she'd been in a situation where her very life depended on revealing the truth.

"Married or not, Nick Hopkins has taken what I wanted—and what you agreed to give."

Grace stumbled back, desperate to get as far away from this devil as the close confines of the cabin would allow. "If I remove my clothes, then are we done?"

"Ah, time now for bargaining." He lowered the gun and placed it carefully on top of the nail keg with the barrel still pointed directly at her as she stood before the fireplace. "You would agree to that? To completely disrobing?"

"I might." She was bargaining all right—for time to think how she might raise an alarm and escape.

"There are three pieces to my plan for you today, my sweet. First, you will undress. Next, I will open my trousers, and you will kneel before me. And finally, you will pleasure me without my needing to sully myself by entering your defiled body. And once I am satisfied, you may leave. I am an honorable man, Grace, and I have given you my word. Those are my terms, and they are not up for discussion."

"But—"

The slap came seemingly from nowhere, and while she was still in a state of shock from the blow, he grabbed her hair and twisted it so that her face was less than an inch from his. "You are wasting my time, Grace. I suggest you get on with it."

She fought against giving him the satisfaction of her crying out. He was pulling so hard, it felt as if he intended to pull her hair from her scalp. She licked her lips and tasted blood. And seeing no other option, she nodded.

He shoved her back so hard that she had to grab onto the shelf above the fireplace to keep from falling into the fire itself. The heat was insufferable. He had built the fire with stacks of woods and kindling—a fire designed to roar for at least an hour or more before fading. But on the shelf, her fingers closed around something. It was the poker, a rusted and bent piece of metal Nick used to stir the embers.

Carefully, she eased her fingers away from the poker, praying it would not roll forward. She removed one glove and touched her lip, which was beginning to swell.

"You'll have to say you fell," Perkins said and then waved his hand at her. "The other glove, please, and then your coat."

Lily's coat.

She took it off and folded it carefully. "It belongs to a friend," she said. "I don't want to soil it."

He reached over, grabbed the coat from her, and tossed it aside. "Stop stalling, Grace. This is going to happen. And in the end, you will have learned a new technique for lovemaking, one that I assure you will thrill and delight your cowboy."

By the light of the fire, she could see that he was sweating profusely. His eyes were wild, his lips slick with drool. Never in her life had Grace seen anything more disgusting, and her disgust fueled her courage. She would survive this ordeal.

She opened the buttons of her shirtwaist slowly, watching him the entire time. "Jasper," she whispered, trying to make her tone sweet and seductive. She could see he was fighting not to come prematurely. But the bulge in his trousers suggested he was losing that battle.

"That's better," he whispered. "Let me hear you say my name."

"My skirt fastens in the back, and I can't seem…" Deliberately, she turned her back to him, placing her hands on the shelf as she looked over one shoulder at him. "Help?"

He stumbled forward, eager to rid her of the clothing. Her fingers closed around the poker. Perkins muttered to himself as he wrestled clumsily with the hooks that held her skirt closed. He was squatting behind her. "Turn to the light," he instructed.

She grasped the poker with both hands and spun away, striking out as she did. The weapon made a satisfying thud when it crashed into his back. She dropped the weapon and ran for the door, tripping on her unfastened skirt as she did.

With a growl, Perkins lunged for her, catching her by the ankle and dragging her back just as she managed to throw the door open. She screamed. The door slammed, and he hit her again. "You little whore," he muttered as he laid his full weight over her, pinning her with his lower body. He ripped open her shirtwaist and camisole and grasped her bare breasts, squeezing them until she cried out in pain.

He grinned. "That's right, Gracie, you holler. I promise you'll be yelling for pure pleasure in a minute." He pushed her skirt up and tore at her pantaloons, ripping them in his frenzy. When she fought back, he hit her again. Once he had her exposed, he stood and opened his trousers. "You have brought this on yourself, my dear."

Grace closed her eyes. She was going to be raped. Her head rested very near the fire where she'd landed when he dragged her back. She spotted a small piece of kindling. She tried to roll toward it. He kicked her.

"Lie still," he ordered.

When he knelt and then leaned close, ready to push into her, she no longer cared whether or not she suffered burns. She closed her hand around the charred and still burning stick and ground it into his face. When he screamed and leaped away, she tried to get up, but he was blocking her against the wall, so she shouted as loudly as she could.

"Help!" she yelled, hoping someone might be passing by and hear.

Blinded by pain, Perkins thrashed about and picked up the poker. He couldn't see clearly, and Grace scrambled away. He swung the poker wildly, upsetting the balance that held the logs in the fireplace. Embers scattered across the cabin floor, igniting stray pieces of paper and straw and finally the blanket Grace and Nick had left there. In no time at all, the cabin filled with smoke.

Nick, she thought desperately. What was the point now of all the time they had wasted? And all because she stubbornly refused to give up her work. Her family would have found a way through their hard times. Hadn't her mother told her to save her money and not send any more? What made her think she needed to be anyone's savior?

She heard Perkins choking on the smoke and staggering about as she curled herself into a ball, hoping to evade him. Just when she had given up hope, someone tried to lift her. Perkins! The smoke made breathing difficult and shouting for help impossible. He was going to win. She fought with what strength she could muster. But it was no use. The hands that lifted her were strong and determined. *Would this nightmare never end?*

Chapter 13

WHEN NICK ARRIVED AT THE HOTEL, HE HAD A PLAN. He would surprise Grace by simply walking into the dining room, knowing she would be there finishing her final chores. But it was Jake, not Grace, who glanced up and frowned at the sight of him.

"Nick, what are you doing here?"

"Well, I thought I was surprising Grace."

"But you sent that kid with the message for her to meet you."

"I didn't send any kid or message." Nick stared at Jake, alarm coursing through his veins. "Where's Grace?"

"She ran outta here maybe twenty minutes ago on her way to meet you at the usual place. That's what the kid said and what I told her. She was all excited and happy and—"

Nick was already headed for the kitchen. "Jake, get the sheriff and Aidan and meet me at that old abandoned cabin at the back of the property." Thankfully, Jake didn't ask questions, just nodded and started back through the kitchen to find Aidan. Nick was already running for the cabin when he heard shouts of "Fire!" and realized other people were also headed in the same direction.

He smelled the smoke before he saw the flames. Around him, there were calls for "Water!" and the general chaos of people rushing around, unsure of what to do. Pulling a bandana from his pocket, he covered his mouth and nose and ran inside the burning cabin. The place was full of thick, pungent smoke and smoldering debris, but he made out a figure standing near the fireplace—a man.

"Where's Grace?" Nick tried to ask, but his words clogged in his throat.

The man stood there, frozen, and when Nick reached for him, he saw that it was Jasper Perkins, holding the poker Nick had so often used to stir the fire when he and Grace were there. Dodging the swipe of the poker, he bent low and felt around for anything that would mean he'd found her, praying she had somehow made it outside and was too dazed to let anyone know. His hand closed on fabric, then a foot that kicked out at him.

Grace!

She lay huddled in a corner, shielding herself with her arms. When he tried to gather her to his chest, she fought him and continued to flail and struggle as he lifted her. Disoriented, he searched for the door—the only exit.

"Come on," he tried to say to Perkins, who was bent over the rough mantel of the fireplace, coughing as if his guts might actually come tumbling out.

A splash of water thrown through the doorway showed him the escape route. Grace had gone still, slumped against him, and he ran for the exit, emerging into the daylight just as one wall of the cabin collapsed, followed by a popping noise that sounded a lot like gunshots.

When the fresh air hit them, it seemed to revive Grace some, but she was still coughing and gasping for air. Her eyes were squeezed shut, and she flailed about, pointing back toward the cabin. "J…J…Jas…"

Nick was tempted to let the man burn in the hell of his own making, but he knew Grace would find a way to blame herself. He turned her over to the care of Aidan and Frank and ran back inside.

The banker was now lying near the hearth. He wasn't moving. Never in all his years had Nick wanted to kill a man more than he did this man right now. Holding his breath, he grabbed Perkins by his ankles and dragged him to the door and outside. As soon as Nick got him a safe distance from the danger of the fire, he let go and went to check on Grace.

That was when he realized that her clothes had been ripped and her lip was swollen and caked with soot and blood. Miss Kaufmann and Aidan were busy tending to her, pulling her clothing back into place, and wrapping her in Aidan's coat. She mumbled incoherently, her eyes darting around without seeing anyone. Nick clenched his fists and strode back to where he'd left Perkins.

"He's dead, Nick. He's been shot." Frank and the sheriff both glanced at Grace.

"She had nothin' to do with this, if that's what you're thinkin'," Nick said. "Whatever happened in that cabin today, Grace is the victim."

"Still have to investigate what happened, Nick," the sheriff said. "Doc Waters is on his way here now. Let's let him check her out, and then we can decide what comes next. Meantime, I need to go give Mrs. Perkins the news."

Nick watched him walk away. Cody Daniels was new in town. He'd taken over as sheriff after the man he'd succeeded was killed in a gunfight with train robbers. The West might be changing, but some things seemed like they never would.

"Nick?" Grace's voice was weak, and she barely managed to call to him before she started coughing. "Oh, Nick, I'm so sorry—" Her voice broke as she collapsed against Aidan.

"We need to get this young lady inside," the doctor said, addressing his comment to Aidan and Miss Kaufmann.

"I've got her," Nick said, stepping between the doctor and Aidan to lift Grace into his arms. She curled into him and rested her head on his shoulder. "The hotel?" he asked.

"My office," Doc Waters replied and led the way.

While the doctor examined Grace in a small room off his reception area, his wife brought tea for the three of them in the waiting room.

"Thank you, ma'am," Nick murmured, warming his hands on the cup without drinking any.

"I simply don't understand what Grace was doing there," Miss Kaufmann said. "How did she even know of that place? You don't think Mr. Perkins—"

"We all think that, Bonnie," Aidan said. "I don't

wish to speak ill of the dead, but in the case of Jasper Perkins, we've certainly all heard rumors."

It was the first time Nick had ever heard anyone refer to the head waitress by her given name. It softened her usually stern demeanor, and he realized she was close to tears.

"Perkins tricked her," he said. "She thought she was coming to meet me."

"You? In that place?" Bonnie Kaufmann pursed her lips with disapproval. "Really, Nick, I thought better of you."

He studied the burns beginning to blister on his hands. "We love each other," he said softly.

"Even so."

Nick was close to announcing that he and Grace were married and he would meet her anywhere he damned well pleased when the doctor emerged from the examining room.

"She inhaled a lot of smoke," he said, "so it will take some time for her lungs to clear. Once they do, I can better assess any permanent damage."

Nick was on his feet, his eyes riveted on Doc Waters. "You're saying she might not—"

"I'm saying nothing of the sort." He glanced at Aidan and Miss K. "However, it might be best to contact her family."

"I'm her family," Nick blurted.

The room went quiet, and everyone's attention was on him. There was no reason now to continue hiding the fact that he and Grace were married. She was going to need time to recover, and there was no chance she would be able to go back to work anytime soon. Her contract would run out, and now that the Lombards had—

"What do you mean you are Grace's family?" Miss K asked.

"Grace and I are married." He turned to the doctor. "So if you don't mind, I'd like to see my wife." He didn't wait for permission but opened the door to the examining room and closed it behind him.

She was lying on a cot, one soot-blackened arm covering her eyes. Outside, it was dark, but he walked to the window and pulled down the shade anyway before setting the single chair close to where she lay.

"Grace?" He pulled her arm away. Tenderly, he ran his fingers over the cut lip, the swollen cheek.

She clutched his hand. "He tried…he wanted to…"

"Shhh. It's over, Grace. He can't hurt you. I'll never let anyone hurt you again."

She started coughing and choking, so he helped her to a half-sitting position, grabbing whatever pillow or blanket was available to support her. On a table near the door, he spotted a pitcher of water and a glass. He filled the glass halfway and brought it to her. "Take it slow," he instructed, holding the glass to her lips.

"I'm so sorry," she whispered. "I was a fool. I should have…"

Nick was stunned. Grace was blaming herself for what that old man had tried to do—maybe had succeeded in doing.

Her eyes widened. "Will I be arrested, Nick?"

"For what?"

"I heard the sheriff say Jasper Perkins died of

a gunshot wound. He had a gun with him, but I never…I could never…"

Nick abandoned the chair to sit next to her on the cot, taking her in his arms as he rested his back against the wall. "We'll get it all sorted out." He wasn't entirely convinced of that though. The truth was, the sheriff seemed inclined to believe Grace had in fact shot Perkins. He might even go a step farther and accuse her of setting the fire deliberately to cover it up.

In a desperate attempt to turn her thoughts to other things, he said, "Did you know Miss Kaufmann's given name is Bonnie?"

She looked up at him and frowned. "Don't try to distract me, Nick. Am I in trouble or not?"

"Right now, the only thing you need to worry about is getting well."

She was quiet for a moment. "How on earth did you learn Miss K's first name?"

"Might have been something Aidan said—or maybe it was when they heard me tell Doc that you and I are married."

She stiffened and then slowly relaxed. "It had to come out some time, I suppose," she said. "So we've got more problems than the possibility I might go to jail? I'll have no pay, and we still have nowhere to live."

"Not really. Truth is that side of things is looking pretty good." He told her about his meeting with the Lombards. "That's why I came to town today—so we could celebrate."

"Some celebration," she whispered as she stroked his cheek. "But wonderful news for you," she added.

"For us," he corrected her.

There was a light tap on the door, and Doc opened it enough to look in on them. Nick stood as the doctor stepped fully into the room and left the door open so that Aidan and Miss K could look in as well. "Grace, your employers and I feel it might be best if we move you to the hotel where you can recuperate while this whole business…while things…"

"Thank you," Grace replied. She made a show of trying to sit up straighter and then realized her clothing was ripped and covered in soot. "Perhaps, Miss Kaufmann, if it isn't too much trouble, you could bring me some fresh clothing and let Emma and Lily know I'm fine. I'm sure they must have heard any number of terrible tales by now."

"Of course," Miss K said, and she seemed relieved to have some task to do. "I'll go straight away."

"And, Grace," Aidan said, "you are not to worry about your position. We can cover your shifts for now and—"

Nick knew the exact moment Aidan Campbell recalled that Nick and Grace were married, the moment he realized Grace could no longer be considered a Harvey Girl.

"I'll just…" He edged back from the doorway. "I'll see to a room for you in the hotel," he promised and left.

Doc busied himself putting away the supplies he'd used to treat Grace's wounds and examine her. "Sheriff Daniels will want to question you, Grace," he said as he worked. "But I'll make sure we put that off as long as possible."

"Thank you."

"As for you," the doctor said, turning his attention

on Nick, "your wife is going to need care. I understand that you just want to have her with you, but you need to consider what is best for her, and right now, that means keeping her in town where I can check in on her regularly. It looks like her friends at the hotel are willing to provide the care she'll need in the next week or so. I assume I can count on you not to interfere with that?"

Nick bristled. The doctor was a small man of about fifty who peered over the top of half-glasses with thick lenses. When they'd been standing next to each other in the reception area, Nick had towered over him. But now he was talking to Nick like a father to an errant son.

"I will do whatever is best for Grace," he replied stiffly.

Waters smiled. "Excellent. Then wait here until Miss Kaufmann returns. She can assist Grace in changing. In the meantime, I have a wheelchair for transporting her to the hotel."

"No need," Nick said. "I'll carry her."

When Doc seemed inclined to object, Nick moved a step closer to Grace.

"Very well, but I am warning you, young man, she needs rest. This is going to take some time."

"I understand," Nick replied.

Doc nodded and left the room.

Nick sat down again and held Grace. "I'd sing you a lullaby, but the hands at the ranch say I have no voice for singing."

"Hum then," she croaked, snuggling closer to him.

He chose a song he suddenly recalled his mother humming to herself as she went about her chores.

He'd forgotten the words, if he ever knew them. Grace's head grew heavy against him, and he knew she would soon be sleeping.

But when Bonnie Kaufmann came bustling in with a bundle of clothing and greetings from Emma and Lily, Grace roused herself.

"I'll be just outside the door," Nick promised as he left the room, closing the door behind him. In the reception area, the doctor was sitting at his desk, making notes. "What do I owe you?" Nick asked.

Doc looked up and actually removed the half-glasses as he studied Nick. "Save your money, Mr. Hopkins. Once your wife is settled, you'll have need of it to purchase these compounds I'm ordering from the pharmacy." He tore a paper from the pad and handed it to Nick. "I added a salve that will help heal those burns on your hands."

Nick scanned the script without understanding any of the words. "What are you going to tell the sheriff?" he asked.

"I first need to examine the body of the deceased." In addition to his role as the town's doctor, Tom Waters served as Juniper's coroner and funeral director. "But after speaking to your wife briefly, it is my opinion that whatever happened in that cabin this evening, none of it was her fault."

Nick felt the full force of the emotions of the last several hours settle into a hard lump in the middle of his throat. His legs threatened to fail him, so he grasped the back of a chair to steady himself. That's when he realized tears were plopping like raindrops after a long drought onto the front of his shirt.

Doc stood and led Nick to sit down in the chair. "She's young and strong, Nick. Your wife is going to be all right," he assured him. And then he said the same words Nick had used in trying to console Grace. "The important thing to remember is that her ordeal with Perkins is over."

Only Nick was pretty sure it wasn't.

Grace was vaguely aware of Miss K helping her undress, washing away soot and dirt, and putting her into the heavy flannel nightgown and robe. But when Miss K wadded the clothing she'd been wearing and seemed to be looking for a place she could dispose of it, Grace once again found her strength. "No. Bring it," she said. "Better yet, give it to the sheriff. Let him see what that horrid man tried to do to me." She choked on fresh sobs as the memories of her ordeal overwhelmed her.

"Calm yourself, Grace. I'll make sure the sheriff sees the clothing." Miss K placed a blanket around Grace's shoulders and then opened the connecting door. "Nick, she's ready."

When he lifted her and started for the hotel, for some reason she thought of that day they'd first met on the train—the way he had stored her suitcase in the overhead rack, lifting it as if it weighed next to nothing. How long ago that all seemed now.

Inside the hotel—through the front entrance as if she were a paying guest—Aidan directed Nick to a room on the first floor, close to the lobby. It was beautifully furnished with a double bed, a dresser, an upholstered chair, and a writing table. The walls were covered in weavings done by local native people. Nick laid her on the turned-down bed and pulled the covers over her. "What do you need?" he asked, stroking her hair back from her temple.

"You," she whispered. But her eyes were fluttering closed. She was so very tired. She fought, but sleep won the battle.

When she woke, the sun was just beginning to rise. Nick was asleep in the chair, his boots off and feet propped on the table. He needed a shave, and his shirt was spotted with soot. It occurred to her that in saving her and returning to bring out Perkins's body, he could have been seriously hurt. She pushed herself to a half-sitting position, trying to examine him for burns, but the movement sent a wave of dizziness and pain through her, and she collapsed back onto the pillows with a whimper.

Nick woke at once and looked around, getting his bearings. When his gaze settled on her, he stood and came to her. "Good morning, Wife," he said, leaning in to kiss her forehead. "What can I get you?"

"Just you," she repeated the answer she'd given the night before. Then she started to cough, the strangling sound reverberating throughout the room as Nick hurried to get water. The door opened, and Miss K brought her a foul-looking concoction in a glass.

"Good morning, Grace. Time for your medicine." She gave the liquid a final stir and handed Grace the glass. "Down the hatch," she instructed. "Come on. Drink it all down. Polly is preparing an orange juice chaser."

As if she'd heard her name, Polly entered the room, looking anywhere but at Grace. She carried a tray with a glass of fresh squeezed orange juice resting on a bed of ice. *The Harvey way*, Grace thought, nearly choking on the medicine. Nick stood by looking worried and helpless.

"Go get some breakfast, Nick," Grace managed to croak as she exchanged the medicine glass for the juice. "When's the last time you ate?"

Polly waited by the door. "Best listen to your wife," she murmured as they left the room.

Grace turned to Miss K. "Everyone knows?"

"It seemed the lesser of two evils. Rumors were bound to spread. Besides, everyone is very happy for you and Nick. Well, perhaps not Polly, but she'll come around in time. She's a good person, Grace." She sucked in her breath and added, "I must say I am disappointed that you felt you could not confide in me."

"You would have had to terminate my contract, and I needed to see it out."

"Yes." She paced the room as if there were more she wanted to say. "Did Mr. Perkins know about your marriage?"

"Not until I told him. I thought if he knew I was married and no longer...pure, then he would want nothing more to do with me, but he became so enraged. He called me such horrible names, and he—" She choked again, but this time, it was on the tears she thought might never stop sneaking up on her whenever she recalled the fear and panic she'd felt in that cabin.

She realized Miss K's eyes had also filled with tears.

"Oh, Grace, I only wish… This never should have happened. I feel I have failed you."

"Not at all. It was you and Emma and Lily who helped me through those times."

Miss K brightened and removed two envelopes from the pocket of her apron. "Speaking of Emma and Lily, they want to visit, of course, but until we can be quite sure their illnesses have passed, Dr. Waters says they must make do with notes."

Eagerly, Grace opened the first note. It was from Lily.

> You're married??? And here I had you pegged as far too innocent and shy to ever allow Nick Hopkins to persuade you to break the rules. Proud of you, girl! We must plan a proper party as soon as you are up to it.
>
> Love,
> Lily

Emma's note was more serious.

> Grace, we are here for you, whatever you may need—you and Nick. Lily and I are so happy for you both, but you must allow yourself to heal properly. We will visit soon. In the meantime, follow the doctor's orders and tell Nick to do the same.
>
> Your friend,
> Emma

Grace folded the notes and handed them back to Miss K, who placed them in the drawer of the bedside table. "Could you let them know I got their letters and I can't wait to see them?"

"Of course." Miss K fluffed the pillows and rearranged the covers. "Now you get some rest. The doctor will stop by later."

"And the sheriff?"

Miss K frowned. "No word on that, but Aidan—Mr. Campbell—will make sure you have plenty of warning." She patted Grace's shoulder, then gathered the medicine and juice glasses and walked to the door. "Grace, would you like me to contact your family?"

"No. I don't want to worry them. I'll write them once—" The tears started again.

Miss K bit her lower lip and left the room.

When Nick returned after having breakfast at the lunch counter, Grace insisted he go back to the ranch and get some rest. "I'll probably sleep much of the day," she said. "Besides, the doctor will check on me later." He still looked torn. "Go. We can't afford to both be out of work." She tried to make her tone light but failed.

"I'll be back this evening," he promised as he leaned in to kiss her. He skimmed his forefinger over the bruises and cut on her lip, and his expression changed from tenderness to a rage that scared her.

She clasped his forearm. "I am fine," she told him. "A few scrapes and such that will heal in a few days."

"You could have died, Grace. That man tried to—"

"That man is dead and can no longer cause harm to me or anyone else. You said yourself that it's over.

Please do not allow Jasper Perkins to haunt either of us from the grave."

He started to say something—no doubt to remind her of all the terror the banker had put her through—but then he lifted her hand to his lips and kissed it. "You're right," he said. "What can I bring you when I return? Mrs. Lombard will want to send something, I'm sure. How about some of Hattie's ginger cookies?"

Grace felt a new wave of emotion threaten to overcome her. She was not used to being cared for. On the farm, she was the one others had turned to when they needed something. "Ginger cookies sound nice," she managed. Then she squeezed his hand. "Now go, or you'll just get there before you need to turn around and return."

"Yes, ma'am. You know, if I'd thought you'd be this bossy, I might have thought twice about marrying you?" He smiled, and she realized it was the first time she'd seen him smile openly in a long time.

"Too late, cowboy. I'm all yours. Now go."

He was chuckling as he stepped into the hall and closed the door. Grace sighed with relief and pulled the covers to her chin.

She had no idea how long she slept. She was vaguely aware of people coming and going—the doctor, who advised letting her sleep, followed by Emma and Lily, who whispered to each other as they stood in the doorway, keeping their distance lest they pass on their illness to Grace.

"She looks peaceful," Lily said.

"She's not dead and lying in her coffin," Emma countered.

"I never said she was. I just meant—" And then Lily started to cry, and Emma comforted her as they left the room.

Later, someone pulled the drapes shut, casting the large room in the dimness of late afternoon. Grace tried to bring herself awake, but every movement sent a shot of pain through her body, and it seemed to take all her strength just to turn onto her side. She dreamed of her parents and the farm, and then it wasn't the farm but that cabin, and Jasper Perkins was there, leering at her, threatening to do unspeakable things to her, touching her—

With a cry, she sat up and looked around, trying to get her bearings. A man entered the room, but it wasn't anyone she knew. "Who are you?" she croaked.

Chapter 14

HE REMOVED HIS HAT AND APPROACHED THE BED. "I am Sheriff Cody Daniels, Miss Rogers. I was wondering if you felt up to answering a few questions?" He turned on the bedside lamp. "Mr. Campbell is just outside there if you'd prefer he be present."

"Yes, please."

When Aidan entered the room, Grace asked, "Is Nick back yet?"

"Not yet. Grace, if you're not feeling up to this…"

She let out a breath, which sent her into a coughing spasm and had both men reaching for the water at her bedside. She took a sip, cleared her throat, and pushed herself higher against the headboard, pulling the covers up to her chest. She focused her attention on the sheriff. "Let's get this over with," she said. "As you will see, it is not an incident I relish reliving."

The sheriff nodded and pulled a small pad of paper and pencil from his pocket. "Do you mind if I sit, Miss Rogers—or rather, I understand it is Mrs. Hopkins?"

"Please sit, and call me Grace."

The sheriff frowned. "I think we may need to

maintain a bit more formality, Mrs. Hopkins." He opened the notepad to a fresh sheet and wrote something at the top of the page. "All right, how did you come to be in that cabin with Mr. Perkins?"

Over the next hour as Sheriff Daniels questioned her, she told her story in as much detail as she could manage, going back as far as that first encounter at the Lombard party. Behind the sheriff, Aidan paced. From time to time, he would glance at her with alarm, especially when she told the part about fighting Perkins and burning him with the kindling. The sheriff remained stoic and expressionless throughout the interview. He asked questions and took notes, and he rarely looked directly at her.

"I think that's everything," she said after recalling Nick's arrival and rescue and how he went back for the banker.

Sheriff Daniels turned the page on his notepad. "Not quite. Let's talk about your upbringing—your past before coming to work at the hotel."

She bristled, suspecting he was looking for some scandal or behavior that might have led Perkins to believe she was encouraging him. "My parents are farmers. I am the eldest of six children. Just after I completed my schooling last spring, I saw the advertisement Mr. Harvey placed in our local paper, and I applied to become a Harvey Girl. I was accepted, went through a month of training in Kansas City, then boarded the train that brought me here. During the time I have been here, I worked first at the counter and later in the dining room. As Mr. Campbell will attest, we have little opportunity for…frivolity."

Aidan smiled.

"And yet you somehow found time to meet and marry Nick Hopkins." Sheriff Daniels looked directly at her for the first time since beginning the interview. "Had you and Mr. Perkins had any…interaction prior to your decision to step out with Mr. Hopkins?"

"That's enough," Nick growled. None of them had been aware of him standing just outside the door. He opened it fully and crossed the room to stand in front of the sheriff. "You've asked your questions, Cody. Now leave my wife to get some rest."

The sheriff stood. He turned to Grace. "Just one more question, ma'am." He consulted his notes. "You say that Mr. Perkins brought the weapon to the cabin?"

"That's right."

"Then how is it he's the one who ended up shot?"

"I have no idea, Sheriff Daniels." She met the law-man's gaze directly as Nick took a step closer. "What I know is that when the fire raged out of control, we were both there, and neither of us had the gun. I could hear Mr. Perkins coughing as he tried to escape the fire—with, I might add, apparently no thought of me. For my part, I was struggling to come to terms with the fact that the fire that had saved me might well kill me in the end."

No one spoke for a moment, and then the sheriff tucked his pad and pencil back into his pocket and put on his hat. "Be that as it may, Mrs. Hopkins, the fact remains. There were only two people in that cabin with that gun, and now one of them is dead."

Nick felt Aidan grip his arm, restraining him from punching the lawman as he stepped past them and left the room.

"That man thinks I killed Jasper Perkins in cold blood," Grace said.

"He's just doing his job," Aidan said in a tone intended to defuse Nick's rage and soothe Grace's fears.

"I'll soon set him straight," Nick muttered as he headed for the door.

"Nick, no," Grace called and then began coughing so hard, Nick hurried back to the bedside, his arm around her as he held out his hand for the water glass Aidan was refilling.

Nick thought back through every detail of the seconds he'd spent inside the cabin—both rescuing Grace and then returning to drag Perkins out. He tried to remember if there had been a gun anywhere near either of them. Maybe Perkins had shot himself, knowing his behavior would be exposed. But that made no sense. Although no one had openly admitted it, there were rumors all over town that Grace was not the first girl he'd pursued. It made Nick wonder if there were other women—perhaps even still living in Juniper—who'd been victims of the banker's vile obsessions. Of course, even with him dead, it would still be a Missouri woman's word against a respected leader of the community. Mrs. Perkins would garner sympathy, having just buried her husband. Nick was pretty sure even if there were others in town who knew what Grace had faced, they would not come forward. Why should they?

He sat with Grace while she ate a little of the soup

Jake had brought her. When she pushed the bowl away and said she simply wasn't hungry, Nick didn't argue. "You don't mind if I get something to eat while you rest?"

"Of course." She stroked his cheek. "You go. All I seem capable of right now is sleeping."

He helped her settle on the pillows, kissed her, and smoothed her hair away from her face. Her eyes fluttered closed. "I'll be back," he promised, but she was already asleep.

He left the hotel and headed straight for the ruins of the cabin. Although it was after sunset, there was still enough light from the hotel and a full moon to make out details. In his mind, he reconstructed the space. The hearth of the fireplace still stood, so that gave him perspective on distance. There'd been a window there, beneath which he'd found Grace. He closed his eyes and mentally retraced his steps. He'd entered the cabin, protecting his mouth and nose with his bandana, searching for Grace. He'd seen a figure he now realized was Perkins standing by the fireplace. He'd found Grace, picked her up, and run, all while Perkins was on his feet.

And *that* was when he'd heard the shots. Grace was already outside, gasping for breath, nearly unconscious. He was sure of it. She could not have shot Perkins. Others would remember as well. His heart swelled with hope as he ran back past the hotel and across the plaza until he reached the sheriff's office. "She didn't shoot Perkins," he blurted as he threw open the door.

Cody Daniels got to his feet. "Sit down, Nick."

Nick refused the request. Instead, he leaned his

hands on the small wooden table that served as the sheriff's desk and laid out his proof. "She could not have shot him. She was already outside the cabin when the shots went off. The heat of the fire…"

"No doubt, and yet it seems convenient that a shot set off by the fire could find its mark directly in Mr. Perkins's chest."

Nick felt his forearms go weak, and he slumped back into the chair the sheriff had offered. "She did not shoot him," he said.

"Look, Nick, I believe you—and your wife. However, at the moment, we need proof. Mrs. Perkins is insisting on a full investigation. She claims your wife made advances toward her husband one evening when they had invited three of the Harvey Girls to their home. She gives quite a convincing account of how her husband went to the kitchen sometime after dinner to prepare coffee for the guests and your wife insisted on helping, leaving her to entertain the other two women."

"She lied. He was the one who tried to—"

"Nevertheless, Mrs. Perkins reports that once you and your friends showed up, your wife returned from the kitchen in a state of some disarray—her hair mussed and clothing askew."

"That's not true. I saw it all."

Cody raised an eyebrow. "How?"

Nick gave him the details—how he, Jake, and Aidan had gone there to see the girls back to the hotel, how he had not seen Grace sitting with Mrs. Perkins and Emma and Lily and suspected something amiss, and how he had gone around to the back of the house and through the window observed Perkins pressing Grace against the sink, trying to kiss her.

"And your friends also observed this?"

"No, they stayed in front."

Cody sighed and leaned back in his chair. "You understand that because you are married to Grace, your testimony raises questions?"

"But it's what happened."

"And Mrs. Perkins claims her husband told a different version of the incident. Who do you think a jury will believe? A grieving widow or a man trying to save his wife from going to prison?"

Jury? Prison?

"You're going to arrest Grace?"

Cody Daniels sighed. "I can hold off for a while, but the circuit judge will be here at the end of the month. Unless we can find a way to get this business cleared up and get everyone—including Mrs. Perkins—to agree that her husband's death was a terrible accident, I may have no choice."

It dawned on Nick that Cody was not their enemy. For what it was worth, he seemed to believe Grace's version of things. "What evidence would you need to make that happen?"

The sheriff gave him a wry smile. "The evidence we need has been lost in the fire. We got the gun, but all the bullets had been fired. We know one is lodged in Jasper Perkins's chest, but—"

"The shots went off as I was bringing Grace out from the cabin," he insisted. "He was standing when I got Grace and on the ground when I went back in."

"Meaning?"

"If he was standing, trying to find his way out, and the gun went off, wildly firing shots in the small space…"

Cody looked up at the tin ceiling of the office. "I suppose it helps give credence to the idea that he was shot accidentally. But it still doesn't prove he hadn't already been shot once before you and others spotted the fire and showed up." He looked over at Nick. "I don't want to arrest your wife, Nick, but the facts point to the possibility that she did it."

"Look, Cody, I appreciate everything you're trying to do for Grace. You're in a tough spot, but I'd be mighty grateful if you could just see your way clear to leaving her be until she's had a chance to regain her strength."

The sheriff nodded. "Not likely she's gonna go around shooting up the town. Truth is, from rumors circulating about Perkins, she'd have a good case for self-defense even if she did pull the trigger."

"Which she didn't," Nick said, wanting to make sure the sheriff wasn't talking himself into believing Grace had killed Perkins.

Cody stood and extended his hand. "You have my word, Nick, that unless somebody goes over my head, your wife will be free at least until the circuit judge shows up. If this entire business hasn't been sorted out by then, Judge Evans will hold a hearing and decide whether or not to bind your wife over for trial."

The two men shook hands. Nick realized Cody was almost as exhausted as he was. "I'd best get back," Nick said. "Doc Waters is supposed to stop by to check on Grace."

Cody walked him to the door. "Hope everything turns out for you, Nick."

When he got back to the hotel, anxious to reassure Grace that Sheriff Daniels seemed to be on their side, Doc Waters was in with her, and Miss Kaufmann was standing guard outside the door.

"Get something to eat, Nick," she replied when he argued that he was, after all, Grace's husband. "She'll still be here after. And a word of advice, young man. Grace broke her contract, and I'm not sure how that will play with management back in Kansas City. I'm holding off doing anything until we know she'll fully recover, but do not push me."

"Yes, ma'am." Nick gave her a sheepish smile and crossed the lobby to the dining room.

With Emma and Lily ill, Polly was his waitress, and that night, she seemed unusually distracted. "Sounds like Grace will be all right, Nick. We're all praying for her," she said after she'd taken his order and set his cup upright for the drink girl to fill with coffee.

"Thanks. Doc's with her now."

Polly hesitated. "So it's true? You two are really married?"

"Yeah. Things are pretty rocky for Grace right now—her health, of course, but she also really wanted to finish her contract."

"She'll be all right. You both will," Polly said. "Girls like Grace always land on their feet." She went off to fill his order, and her remark nagged at him until the time she returned.

"Grace has been through a terrible ordeal, Polly. Perkins… There was nothing she could do. As a man, I can't imagine what that must have felt like."

"Surely he didn't… I mean, she wasn't…" She

stumbled over words and finally gave up, but Nick knew what she was asking. Her hand shook as she set the plate of meatloaf, mashed potatoes, and green beans in front of him.

"You're right, Polly. She'll get past this. We'll find a way together."

Polly regained her composure and gave him her bright Harvey Girl smile. "Of course you will. She's got you by her side, so how could she not? Enjoy your dinner, Nick. I think there's one more piece of lemon meringue pie left. I'll go set it aside for you." And with that, she was gone.

As he ate, Nick kept running over the conversation with Polly. Something was off about the way she'd kept the conversation going—the way she didn't seem satisfied, as most people might be, to learn that Grace was recovering and in good hands. Most folks knew only that Grace had been caught in the fire and was suffering from the smoke. If they'd heard Perkins was there as well, they'd apparently assumed he'd been the one to discover the fire and had tried to save Grace. But Polly had specifically mentioned the banker's name—and she had done so in the context of worrying he might have harmed Grace.

He thought about the waitress, recalling she had worked at the hotel for some time now. And instead of taking a position in the dining room—the goal of most Harvey Girls—she had stayed at the counter. Perkins rarely ate at the counter. Nick might be grasping at straws, but something told him Polly Forrester might know something about Jasper Perkins that could help clear Grace's good name.

He gobbled down his food and waited for Polly to bring the slice of pie, but it was another girl who delivered his dessert and refilled his coffee. "Everybody just loves Grace," she told him. "We all hope she'll be back on her feet soon."

Nick thanked her, ate his pie, and lingered over his coffee. He wanted to get Polly to agree to meet him so they could talk in private, but the waitress never returned to the dining room. All thoughts of Polly evaporated when Doc Waters pulled out the chair opposite him, signaled the drink girl for coffee, and sat down.

"How is she?" Nick asked.

"She's improving. You're gonna need to be patient, Nick. These things take time."

Once his coffee was served, Doc took his time adding cream and sugar. It seemed to Nick that there was something the older man wanted to say but was having some trouble spitting out. "What else?"

"I assume there is every possibility that Grace could be with child?"

Nick's mind shot immediately to their wedding night six weeks earlier—the night he'd had every intention of preventing her from getting pregnant. The night he'd gotten so caught up in their shared passion that he'd failed to protect her. Since then, he'd made sure they were safe, and as the weeks passed with no sign, he'd been relieved.

"There's one," he admitted.

"That's all it takes," Doc muttered as he blew on his coffee before taking a swallow.

"Wait a minute—how do you know? Did Grace say something?"

"Given Grace's account of what happened with Perkins, I felt it prudent to examine her quite thoroughly." He waited a beat to make sure Nick understood the full extent of such an examination. "There were signs. I asked her a few questions about her appetite in recent weeks and how she'd been feeling in general, and her answers tended to confirm my suspicions." He drank the rest of his coffee. "Congratulations, Nick. I'd say by late summer, you and Grace will be welcoming your first child." He stood, laid some coins on the table, and picked up his black bag. "I'll stop by tomorrow. Have a good evening, Nick."

"Does Grace know? I mean about the baby?"

"I didn't say anything, but I've never met a woman yet who couldn't figure things out on her own."

Miss K stayed after the doctor left, telling Grace that Nick was having his supper and would be in to say good night before heading back to the ranch. She fussed with the pillows and rearranged the items on the side table that Doc had pushed aside to make room for his bag.

"Thank you, Miss Kaufmann," Grace said softly. "You've been so kind. Everyone has."

"And why wouldn't we?"

"Well, I sort of violated the whole Harvey code, didn't I?"

"We're not going to dump you in the street." The older woman paused in her task of refolding a stack of towels and looked at Grace. "I do wish you hadn't broken your word, but I can see that you and Nick Hopkins are very fond of each other. I may be an old spinster, Grace, but my heart still warms to the sight of two young people in love."

"I do love him," Grace said softly.

"And it's quite evident that young man is over the moon for you."

"It all came upon us so suddenly. One day, we were strangers on a train, and then we began spending time together…one thing led to another—"

Miss K held up both hands as if trying to stop a runaway wagon. "That is more than I need to know, Grace. The question is where will the two of you go from here?"

Grace had thought of little else. "Will I need to find a way to pay back the wages I received before—"

"Heavens no, child. That money was fairly earned. You worked hard. You are…*were* one of our very best girls."

"That's very kind of you to say."

Miss Kaufmann snorted. "I speak truth only, Grace. You know that." She glanced around the room and, finding nothing more that needed her attention, opened the door to the hall. "I'll go see what's keeping that husband of yours. Sleep well, Grace."

"Good night, Miss Kaufmann."

She had her hand on the doorknob but hesitated. "Grace, it occurs to me that in light of our new relationship, could you call me by my given name? It's Bonnie."

"I'd like that. Thank you, Bonnie."

After the door closed, Grace heard voices in the hall, and then the door opened again. Nick stood there a minute staring at her as if she had somehow changed in some marked way.

"What's the matter, Nick?"

He closed the door and then pulled the chair close to the bed. "Had a talk with Doc Waters. He says you're coming along."

"I do feel better," she said.

"He also thinks we're going to have a baby sometime this coming summer."

So that's why the doctor had kept asking questions about her appetite and how she'd been feeling before this whole business with the fire and Jasper Perkins happened. The truth was, Grace had briefly entertained the idea that she might be pregnant when she realized how tired she had been getting and how short-tempered. But she had dismissed the idea as unlikely. After all, they had been so careful—so frustratingly careful.

"Oh, Nick, I never meant...I mean, maybe Doc is wrong."

"Do you want him to be wrong?"

"Do you?"

He sat on the bed next to her, taking her in his arms. "No, Mrs. Hopkins. I can't think of anything more wonderful than you being the mother of my son."

"Or daughter," she reminded him, but she was laughing with relief.

"We're going to be just fine, Grace, all three of us." He told her about his talk with Cody Daniels and how the sheriff seemed to be on their side.

"But Mrs. Perkins—" Grace protested.

"She's in shock and grieving. My guess is she's known about her husband's activities but chosen to ignore them. Besides, I've got a plan. Not fully developed yet, but I don't want you worrying, all right?"

Other than her father, there had never been a man Grace trusted—or loved—as she did Nick. She relaxed against him. "Can you stay until I fall asleep?" she asked.

"Depends," he said. "How long we talking?"

"Maybe five or ten minutes," she admitted.

He chuckled and settled himself more fully on the bed next to her. "Take your time," he said as he kissed her temple.

Chapter 15

THE FOLLOWING DAY, GRACE WAS SITTING UP IN BED, feeling better for the first time since the fire, when she heard a light knock at the door. "Yes, come in," she called.

Bonnie Kaufmann entered, looking quite distressed. She was holding a telegram and looking anywhere but directly at Grace.

"Bonnie, is everything all right?"

"I'm afraid I have some bad news for you, Grace."

Her heart filled her chest, making breathing even more difficult than it had been with all the smoke. "More bad news?" She tried a smile but could see this was no time for lightness.

"Mr. Campbell received this wire a few minutes ago."

Grace focused on the thin, crumpled paper clutched in Bonnie's hand. This was it, then. Perkins's wife had set things in motion that would destroy any chance she might ever have for happiness.

Bonnie sat on the edge of the bed and placed her hand on Grace's forearm. "There is no easy way to deliver such terrible news, Grace, so I shall simply say it. According to this message, your father is quite ill." She smoothed out the telegram and handed it to her. "There are no details, but of course you'll want to leave for home as soon as Doc Waters gives you clearance. Mr. Campbell can make arrangements for a ticket on the ten o'clock train the day after tomorrow, as long as the doctor says you're well enough to travel. Emma and Lily can pack for you. There's no need to take everything. I mean, you and Nick are married. Surely you'll come back. New Mexico is his home—your home now."

Grace fixed her gaze on the typed words on the paper, words that made no sense and gave her no answers. Her father ill? Impossible. He was the strongest man she'd ever known, except for Nick. "I have no money," she said, realizing that now that she had violated her contract, she could no longer ride the train for free. She had counted on her January wages and had spent what little she hadn't sent to her mother on Christmas presents. Not only that, but she still owed Mr. Tucker for the balance on Nick's pocketknife.

"There'll be no charge for the trip, Grace," Bonnie assured her. "I discussed the matter with Aidan, and we are agreed. You've suffered quite enough already, and now this."

"Thank you, Bonnie." Grace scooted to the edge of the bed and swung her legs over the side. "I need to get up and walk a bit if I'm to be in any condition to travel. My strength—"

"Wait for Nick. He can walk with you, and if you feel dizzy or weak, he can get you safely back to bed."

"Would you send for him, please? He needs to know about my father."

"Of course. Don't worry, Grace." Bonnie left the room, closing the door softly behind her.

Once Grace was sure Bonnie was gone, she pushed herself to her feet, grasping the bedpost for support. A wave of dizziness rolled through her, but she waited, and it passed. She took one step toward the window and then another. From outside, she could hear the whistle. That would be the four o'clock train pulling into the station. The passengers would head straight for the hotel, where Lily, Emma, and the others would already be at their stations, ready to serve. Grace closed her eyes, imagining the scene—all in readiness in the dining room and kitchen. She was going to miss this. And even though she and Nick would settle in the area and perhaps occasionally come to the hotel for lunch or dinner, it would not be the same.

She realized she was still holding the telegram. She sat in a chair positioned near the window and read the message again.

NEED TO RETURN HOME STOP FATHER VERY ILL STOP COME SOON STOP

The message was addressed to her, in care of the manager at the Palace Hotel, Juniper, New Mexico. It had been sent by Bill Ferris, their neighbor and her father's closest friend. She scanned the message again as if a deeper explanation might magically appear. But there was no denying the urgency underlying the few words that were there.

She gazed out the window at the train waiting for the passengers to return from their meal. Closing her eyes, she calculated the length of the journey. If she took that late-afternoon train and traveled overnight, she could be home late the following day, assuming she could make the change of trains in Kansas City. Bill Ferris would be waiting to take her to the farm if she let him know the schedule. Of course, it was winter, and the snows would be deep, the roads possibly impassable in places, but Bill could bring a wagon with runners and travel cross country, cutting the distance.

She opened her eyes and briefly wondered if there were any possibility she could be on this train, tonight. But there were too many obstacles. For one thing, she was only wearing a nightgown, and her ruined clothes had been taken to Sheriff Daniels as "evidence." Fresh clothes were all the way up on the third floor, and although she had made the distance from the bed to the chair by the window without incident, climbing two flights of stairs might be more than she could manage.

Lily and Emma were on duty and would not be done for hours yet. Nick was at the ranch. She may as well face facts. She was not going anywhere tonight. But tomorrow…

It had been a while since Nick had pulled night watch, but with everything going on in town with Grace, the other cowboys had been spread thin covering for him. So that night, he'd told Smokey to get some sleep and relieve him come dawn. The truth was, he liked the solitude of being out with the herd, alone, in the darkness. He rode slowly over the grazing pasture, staying close to the fencing with an eye out for any signs of the rustlers at work. Across the vast span that was Lombard land, he knew Slim was doing the same thing. The difference was that Slim hated night duty. The least little thing could spook him. Nick smiled, recalling the night the other cowboys had dressed up Smokey in a sheet and pretended he was a ghost, riding hell-bent for leather across the mesa that bordered one side of the land. Slim had never entirely forgiven his friends for that. John Lombard had reprimanded the men, reminding them they could have spooked the herd as well as Slim, but Nick recalled the hint of a smile on the older man's face as he returned to the ranch house. And a few minutes later, Nick had heard Rita Lombard laughing uncontrollably.

Now, in the dark of night, Nick let his thoughts turn to Grace. He looked forward to the days when he would be the one coming home to her to share tales of the workday. He imagined her meeting him as he rode into the yard after a day on the range. She'd be holding their baby, and he'd slide from his horse's back and embrace the two of them. She would tease him about needing a bath and a shave. He would take the baby from her and wrap his arm around her shoulder as together, they went inside the foreman's cabin they had turned into a real home. The very thought of that scene gave him such a sense of peace. But the truth was, they were a long way from playing out that particular tableau.

She was going to be all right according to Doc Waters, but Cody Daniels had not been as reassuring. There had to be some way to persuade Perkins's widow not to pursue charges against Grace. In his gut, he had a feeling that Polly Forrester knew something she wasn't telling—and his gut was rarely wrong. Maybe he could get her to open up. Unless she wasn't in the mood to forgive him for marrying Grace. She'd clearly thought one day she might be the one to become Mrs. Nick Hopkins, although he'd never given her any reason to come to that conclusion.

As the sky in the east lightened to a pale gray, streaks of pink promising another clear day, Nick saw Smokey riding his way. He knew Smokey was coming to relieve him, but there was something about the jagged way he was riding that gave Nick pause. Something had happened. He spurred Sage and took off to meet the cowboy.

"What's up?" he shouted when he thought they were near enough for Smokey to hear.

"You got a message." Smokey reined in his horse and dug a paper out of his pocket. "That young kid from the hotel brought it. Grace—"

Nick snatched the paper from the cowboy's hand.

> *Nick,*
> *Grace's father has taken ill. She needs to return to her family as soon as possible. She seems determined to leave today or tomorrow at latest. Thought you'd want to come talk sense to her.*
>
> *Aidan*

"Is Grace worse?" Smokey asked.

"No. It's her pa back in Missouri. I need to get to town."

"I got this," Smokey said, and Nick took off.

At the ranch, he stopped long enough to let the Lombards know what was happening.

"Go," Rita urged him. "We're not so short-handed we can't manage for a while. Grace and her family are your main concern. Stay as long as necessary."

He did not stop to wash up, shave, or grab a clean shirt. As he rode cross-country, taking the most direct route to town, he planned what he would say to stop Grace from risking her own health—and their baby's—in her zeal to get back to Missouri. He couldn't go with her. Once there, it could take weeks for her to sort things out, and as generous as the Lombards were, he could not expect them to simply leave his absence open-ended, not with spring coming. Spring was the busiest time for ranchers—branding, calving, moving the herd to higher, cooler ground for the summer, and hiring cowhands to help do all that.

By the time he reached the edge of town, the sun was almost fully up. He headed straight for the hotel, tied Sage to a hitching post, and entered the lobby. Aidan was at the front desk again. Did the man ever sleep?

"Aidan!"

The hotel manager looked up and seemed to release a breath of relief. "Thank goodness. She simply will not listen to reason." He and Nick walked down the hall to the room Grace had occupied since the fire. "Doc says she can travel, but—"

Nick opened the door and froze.

Grace was leaning over the side of the bed, retching into a basin Emma held, while Lily knelt behind her, holding back her hair.

"Morning sickness," Lily explained. "Perfectly

normal at this stage of things, according to Doc. Good reason to reconsider the whole having kids idea, if you ask me."

Blindly, Grace reached for a towel lying on the bed beside her. She wiped her mouth as she sat up. "Sorry," she murmured, her voice raspy and raw.

Emma set the basin aside and handed Grace a glass half filled with water. "Small sips," she instructed.

Nick had no idea what to do. Emma and Lily seemed to have everything under control, and there certainly was no room for him on the bed or even sitting next to Grace. Nevertheless, this was his wife, his baby causing all the fuss. He tossed his hat on the bureau near the door and crossed the room. "Grace?"

She looked up at him and smiled. "Don't look so alarmed, Nick. Lily's right. It's all part of the process."

Well, he sure didn't have to like it, and seeing her like this did more to reinforce his determination to keep her from traveling than anything else could.

"You heard?" She allowed Emma and Lily to ease her back onto the pillows and reached out her hand to him.

Nick nodded as he sat on the side of the bed and brushed her sweat-damp hair away from her forehead. "I'm sorry, Grace. Has there been any more news? I mean maybe—"

"I have to go, Nick. My family relies on me, and with my father—" Her voice caught, and Nick swallowed his protest that he was her family now.

"We'll see," he said. It was a promise that could go either way.

She saw right through him. "I'm going," she said firmly. "Doc says if I take it easy—"

"And how are you going to do that? Traveling alone? With luggage?" He spotted the sick basin and pointed. "Morning sickness? Emma and Lily won't be there."

"I'll manage. I'm not helpless, you know." She sounded annoyed and exhausted. "I am getting on that train tomorrow."

"I'm afraid I can't allow that," a male voice announced from the doorway.

Everyone in the room looked up and saw Sheriff Daniels. "Grace Hopkins," he said, stepping fully into the room, "I am placing you under house arrest."

Grace felt the urge to laugh and knew it was not humor but hysteria driving the feeling. Wasn't it impossible for so much trauma to befall a single person in such a short time? She bit her lip and gripped Nick's hand. Her hold was partially to steady her nerves but more to keep him from attacking the sheriff. His body tightened beneath her touch, and she saw his eyes harden. "Nick, no. He's just doing his job," she said just as Lily crossed the room and stood toe-to-toe with the sheriff.

"Have you any idea what this poor woman has been through already? Any idea what she's facing now? How dare you!"

"And you are?" Cody asked with a frown as if trying to place her.

"Lily Travis."

"I mean who are you in relation to Mrs. Hopkins?" He glanced from Lily to Emma, including both in his query.

Emma stepped forward. "I am Emma Elliott, and this is Lily Travis. We are Grace's friends." Grace watched as Emma offered a handshake to the sheriff as if this were a social occasion and they were being formally introduced. *Dear Emma*, she thought.

"Like sisters, we are," Lily added, folding her arms firmly across her chest. Clearly, she had no intention of offering a handshake.

"What's changed?" Nick directed his question to Cody.

The sheriff stepped around Emma and Lily to address Nick and Grace directly. "Mrs. Perkins went over my head. She contacted a friend of her late husband who serves in the state legislature. One thing led to another, and this morning, I received word that Mrs. Hopkins was to be formally arrested. I was able to explain that Mrs. Hopkins was still recovering from injuries suffered in the fire—"

"And at the hand of that monster," Lily added.

"At the moment, that's still unproven, miss," the sheriff replied.

Nick was on his feet at once, and there was no way Grace could have stopped him. "Are you telling me we have to prove she didn't give herself this split lip and black eye? That she ripped her own clothes?"

"It's the law, Nick," Cody said softly, almost apologetically. "The circuit judge will determine whether or not she's to be bound over for trial, in which case she'll be transferred to Santa Fe, and it will be out of my hands."

"Thank you, Sheriff," Grace said. "I know you're doing your best to try and keep me out of jail.

However, I do need to go to Missouri. I promise I'll be back in time for a trial if that's what needs to happen, but my father—"

"Mrs. Hopkins, there is only so much I can do for you. Allowing you to leave town is not one of those things. I am genuinely sorry."

"I'll go," Nick said, turning back to her. "I'll take the afternoon train."

"But you don't even know my family, and they don't know we're married and especially about the baby."

Nick smiled and cupped her cheek with the palm of his hand. "Then I'll hopefully be bringing news with me that might make things there seem a little brighter. Grace, let me do this. Let me go there and find out what's going on while you stay here and regain your strength."

"But your job, the ranch… You told me this is coming onto the busiest time, and with your new responsibilities—"

"The Lombards understand."

"And if they can't afford to be without you?"

Nick shrugged. "Then they will find another way. Come on, Grace. It's not the best solution, but it gets us closer to one."

She glanced around the room and saw by their expressions that Emma, Lily, and Aidan all agreed with Nick's plan. She was outnumbered. "Help me over to the chair there and bring me some stationery and a pen," she said. "At least I can send you there with a letter of introduction."

Nick looked to Aidan, who went off to get the paper and pen. Emma pulled the chair closer to the table. Grace pushed back the covers and reached for her robe, but when Nick seemed prepared to carry her to the chair, she shook her head. "I can walk." With Nick at her side, she made her way to the chair and sat down.

Aidan returned and placed the writing materials on the table. "Anything else, Grace?"

"No, thank you." She looked at each person. "Perhaps if I could have some time? I need to compose my thoughts."

Emma, Lily, and Aidan followed Sheriff Daniels from the room. Emma closed the door behind them. Grace looked at Nick.

"I'm staying," he said, taking the straight chair from next to the bed and setting it down across from her.

"Good," she said softly and began to write the letter that she hoped would explain everything.

Almost before the train pulled out of the station, Nick had leaned his head against the window and fallen asleep. He'd been up all night watching over the herd, and the day had been filled with a whole bunch of upsetting news followed by hurried arrangements for the trip. He'd had to get word to the Lombards and stop by the mercantile for a new shirt, which he'd only put on once he'd washed up and gotten a haircut and shave, at Grace's insistence.

"I can't have my folks thinking I married some bum," she said. "It would only go to prove their worst fears when I took this job."

After getting Aidan's promise to wire him immediately should anything change concerning Grace's
physical or legal condition, Nick stopped by her room
to get the letter he would carry to her parents—and a
kiss passionate enough to sustain him on the journey.

"I'll be back by the end of the week," he promised.

Her eyes filled with tears. "Tell Papa that…"

"Tell him yourself. We'll go back for a proper visit
once this is all finished," he told her.

Emma and Lily had promised to make sure she
didn't overdo things, and Aidan assured him that Grace
could stay right where she was as long as necessary.

Because Nick was traveling on his own nickel, he
did not ride first class. Instead, he spent the night sitting up and was stiff and sore when the train stopped
for breakfast early the next morning. He followed the
other passengers to the eating house where he drank
three cups of black coffee and downed eggs, bacon,
and fried potatoes along with four biscuits that he
smothered in butter and honey—all served to him
by a Harvey Girl whose smile only reminded him of
Grace. Back on board, he stared out the window as the
train continued on to Kansas City. The farther north
they traveled, the more the scenery changed. Having
been raised in the desert, only traveling this route for
business in late summer or early fall, Nick found the
change mesmerizing. So many trees—whole forests of
them—with black leafless branches stretching above
rows of evergreens like arms reaching up to heaven.
Frozen creeks followed along the railway tracks,
winding through snow, seemingly mountains of the
stuff. The cold seeped through the train window, and

he heard the whistle of the wind. The train passed through a bunch of small towns where people hurried along, their bodies bent against the chill, their faces covered with heavy woolen scarves.

Finally, late that afternoon, they arrived at Union Station in Kansas City. It was snowing when he stepped off the train, intent on finding the connection he would take to Galax, Missouri, the town nearest the Rogerses' farm. There, he would rent a horse and rig and head for Grace's parents' home. He patted his chest, checking for the fat envelope with Grace's letter that he'd put in his inside pocket.

"Nick Hopkins?"

For a minute, Nick thought someone he'd met in his business dealings in Kansas City had recognized him. He turned with a smile, prepared to greet the man and then explain he had to move on. But the man standing behind him was a stranger.

"Are you Nick Hopkins?" The man was wearing a battered and misshapen felt hat and a heavy coat with a frayed collar.

"I am," Nick replied cautiously.

"Bill Ferris," the man said with a huff of relief and a grin. The name was familiar at least—Grace had described him as her family's neighbor. "Figured that might be you. Grace sent word, describing you as tall and wearing a black hat and fancy stitching on your boots. You got any luggage?" He glanced around.

"No. Not planning on staying long. Just came to check on Grace's folks. She's a little under the weather."

Bill nodded and started walking toward the exit.

"Got a sled wagon waiting. If we get going, we can make it to the farm later tonight."

Nick followed the farmer out the door.

"How's Mr. Rogers doing?" he asked once they were on their way. He had to shout to be heard over the wind.

"It's his chest. Took sick with the pneumonia not long before Christmas and just never seemed able to get past it. Weak as a newborn calf, he is." Bill shook his head and concentrated on driving the wagon.

Further conversation seemed like too much effort, so Nick hunkered down and let Bill handle the team. When they finally passed through the town of Galax, Nick saw that it was really more of a village. There was a store, a livery stable, a Wells Fargo office, and not much else. After that, they traveled past fields lying fallow, dried cornstalks poking through the snow as the night surrounded them. Once Bill turned onto a narrow, rutted lane, Nick saw a small house, smoke rising from the chimney. There was a barn and a chicken coop. "Whoa," Bill shouted as he pulled hard on the reins.

Nick saw a white lace curtain move, and a moment later, an older woman stepped outside, clutching a shawl tight around her shoulders. She focused her attention on Nick, so he jumped down from the wagon and crossed the yard. "Mrs. Rogers? I'm Nick Hopkins—Grace's husband." A strong north wind made it necessary to shout, but Nick tried to soften that with a smile.

Grace's mother eyed him with skepticism. "So you say."

Nick was aware he was being observed from several

locations. A girl of about thirteen was peering out from the doorway to the small farmhouse. An older boy stood at the entrance to the barn, and two more children, a boy and a girl, stood just behind their sister. He stepped forward, pulling the letter Grace had written from his pocket and handing it to Mrs. Rogers. "I appreciate that you don't know me, ma'am. Grace asked me to come in her stead. It's all explained in this letter."

Bill Ferris stepped closer to Mrs. Rogers. The wind threatened to rip the pages from her bare fingers as she pulled the letter from the envelope. "Mary? Maybe it'd be best to get back inside. You've no gloves and that shawl…"

Mary Rogers glanced at Nick, then turned on her heel and marched back to the house. "Get inside, all of you," she instructed the children. "And shut that door."

If Bill hadn't motioned him forward, Nick would have figured he was being left—literally out in the cold.

Once inside, he took a moment to look around while he removed his gloves and hat and opened his sheepskin-lined jacket. The house was neat as a pin despite being so small for accommodating such a large family. They stood in the front room where two chairs faced the fireplace, a braided rug under them covering a floor made of wide planks and polished to a high sheen. In one corner next to the fireplace, he noticed a small bookcase crammed with books. There was also a child-sized table and chairs and two other adult chairs, one of them a rocker. The furniture looked handmade, and Nick wondered if Grace's father was a carpenter in addition to being a farmer.

"How is Mr. Rogers?" he asked, his voice seeming to fill the small room.

Grace's mother held up a finger to silence him as she perched on the edge of a chair and read Grace's letter. Twice, she glanced up at him and then returned to her reading. Her first words were to her neighbor. "Have you read this?"

"No. Just the telegram she sent asking me to meet Nick. Grace said he would explain everything."

From a room down a dark hallway came the sound of a man coughing. The girl who'd been standing at the door hurried toward the sound, the two smaller children right behind her. Nick heard a door open, magnifying the racking cough, and then close again. He turned his attention back to Mrs. Rogers.

"Grace is expecting a child?" she said.

Nick fought a smile. "Yes, ma'am."

"Your child?"

"Yes, ma'am."

"Did you get her in the family way before marrying her?"

Suddenly, Nick wished he'd read the letter. What on earth might Grace have said to give her mother that impression? "No, ma'am. Grace and I love each other, and it was because of that that we decided to marry."

She grunted and looked back at the letter. "She says she was prevented from coming herself and that's why you're here. Is it the baby? Grace herself has a strong constitution, but…"

From the way she kept focusing on the pregnancy, Nick guessed that Grace had not written anything about her ordeal with Perkins or the fire or the fact that she was currently under house arrest. "May I?" he asked, indicating the chair opposite hers.

Mrs. Rogers nodded, and Bill Ferris took up a position just behind her chair. The two of them stared at him as if expecting the worst. Nick was glad the neighbor had stayed. As he told them the story—Perkins stalking Grace for weeks and then tricking her into meeting him, the gun and threats, the fire, the rescue, the sheriff trying to help, the staff at the hotel caring for Grace—he made no effort to sugarcoat what had happened even when tears trickled down Mrs. Rogers's cheeks. But then he decided she'd heard enough. He wouldn't tell her the worst: that Grace could be tried for murder.

"The doctor felt it would be dangerous for her health—and the baby's—for Grace to travel, so she sent me in her place."

To his surprise, Grace's mother reached across the space that separated the two chairs and took hold of his hand, turning it over as she examined it. "You have burns," she murmured, and he knew her gesture had been one of seeking confirmation that the wild tale he'd just relayed was fact.

"They'll heal," he said, then closed his fingers around hers. "The important thing to remember is Grace is going to be fine." She did not pull her hand away, just sat there crying softly, her tears spotting the ink of Grace's letter. "Mrs. Rogers, Grace is worried about you—and her father."

Mrs. Rogers snorted back her tears. "That's Grace. Always trying to do for others. You'll learn that soon enough, young man, if you haven't already." She pulled her hand free of his and clutched the letter. "The way she speaks of you, I can tell she loves you. I just hope you can live up to what she needs from you."

"I plan on spending the rest of my days doing just that, ma'am."

She stood. "You should eat something. It's been a long, hard day for you. Bill, you'll stay for some supper before going on?" And not waiting for her neighbor's reply, she left the room, still offering Nick no information about her husband's condition.

Bill Ferris sat in the chair she'd just vacated. "Jim is bad off," he said, studying the knuckles of his hands. "Doctor says he might not make it through the winter. The one thing he wants is to see Grace. She's always been his favorite. And once he knows there's a grand-baby on the way…"

"Grace and I can come once—"

But Bill wasn't listening.

"Can't seem to catch his breath," he muttered as if trying to make sense of things. He looked up at Nick. "Doctor says this weather is not helping—the cold and the damp. Goes right through him."

"And there's nothing to be done?"

Bill shrugged. "Hope he makes it to spring. The warmer weather would give him a chance to rebuild some strength. 'Course spring is still damp in this part of the country. We get more than our fair share of rain most years."

Nick quickly compared the weather he was experiencing and Bill was describing to the drier, warmer weather of New Mexico. And from there, it was an easy leap to an idea that just might solve everything—at least as far as Grace's father was concerned. He'd heard stories of people coming to New Mexico for their health. Maybe… "Does the doctor stop by often?"

Again, Bill gave him a noncommittal lift of his shoulders. "Not much call for him to come over unless Jim takes a turn for the worse. I expect he's due though—the doc, that is. He usually comes by whenever he's got a call out this way, and word has it the Turner girl two farms over is having her baby." He eyed Nick with suspicion. "Why do you ask?"

Nick wasn't ready to share his idea with anybody until he'd had a chance to discuss it with the doctor. No sense raising false hopes. So this time, he was the one to shrug. "Just thought it might give Grace some peace to know I spoke to the doctor directly."

The older girl edged her way into the front room. "Pa wants to meet you," she said, glancing at Nick and then back down at the floor.

"Sure," Nick said, instinctively running his hands through his hair and straightening his shirt collar. "Lead the way, Angie." She whirled around with a wide-eyed stare when he used her name, and he smiled. "Grace talks about you and the others—Reuben out there in the barn, the twins Darla and Douglas, and there's one more—another boy." He counted them off on his fingers, murmuring the names.

"Walt," Angie said. "You forgot Walt. He's between me and Reuben. You'll meet them at supper."

"Walt," Nick repeated. "Are you sure your father is up to me stopping in, Angie?"

"He says he wants to meet you, and we don't like to upset him. That sets him to coughing and choking.

Grace is his favorite," she added. The statement came out of the blue and sounded more like a warning than information.

"Well, we've got that in common," Nick said as he followed her to a partially open door. "She's my favorite too," he added as he slipped past Angie and approached the high bed that dominated the small room.

Chapter 16

GRACE'S FATHER RESTED AGAINST A STACK OF PILLOWS in a half-sitting position. He turned his head toward the door, beckoned Nick closer, and stuck out his hand. "Jim Rogers," he managed, his voice a raspy whisper.

"Nick Hopkins," Nick replied, accepting the man's handshake.

"Sit." Jim pointed to a small wooden side chair, waited for Nick to do as he asked, and then said, "You married my girl?"

"I did. I love her."

"Are you worthy of her?"

The question was unexpected. Nick stumbled for an answer. "Probably not," he admitted. "But I've got a good job, a secure future. I can provide for her."

"And the baby?"

"All the babies," Nick said, trying to temper the hint of defiance he felt at the man's probing.

A hint of a smile tugged at the older man's chapped lips. "Tell me about yourself, son. You do the talkin', and I'll do the listenin', if that suits."

Nick could see that every word the man uttered

came with a price, so he was more than ready to agree. He told Jim how he and Grace had met on the train, making Jim smile at her refusal to accept the invitation to have supper with him. He told him about the Lombards and how, with his own parents passed on, they were more like family than employers. He told him about how he and Grace had decided to secretly marry and how the news of her pregnancy had caught them both by surprise.

"But we're real excited and looking forward to being a true family," he assured the man.

"No doubt," Jim Rogers muttered. He cleared his throat and pushed himself a little higher on the pillows. Nick's father-in-law was tall and lanky and far too thin. "Now tell me about this business with the sheriff," he said, pinning Nick with clear blue eyes that dared him to sugarcoat the details.

So Nick told him—about Jasper Perkins, a powerful man in Juniper who had pursued Grace for weeks, even though she had rebuffed him over and over again. He told him about the night the girls had gone to the Perkins house and how he and Aidan and Jake had gone to walk them home. He told him what he'd seen that night through the kitchen window.

"I shoulda beat him to a pulp right then and there," he grumbled, his fingers tightened into fists.

"Wouldn't have done any good," Grace's father said. "You just would have ended up in the clink, and then who would protect my girl?" He swallowed hard as if having to work through a large knot in his throat. "Tell me the rest, son. Don't leave out anything. I need to know it all."

Nick told him about the fire and pulling Grace out and her insisting he go back for Perkins. He did not mention her arrest or trial. Instead, he told him how Doc Waters, Aidan, and the others at the hotel had insisted on caring for her at no charge. "She is much loved by everyone there," he said.

Her father smiled. "So it was when the doctor was treating her for her injuries that he figured out that she was with child?"

Nick nodded. Maybe Jim would assume that the reason she couldn't come was because the doctor thought it too risky. Maybe he didn't have to tell them the worst—that their beloved daughter was under arrest and facing a trial for the murder of the banker.

But just like Grace, Jim Rogers saw through him. "What else?" he asked. "There's one more thing you don't want to say. Say it."

So Nick told him. But the moment he saw silent tears leaking down the deep crevices of the man's face, he wished with all his heart that he'd lied instead.

A light tap at the door broke the silence between the two men. Mrs. Rogers opened the door. "Dr. Rove is here, Jim. Nick, your supper's getting cold."

Nick squeezed his father-in-law's shoulder as he stood and left the room. Grace's mother stayed behind, so he walked down the hall to the kitchen where the twins, Angie, and the two older boys sat around the table eating their supper. A place had been set for him. "Smells mighty good," he said, then pulled the chair closer and dipped his spoon into a bowl filled with a stew of meat, potatoes, and onions. Angie passed him a wooden board that held half a loaf of bread. The other four children just stared at him.

Reuben and his brother wolfed down their food. He judged them to be about seventeen and fifteen respectively, based on the fact that Grace had just turned nineteen. Angie was maybe a year or two younger than Walt, and the twins were several years younger. He wondered if there had been babies in between—infants who hadn't made it.

Reuben slid his chair back as he wiped his mouth on the sleeve of his flannel shirt. "We got chores," he muttered, giving Walt a nudge.

"I'll help," Nick said, downing the last of his food and standing.

The two boys glanced at each other, unsure of what to say.

"I mean, with your pa down, I expect you're short-handed," Nick offered.

"You ever work on a farm?" Reuben asked, his tone challenging.

"Where I come from, working a ranch is much the same as you working a farm. Anything different, I figure a couple of men like you can show me."

At his calling them "men," Reuben straightened to his full height—tall like his father—but he still didn't smile. "Get your coat. We'll be in the barn. Come on, Walt."

Nick drained the last of his coffee and grabbed his coat. He helped the boys feed the livestock and was shoveling a path from the back of the house to the chicken coop when the doctor left by the front door.

"Just keep him resting, Mary," the doctor said as Grace's mother stood on the front stoop, once again wrapped in her shawl. "Calm is the only medicine I can offer right now."

Nick heard the door to the house close and the jangle of the harness as Dr. Rove climbed into his wagon. Knowing the doctor would come past the coop and the barn, Nick waited.

"Excuse me, sir," he called.

Dr. Rove was an older man with unruly white hair and a posture that looked as if he'd seen far too much in his years. He pulled the wagon to a stop and looked down at Nick.

"You're Grace's husband," he said.

"Yes, sir."

"I heard the story from Jim. Sounds like this family's got more than its fair share of trouble to deal with right now."

"I'm thinking maybe there might be a way to ease that some," Nick replied and saw the doctor's eyes widen with interest. "Come inside the barn where it's warmer, and hear me out if you will."

Dr. Rove nodded and snapped the reins, and the horse started for the barn. Once the two men walked inside, Reuben glanced up.

"This involves you and Walt as well, Reuben, so let's talk," Nick said, motioning the boys to join the doctor and him by the fire they'd built in the potbelly stove in one corner of the barn. "I might have an idea that will help your pa."

❧

With each passing day, Grace grew stronger—and more anxious. The judge would arrive any day now, and in spite of everything Sheriff Daniels had done to find evidence she could not have fired any of the shots, she might still stand for trial, accused of murdering Jasper Perkins.

"It's all circumstantial, Mrs. Hopkins," the sheriff told her as they sat on the veranda outside the hotel with Emma and Lily one evening after the dining room had closed for the day. "I've found no clear proof. But the problem with that," he added, "is things can go either way."

Lily was beside herself. "But if there is no solid proof that she's guilty... I mean, isn't the law 'innocent until proven guilty'? And anyone who looks at her knows there is no way Grace could ever..."

Cody Daniels leaned back and stared out at the passing traffic on the street. "That's the law in theory, but the truth is, sometimes things can go the other way, depending on how a jury sees things. I mean, if it comes to that."

A jury. Of course. If the judge decided to order her case to trial, twelve men would decide her fate. Men she might have served in the dining room. Men perhaps beholden to Jasper Perkins for the bank loans that helped them build their livelihoods.

"Grace, have you consulted with Oscar Brooks?" Emma asked quietly.

Oscar Brooks was the sole attorney in Juniper. He often dined at the hotel—and frequently with Jasper Perkins. "I doubt he would see my side of this," Grace said. "Besides, I can't afford a lawyer."

Lily snorted. "We'll raise the money. You have friends, Grace—people who care a good deal about you."

"If we could just find someone willing to step forward," Emma mused. "Someone to testify that what Perkins did to Grace was part of a pattern—that he's hurt girls before. That's been the rumor."

"I thought of that," Cody said. "I've heard a lot of talk, but it sounds like any other girl he's supposedly accosted has either left town or has settled into a life she wouldn't want to jeopardize. That's a long shot, I'm afraid."

"But it could make a difference," Lily insisted.

The sheriff stood. "It could, but, ladies, I have to warn you. It's not only a far-fetched idea, but you'd be playing with the lives of others. Maybe ruining reputations, even marriages if the woman never told her husband." He put his hat on and tugged it tight. "I'll be in touch," he said, addressing his comment to Grace.

"Thank you," she replied. Cody Daniels was clearly torn, and her heart went out to him.

Lily was not quite so generous. "That man could make all of this go away if he was of a mind to do so," she muttered as they watched him cross the plaza on his way back to his office.

"Oh, Lily, that's not his job," Grace replied.

They sat in silence for a long moment, the seriousness of Grace's situation weighing heavily on the three friends. Uncomfortable with having the others assume the burden of her problems, Grace cast about for a way to lighten the mood. "One thing about Cody Daniels," she said, "he's quite nice-looking. And those dimples."

Lily grunted dismissively. "If you like that sort of thing."

Emma started to giggle, then Grace, and finally Lily saw the humor in her comment. The three of them laughed until tears filled their eyes, gasping out comments between fresh bouts of merriment.

"And you do, Lily," Emma managed.

"What?" Lily protested, but she was smiling.

"Like a man with dimples," Emma and Grace replied in unison. That set off a fresh gale of laughter that had passing hotel guests looking their way with curiosity.

"Shhh," Emma whispered, but giggles continued to bubble up from one or all three until they settled back in their chairs and let this new silence envelop them—the comfort of friendship.

"It's going to be all right," Lily said softly as they stared up at the stars.

Grace was not so sure, but she was grateful for their support. These two women had become her sisters as much as Angie and Darla were. "Thank you," she murmured, reaching out to each of them and clasping their hands.

Two days later, Bonnie Kaufmann brought the news that Grace had been dreading. The judge was arriving on the morning train.

Bonnie took hold of Grace's hands. "Sheriff Daniels says it will take time for him to settle in and review all the cases he's come to hear. It's unlikely you will need to be in court until Thursday."

Nick had sent word that he would be back by the weekend. Would he be in time? "Surely they will not start the hearing until Nick can be here? He was a witness."

"Unlikely, I'm afraid." Bonnie pursed her lips. "Aidan told me the judge has a schedule to keep and is determined to finish his business here and be on his way. Apparently, there is a trial in Santa Fe involving a gang of outlaws who murdered a rancher."

Grace's lip trembled. She was frightened, and without Nick at her side…

"Are you sure you wouldn't like Aidan to contact an attorney he knows in Santa Fe?"

"I am innocent, Bonnie. I have to hope that others will see that."

The older woman frowned, clearly not as trusting as Grace was. *If only I could speak privately with Mrs. Perkins*, Grace thought. And why shouldn't she? She picked up her hat and began pinning it in place.

"You're going out?" Bonnie asked.

"For a walk. I just need to clear my head. I won't go far."

"Shall I have someone accompany you?"

Grace squeezed Bonnie's hand. "I'll be fine, thank you. I'm feeling stronger every day, and I can't just sit here. I want to let Nick know the judge has arrived, so I'll just walk to the Western Union, send the wire, and come back again." She did not add that she planned to stop at the Perkins house, located just half a block from the telegraph office.

Bonnie smiled. "Of course." She stepped aside and waited for Grace to go ahead of her into the lobby.

Once outside, Grace felt a little of what she had felt the first time she'd stepped off the train in Kansas City, before her interview and before she had been hired as a Harvey Girl. She had been as nervous then as she was now, as unsure she was doing the right thing. But that had turned out to be one of the best things she'd ever done. *Trust your instincts*, her father had once told her, and with those words ringing in her ears, Grace walked briskly across the plaza and on down the street to the Perkins residence. Maybe she would have good news to add to her message to Nick. Maybe Mrs. Perkins would relent and rescind her accusations. Maybe…

The doorway was draped in black crepe, and the curtains on every window were closed tight. There was no sign of anyone being home, but Grace raised the knocker and let it fall on the polished brass plate.

After a long moment, the door opened just enough for Mrs. Perkins to peer out. "You!" She prepared to shut the door.

"Wait. Please." Without thought, Grace placed the flat of her hand against the door and pushed.

Mrs. Perkins had always been a thin waif of a woman. Now, her eyes were puffy and swollen from weeping or lack of sleep or both, and she had disintegrated into a state of such ill-health that Grace easily pushed the door open.

"Please," she said again, unwilling to force her way into the dark house. "Let me come in so we can talk."

Mrs. Perkins stepped away from the door, allowing it to swing open as she walked into the front dining room. Grace followed.

"You will not speak ill of my husband," the widow

hissed. She stood behind one of the large carved wooden chairs as if it would shield her from an attack. "Not in this house. I know what you've been saying— the lies, the dishonor you've heaped on his memory, when it was you! You and the others who—"

Grace's mind locked on the single word—*others*. Had Mrs. Perkins known what her husband had been and what he had done? Had she somehow found a way to twist the facts around until Jasper Perkins became the victim?

"Others?" she asked quietly.

"Oh, do not play games with me, young woman. You so-called Harvey Girls are supposed to be so respectable, so moral and above reproach! Well, you don't fool me. You never did. From the day that hotel was built and your kind started showing up, it's been the same. You see a wealthy pillar of the community and set your sights on him—no matter that he's already married. You're not above blackmail, are you? Is that what happened? You lured my husband to that cabin to compromise him? Everyone knows about your family back in Missouri, how you send money to support them. Was it not enough? Did you need more and think my husband was an easy target?"

"Mrs. Perkins, you've got it all wrong. I never—"

"Stop!" she shouted. "Just stop your lies. I knew the minute you showed up for supper that night that you were trouble. I saw how Jasper was around you— nervous and unsettled. And attracted, yes. Of course. He's a man after all. They have urges, but you played on those urges, didn't you? And now he's dead." The woman was ranting, completely beyond reason.

Grace had made a terrible mistake coming to her house. She began backing toward the front hall. "I'm going now, Mrs. Perkins."

"Yes, go. Enjoy your last breaths of freedom, you Jezebel. Judge Evans is here, and he will see you for who you really are. He will order you to be tried, and if there is justice in this world, you will be taking your final walk to the gallows." Mrs. Perkins followed her to the door and shrieked at her while a couple passing the house and a neighbor sweeping her walk turned to look. Grace hurried down the steps.

"And I'll be there watching," Mrs. Perkins screamed before slamming the door so hard the frosted glass panels to either side rattled.

Grace was shaking so badly that she wasn't sure she could make it back to the hotel, much less to the telegraph office. Instead she walked to the plaza, found a bench, and sat.

"Grace?"

She had no idea how long she'd been sitting there when she looked up and saw Polly Forrester standing in front of her. Polly sat next to her and took hold of her hands. "Are you unwell? Should I send for the doctor?"

Grace shook her head, finding it hard to put words together. "I'll be fine. Thank you." She noticed Polly's uniform at the same time she heard the train approaching the station. "I don't want to keep you. The train's coming."

"Walk with me back to the hotel," Polly urged, pulling Grace to her feet and linking arms with her, "and tell me what has you so upset. Is it that the judge is in town? Because you know, Grace, everyone says he's a fair man and—"

"I went to see Mrs. Perkins," Grace admitted.

There was a beat, and then Polly said, "You shouldn't have done that."

"I know, but, Polly…" And Grace found herself telling Polly everything Jasper Perkins's wife had said. "There have been other girls, and she knows who they are. I'm sure of it."

They had reached the hotel, and Polly had asked no questions, made no comment. "You should go in and rest," she said, preparing to leave Grace at the front steps while she went around to the staff entrance in back.

"But, Polly, you've been here since the hotel opened. You must have heard—"

"I have to go," Polly said, her face ashen. And she fled.

And that's when Grace guessed that Polly Forrester had been one of the girls Perkins had gone after. Polly knew what Grace knew. Oh, how she wished Nick were here! He could persuade Polly to tell the judge what she knew. He could persuade Polly to testify on her behalf. But Nick wasn't here, and she was pretty sure Polly was not going to give up any secrets that could get her fired and ruin her reputation, especially now that it was rumored Bonnie was considering retiring and moving back to Virginia to be closer to her nieces and nephews.

Grace entered the lobby. Aidan looked up from his position at the front desk and frowned with concern. She raised her hand in greeting and hurried on to the room she'd occupied since the fire, closing the door behind her and leaning against it as the tears broke. In the absence of anyone to speak for her, she understood for the first time, Mrs. Perkins's prediction that she would hang might just be the way this all ended.

Once Reuben and Walt assured him they and Angie were fully prepared to run the farm, Nick returned to the house, prepared to discuss his idea with Grace's parents. But while the doctor saw the possibility of his plan, persuading Grace's mother was not going to be nearly so easy. They were seated in front of the fireplace. Nick perched on the edge of one chair, while she sat huddled in her shawl in the other. Dr. Rove had left, and now Nick wished he'd asked the man to stay and help him make the case. "It won't be easy," the doctor had warned, but Nick had thought he was talking about the logistics of getting the move organized. Now he was pretty sure the doctor was warning him he'd have his hands full with Grace's mother first.

"Move Jim to New Mexico?" She gave him a look of pure panic. "He's far too ill to go from the bed to the front room, much less halfway across the country."

"Please hear me out, Mrs. Rogers."

"You want to pack Jim up and take him back to New Mexico," she said. "That's the gist of it."

"And you. The two of you would come. Dr. Rove agrees the drier and warmer weather there might just be the cure Mr. Rogers needs. It wouldn't be forever, just time enough for him to regain his strength. Grace will be there," he added, hoping to turn the tide with that reminder.

"And who would be here, young man? Who would run this place?"

"Reuben and Walt are running it now," he said gently. "Have been for all the time your husband has been ill. Angie would stay to cook for them and care for the twins."

She chewed her lip, gazing at him with suspicion. "And you have a place there?"

He thought about the anteroom where he'd planned to live with Grace and the baby. Could they make it work for Grace's parents as well? Especially when her father might be bedridden for some time?

When he hesitated, Mrs. Rogers snorted and turned her sharp eyes to the fire. "You haven't thought this through, have you? Never mind where we'd live, what about the train fare? We've living hand to mouth here, in case you didn't notice. I told Grace to stop sending money, because with Jim down, it won't make a difference. Come spring, maybe it will be a good year for the corn and wheat and all, but farming is a gamble. You bet against the weather."

"Yes, ma'am. Ranching's like that too." He was grasping at anything that might give them a connection. "And I have the money for the train fare."

She shot him a look. "We don't take charity."

"I'm family now, Mrs. Rogers. Me paying for the tickets is no different from Grace sending money. But if you're not comfortable with the idea of that, we can consider it a loan."

She waved a dismissive hand. "It won't work. Jim's far too ill to be moved."

Nick decided he had no choice but to play his

trump card. "There's something Grace hasn't told you—that she asked me not to tell you," he said. "She doesn't want to add to your worries, but the truth is your daughter needs you and her father."

Mrs. Rogers sat forward, the shawl slipping unnoticed from her bony shoulders. "The baby?"

"No. Far as I know, that's all fine." He took hold of the older woman's hands. "Grace has been accused of killing the man who assaulted her. And she's about to go on trial." Nick told her the rest of the story then, leaving no detail out, and when he was finished, he waited for her reaction.

"I knew her going to work for that outfit was a mistake," she muttered as if talking to herself. "She could always get around her father, so we let her go, and now this." She looked at him as if suddenly realizing something. "This is why she couldn't come. It wasn't the baby. It was this?"

Nick nodded but said nothing. He wanted to give her the time she needed to digest what he'd told her and come to some conclusion.

"And Dr. Rove agrees Jim is up to the travel?"

"No guarantee, but he believes it's worth a try. He told me he has nothing more he can offer."

She studied her clasped fingers. "He's been telling me for ages now that it's just a matter of time." Tears filled her eyes. She pulled her hands free of Nick's hold and swiped the wetness away, then stood and let out a long breath of resignation. "I'll talk to Jim about it," she said. "For now, you should get some sleep. I can offer the chair here or the barn. Otherwise, I'm afraid we're full up."

Nick smiled. "No room in the inn," he said and saw the spark of humor light his mother-in-law's eyes.

A half smile twitched the corners of her mouth. "Something like that. Good night, Nick."

"Good night, Mrs. Rogers."

She hesitated before leaving the room. "Maybe in light of circumstances, you might call me something like Ma Rogers?"

He tried it on. "Ma Rogers. Sounds good to me." He had an urge to kiss her weathered cheek but knew instinctively that would be going too far. "I'll stay here for the night," he added, indicating the chair. "If you need anything at all, let me know."

She nodded and walked away.

He slept more soundly than he would have thought possible. He woke only when the two older boys came down from the loft before dawn and started donning their coats, hats, and gloves before heading out to do morning chores. Nick made sure the fire in the kitchen was going, put on his coat and hat, stopped by the outhouse, and then headed for the barn. He and the boys worked mostly in silence, milking the cows, pitching fresh hay, breaking the ice that covered the trough, and gathering eggs from the coop.

"Thanks," Reuben muttered as the three of them headed back to the house, their shoulders hunched against the cold. Inside, the smells of biscuits baking and bacon frying hit them right along with the warmth of the fire. Angie and her mother were working in the kitchen, dressed in calico dresses similar to the one Grace had worn that day they'd gone on the hayride. The younger children were already seated at the table.

"Smells mighty good," Nick said as he stamped the snow from his boots and hung his coat and hat on a peg near the back door.

"Jim would like to see you," Ma Rogers said.

A flicker of hope flashed through Nick's chest. "Now?"

She nodded and turned the bacon without looking at him, but both Reuben and Angie glanced from their mother to him and back again, their curiosity held in silence.

Nick knocked lightly before turning the knob to the sickroom door. As before, Jim Rogers was reclined against a stack of pillows. "Come in, son," he said. "Let's figure out this grand adventure you and my wife have come up with."

Chapter 17

GRACE DECIDED TO BIDE HER TIME, WAITING FOR Polly's shift at the lunch counter to end so she could catch her alone and question her. Polly had a reputation for knowing all the gossip, although she herself rarely spread any rumors. If Polly was unwilling to tell the judge her story, at least she would know who among the girls—maybe some who were still in the area—had caught the banker's fancy.

Finally, the last customer paid his check and left, and Polly immediately began the cleaning—the part of their work few customers ever saw or thought about. She was polishing one of the coffee urns when Grace walked to the counter. "Could I help?"

Polly hesitated, then shrugged. "Suit yourself. As long as you don't expect me to share my tips."

"No. Just restless. I've been cooped up now for what seems like weeks." She found a clean cloth and began polishing the second urn. "I should never have gone to see Mrs. Perkins," she admitted.

"That was dumb," Polly agreed.

"Yes, it was."

Polly glanced at her. "Are you scared, Grace?"

"Wouldn't you be?"

"I guess I never thought you'd be accused. Of course, it makes sense. The only way that woman could get through life was to pretend it was the girls, not her husband."

Grace's ears perked up. So Polly knew how Perkins's wife rationalized his behavior. "Like I said, she suggested there had been other incidents."

Polly paused in her polishing but did not look at Grace. "I wouldn't know. Firsthand, I mean. There are always rumors. Juniper is a small town, and people talk and all." Her cheeks had flushed to a mottled red, and her hands were shaking.

Grace was sure Polly was lying. Challenging that was a long shot—or maybe not. Maybe Polly would be relieved to finally tell someone. And who better to tell than the woman who had come close to being raped by that monster? She stepped closer and put her hand on Polly's shoulder. "Polly, did he ever...I mean, were you someone he—"

"You should go," Polly whispered. "I don't know why you're here, and if Miss K catches you...me..."

Grace hesitated. Polly was trembling, and Grace was sure it wasn't Bonnie Kaufmann she feared. "Tell me what happened, Polly."

"No! You want me to risk my reputation to save yours. Well, we aren't friends, Grace. We never were. Coworkers. Rivals for Nick's affections, but never friends. So please just leave me out of this. You'll be all right. Your kind always are." And with that, she dropped her cloth and fled to the kitchen.

Grace watched her go. Even knowing Polly had feelings for Nick, she had hoped that in time, they might find a way to get along. After all, Jake had unrequited feelings for Lily, and they were the best of friends. But in a way, she understood Polly's ill will toward her. If the shoe had been on the other foot and Nick had chosen Polly, would she be so quick to set aside her disappointment and bitterness?

She finished polishing the two urns. She wiped the counters and made sure everything was in its proper place, ready for tomorrow's onslaught. It occurred to her that she had performed these tasks that had become such a part of her routine for the last time. She walked to the window and lifted the edge of the lace curtain.

Outside, people were going about their business. Frank Tucker had paused while sweeping the board-walk in front of his store, leaning on the broom to pass the time with two railroad workers. And Cody Daniels was striding across the plaza, headed straight for the hotel. The way he was moving looked like he had some news he was intent on delivering, and her heart quickened. Perhaps her visit with Mrs. Perkins had not been a mistake after all.

She heard his deep voice addressing a question to Aidan and the bellboy, Tommy, volunteering, "She's in there."

Grace opened the door that led to the lobby. "Are you looking for me, Sheriff?"

"Are you trying to get yourself hanged, Mrs. Hopkins? Because if you're not, then why in the world would you call on the widow?" He kept his voice low, but his demeanor attracted stares from guests passing through the lobby.

"Has something happened?" Aidan stepped away from the front desk and approached them.

"It's all right, Aidan," Grace said, knowing from the look on the sheriff's face that it was a lie.

"Grace Hopkins, please come with me," he said as he took her elbow and guided her across the lobby, out the door, past the railway station, across the plaza, and directly into his office. Without releasing her, he opened the door to one of three small cells and indicated she should enter.

"But—"

"Mrs. Perkins has questioned why someone accused of shooting her husband in cold blood is free to walk around town. Judge Evans agreed. He insists you be locked up." He closed the cell door and turned the key, and then he seemed to finally drop his official attitude. He looked down at his boots and then away toward the window across from his desk. "Is there anything you need? Anything I can ask Bonnie Kaufmann to get for you?"

"I'm fine," she replied softly.

"The judge will hear your case the day after tomorrow," he said. "You might want to think more about getting yourself a lawyer."

"I'm innocent, Sheriff."

He turned his gaze on her. "That may be, but you'd be surprised how many innocent people go to jail or to the gallows because they have no one to speak for them."

"We both know it's too late for me to find

representation now. Surely the judge will postpone
the proceedings until Nick can be here to testify."

The sheriff let out a long breath. "That's not happening, Grace. Mrs. Perkins has friends in high places.
The territorial governor himself sent word that the
judge needs to get on with it."

"Will you let Nick know? About the hearing, I
mean?"

Cody Daniels studied her for a long moment and
then nodded, checked to be sure the cell was locked,
and left the building.

Nick knew it wouldn't be easy getting Grace's parents
to Juniper, but he'd drastically underestimated the
level of the struggle. Ma Rogers was a nervous wreck,
while her husband seemed to handle every challenge
with a kind of stoic humor intended to calm his wife.
But Nick wasn't fooled. Every movement for the man
was akin to climbing mountains.

The struggle began as they met with Bill Ferris
and Dr. Rove to decide how best to get Jim to the
train. There was no possibility the man could sit up
on the hard wooden seats of second class from Galax
to Kansas City. And what of the transfer there? The
wait between trains? The overnight travel from there
to New Mexico?

"We'll book a sleeping compartment," Nick said.

Ma Rogers stared at him, her mouth open without
the ability to form words. But she gathered herself.
"I don't know what you think you've married into,

young man, but let me assure you, it is not money. We can barely afford the cheapest seats, and now you want to talk about a private compartment?"

Nick had used part of the money the bank had returned to him from his payments on the land for the trip to Missouri. There was enough left to get Grace's parents to New Mexico if he went second class. What better use did he have for the money than that? "I've got everything covered, Ma Rogers. You just worry about getting packed and ready to go."

The room went quiet as the doctor, Bill, and Nick's mother-in-law stared at him, and Jim Rogers chuckled. "Looks to me like it's us who've married into money," he said. "We'll pay you back, son." He started to cough and choke then, and for that day, any further discussion of how they might manage the trip was over. Later, Nick wrote out a message he asked Bill to send to John Lombard, asking him to wire the money Nick had given him to hold—the money he'd saved for the land he would never own.

"You're going to kill him," Ma Rogers argued when she and Nick were alone in the kitchen the next morning. She spoke in a fierce whisper, designed to keep her husband from hearing.

"And yet he seems determined," Nick reminded her.

"He's stubborn. You'll learn soon enough the apple doesn't fall far from the tree. Grace is just like him."

That made Nick smile, because he knew his mother-in-law was right. On the surface, Grace might seem delicate, but beneath, there was a fierceness about her, a survival instinct that had made her drive a burning stick straight into the face of her attacker.

"He wants to go, Ma Rogers. I expect he wants to see Grace, and knowing she can't come here—"

"That and he wants to see his first grandchild, assuming he lasts that long." She gazed out the kitchen window. The sky was a gunmetal gray, promising more snow by nightfall. "Well, I've had my say, not that Jim or anybody else pays me any mind. Maybe the weather will bring all of you to your senses."

As it turned out, the weather gave Mary Rogers the reprieve she hoped for. It snowed through that night and all the next day. And when it finally stopped snowing, the temperature dropped to frigid numbers that made travel of any sort impossible.

After two days of being cooped up in the small house and no way to know what was going on back in Juniper, Nick thought he might go crazy. He got through the endless daylight hours helping the boys with chores, repairing harnesses and sharpening tools, and in general staying in the barn as much as possible. The nights were harder. He lay awake in his chair, listening to the silence that crept over the house in between Jim's coughing bouts, and thought about Grace.

He knew she wanted him to be there with her family when she couldn't be, but dammit, he wanted to be with her. He barely knew her parents and siblings, and yet slowly, he was being drawn into their lives. Reuben sought his advice the way he might have asked questions of his father. Walt watched everything he did, and Nick had heard the boy repeating things he'd said or the phrases he used. Angie quizzed him about New Mexico and her sister and the Harvey Girls, and every time she did, her mother looked over at him with a warning in her eyes that made him keep his responses brief. In the evenings after supper, the twins snuggled against him as he sat in their father's chair near the fire, begging for stories. He ran out of appropriate stories about the ranch early on and started making stuff up about Slim and Smokey that made the little ones laugh.

One evening, just as he and Reuben were headed to the house for supper, they heard a wagon and saw Bill Ferris headed down the lane. "Got a telegram for you, Nick," he called out. "Also, the clerk at the telegraph office is holding that money you asked your boss to send."

Nick's heart started to race. Finally, news from Grace. He reached the wagon before Bill had had a chance to climb down and held out his hand for the message. Bill and Reuben waited while Nick scanned the thin paper by the light of a lantern Bill carried on his wagon.

MRS IN JAIL STOP DOING MY BEST STOP

It was signed "Cody." But what did it mean? His best to do what? Protect her? Get her released? Nick knew he had to get back to Juniper.

"How are the roads to town?" he asked Bill.

"Passable."

"Trains running?"

"Mostly."

"Then we go tomorrow." Nick headed for the house. Reuben and Bill followed him. He heard Ma Rogers and Angie in the kitchen, but he went straight to his father-in-law.

"Jim, there's been a change in plans. I need to get back to Juniper as soon as possible. Next train is tomorrow morning. Are you up to making that?"

Jim frowned. "What's happened? Is it Grace? The baby?"

"It's just—" He knew Bill would tell Jim about the telegram, and he didn't know whether or not the man might have read the message. "I got word from the sheriff. Grace has been put in jail instead of being allowed to wait at the hotel, so something has changed, and it can't be good."

Jim nodded. "Let's get Mary and the children in here and figure out what needs doing."

"Thank you, sir." There was no doubt in Nick's mind that Jim Rogers would do whatever was necessary for Grace, no matter what the cost to his health. He turned to Bill. "Can you book a sleeping compartment for Jim and Mary and a coach ticket for me? One way for now—we'll worry about a return later."

"Got it," Bill said. "I'll head back to town now and be back at first light tomorrow to get you to the station."

"Thanks," Nick and Jim said in unison.

Having heard the commotion, Mary Rogers was outside the bedroom door when Bill turned to leave. "What's going on?"

Jim held out a hand to her. "Come here, darlin' girl."

She hurried to his side, clearly prepared for some worsening of his condition. "What?" she demanded.

"How about you and me take that honeymoon we never got around to?" He grinned at her, but his words came in huffs of breaths, each one a struggle.

"Stop being an old fool," she groused, but he caught her hand and held on, and she sat on the side of the bed and stroked his whiskered cheek.

Nick felt his presence was an intrusion, so he stepped into the hall, softly clicked the door shut, and went to the kitchen. There was every chance Jim Rogers would not live through the trip, but there was even more certainty that his days would run out faster if he stayed. Nick wished he could talk it through with Grace. Like her father, she had a way of looking at things from both sides and understanding the true meaning of being caught between a rock and a hard place.

Emma, Lily, and Bonnie visited Grace between shifts. During those visits, the sheriff opened the cell door and left them to their conversations, noting he would be just outside.

The first time he'd made the announcement, Grace sighed heavily. "Well, that's disappointing. I was definitely planning to make a run for it."

He froze and slowly turned to face her while her friends hid smiles behind their hands. He scowled at each of them in turn. "This is no laughing matter, ladies," he said sternly.

"No, it is not," Grace replied, meeting his eyes steadily. "But you will forgive us for trying to lighten the mood a bit, Sheriff Daniels. When my friends come calling, I'm going to try to find ways to brighten their long and worried faces."

Cody glanced at the other women, somber now, their hands at their sides or crossed over their chests as they studied him, daring him to do anything that might upset Grace. "Mrs. Hopkins, you are absolutely right." He tipped his hat to the four of them. "Enjoy your visit, ladies. I'm just going to step across the street to the mercantile."

Once he was gone, Lily turned to Grace. "That man…"

"…makes you glow," Grace finished, and Emma and Bonnie nodded.

"With annoyance," Lily protested. "He can be so darned…"

"Frustrating?" Bonnie offered.

"Arrogant?" Emma suggested but shook her head, then snapped her fingers. "Ah, got it. He can be so darned charming."

"I was going to say sweet," Grace added. "He's got a job to do, but he's taking risks to make sure I'm comfortable. He sent a telegram to Nick to let him know about…" She motioned to the cell as her eyes brimmed with tears.

Bonnie produced a handkerchief.

"Did Nick reply?" Lily asked.

Grace nodded. "They started out this morning—my parents and Nick. They should be in Kansas City later today. They'll have a layover of several hours, travel overnight, and…"

"…be here tomorrow," Bonnie finished. "Well, finally, some good news."

"This calls for a celebration." Emma reached into the large satchel she brought with her for every visit. It was always filled with goodies Jake had sent from the kitchen. Today's treat was peaches au gratin.

"My favorite," Grace said with a smile. "You must thank Jake for me. How is he?"

They all turned to Lily.

"He's fine," she said softly. "You know, in spite of the fact that my feelings for Jake don't match his, he says he's all right with that. He says if all we can be is friends, he'll take that. I never knew a man like that."

"You're lucky to have him in your life," Emma said.

Lily smiled at them, then bit her lip. "I am, aren't I? But am I being fair to him?" Tears brimmed, but she kept them in check.

"Lily, if you have been honest about your feelings for him and he has accepted that, don't question it," Bonnie advised. "Jake is a good man—a man you will always know you can count on. That's so very rare."

Emma nodded. "Besides, the other day, he actually said to me that maybe you and our handsome sheriff would be a good match."

Lily's eyes widened with dismay. "Mr. Law and Order and me? I don't think so."

"Never say never," Grace advised and got up to get a glass of water. "May I pour?" she asked, holding up the dented tin pitcher and giving them her best Harvey Girl smile.

"Put that down," Lily instructed. "We brought milk for our farmer's daughter and her baby." Lily produced a pint packed in ice.

Grace felt the twinge of nerves she always felt whenever the baby was mentioned. She couldn't help wondering if her child would be born in jail or perhaps, if Dolly Perkins got her way and Grace was sentenced to hang, not at all. Surely the authorities would not kill an innocent child for the mother's crime. No, they would hold her in jail until her time, deliver the baby, and then hang her. She shuddered.

Bonnie immediately removed her shawl and placed it around Grace's shoulders. "We really must speak to Sheriff Daniels about the draft in this place," she muttered, then turned to Emma. "Well, have you a spoon in that bag? Grace can hardly eat her peaches with her fingers."

They all understood Bonnie's tone. Everyone was on edge, trying to pretend they weren't as worried as Grace was. Emma handed Grace a spoon, and because she didn't want to disappoint them, she took a bite of the luscious dessert. The cool sweetness soothed her throat, still raw from the smoke she'd inhaled.

"If Nick is coming tomorrow, you need a change of clothes," Lily announced. "And we really must do something about your hair. We'll wash it and put it up. Where are those combs he gave you?"

Leave it to Lily to turn somber to cheerful. And as everyone offered ideas for how best to manage the washing of Grace's hair and considered what dress they might bring for her to wear, she consumed all the peaches and milk.

When Cody Daniels returned, they all turned to him with demands. "We will be here early tomorrow morning," Emma stated.

"Well, not that early," Lily cautioned.

"Grace needs to wash her hair and attend to other

assorted matters of personal care that a man simply would not understand," Bonnie said. "So please arrange for there to be some sort of screen behind which Grace can change. Oh, and a wash basin and pitcher—"

"Two pitchers of water," Lily interjected. "One for washing and the other for rinsing. Are you going to remember this?" she asked, stepping closer to the sheriff and peering up at him doubtfully.

"Privacy screen, two large pitchers presumably filled with warm water, a basin." He ticked the items off on his fingers. "Anything else?"

"We'll bring the towels," Emma said, then glanced at Grace's cot, "and clean linens for this so-called bed."

"Plus a proper blanket," Bonnie added. "Do you appreciate how drafty this jail is?"

"It's not meant to be the hotel," Cody muttered defensively. "Most who stay here don't notice."

"Well, our Grace is not most prisoners, Sheriff," Lily said. "She is special."

"Stop badgering the man," Grace said. "He's done a good deal for me already."

"Well, that may be but—"

"Bring your things, ladies," Cody interrupted. "I'll have what you need." He opened the door, signaling that visiting hours were over.

"We'll be back later today," Bonnie said as she followed Lily and Emma out the door.

"No doubt," Cody said wearily, closing the door.

"They mean well," Grace said as she pushed one of the three chairs into her cell and then sat on her cot. To her surprise, he sat on the chair.

"The judge will hear your case tomorrow," he said.

"Oh. I see." So it was finally here—the hour of reckoning.

"Juniper has no courthouse as such. The judge usually holds court at the hotel."

Grace nodded. "What will happen?"

"Since you have no attorney, Aidan Campbell and Jake Collier collected letters of support from several people. On the other hand, Oscar Brooks will have the right to call witnesses and lay out the case against you. This is just a first hearing, so there will be no jury, just the judge. Should things go... should you..."

"I'll be bound over for trial?"

He nodded.

"Will I need to testify? Will Nick?"

"Oscar Brooks may call you to the stand. If he doesn't, you don't need to worry."

Grace gave him a sardonic smile. "Sheriff Daniels, we both understand that whatever happens tomorrow, for now, I need to worry."

He looked down at his folded hands and then back at her. "Are you up to this? I mean if perhaps you were to experience problems with—" He nodded toward her stomach.

Grace shook her head. "The waiting is its own sentence," she said. "Let's get this over with one way or another."

Cody stood, stepped outside the cell, and closed the door. "Nick Hopkins is one lucky man," he said as he tipped two fingers to his hat.

"Will you let Mr. Campbell know my parents will be arriving with Nick on tomorrow's noon train? My father is quite frail, and Nick will need help getting them settled."

"I'll see to it. You should rest. Big day tomorrow."

Grace lay down on the cot and pulled the thin blanket over her. "Thank you, Sheriff."

"My pleasure, Grace," he replied.

It was the first time he'd called her by her given name.

Chapter
18

By THE TIME THEY REACHED KANSAS CITY, MARY Rogers was a bundle of nerves, and Nick really couldn't blame her. It was pretty clear that her husband was barely holding on. Their salvation turned out to be Ollie, the conductor Nick knew from his previous trips for the Lombards.

"Leave everything to me," Ollie told him, then turned to Mary. "Ma'am, I'm going to personally see that you and your husband travel in comfort."

"Thank you," she mumbled, looking around at all the activity surrounding the station. "This is all very… unsettling."

"It can be, but you just wait right here while I get everything in order. I won't be long."

True to his word, Ollie returned moments later, leading a group of red caps and porters, one of them pushing a wheelchair. Two of the men lifted Jim into the chair and covered him with blankets around his shoulders and over his knees. Two more men took charge of the luggage, and Ollie held Mary's elbow as he led them all down the platform. On board, there were two more porters waiting to transfer Jim to the bed they had made up for him and bring Mary hot tea. Ollie even told them there was a doctor traveling on board, and he'd already alerted him to the possibility of a need for his services. The color that had drained from Mary's face after the nightmare of the trip from Galax to Kansas City returned.

"I recall your daughter, sir," he said to Jim. "Pretty little thing. I knew this cowboy here had his eye on her from that first day." He chuckled. "Looks like it all turned out for the best."

Jim offered Ollie a weak handshake and thanked him. Mary Rogers gave him a hug.

Once Nick was sure Grace's parents were settled in their compartment, he found his seat in second class and breathed a long sigh of relief as the train pulled away from the station. They were on their way. By this time tomorrow, Grace and her parents would be reunited. More to the point, he would be able to find out what exactly had made Cody Daniels lock his pregnant wife up in a cold, cramped cell.

The following day, Grace was as ready as she was going to be. Accompanied by Sheriff Daniels, she crossed the plaza and entered the hotel. Emma and Lily had helped her get ready and assured her she looked fine.

"Innocent," Lily added. "Like a woman who is about to walk free in time to meet her husband and parents getting off the afternoon train."

She glanced at the station on her way to the hotel. Nick and her parents were scheduled to arrive in an hour, and she wondered if Lily's prediction would come true. She imagined waiting on the platform, scanning the windows of the cars as they rolled by until she saw Nick's face—and then her mother's. She would know with one look at her mother how her father had fared on the strenuous journey.

"This way," Cody said softly as they entered the hotel lobby. He looked neither left nor right but walked toward the small room usually designated for letter writing or reading.

As she hurried to keep pace with the sheriff, Grace glanced toward the lunch counter, where every seat was taken. Polly peered at her for a moment before pointedly turning away. Bonnie stood in the doorway leading to the dining room, not yet open for lunch. She forced a smile that was more of a grimace, one that reminded Grace of that first day she'd come to work at the hotel.

Her life had changed in so many ways since that day, and yet this place and the people she had gotten to know felt more like home than the farm did.

Cody led her to a single chair at one of two small tables. Both tables faced a larger, longer table where she assumed the judge would sit. Chairs arranged theater-style, presumably for witnesses and other interested parties, filled the rest of the room. Mrs. Perkins sat in the front row of chairs just behind the other small table. Next to her was her sister, Rita, along with John Lombard. Mrs. Perkins was speaking to a man of about forty who seemed to be trying to reassure her.

"That's Oscar Brooks," Cody muttered. He pulled out a chair for Grace. "Sit until the judge comes in, then stand until he tells you to sit again. I'll be right over there." He took up his position near the windows.

Grace nodded. Aidan entered the room and then exited again through a side door she'd never really noticed before. Grace folded her hands and rested them on the table, the smooth surface inlaid with a game board for checkers or chess. Behind her, she heard people whispering as they filled the empty seats, but she did not turn around.

Aidan opened the side door and stepped aside as the judge entered the room, followed by a man carrying a stack of folders. Immediately, Grace was on her feet, her hands at her sides, her clenched fists hidden in the folds of her skirt.

"Be seated," the judge said without looking at anyone in the room. Instead, he studied a file his aide handed him. After what seemed a long time, he leaned back and focused his attention on the lawyer. "Mr. Brooks, have you witnesses to call?"

"I do, Your Honor." Brooks was a wiry man with a good deal of nervous energy. To Grace's ears, he spoke far too loudly. As the man passed her on his way to stand closer to the chair for witnesses, he smirked at her.

"Then let's get on with it." By contrast, the judge seemed weary, as if he had seen far too much and most of it unpleasant.

"I call Frank Tucker," Brooks bellowed.

The judge flinched. "We are all of good hearing, Mr. Brooks, and it's a small room. No need to shout."

Frank Tucker approached the witness chair. The

judge's aide had him swear to tell the truth and then indicated he should sit. The lawyer asked him questions related to the fire—when he had first become aware of it, when had he arrived on the scene, what had he observed. Then Brooks started questioning the shopkeeper about Grace—had he ever observed her with Mr. Perkins or any other man in town? What was her demeanor like on those occasions?

He repeated this process with several other witnesses, all men she had served either at the counter or in the dining room. Some of them were good friends of the banker, and as they testified, they kept glancing over at Perkins's wife. Grace they dismissed as another girl who no doubt had come to work at the hotel hoping to marry a wealthy man. Several of them mentioned they had heard that her family farm was failing and that she was desperate to send money back to them. Most of them did not know the first thing about her except that she was a Harvey Girl and they'd heard she needed money.

As witness after witness testified and Brooks twisted the words of those who she knew had come to speak in her support, she understood how foolish she had been not to engage a lawyer of her own. Of course, how would she ever have paid the man? Her hopes for anything approaching a positive outcome plummeted.

Then Brooks called Dolly Perkins to the stand.

The train pulled into the station right on time. Jake was on the platform, having been sent by Aidan to meet them. "I got this," he said, motioning toward the porters transferring Grace's father to a wheelchair. "You need to get to the hotel. It's not going well, Nick. Grace needs you. That lawyer is making it look like Grace—"

The man had not finished the sentence when Nick took off at a run. "Get Doc Waters to check on Grace's pa," he shouted over his shoulder.

Inside the lobby, he paused for a minute, looking around and trying to figure out where Grace might be.

"In there," Polly said.

"Did the lawyer call any of you girls to testify?"

"Not yet, and I think he's about finished. I heard somebody say he'd saved Mrs. Perkins as a cincher for last."

Nick hesitated. "Look, Polly, if you know anything—"

"I've got customers, Nick." She turned away.

Every stool at the counter was empty.

Nick strode across the lobby to the reading room. He heard Dolly Perkins sobbing as she told her version of the night Grace and the other girls had come for supper. He entered the room and would have marched straight to the front had Aidan not caught his arm and held him back. As he leaned against the back wall near the door, he spotted the Lombards sitting in the front row. Of course, Mrs. Lombard would be there for her sister, but their presence on that side of the room did not bode well for Grace. John Lombard was one of the most highly respected men in the area, and if he was sitting with the accuser, folks were bound to think there might be some validity to what Mrs. Perkins was saying.

Grace sat alone. She looked so small and fragile, and yet she sat straight and tall and listened carefully to everything Dolly Perkins said—all of it some concoction of her need to believe in her husband's innocence.

"Can I testify?" Nick whispered to Aidan.

"Probably wouldn't help. You're Grace's husband."

The judge cleared his throat as the lawyer helped Perkins's wife back to her seat. "Do you have any further witnesses, Mr. Brooks?"

"No, Your Honor." He gave Grace a triumphant look as he took his seat.

"Good. Now, Mrs. Hopkins, I see you are without representation. That is unusual. Would you like to make a statement?"

Nick saw that this possibility had never occurred to Grace.

"No, sir," she said, her voice barely audible.

The judge was obviously nonplussed. He looked over those gathered in the crowded room and waved a stack of papers. "I have all these letters from local citizens. Does no one here wish to speak on Mrs. Hopkins's behalf?"

Aidan stepped forward. "I do."

Then Frank Tucker stood. "Me too."

Three other men stood as well—railroad workers who were regulars at the lunch counter.

One by one, the judge had them sworn in, and then he deftly guided them to speak their piece. Near Nick, several Harvey Girls crowded in the doorway.

"Anyone else?"

Nick saw John Lombard stand. "Perhaps I could clarify an incident that my wife and I witnessed involving Mr. Hopkins," he said.

The judge motioned him forward, and in clear, concise detail, Nick's employer gave the judge the facts of what had happened at the party. "My brother-in-law tended to overindulge in social situations," he said. "And more than once in such situations, I witnessed his focus settling on someone who was without the power to object to his attentions." He looked straight at Grace and then left the stand.

"Very well," the judge said, apparently assuming Lombard was the last witness for Grace.

Then Bonnie Kaufmann stepped forward. "I would like to make a statement," she said. Without invitation, she marched to the front of the room, raised her right hand, and waited for the aide to swear her in. The judge asked who she was in relation to Grace.

"I am her supervisor—and friend," she replied. "However, I am not here to talk about Mrs. Hopkins. You have heard enough to know that she is a fine, upstanding young woman. I am here to tell you about Jasper Perkins."

An audible gasp ricocheted through the room. The judge banged his gavel, calling for order. "Mr. Perkins is not on trial, Miss Kaufmann," he reminded her.

"Perhaps he should be," Bonnie muttered, then recovered her composure and faced the judge. "Nevertheless, you need to hear me speak."

Nick saw Aidan shake his head and knew they were thinking the same thing. Once Bonnie Kaufmann made up her mind to do something, there would be no stopping her.

"When I first arrived in Juniper ten years ago, Mr.

Perkins took an interest in me, very similar to the interest he took in Mrs. Hopkins."

"I object," Brooks shouted.

"I want to hear this," the judge replied, "so sit down, Mr. Brooks. You had your moment." He leaned toward Bonnie. "Go on, Miss Kaufmann."

"I was younger and probably a good deal more attractive in those days, although I don't think that mattered much to Mr. Perkins. Like Grace, I was straight off the farm and innocent. He seemed so nice, and as a stranger here, I needed a friend—a mentor. He invited me to stop by the bank one evening so we might discuss how best to manage my finances, and I went."

She sat stone still, chewing her lower lip, her eyes fixed on some distant memory. "When I arrived, I could tell he'd been drinking. As soon as he touched me and I realized this was no business meeting, I tried to leave, but he stood between me and the door. He…" She faltered, and her voice was so low, Nick suspected only the judge could hear her clearly. Nick caught enough words to know what Bonnie was saying. *Undressed. Dark. Mouth covered.*

Once again, she went silent. Nick realized everyone in the room was leaning forward, waiting for her next words.

"I must have passed out. I remember being so very afraid and so very shocked that this was happening. When I came to myself, he was gone. My clothing was undone, and there was…" She swallowed hard. "After examining myself, I realized I had been violated."

"Why did you not report this?" The judge was indignant.

"I did. The sheriff—not Sheriff Daniels but his predecessor—told me I had no proof that he had forced me. By my own admission, he was not there when I awoke, and the office was unlocked." She looked at the judge wide-eyed. "The sheriff did not believe me. He actually said he'd seen this before, where a girl makes a mistake and then regrets her action and cries 'foul.'"

"She's lying," Dolly Perkins shouted. "They all lie." Nick saw Rita Lombard try unsuccessfully to calm her sister.

"All?" The judge looked up sharply, then at the women seated in the room, including those Harvey Girls who had crowded into the room still wearing their uniforms. "Are there others among you with a similar experience?"

Someone nudged Nick from behind, and as he turned, Polly Forrester squeezed past him. She hesitated.

"Well?" the judge demanded.

"I'm not doing this for Grace," she murmured to Nick. "I'm doing it for myself." Nick couldn't have been more surprised as Polly stepped to the front of the room, stopping next to the table where Grace sat. She raised her hand. "As God is my witness, Jasper Perkins raped me, Your Honor, and I can give you the names of at least three others who will testify to the same thing." Her voice broke, and she staggered a bit.

Grace was on her feet immediately. She wrapped her arms around Polly and led her to the nearest chair. Once she'd handed Polly the glass of water she hadn't touched, she turned to the judge.

"Your Honor, I would like to speak after all, if I may."

"Please," the judge said.

Grace approached the witness chair and looked at the judge's aide, who scrambled to grab his Bible and swear her in. Nick was torn between protesting her decision and cheering her on.

"The facts I am about to relate are true—as true, I suspect, as the ones you have just heard from my friends. They will be painful for Mrs. Perkins to hear, and yet I believe in her heart, she knows the veracity of them. I believe, like any devoted wife, she sees it as her duty to protect her husband's name and memory. But there is a pattern of behavior here that goes back years, and the only individual who was present in each instance we have heard today was Jasper Perkins."

Grace paused and looked directly at the judge, speaking to him as if they were alone in the room. "As you have already heard, Your Honor, when Mr. Perkins first approached me, I was serving at a private party at the Lombardo Ranch. Our first encounter was witnessed by many of the guests that night. Unfortunately, the harassment continued, often in public places such as the lunch counter here at the hotel or once on the street just before Christmas, but never in such a way that others might overhear or have reason to be concerned. During those encounters, he threatened my husband, and he threatened me."

From her pocket, she pulled a folded envelope. She handed it to the judge. "This was on my bed one night after he demanded I meet him alone at the bank after hours and I did not go."

The judge removed the contents from the envelope,

read the message, then passed it to his aide to hand to Mr. Brooks. "Go on," he coached Grace.

"Because he had told me my appeal for him was my innocence, once I had married, I thought if I told him, that like any new bride…if he knew…"

"I understand. The day of the fire, what happened then? Why were you at the cabin?"

Every muscle in Nick's body tensed as Grace related the details of that horrible encounter. She left little out, but whenever she reached a detail that was embarrassing or upsetting, the judge nodded and gently prodded her to continue.

"I cannot say how he was shot, Your Honor, but I can say with all certainty that when my husband carried me from that burning building, Jasper Perkins was alive."

"And yet according to testimony we have heard, you sent your husband back in to the fire for him," the judge noted. "Why? With his death, your problems were over."

Grace gave him a tight, sardonic smile. "I would respectfully disagree, sir. For it is I who am on trial here, not the man I had hoped would finally have to face justice for his crimes. I wanted him to have to face me and perhaps these women and others who, like me, he had harassed and violated. You may accuse me of hating him and of causing harm to him in order to escape, for I did all those things. But I did not kill him. In the name of justice, not just for me, but for all his victims, I ask that you put this matter to rest. Let us get on with our lives."

She folded her hands in her lap and sat dry-eyed and composed, still facing the judge. She was magnificent, and Nick could see there wasn't a person in the room—save Perkins's widow and her lawyer—who didn't agree.

Brooks got to his feet. "Your Honor, may I have permission to cross-examine this witness?"

"That's your right, Counselor."

Brooks approached her. He smiled. "Mrs. Hopkins, I am sorry for the ordeal you endured during the fire. I do hope your health has improved?"

Grace met the lawyer's eyes. "Yes, thank you," she replied.

"I would like to bring our focus away from the sordid stories you and your friends have asked us to believe—of a man who was a pillar of this community, I might add."

"Get on with it, Brooks," the judge muttered.

"Let's talk about the shooting of Mr. Perkins. Is it your testimony that you feared for your life?"

"Yes, sir." She eyed him suspiciously, as if unsure of where he was headed with his question.

"And is it safe to assume that if you could have gained access to the pistol in question, you would not have hesitated to use it to defend yourself?"

Grace straightened and faced her accuser directly. "Mr. Brooks, I never touched that gun. It was pointed at me. It was placed quite forcibly against my person. The last I saw of it, Mr. Perkins had placed it on top of a nail keg so he could…" Her voice broke, but she lifted her chin and continued. "Your Honor, I am guilty of bargaining for my life, but I did not shoot Mr. Perkins."

The lawyer seemed at a loss for words. He turned

back to the table where he'd sat and shuffled through some papers.

"Mr. Brooks?" the judge said. "Was there something more for this witness?"

Brooks waved a paper in the air. "I have here the sworn statement of Mrs. Dolly Perkins that Mrs. Hopkins not only pursued her husband, but also threatened her."

The judge sighed heavily and motioned for Brooks to hand him the paper. Then he held up a sheaf of papers from the folder his aide had carried into the room when they arrived. "And I have here statements from a number of citizens who witnessed the fire. I will certainly take Mrs. Perkins's statement under consideration. So unless you think you have anything to add, I am prepared to retire to consider my decision. Mrs. Hopkins, you may return to your seat." He motioned to Grace, who faced the lawyer with her jaw set and head high, as if daring him to doubt a word of her testimony.

Nick actually felt a little sorry for the guy, who fumbled with his pen and notepad for a moment and then sat down again.

The judge gathered his papers and stood. "We are in recess. Mrs. Perkins, I would like to speak privately with you and Mr. Brooks." He left by the side door, and the room erupted in chatter.

Brooks escorted Mrs. Perkins to the side door, and the Lombards went with her. Grace returned to her place without looking at anyone. Nick knew she hadn't yet seen him, so he started toward her, only to have his way blocked by Cody Daniels.

"She's still in custody, Nick."

Hearing his name, Grace turned. Her smile was radiant as she ran to him. Nick realized he might have had to punch Cody to get to her, but all Grace had to do was push past the sheriff with a soft "excuse me," and Cody was beat.

"She stays right here," Cody ordered as Nick folded his arms around her and felt her tighten her hold on him.

"We're not going anywhere," Nick assured him, leading Grace to the closest chair and sitting next to her. "You were—"

"My father?" she asked at the same time.

"Jake took charge the minute we arrived. I expect he and Ma Rogers are already settled in a room and Doc Waters is examining your father for any ill effects from the trip."

"Ma Rogers?" She smiled, then frowned. "Tell me, was the trip awful?"

He realized she needed to focus on her parents—on anything but her current circumstances. "Remember Ollie?"

"The conductor who liked you so much?"

"He sends his regards. He took care of everything once we reached Kansas City." He told her every detail he could recall of the journey.

The side door opened, and the aide stepped to the front of the room. "If everyone would please take a seat, the judge is ready to deliver his decision."

It had been less than fifteen minutes. Most people had left the room thinking they had time to step outside for a breath of air or perhaps get a cup of coffee at the counter.

Cody stepped up to Nick. "She needs to be in her place," he said.

Nick wanted more than anything to sit next to her at that lonely table, but he knew Cody would never allow that. Instead, he watched Grace return to her table, standing as she waited for the judge. He took a seat in the row just behind her. The judge came through the door, followed by his aide and the lawyer. There was no sign of Dolly Perkins or the Lombards.

"Mr. Brooks, is it my understanding that your client has decided to drop all charges related to Grace Hopkins?"

"Yes, Your Honor."

"And further, Mrs. Perkins has agreed not to pursue any of her late husband's accusers by filing similar charges?"

"Yes, Your Honor."

The judge turned to Grace. "Then, Grace Hopkins, you are free to go on with your life." He slammed down his gavel. "Case dismissed. Next case," he called, and his aide rushed to his side, rummaging through papers. Those few who had heard the decision scurried for the doors, anxious to spread the word.

Upon hearing the judge's decision, Grace bowed her head and rested her hands on the table in front of her. Nick realized she was shaking and hurried to her side.

"It's over, Grace." He pulled her against him. "You're free, darlin' girl."

Her bewildered expression and half smile told him she was having trouble believing that at long last, the nightmare had come to an end.

A single large tear fell from each eye and made a

slow trail down her cheeks, and then that smile he'd first noticed on the train blossomed—that smile that had set his heart skipping all those months ago.

He scooped her high in his arms. "Mrs. Hopkins, what say we go see your folks and give them the good news?"

Chapter 19

AIDAN HAD PUT GRACE'S PARENTS IN THE ROOM SHE'D occupied after the fire. It occurred to her that he thought either she would be set free, in which case she and Nick would head for the ranch, or she would be bound over for trial and returned to jail. In either case, she would not be occupying the hotel room.

"I'll wait here," Nick said after opening the door and stepping aside. "Take some time."

Her mother sat by the window, gazing out at the unfamiliar landscape. Her father was in the bed, his eyes closed.

"Mama? Papa?"

"Grace!" They said it in unison, their faces wreathed in relieved smiles. Her father opened his eyes and tried without success to sit up.

"Is it over?" her mother asked as she crossed the room and hugged her.

"All over," Grace assured them. "The charges were dropped." She studied her father. He was so very gaunt. "How are you doing, Papa?" She went to the side of the bed and took hold of his hand.

"He's worn out," her mother replied. "The trip was hard on him."

"But I'm here and still in one piece, and everyone has been so kind. That young man you married is blue-chip all the way, Grace." Her father's approval of Nick meant the world. Not that she had expected anything less, but to hear him say it was a gift. "And what's this I hear about you making me a grandpa before my time?" he teased.

This time, Grace blushed. "I think this baby caught Nick and me both by surprise," she admitted, laying her hand over her flat stomach.

"Like you did your mother and me," her father said, chuckling.

"Jim!" It was Mary Rogers who blushed now. "That's not for—"

Jim waved her protests away. "Just proves how much I loved you, Mary. Still do." He squeezed Grace's hand. "And look how well things turned out for us." He started coughing then, racking noises that came from somewhere deep in his chest and went on far too long.

"I'll get the doctor," she said and headed for the door.

"He's been here," her mother replied. She sat on the side of the bed, raising her husband enough so he could take a sip of water.

Grace waited for the coughing spell to abate before peppering her mother with more questions. "What did the doctor say? What does he recommend? Does he agree with Dr. Rove back home?"

"He said your father needs to rest and regain his strength. He's sending over some medicine—a tonic of some sort. In a day or two, he wants us to spend part of each day outside, sitting in the sun. And yes, he and Dr. Rove are in complete agreement that we have done the best we can. Now it's just a matter of waiting to see if the change of air works."

"Where's that husband of yours, Grace?" her father asked. He had collapsed back onto the pillows, and each word took effort.

"He's right outside the door."

"Well, get him in here. We've got plans to make, starting with getting your mother and me out of this fancy hotel."

Grace and her mother mostly listened while Nick and her father discussed the future, but Grace was adamant about one thing. "I don't want to be miles away, at least not until Papa's health shows definite signs of improving. Besides, Mama needs me. She can't manage his care by herself—lifting him and such."

"I have a job, Grace," Nick reminded her. "And that job is miles from town—as is our home."

"Nick's right," her father said. "You too have been married now for what, a couple of months? High time you started acting like it. Gracie, that means this man comes first. Your mother and I will be fine. Nick, there must be a boardinghouse in town. Mary and me can take a room there. We've done just fine up to now without you, Grace."

"But you had Angie and the boys and—"

"There's no boardinghouse," Nick interjected, "but I've got an idea. I'll be back in a bit." He kissed Grace's cheek and left.

"That boy's a real hard worker," her father muttered and chuckled before closing his eyes and drifting off.

While Nick was gone and her father slept, Grace told her mother all about the trial and especially how Bonnie and Polly had come forward about their experiences with Jasper Perkins. "They were so brave," she said. "I mean, they've only known me a few months. And frankly, I never thought Polly liked me."

"I'd like to meet your friends," her mother said. "Emma and Lily especially. Whenever you wrote of them, I was so relieved to know they were here with you."

Grace checked the clock on the mantel above the small fireplace. "They'll just be setting up for dinner now. I'll be right back."

She found Emma and Lily in the kitchen. "My mother wants to meet you," she told them after they'd exchanged hugs and happy exclamations.

"How about we stop by after our shift? The five o'clock will be pulling in any minute."

"Of course," Grace agreed. "After supper will be fine. Bring Miss K, will you?"

Grace turned to go and practically ran into Polly.

"Congratulations, Grace," she said.

"Oh, Polly, how can I ever thank you? I'm sure I could never have been so brave."

Polly met her gaze, and for perhaps the first time, Grace saw something that resembled respect in the other woman's eyes. "I did what I did for myself, Grace. I have carried that horrid secret with me for so long. I realized it had changed me. I need to rediscover the happy, innocent young woman I was when I took the job with the Harvey Company. And to that end, I've asked for a transfer—a fresh start."

There were no words Grace could find, so she reached out and hugged Polly. "Be very happy, Grace," Polly whispered. "You deserve it."

She hurried away then, through the kitchen and up the back stairs. Grace thought of going after her but decided not to. They had made their peace. There was no more to say.

As she crossed the lobby to return to her parents, Nick entered the hotel, grinning like he had a secret.

"What?" she asked when he wrapped his arm around her shoulders and led her to a settee. His good mood was contagious, and she found herself smiling and feeling lighter than she had in days.

"I caught up with the Lombards before they headed back to the ranch. I wanted to thank them for everything they've done for us, especially for you today."

"Oh, I wish I could have been with you. I want to thank them as well."

"You'll have your chance, once we all get back to the ranch."

Her high spirits plummeted. Had he not understood? "Nick, I—"

"You're supposed to ask me who 'we all' is, Grace," he said softly.

She felt a pang of irritation. "You're talking in riddles."

"There's you," he said, ignoring her comment and holding up his forefinger. "There's me—that's two. Then there's your ma and pa—that makes four." He waggled four fingers at her.

"You said the foreman's quarters are barely big enough for us and the baby," she reminded him.

"Yep." He was still grinning. It was maddening.

She had fallen in love with that smile, but at the moment, she found it annoying.

"Then what?"

"Before they built the big house, the Lombards lived in a cabin near the falls. A well-kept cabin that nobody's using. What if you and me stayed there, and your folks moved into the foreman's place at the ranch?"

"But you need to work and—"

"The cabin's less than half a mile away from the ranch. It'll be an easy ride to and from—for me to do my job and for you to check on your folks. Best of all, it gives us some time, and some privacy."

"My father will want to pay. My parents are proud people, Nick. They won't take charity. They don't even know the Lombards. Neither do I, for that matter."

Nick's grin faded. "I just thought…"

That was the moment Grace realized that Nick had done everything he could. For her parents, for her siblings, but most of all, for her. He had put his job at risk. He had gone to Missouri and possibly come up with a way to save her father's life, and now he was trying his best to give her what she wanted.

This was her husband. This man, so eager to do whatever he thought was necessary to ensure her happiness, was what true love looked like.

She touched his cheek. "Yes," she said softly. "It's a wonderful plan, and we'll make it work. Together."

They were lost in each other's eyes and smiles when Aidan cleared his throat. They looked up to see the hotel manager standing next to Bonnie and Jake just a few feet from the settee. "Congratulations, Grace," Aidan said.

"How blessed I am to have such dear friends,"

Grace replied. She stood and hugged each of them. "Thank you for everything you've done for me and my parents."

"We'd like to do one more thing, if you and Nick agree," Bonnie said.

"Oh no, you've done more than enough. We couldn't possibly—"

"We'd like to stage a proper celebration of your marriage here at the hotel," Jake interrupted, and Aidan nodded. He was wearing his do-not-debate-this expression.

"Yes. With your parents here, Grace, perhaps the two of you should renew your vows," Bonnie added.

"Shall we say Sunday night in the dining room?" Aidan asked.

"That's the day after tomorrow," Grace protested.

"Then we'd best get busy," Bonnie said. "Emma, Lily, and I will take care of everything." She studied Nick critically. "You'll need a haircut—and a shave."

"Yes, ma'am." Nick shook Aidan's hand, then hugged Bonnie. "Thanks—for everything."

"We'll do this up right," Jake assured them, then smiled. "The Harvey Way."

"Mama," Grace said the next morning as her mother finished giving her father his sponge bath and got him to eat a few bites of oatmeal. "Let's you and me take a walk through town. There are some people I'd like you to meet, people I need to thank."

"Your father—"

"Is practically asleep already," Grace said quietly.

"Go on, Mary," her father said, his eyes closed. "I'm not going anywhere. It'll do you good to get out for a bit."

"I suppose."

"Good." Grace got her mother's sunbonnet. "We won't be long, I promise."

Once they were outside, Grace smiled as her mother blinked in the bright sunlight. "It takes some getting used to," she said. "But, Mama, feel the warmth." She turned her face to the sky and closed her eyes.

"People are looking, Grace," her mother whispered.

"I suppose I'll need to get used to that, at least for a while. What with the hearing and all." She linked her arm through her mother's and headed across the town plaza. "Come on. I want you to meet Sheriff Daniels."

Cody was seated at his desk, bent over some paperwork, but the minute he saw Grace, he stood and smiled. "My favorite prisoner," he teased.

"Cody, this is my mother—Mary Rogers. Mama, this is Sheriff Cody Daniels."

"It's my pleasure to meet you, ma'am," he said.

Mary studied him for a moment. "I have to admit, young man, when my daughter got it into her head to come all the way out here, I feared for her safety. Ruffians and outlaws and such. But you seem capable of putting the order into law and order."

Cody blushed. "Well, now, ma'am, these days, the Wild West is not nearly as wild as it once was."

"Aidan Campbell has insisted on throwing a party for Nick and me tomorrow at the hotel, Cody. I do hope you'll come."

"Got my invite right here," he said, holding up an envelope on his desk. "Tommy delivered it this morning. Looks like everybody in town will be there."

"You should bring your wife, young man," Mary said.

"Not married, Mrs. Rogers. Maybe you've got another daughter as spirited as Grace here?"

"I have another daughter, but she's far too young for you, Sheriff," Mary Rogers teased. "Perhaps one of Grace's friends?"

Grace was stunned. Her mother knew how to flirt. She was flirting with Cody. Her eyes twinkled and her cheeks had more color than Grace had seen in them since her parents had arrived. For the first time, she saw her mother as her father must have first seen her. What a pretty and spunky young woman she must have been.

Cody grinned and winked at her. "Well, I hope maybe you'll save a dance for me, Mrs. Rogers?"

"Maybe I will." She turned to Grace. "We should let the sheriff get back to work, Grace. You said there were others you wanted me to meet?"

Cody walked them out, tipping his hat when Grace's mother glanced back at him and waved. Grace led the way down the boardwalk to the mercantile. When they entered the store, Mr. Tucker was busy with another customer, so Grace gave Mary a tour of the wares. "And he even sells ladies' hats." She pointed to the selection, noticing the brown straw Nick had picked out for her that day was still there. "Here, try this one on." She plucked the hat from the shelf and set it at a slight angle on her mother's gray hair, then held up a hand mirror Frank kept on the shelf. "It's lovely, Mama."

"Well, now I understand why it hasn't sold," the store owner commented as the other customer left and he joined them by the display. "Every hat needs the perfect model."

Grace made the introductions, again surprised by how the years seemed to have fallen away as her mother smiled at Frank Tucker. "It's a lovely hat," she said, removing it and handing it back to him.

"I could box it up for you," he offered.

To Grace's amazement, instead of refusing the offer outright, her mother turned the price tag over and seemed to be doing some mental figuring. "No, thank you. It's very nice, but the last thing I need is a new hat."

"Mama, if you—"

"Tell you what, Mrs. Rogers," Mr. Tucker said. "I've got new stock coming in the end of next week, and I need the space. This hat has been here for several months now. If you want it for half the price, it's yours."

"For the party, Mama," Grace urged, digging in her pocket for her change purse. "And in this sun, you'll need a hat like this one with a broader brim," she added. She counted out the money, adding extra to the pile. Mr. Tucker lifted an eyebrow. "I still owe you the balance on that pocketknife," she said.

She was now completely broke, but since Nick's job was secure and he didn't have to make the land payments, their worries were gone.

Frank counted out the amount necessary to pay for the hat and pushed the rest back to her. "Wedding present," he muttered and turned away to place her mother's hat in a box.

Grace realized to argue with him would be to insult

him. The way this man was always giving people special deals, she had no idea how he stayed in business. But then maybe because people knew he was fair and generous, they were loyal customers who chose to shop with him rather than at other stores in town.

Her mother made sure he and his wife planned to attend the party, and when he told her his wife had died a few years earlier, she promised him a dance. After they left the store, she said, "Two good hardworking men who should be married. What's the matter with the women in this town?" She shook her head. "I simply do not understand that."

They walked back to the hotel. Along the way, people stopped Grace to say how happy they were for Nick and her and how relieved they were that she had been set free.

"You've found your place here, Grace," her mother said. "Anyone can see that. It's not just Nick. You've found friends you can rely on, and that gives me a good deal of comfort. I worried knowing you were so far away and all."

"So you agree I made the right decision?"

"I didn't say that. You took a huge risk, and as it happens, it has paid off. Do not go puffing out your feathers thinking you know best."

And suddenly, the girlish Mary Rogers who had flirted with both a man half her age and one a few years older was once again Grace's mother—stern and rigid without a trace of a smile.

Grace hugged her, not taking the rebuke to heart, and opened the door to the hotel.

Chapter 20

THE DAY OF THE PARTY, NICK ARRIVED AT THE HOTEL around noon, but Lily and Emma refused to let him anywhere near Grace.

"It's bad luck, cowboy," Lily said, wagging her finger at him.

"We're already married," he reminded her.

"Not the Harvey Way, you're not," Emma chimed in. "Now scoot. We've got a lot to do and not near enough time to get it done."

He thought about heading over to the saloon where Slim and the others were quenching their thirst, but he wasn't in the mood for any more of the good-natured ribbing he'd suffered through the night before in the bunkhouse. Besides, he was wearing his best suit and shirt, not to mention a collar that was far too stiff and tight for his taste. He wasn't about to risk having beer spilled on any of it. He wandered out to the veranda that surrounded the hotel and was surprised to see John Lombard sitting in one of the rocking chairs.

"Nick! You look like you could use a drink. All I can offer is a glass of this lemonade." He nodded toward the pitcher on the small table beside him. "Help yourself and have a seat."

Nick did as his boss suggested. "Long day," he muttered as he downed the lemonade and then refilled his glass.

"I expect it seems that way," Lombard said. "Truth is, it's no longer than any other." He set his chair to rocking and stared out at the horizon. "I remember the day I married Rita. I thought we'd never get through it."

"Grace and I are already married," Nick said, wondering why it was he seemed to have to keep reminding everybody of that. "So I don't understand why—"

"It's the ladies, Nick. They do love their little superstitions—traditions, they would call them. My advice? Play along. And because you and Grace are just going through this for her folks and friends, all you have to do is relax and enjoy the celebration."

Nick grunted.

"You want me to get started with the branding tomorrow?" he asked after a while.

"It'll wait. Next week's plenty of time."

"What about that outfit you had me look into out in California?"

Lombard studied him for a moment and then smiled. "Okay, Nick, let's talk business—and get your mind off whatever's got you jumpy as a cornered jackrabbit."

An hour later, Nick saw Aidan close the doors to the dining room and post his assistant manager as sentry with strict orders to allow no one in. Nick's mood darkened like thunderclouds over the mountains. All this fuss when what he thought he'd agreed to was a simple repetition of their vows, a short reception to follow, and then they could be on their way home to the ranch—and to christen their cabin by the falls.

He loosened the collar that was beginning to feel like a noose, shoved his hands in his pockets, and paced.

After what seemed like forever, the door to the room where Grace's parents were staying opened, and Mary Rogers slipped out. She headed across the lobby to the reading room.

"Ma Rogers," he called out, drawing the attention of a few hotel guests lingering in the lobby.

Grace's mother glanced from him to the closed door and back again. "Nick, why don't you keep Jim company while I go help Grace get ready?" She took his arm and steered him back to the room she'd just left. "Go on now. It will help pass the time," she assured him.

She stopped just shy of shoving him into the room before shutting the door behind him. From the bed, he heard Jim Rogers let out a combination of chuckle and cough.

"It won't be long now," his father-in-law assured him once he'd cleared his lungs.

"It's a circus," Nick grumbled.

Jim motioned for him to come closer. "Want to help me with a little surprise for Grace?"

Nick nodded. Right about now, he'd do whatever it took to get his mind off things he clearly could not control.

❈

Grace stood before the floor-length mirror. Emma knelt at her feet, a row of straight pins clenched between her lips. Lily circled her, a frown drawing her usually laughing mouth down at the corners. Grace's mother stood to one side, one hand resting on her cheek as she slowly shook her head.

"It just doesn't look like a wedding gown," she observed.

"That's because it's a tablecloth, Mama," Grace said. "Lily, I love that you're so inventive, but a tablecloth?"

"It's lace, and it's white," Lily replied. "Well, almost—a few minor stains no one will see."

"How you ever persuaded Jake to let you have this—much less cut it up for a gown—is beyond me," Emma muttered. "Turn," she ordered.

"Jake pulled it from the discard bin. It was his idea to use it for your wedding dress. Aside from the stains, there are some tears, and you know the Harvey rule—nothing but the best, so no mending the linens. Discard and replace."

"What would any of us do without that man?" Grace said as she followed Emma's instructions and turned. "On the other hand, I could always wear what I wore when Nick and I married the first time," she pleaded.

"No. You can wear that for the trip to the ranch," Lily replied flatly, and then she smiled. "I've got it." She nudged Emma aside as she began removing the pins, allowing the fabric to fall in a heap around Grace's feet.

"Lily, the clock is ticking," Emma reminded her.

"Or I could wear this lovely jacket Bonnie loaned me and a plain navy skirt," Grace said, continuing to offer suggestions. The jacket was made of a cream-colored heavy cotton faille fabric with a high neck and long sleeves, each finished off with lace trim.

Lily ignored her, examining the tablecloth, turning it this way and that. Then she gave a yelp of victory, found the center point, and placed it against Grace's waist. "Hold that right there," she instructed. "Emma, take this end while I take the other."

As if Emma had seen Lily's vision, the two women drew the fabric tight and began pinning the fabric onto Grace's corset to fashion it into a skirt that fit Grace's slim waist and fell straight to the tops of her shoes. The scalloped edges of the fabric accented the hem. In back, they arranged the fabric into a cascade of ruffles—not quite a train, but certainly elegant beyond anything Grace had ever imagined. They held the faille jacket for Grace to slip into and helped button the front.

"Ta-da!" Lily stood back and admired the result.

"You have missed your calling, Lily," Mary Rogers said. "It's beautiful. Perfect."

Lily stepped back and admired her work. "Let's get it sewn up," Emma said and set to work.

"I'll be right back," Lily announced.

She was gone long enough for Emma and Grace's mother to stitch the draped tablecloth into a beautiful trained skirt. As Grace tried on the garment for one final fitting, Lily burst back into the room, clutching a package. "The finishing touch," she announced as she tore the wrapping away and shook out the most delicate white lace mantilla Grace had ever seen.

"Lily, where on earth…?"

"I have my sources," she said mysteriously. "Now turn around."

When tears sparkled in her mother's eyes, Grace knew that Lily and Emma had been right to insist she needed a proper wedding. Slowly, she turned to face the mirror and gasped. "Oh, Lily, I look so…"

"Bridal?" Emma offered.

"Lovely," Grace's mother whispered.

There was a light tap on the door, and Bonnie stepped inside. "Oh my," she said when she saw Grace.

"Is everything ready?" Lily asked, glancing at the clock.

Bonnie nodded. "The musicians are here, as are the guests. Nick's friend the judge just put on his robe."

"I'll get my hat," Mary Rogers said, her voice trembling with excitement.

After she and Bonnie left the room, Emma and Lily did one last check to be sure everything about Grace was perfect. "Thank you both," she murmured. "I am so blessed that I sat down with the two of you that night."

Tears welled in the eyes of all three Harvey Girls as they hugged each other.

"Come on, Lily," Emma said. "Grace, wait here, and we'll come get you when we're sure Nick is in place."

After they left, Grace couldn't resist taking one more look in the mirror. A moment later, the door opened, and Bonnie, dressed in her uniform, smiled. "Ready?"

"I…"

Outside the door, all the Harvey Girls, including Polly, had lined up at the double doors leading into the dining room, all in perfectly pressed uniforms. Jake ushered Grace's mother to her place, and then her father—seated in a wheelchair with Aidan pushing—emerged from the guest room.

"Papa?"

"You didn't think I'd miss a chance to give away my daughter, did you?" he said. "Aidan, if you please, let's get these young people married—again."

Bonnie handed Grace a small nosegay of flowers and then nodded to Lily, who led the Harvey Girls down the makeshift aisle. Grace took hold of her father's hand, keeping pace as Aidan slowly wheeled him into the dining room. He paused in the doorway, waiting until all the girls had taken their places.

And that's when Grace saw Nick. He had slicked back his hair, and Grace smiled as she thought what fun it was going to be to muss it up again once they were alone. But her smile faded when she realized that Nick was scowling, digging his forefinger between his neck and collar.

When his gaze locked on hers, his features softened, and slowly—like a desert sunrise—he gave her that smile that had set her heart fluttering that first day on the train. They'd have their fair share of challenges to be sure, but they would face them with a love that had already proven to be indestructible.

She'd left home seeking the opportunity to help her family with the hope of finding some adventure in the bargain. Little did she ever imagine that in becoming a Harvey Girl, she would find both and a good deal more—dear friends she would cherish for all her days and, best of all, the love of her life.

Author's Note

The hotels named in this story are fictional, although they are written in the spirit of a Harvey establishment. While Fred Harvey and his sons eventually became famous for their hotels and restaurants and even guided tours that helped the West become a major destination for travelers, it was his eating houses along the Santa Fe Railway that started it all. Thanks to George H. Foster and Peter C. Weiglin, many of the recipes for the dishes made famous by the Harvey Company have been preserved in *The Harvey House Cookbook* (Atlanta: Longstreet Press, 1992). With the publisher's permission, here are three of those delicious recipes.

Peaches au Gratin

George Burnickel, Chef, California Limited

- Peaches
- Sugar
- Butter
- 2 teaspoons lemon juice
- Bread crumbs
- 3 tablespoons drawn butter
- 3 tablespoons whipping cream

This dish can be made from either canned or fresh peaches; if the latter are to be used, they must be cut into halves and stewed with plenty of sugar and a small quantity of water. Thickly butter a baking dish; drain the peaches from the syrup; lay them in the dish (cut side down) and strew over them plenty of grated bread crumbs. Mix with the syrup two teaspoonfuls of lemon juice and pour over the peaches; strew more bread crumbs over the top and baste them with a few tablespoonfuls of drawn butter. Put the dish in a hot oven and bake until lightly browned over the top. Serve with whipped cream.

Fred Harvey Coffee

The secrets of good coffee are that it be:

- » Made strong enough
- » Served hot enough
- » Brewed correctly
- » Always freshly made
- » Made from good coffee
- » Drip coffee

Use one rounded tablespoon of regular grind to each six-ounce cup of fresh boiling water. Scald your coffeepot with boiling water. Put the coffee in the coffee basket; replace in pot and cover with water container. Slowly pour boiling water into it. Keep warm while coffee drips through, then remove upper sections, stir, cover pot, and serve.

Harvey Girl Special Little Thin Orange Pancakes

Henry Stovall, St. Louis Union Station, Missouri

- 1 cup pancake mix
- 1 cup orange juice
- ¼ cup diced orange sections and juice (½ orange)
- 1 teaspoon grated orange peel (½ orange)

Combine all ingredients. Bake small pancakes on hot griddle, using one tablespoon batter for each pancake. Serve with maple syrup, honey, or jelly. Serves twelve; three (2¾-inch diameter) pancakes per serving.

About the Author

Award-winning author Anna Schmidt resides in Wisconsin. She delights in creating stories where her characters must wrestle with the challenges of their times. Critics have consistently praised Schmidt for her ability to seamlessly integrate actual events with her fictional characters to produce strong tales of hope and love in the face of seemingly insurmountable obstacles. Visit her at joschmidtauthor.com.

Last Chance Cowboys

*These rugged, larger-than-life cowboys of the sweeping
Arizona Territory are ready to steal your heart.*
By Anna Schmidt, award-winning author

The Drifter

Maria Porterfield is in for the fight of
her life keeping a greedy corporate
conglomerate off her land and drifter
cowboy Chet out of her heart.

The Lawman

As the new local lawman, Jess Porterfield
is determined to prove his worth…
and win back the one woman he could
never live without.

The Outlaw

Undercover detective Seth Grover can't resist the lively Amanda Porterfield...especially when she's taken hostage, and Seth is the only one who can save her.

The Rancher

Facing a range war, Trey Porterfield thinks a marriage of convenience to Nell Stokes might be their best bet. But can their growing love be enough to keep them safe?

"A feisty heroine and a hero eager to make everything right. What more could a reader want?"
—**Leigh Greenwood,** *USA Today* **bestselling author,** for *The Drifter*

Runaway Brides

*Meet the rugged cowboys of the West…and the
ladies of the East who steal their hearts*
Amy Sandas, *USA Today* Bestselling Author

The Gunslinger's Vow

Malcolm Kincaid has no desire to
escort a pampered Eastern lady to
Montana, but the longer he and
Alexandra Brighton travel together,
the harder he's falling…

The Cowboy's Honor

Courtney Adams is still in her
wedding finery when she leaves her
groom at the altar and finds herself
mistaken as a mail-order bride for a
cowboy who makes her blood burn.

"Sandas will leave you breathless."
**Linda Broday, *New York Times* and *USA Today*
bestselling author, for *The Gunslinger's Vow***

For more info about Sourcebooks's books and authors, visit:
sourcebooks.com

The Outlaw's Mail Order Bride

*Can these outlaws open their hearts? First in a new
series from bestselling author Linda Broday*

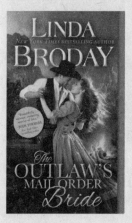

When Clay Colby's hard-won homestead is set ablaze on
the eve of his new bride's arrival, he's heartbroken. But
Tally Shannon doesn't mind—not when he makes her feel
so safe. Yet it's only a matter of time before the ghosts of her
past come calling…and her loving cowboy must defend his
new bride to his very last breath.

"Outstanding…an unforgettable journey."
—Booklist for *To Marry a Texas Outlaw*

For more info about Sourcebooks's books and authors, visit:
sourcebooks.com

Logan's Lady

An epic love story from beloved bestselling author Rosanne Bittner

Ill-mannered and seemingly ruthless, Logan Best exorcises his dark past by hunting wanted men. There's nothing about a pampered Englishwoman that should tempt him.

Lady Elizabeth longs for adventure. She leaves for America full of hope…only to be swindled by a gentlemanly thief. Now, Logan is her only hope—a man whose rough manners and dark eyes thrill her to the core…

"Unforgettable."
—RT Book Reviews TOP PICK for
The Last Outlaw, 4.5 stars

For more info about Sourcebooks's books and authors, visit:
sourcebooks.com

Cowboy Charm School

Stop that wedding!

Texas Ranger Brett Tucker hates to break up a wedding, but the groom is a danger to any woman. So he busts into the church, guns blazing…only to find he has the wrong man.

Guilt-ridden, he's desperate to get the bride and groom back on track—but the more time he spends with Kate, the harder he falls…and the more he wants to convince her that he's her true match in every way.

"A great story by a wonderful author."
**—#1 *New York Times* bestselling author
Debbie Macomber for *Left at the Altar***

For more info about Sourcebooks's books and authors, visit:
sourcebooks.com

Someone Like You

Love and redemption are all he ever wanted… From celebrated and bestselling author Leigh Greenwood

When Rafe Jerry's father ordered him off the family's California ranch, he swore never to return. He ran away to war, where the harsh realities of battle hardened his heart and a traitor ruined his reputation. But now, Rafe must return to his old life, where an unexpected spark ignites hope for the future. When all else seems lost, Maria de la Guerra is the only one who can free Rafe of the pain of the past…

"An emotional, rich, adventurous romance."
—RT Book Reviews for *Forever and Always*, 4 stars

For more info about Sourcebooks's books and authors, visit:
sourcebooks.com